Champ

Six months in the life of
a twelve-year-old boy

A. Flitcroft

Champ & Co
First published in Wales in 2014
on behalf of the author
by
BRIDGE BOOKS
Pear Tree Cottage
Worthenbury
Wrexham
LL13 0BF

ISBN 978-1-84494-099-8

Cover photograph: Nant Mill, Coedpoeth
© Geoff Jones

Printed and bound
by
Printondemand-Worldwide
Peterborough

Contents

Part One: A New Home, June, 1953

Alan Fletcher could not believe the letter his mum was reading to him and his sister. Up till now it had only been a rumour, but Chester City Council was going to knock his house down along with the rest of the row, and soon. They wanted to build a new road and a bicycle factory. There were three cheers for the City Council.

Twelve-year-old Alan was very happy with the news as for him and his mates the place was a dump. The only thing they had going for them was the youth club, where, on Tuesday and Thursday evenings, he learned judo. The instructor, a black belt, was his 25-year-old Uncle Dave. But the youth club had shut down the previous month so there was nothing to do once school was over — not that school was very inspiring. The only thing Alan was any good at was running and doing his sums. So, with the youth club and his judo training which he loved both gone, Alan and his mates were now roaming the streets full-time and getting up to all kinds of mischief. Knocking on doors and running away ended up with them being chased by angry residents.

Alan and most of his friends were known to the police and he was convinced that Sergeant Gledhill, who had an enormous handlebar moustache, was deliberately picking on him. Every time they met, he had to declare what he had been up to and with whom. His mum's news about the house was therefore music to his ears.

Number 17, Price's Lane where Alan lived was a dump, infested by not only mice, but also cockroaches. If you had to use the outside lavatory after everyone had gone to bed, you would hear the cockroaches scampering over the floor as you made your way downstairs — there were hundreds of them. You always made sure your shoes were at the top of the stairs in case you had to go to the john in the early hours and the first job his mum had to do in the morning was to shovel up the dead cockroaches and mouse droppings. Not only that, but the windows would not open, half the doors would not close properly unless you slammed them and the walls were mouldy and damp which caused the wallpaper to peel off. Because of this, eleven-year-old Jeannie was always coughing and hated having to have goose fat smeared over her chest. The smell was horrible, but the doctor said it was good for her.

So, if a new road and a bicycle factory were going to be built when the row was knocked down, where was everyone going to live? Mrs Fletcher's request to be re-housed, not in Chester with the rest of the row, but in a quaint little Welsh village where, for as long as she could remember, she used to spend two weeks of the school summer holidays with her cousin Rachel, was finally granted. The village, with its funny sounding name (The Adwy), consisted of privately-owned houses and some fifty-two council houses which were constructed with the famous red-bricks manufactured in the nearby village of Ruabon, was being extended. The new 'airy houses' where the Fletcher's were going to live were being built with the newly-invented breeze blocks and plaster board. Three miles away was the well-known market town of Wrexham.

Mrs Fletcher smiled and shed a tear when she received the council's letter. She was so pleased that she and her family were going to be living in Wales. She had never forgotten the fields over which she and Rachel and their friends had roamed as children, often picking bunches of buttercups and daisies, nor the wood with its little river in which they paddled and which had been dammed by the older boys and used as a swimming pool. She remembered being there one time watching the bigger lads swimming and being chased by the farmer. Mrs Fletcher had never forgotten her school holidays in the Adwy.

When her children arrived home from school, she broke the news to them, telling them they were leaving Chester for their new home at the end of the week, on Saturday, 6th June, in five days' time.

There was great excitement on departure day which began at 9.30 a.m. with the arrival of the removal van belonging to Dodd's of Chester. It looked enormous parked up outside Number 17, but when the tailboard was lowered it looked half as long again. Alan had never seen a removal van before and its height worried him, making him fearful that it would topple over going into a sharp bend. But, when no-one was looking, he began to jump on the tailboard which was fun and could not wait to begin emptying the house.

It was whilst he was carrying a chair to the van that he overheard his mum telling a neighbour just how much the van was – it was 'costing an arm and a leg' whatever that meant?

The two men who came with the van, plus Alan's two granddads, did all the heavy work but, knowing how she wanted her furniture loaded and unloaded, Mrs Fletcher was in charge. His two grannies, with a list they had to adhere to, were in charge of seeing that the right item was being delivered to the van.

Alan was put to rolling up and tying with string all the rugs that had been made over the years. When one was ready it was hoisted onto his shoulder and, with his grannies' permission, was delivered to the van where it was taken off him and placed wherever Mrs Fletcher desired it. Her aim was for the off-loading to be as easy as possible.

Every time Alan tried to help with the big furniture: the dresser, the sideboard, the beds, he was told to go away as he was a nuisance and ended up being put in charge of tying up all the boxes and seeing they were delivered to the van – but only when permission was given by his grannies.

Jeannie seemed to have the best of jobs. All she had to do was to make sure she had all her dolls and things. Most of her time was spent watching and talking with friends who had come to see them off.

Then at 12.30, with all the furniture in place and roped down, it was time to leave. Friends, family and neighbours were all there to see them off. They were the first residents to be re-housed, the rest of the row, so promised Chester City Council, would be re-housed within a month two at the most.

Having said goodbye to their friends and grandparents, Alan and Jeannie watched their mum saying her goodbyes. There were lots of hugs and kisses, and tears with her mum and dad, the Thompsons, and again with her in-laws, the Fletchers. Then it was time to say goodbye to the friends and neighbours she had known all her married life. Mrs Fletcher was both happy and sad; sad she was leaving friends who had been there for her when she lost her husband, but happy that she and her children were being given a fresh start in life. Doreen Fletcher was 33 years old, five-feet seven inches tall, slim, with mousy coloured hair, and very pretty.

Alan took one last look inside the old house. He wanted to be sure that nothing was being left behind, except the mice and cockroaches.

When his mother closed the door for the last time he said his good riddance, hoping never to see the place again. But when he, his mum and Jeannie climbed in the cab, the driver dropped a bombshell. He said he could not have five people in the cab as it was against the law. The police would stop them.

The problem was solved when Alan suggested he ride in the back. It was, as he said, only a short hop into Wales. Jeannie, who would have loved to have ridden in the back with Alan, had to sit on the edge of the gear-box, which was most uncomfortable. Her mum and the driver's mate shared the passenger seat as best they could. So, amongst a barrage of waves and shouts of good luck from everyone, the Fletchers set off for their new home in Wales.

In what light there was in the back of the van, Alan heard the engine starting up. When first gear was eventually selected (on account of the van needing a new clutch) the Fletcher's little hop to Wales began. But, as the driver began to rev the engine up, Alan began to wonder if he was going to miss his friends. Then, suddenly, he began to laugh, hearing the driver yelling at someone to 'Get out of the way you dozy little so-and-so.' The 'dozy little so-and-so' was Billy Watts who had climbed up onto the front bumper to see inside the cab. But back on the parapet and out of harm's way, Billy shouted his 'so long' to Alan in the hope that it was heard.

Starting off again, the van reached the end of the street and turned left. Twenty minutes on, not realizing the journey was going to be so long, bumpy and dark, Alan tried to amuse himself in what little light there was by setting up a den. He threw his jacket over an upturned chair, crawled inside, and played at being Dick Barton, Special Agent. When he had shot and killed all the baddies, he sat up to play Jack Stones. But the ride was far too bumpy and jerky, especially when the driver changed gear. Alan thought the gear-box was going to either pack in or fall off. It was grinding like mad. It sounded like someone banging on an old pipe.

Putting his Jack stones away, Alan began to think about his future. On leaving school he was going to find himself a good job and proudly put his wage packet on the table. When he was eighteen and old enough, he was going to follow in his father's footsteps and become a soldier in the Royal Artillery. Every time he thought about his dad, he cursed the Germans for killing him in the war. Regimental Sergeant Major David Fletcher, and several soldiers he was commanding at the time, were mown down by German machine-gun fire in 1944 while crossing a French field.

Even though there were no memories, Alan sure missed his dad and often imagined the fun he would have had with a father who would have played football with him. He knew from his mum that his dad was a big supporter of Blackpool and idolised Stanley Matthews. But, thanks to his mum, his dad's memory was being kept alive with stories told on Sunday evenings. He and Jeannie loved sitting on cushions on the floor while supping a nice hot cup of Oxo, while their mum told them how big and strong and handsome their dad was. How smart he looked in his regimental sergeant-major's uniform and how they would walk in the park on Sunday afternoon after church while pushing the pram. How thirteen-month-old Jeannie was her dad's little princess, and how two-year-old Alan was going to be a famous footballer one day and play for Blackpool. Alan hoped that all the photographs of his dad were safe, especially the one of him in his best battledress which was his favourite.

Suddenly, all the bumping and noisy gear changing ceased. The clutch had survived and the van was parked up outside Number 8, Heol Wen, Adwy, Coedpoeth. No one in the van saw the faces peering at them from behind lace curtains, but those faces were soon to become the Fletcher's new neighbours.

With the engine switched off, the two men lowered the tailboard which brought Alan back into full daylight. Mrs Fletcher jumped out of the cab and with keys in hand, opened their gate, and smiling, walked down the three elongated concrete steps and stopped by the front door at the side of the house — the door had been painted a lovely chocolate brown. Thanking God for all his help, she inserted the key into the Yale lock and, liking the sound it made, smiled yet again. Turning the key to the right, she opened the door and told herself that today, 6 June, was the start of the new life she was going to create for herself and her two children.

Stepping into the empty hall, her hall, with her pulse racing, Mrs Fletcher had a quick peep in the parlour and in her mind's eye, imagined how it was going to be. Then, with a quick glance up the stairs, she entered the living room and again visualised it fully furnished. Sighing, she entered the back kitchen, the door having been left open from her last visit. Unable to resist the temptation she opened the pantry door, then the broom-cupboard door. They were empty now but would not remain so for long.

She turned on the hot and cold water taps together and was splashed for turning them on too quickly. Wiping herself down she un-locked and opened the back door of her brand new, three bedroomed council house. She wanted fresh air to circulate all through the house.

She then checked out the coal house, the outside lavatory, and what was going to be a god send, the washhouse. She was more than pleased with her lot. With all the downstairs doors open, she then opened all the windows.

She was particularly pleased with the fireplace and the black-leaded oven (with its wooden handle and swivelling cast-iron cooking hobs). She was over the moon with the built-in cupboards and drawers that were now available to her. She had windows that opened easily, and doors that did not creak or had to be slammed. She absolutely adored the picture rail that went all around the living room.

There was no smell of damp or mould. All the walls throughout the house had been painted in a white emulsion. Comparing this to what she had in Chester, Mrs Fletcher was so pleased she began to cry. Her mind's eye was visualising this room and the rest of the house furnished to her liking. Yes, she told herself, she was very happy with her lot.

When Jeannie jumped out of the cab, having sat on the gearbox, she limped her way to the back of the van to be with her brother. Having had several jumps on the tailboard while the driver and mate filled in their timesheets, Alan and Jeannie had their first view of Heol Wen. Their mum was right. They were going to enjoy living in the Adwy which was so different from Chester. For one thing, everywhere was quiet, there were no dogs barking, no engines being revved, no kids screaming or bus-drivers honking their horns. Alan was already in love with their new home.

With his right arm on Jeannie's shoulder, Alan said he was both impressed and excited. He began to count the houses that made up Heol Wen and found there were eight in all, in blocks of two, with corner houses leading off in both directions to the left and right. There was also a row of houses facing them, and the chimney pots of another row at the back of them. In fact they were surrounded by houses. It was Jeannie who said how wonderful everything was to which Alan could only agree.

Looking up the street they saw what could only be described as an untidy hedge. Both wondered what could be on the other side? When they saw there was a gaping hole in the hedge, big enough for two people to walk through, they again tried to imagine what could be on the other side. Had they taken a look, they would have seen open fields and hedgerows, like the one they were looking at, extending as far as the eye could see. The hedge they were looking at was made up of holly, hazel and blackthorn.

Because there were no trams or tramlines in sight, Alan told Jeannie that this was going to be a great place to live. How quiet it was with none of the hustle and bustle of Chester. Jeannie nodded her agreement.

Suddenly, the faces that had peered at them from behind lace curtains were now peering into the van, showing a keen interest in the Fletcher's furniture. But no one offered to help when the off-loading began with the driver and mate each carrying two straight-backed chairs down the long path. After what seemed like hours, the last of the Fletcher's belongings were taken indoors.

Thanking Mrs Fletcher for a cup of tea and some biscuits, the two removal men wished her and the kid's good luck before reversing down the street, there being nowhere to turn round. After they had driven off, the inside of 8 Heol Wen looked as if a bomb had hit it, despite the furniture having been brought in as planned. There were items of furniture, boxes, rugs and knick-knacks in every room, both upstairs and downstairs. The only items that were put in place were the cupboard and the dresser. The bed frames and their metal headboards were upstairs waiting to be assembled. Telling her children to keep out of the way and with her sleeves rolled up, Mrs Fletcher began the task of straightening the house. But several minutes later someone was knocking on the back door.

'Can we come in *cariad*?' A Welsh-sounding voice said.

Wondering who on earth it could be, Mrs Fletcher said, 'Yee-ss.'

'Hello love,' said the first woman with a big smile. 'I'm Mair, Mair Edwards from next door. And this is Aunty Jinni, top house, across the road.'

Shaking hands with the two women, Mrs Fletcher introduced herself as Doreen and then introduced Alan and Jeannie, adding that they were all very pleased to meet them.

Looking around the room, Mair, the slimmer of the two said, 'Ooh I dare say you wouldn't say no to a little help *cariad*.'

'We've come to see what we can do' added Aunty Jinni.

Smiling and pointing at all the mess, Doreen indicated that their help would be most welcome. So, with their sleeves rolled up and with Doreen explaining what she wanted, the three women went to work. By six o'clock, the living room, the back kitchen and the parlour were something like ship-shape. Seeing the time, Doreen decided that the hall was going to have to be left for the time being. Told to make a pot of tea, Alan and Jeannie handed out the refreshments and the biscuit tin and everyone agreed that a good job had been done.

Knowing her children were hungry, Mrs Fletcher saw the two ladies to the door and again thanked them for their most generous help. Jeannie was then asked to unpack the box numbered '7' and retrieve three soup bowls, whereas Alan was told to look for the box numbered '8' and retrieve three dessert spoons. A pan of pre-cooked lobscouse was being warmed up on the gas-ring which, when ready, Mrs Fletcher, dished out to the children who were sat at the table with their mouths watering. With a thick slice of dry bread each, they all tucked in. The meal was delicious and thoroughly enjoyed by one and all, even though the table cloth was still in the box numbered '3'.

Jeannie washed the pots and put them away in their brand new spacious pantry. When the tea-towel was hung-up to dry on the door knob, she proceeded to carry some of her things up to her little bedroom which overlooked the back garden. She was quite surprised when she saw the view she had of the countryside. Apart from the green fields and hedgerows which were many, Jeannie could also see what she thought were two enormous red banks.

While she was admiring the view and trying to work out what the two banks were, Alan helped his mum as best he could with some of the furniture that was to be taken upstairs, their meal having revived them. By nine o'clock and falling asleep, Doreen decided she was only going to make up her bed and Alan's. The kids could top and tail for tonight.

It was awfully strange being in an empty bedroom that made your voice sound hollow and echoey. There were no curtains on the window, or pictures on the walls, nor any clothes in the built-in wardrobe. Alan and Jeannie were in a completely bare room except for the bed. Both were snuggled up in bed in the middle bedroom on this their first night in their brand new, three bedroomed council house. While chatting about this and that, they both tried to avoid looking at the bright bulb that, as yet, had no shade. But try as they might they were attracted to it like a moth is to a light, even though it hurt their eyes. And they giggled at the way Aunty Mair and Aunty Jinni spoke. It was so different to the way they spoke.

Jeannie thought it was weird being called *cariad* all the time until her mum told her that *cariad* was Welsh for darling. Doreen had learned quite a lot of Welsh during her summer stays with Rachel as a young girl. She was also familiar with the area. There were changes, but she still remembered a lot of it. She knew the Adwy, Coedpoeth and the Talwrn 'like the back of her hand' as Alan would have said.

While lying there top and tail, Alan and Jeannie agreed that the Adwy was going to be a great place to live. But, because of the excitement they were feeling they began to wonder if there was going to be any sleep tonight. But there was. They were both sound asleep when Doreen checked on them on her way to bed. Because Alan had most of the clothes covering him, Doreen gave Jeannie her fair share and then stood in the doorway and listened to their breathing. She cuffed herself for not having put any curtains on the window when she saw the amount of street light that was shining in. That was going to be her first job in the morning. Even so it was hard to believe they were at last in their new home. Doreen had one last peep in the little box room which was going to be Jeannie's bedroom and, ignoring the mess, pulled the door to and turned in. She was asleep in no time.

Alan and Jeannie spent Sunday morning close to the house in case they were needed while their mum went about finishing the work she had started the previous day. The children knew it was going to be one of those days where you made yourself a jam-butty when hungry because their mum was determined that the upstairs was going to be ship-shape by the evening.

Exploring the back garden, Alan found a good supply of sticks for lighting their fire, and for the rest of the row, from a hedge that ran the full length of their garden. He did not know it yet but the hedge that spanned his garden was once a part of the hedge that he and Jeannie had looked at when they first arrived. The Adwy was once a much larger farming community which meant all the fields were separated by hedges.

When the outside washhouse was checked over, Alan discovered that the boiler and fire place were brand new, as was the sink and draining board. He actually peeled the sticky label off the sink and stuck it on the back of the door for good luck. It suddenly occurred to him that this washhouse would also make a good den and, while he was trying to think up ways to use it, Aunty Mair, from next door, while putting some rubbish in the bin, asked how he was and had they all had a good night's sleep? Alan said they had, adding that his mum was still at it upstairs and that he was standing by just in case he was needed.

Referring to Alan as a 'good boy', Aunty Mair, having disposed of the rubbish and making sure the bin lid was back in place, went indoors. Her three children, two girls and a boy, were running in and out of the house playing tick.

Jeannie was upstairs in her little box-room, setting up her doll's house, pretending to be all grown up. She was wearing one of her mum's turbans, one with blue flowers on it, and she had found her mum's high-heel shoes and handbag and was trying to the best of her ability to apply some lipstick without the aid of a mirror. Eleven-year-old Jeannie could not wait to be grown up.

The Fletcher's front garden (and the others in the row) faced the road and the houses across the way were all slightly sloped and fenced off with brand-new fencing wire. The view from Alan's bedroom was nothing compared to Jeannie's. Whereas her view was countryside and two large red-shale banks, Alan's was of the houses that made up Heol Wen. But at least, he told himself, he would be able to see who was about, if and when he made friends with the local kids. The fences that separated the houses were some four feet high and made out of thin upright slats of wood, held together with strong wire on the top and bottom. Alan, never having had a fence before, thought they were much nicer than the front garden fences. In Chester, garden boundaries were brick walls that were too high, too dirty and too dangerous to climb over. He knew the front garden was going to be a lot of hard work to get tidy. Like all new houses that were being built, the front and back gardens had been good dumping grounds for the brickies, plasterers, and joiners.

With his bundle of sticks, Alan looked at their new house and decided it was ten times better than the one they had in Chester. There was no damp in this house nor was there a musty smell. All you had to do when leaving the lavatory, be it the one upstairs or the one next door to the coal house, was to pull a chain and watch as the water flushed everything away. How different to Chester's smelly earth-toilet. Earth-toilets in that day and age were a disgrace. It was 1953 for goodness sake. He and his sister had their own bedrooms which were fantastic. In Chester they had shared the same damp, smelly room. And even though they had their own beds, they still worried when they heard the mice and cockroaches scurrying about.

It was three o'clock and, having just helped him mum carry two large boxes upstairs, Alan was standing in their gateway enjoying a thick jam-butty. His thoughts of how he was going to enjoy living here were suddenly interrupted. A man with a walking stick was limping up the street. Alan watched him and when they were level was given a nod of the head. Alan nodded back and the man, who never spoke, limped up his path and entered the house opposite, Number 7, via the front door. He later learned that he was Mr Thomas.

While looking down the street enjoying his jam-butty, Alan saw three boys his own age running down the yard of the corner house of Heol Wen. When they ran out of sight he began to wonder who they were for a moment or two, and then went back to wondering what was behind the scruffy looking hedge not twenty yards away.

The only part of the hedge he recognised was the hazel. There had been a hazel hedge in Chester where he and the lads used to play and which always gave a good crop of nuts sometime in the autumn. Did this one? He then twigged that the hedge was the same as the one that ran the full length of his garden and the others in the row, but had no idea what the other two species of hedge were. He later learned that they were hawthorn and blackthorn. He was just about to go and find out what mysteries were on the other side of the hedge, when Jeannie called from his bedroom window to say that he was needed upstairs. Their mum was going to rig up Jeannie's bed and would he bring up the box that was on the bottom step of the stairs?

Again there was no fire lit on this, their second night in their brand new home. Sunday night too was going to be an early night.

It was Monday morning and time for the children to attend their new school. Lying in bed, all snuggled up beneath the bedclothes, Alan was trying to think up ways of being let off school for a day or two so that he could do a little exploring. A couple of days off would not harm his education. But there was a problem – his mum! She was adamant when it came to education, deeming it as one of life's greatest gifts.

Alan's first thought was to find out where the shops were, but he did not think that would work because of all the visits his mum had made before they moved. She probably knew where all the shops were. He then thought of pretending to be unwell, but that would not work either. He had gone to bed the previous night as fit as a fiddle. Ah, but what if he offered to find out where the coal-man lived, and have him deliver a couple of bags? Surely that would work and get him a day off school?

Alan lay there fine-tuning his plan while trying to listen to all the muffled chit-chat that was going on downstairs, but was only catching the odd word which did not make any sense. He suddenly heard the hall door opening. 'Alan,' his mum called up, 'it's time you were up love. Come on now. Don't let me have to shout again.' Her voice and the door closing sounded ever so hollow on account of there being no mats down or curtains hung which would absorb the noise. It reminded him of when he and his mates used to play in the air-raid shelter back in Chester. What fun was had in that old, crumbling shelter. He was going to make it a priority to see if there were any in the Adwy. He not only loved the echoey atmosphere, but, once inside, you were also out of sight of prying eyes.

The old shelter had been mostly used for smoking in, not that Alan ever did. His Uncle Dave, being a black belt judo instructor, was always preaching about the dangers of smoking. But Alan loved to think. It was a favourite pastime of his. Most of his thinking was done in the classroom when he was not interested in the subject he was supposed to be learning. But this morning, with the bedclothes tucked up around his chin, he was thinking about all sorts of things, convinced he was going to be let off school to find out where the coal-man lived.

But his thinking was suddenly interrupted by his mother's ever so loud clump, clump, clumping up the bare stairs. When she opened his bedroom door he was nowhere to be seen. Knowing he was teasing, and playing along, Doreen said, 'Oh, it looks as if I'm going to have to eat his breakfast of toasted soldiers and runny egg' – she knew that would bring him out of his hiding place.

Alan leapt out of the built-in wardrobe and begged her not to eat his breakfast, knowing how much he loved his toasted soldiers and runny egg. Doreen kissed him on the cheek and asked how he had slept?

While he took his pyjama top off and threw it on the bed, his mum opened the curtains and enjoyed the view, albeit only the houses across the way. But there were no dogs barking, no engines being revved and no one shouting.

Alan said he had slept very well, but added, how anyone who slept with Jeannie got any sleep at all was a miracle. Sleeping with Jeannie was like sleeping with a giant worm.

Deciding to come right out with it, he then asked if he had to go to school this morning, adding that he could go and find out where the coal man lived and have him deliver a couple of bags. He could start school tomorrow.

'I already know where the coal man lives,' said Doreen, adding that he was delivering two bags this afternoon. 'As for going to school, I'm afraid you have to sweetheart. You know my feeling on education.'

While straightening the bed-clothes she added, 'But I shouldn't worry, knowing you, you'll soon make friends and, besides, I'm relying on you to look after our Jeannie until she settles in. She admitted to me last night that she's missing her friends.' Pulling Alan to her she said, 'Will you do that for me?'

Alan hugged his mum even though she had fought what Alan considered to be a dirty fight, bringing emotions into it. 'Of course I will,' he said, 'and woe-betide anyone who messes with her.'

'That's my boy,' said Doreen returning his hug. Realizing the time, five past eight, she pointed him towards the bathroom, slapped his bottom and told him not to forget his ears and that she wanted him downstairs in ten minutes.

Halfway down the stairs and listening to Alan talking to himself, Doreen shouted up, 'And only the one flush you little monster' (Alan was going through a phase where he was flushing the lavatory for no apparent reason other than to see the water flooding into the bowl and sloshing around).

With breakfast over and with the time at twenty-five minutes to nine, Mrs Fletcher locked the back door and escorted her children to school. She closed their gate, loving the way the latch clicked in the lock; it sounded new. Pleased that she had hung the curtains on all three bedrooms, she led her children towards the gaping hole in the hedge. Stepping through the gap gave them access to a dirt path, but Alan's eyes lit up. There were fields and hedgerows as far as the eye could see. All the greenery and open space gave him a wonderful feeling as there was nothing like this in Chester. Jeannie was also in awe of view.

'Wow!' was all Alan could think of to say as they began to walk up the well-trodden path that ran parallel with the hedge on their left. Turning to Jeannie, he said there was going to be some serious exploring tonight after school. Nodding, Jeannie agreed with him. Suddenly, a large flock of jackdaws looking for worms and things in the grass took to the air and began to squawk, but soon settled down to feeding again a little further up the field.

The Fletcher's eighty-yard walk along the path was open fields and hedgerows on their right, and the building of yet more houses just visible through gaps in the hedge on their left. Voices were heard shouting to one another. While Alan and Jeanie were trying to take all this newness in, their mum was trying to comprehend all the changes that had been made. This area, including Heol Wen, used to be all fields when she had stayed with Rachel. Workmen, banging away with hammer and nails could just be seen assembling joists on several half-built houses through little gaps in the hedge. Two rather large cement-mixers were also busy churning out mortar for the bricklayers. One of the mixers was also billowing out clouds of black smoke and someone was singing on one of the half-built roofs.

Having seen and enjoyed all this greenery before, Mrs Fletcher was very pleased that her children were also enjoying it. Then, suddenly, the hedge that the children had peeped through to see what was going on, ended. The rest had been ripped out by a mechanical digger which was at the moment standing idle, its tracks covered in at least six inches of dirt.

Alan went up to the digger and, looking up into the cab, wondered what it would be like to drive it. He thought it would be great knocking things down, digging things up and making huge piles of dirt. But the uprooting of the hedges did give a fantastic view of the area that would have been hidden to them. Only used to seeing grotty houses and dirty streets, neither Alan nor Jeannie could believe their eyes. It was like looking inside a picture book.

Scattered here and there in the remaining hedgerows and surrounding fields were several large oak trees. Alan pointed out to Jeannie a small wood on their left which could be seen now that the hedge was gone.

Their mum went one better and pointed out Wrexham Parish Church, three miles away, and several surrounding villages.

Both children were so dumbstruck with what they could see that they began to think that someone had plucked the Adwy out of some picture book and placed it here specially for them. It was so idyllic. Mrs Fletcher was also admiring the view, remembering when she used to roam over these very same fields with her cousin.

As they continued along the now slightly curving path to the right, the tops of the Bryn Celyn Farm buildings were just visible on their left. Suddenly, they came to the end of the path and, seeing the footings of other houses and the makings of a road, joined another path which was officially called Lloft Wen Lane. Both Alan and Jeannie saw something they'd never seen before – according to their mum it was a stile made out of sandstone.

Lloft Wen Lane was originally only fifty-yards long, giving access to the privately-owned houses along the lane from the main road side. But now, it and the newly acquired path had merged with the stone stile marking the spot, giving the village a much appreciated short cut to the main road, the A525. Never having seen a stile before, let alone a sandstone stile, the children, while their mum walked on, climbed over it several times making a game of it. It was fun. But then they heard their mum calling, plus other children from the village on their way to school were approaching in ones and twos. They raced after their mum while admiring the privately-owned houses on their left, especially the one on their right, set back a little, which had its very own tree. Never having seen privately-owned houses before, they reached their mum who was waiting for them by the main Wrexham to Ruthin road.

Facing them across the road, on the corner, was the old Co-op, a shop Mrs Fletcher was going to be doing her big shopping in. She and Rachel had bought many a sherbet lollipop from there as youngsters when they were in this part of the village. It was just as Doreen remembered it.

Turning right, they met up with groups of children of different ages all making their way to school. Coedpoeth was lucky in that the three schools in the area catered for the different age groups. The infant school, for the five- to seven-year-olds, the junior school, for the seven- to eleven-year-olds and finally the senior school, for the eleven to fifteen year olds, the latter age being the official school-leaving age. Mrs Fletcher was more than pleased that Alan and Jeannie were attending the same school so that Alan could keep an eye on his sister.

While walking up the slightly hilly main road, Mrs Fletcher pointed out the shops. The first one they came across was a grocery store on their side, aptly named Glyn's. Across the way was another grocery store called Roberts's. Roberts's, had its very own chippy next door to the store which was very popular with the villagers.

They then passed a row of houses at right angles to the main road. Twenty yards on, set back a little, was 'The Three Mile Inn.' Opposite, and the first of its kind to be built in all of Wales was the Adwy Chapel which had been the church that Doreen attended with Rachel when she stayed in the school holidays. Doreen thought it was a most magnificent building. She absolutely loved its huge conical spire and the two gargoyles that had their beady eyes on you whenever you passed. She still remembered the deep sound of the organ that accompanied the singing and loved the gothic appearance of the pulpit.

But my, what had become of the cemetery? It was a disgrace. When Doreen stayed with her cousin it had been well cared for but was now choked with grass, weeds and bramble. Most of the visible headstones were either leaning or lying flat on the ground. Dear, oh dear, oh dear.

Moving on they came across another public house, the Grosvenor Arms, and a row of four, large, privately-owned houses. Across the road and beyond the low lying hedge were fields, again stretching as far as the eye could see.

Passing the four houses with their magnificent gates, they approached yet another small grocery store belonging to Mr and Mrs Ford, who had come to this part of the world from Liverpool.

Crossing over Smithy Lane, a rather steep hill that branched off the main road, they came across Lingard's, another grocery store cum sweet shop. When Doreen had stayed with Rachel, Ford's shop was always the favourite tuck shop with the local kids, but it now appeared to be Lingard's.

It was at this point that Doreen explained to Alan that she knew not only where all the shops were but also where the coalman, Mr Roberts, lived and reiterated that he was delivering two bags of coal that afternoon.

Alan had been well and truly beaten in his fight to have a day off school. But, when several groups of children began crossing over the road, the Fletchers crossed over with them – they being pupils of the senior school.

Alan noted that the red-shale path they were walking along was about to be tarmaced. The council men with their tools were only waiting for the last of the children to pass by before they started their work at nine o'clock. There was already a lovely smell of coal-tar in the air coming from the coal-tar lorry. There were another four houses along the path and Alan hoped there were no children living in them – fancy having to live next door to a school.

At the far end of the path was the school canteen. Turning right, the Fletchers and groups of children walked alongside the building for several yards before turning left and making their way up a concrete path which separated the school field from the school gardens where flowers and vegetables were growing. Moments later, they found themselves being stared at by the children as they walked across the school yard towards the headmaster's study.

Mr Samuels received them in his official cap and gown. He was a large, slightly overweight man with big spectacles that made his eyes look huge, and he spoke as if he had a sinus problem. He thanked them for being punctual and then spoke at length about the school. He ended by telling Mrs Fletcher the names of the teachers whose class her children would be attending. He also said that they would be in very good hands, adding that there was nothing to worry about.

Giving them a hug and a promise of something special for tea, (their favourite lobscouse pie) Mrs Fletcher thanked Mr Samuels and left to do some shopping in Coedpoeth before going home. It was Mrs Fletcher who felt like crying, the children appeared to be excited.

Mr Samuels escorted Alan and Jeannie to the assembly room which was slowly filling up with children of different ages. Seeing them settled and ignoring everyone, the headmaster gave certain trouble makers a hard stare before returning to his study. There were some ten minutes to go before he asserted his authority and brought the school to order.

The moment Mr Samuels disappeared the chattering resumed. Jeannie was approached by two girls her age and was asked if she would like to sit with them? With Alan's approval, Jeannie picked up her satchel and moved over to the girl's section of the room with them. Pleased for her, Alan then began the serious business of sussing out the older, bigger lads – the ones he suspected would be giving him a little trouble later. There were many pairs of eyes on him.

At precisely one minute to nine, a female monitor stood in the middle doorway of the old Victorian building and rang the school bell. Instantly, the assembly hall (converted to its present size by the unfolding of two classroom partitions) filled with bustling children between the ages of eleven and fifteen, all trying to find a seat as quickly as possible.

At exactly nine o'clock, with the appearance of the teachers who sat in their appropriate places in front, the children came to order and were quiet. There was absolute silence and stillness when Mr Samuels made his entry. He very generously gave some stragglers a few extra moments to settle down, then he ordered the outside doors to be closed and brought the assembly hall to order. His gargantuan presence was felt and feared by most of the children.

Mr Griffiths (the history teacher), small in stature, but jolly in nature, opened the piano lid and, taking his cue from Mr Samuels, began to play the introduction to *All Things Bright and Beautiful*. Standing, with books in hand the children burst into song. Miss Griffiths (the music teacher) conducted them very enthusiastically. Her arms waved, her body swayed, she encouraged the children to sing from the heart. She was always going on about singing from the heart and feeling the music. Some children did, some did not. Nevertheless, there was a lovely rendition of *Fight the Good Fight, Stand Up, Stand Up for Jesus*, and *The Lord is my Shepherd*. Then with everyone seated, Mr Samuels read the parable of the Good Samaritan from the Bible. During the reading, had a pin fallen to the floor, it would have been heard; that was how quiet the children were. But when the Bible was closed and his audience given a hard stare (a favourite weapon of his) Mr Samuels mentioned the school's sports day in just over six weeks time. He said he was hoping for better results than last year.

So with the morning's assembly over, Mr Samuels searched for and beckoned his newest pupils to come forward and meet their respective teachers. Meanwhile, in silence and with military precision, under the watchful eyes of the teachers, the children were ordered to their classrooms to begin their lessons.

Alan was introduced to and instructed to follow Miss Williams, the English teacher. Jeannie was introduced to Miss Edwards (religious instruction). Suddenly, two male monitors (fifth formers) returned the Assembly Hall back to classroom size by unfolding the concertinaed sections, making sure that each was locked into place. It was the metallic sound made by the little wheels as they rolled along their tracks that caught Alan's attention. He was so fascinated by it that he forgot to wish Jeannie good luck. When he turned to see where she was, Jeannie was gone.

Following Miss Williams, Alan was taken to her classroom away from the main building, where he was made to stand in front of the blackboard for everyone to see. Miss Williams entered his name in the register book then, with cane in hand, addressed the children. 'Good morning form 2X,' she droned, realizing there were several absentees this morning.

'Good morning Miss,' the children replied drearily.

'For those of you who are still half asleep, we have a new boy. His name is Alan Fletcher.' She paused then said, 'I do hope we are going to make him feel welcome.'

Slamming her cane down on the desk in front of her (making the two female occupants jump) Miss Williams said rather harshly. 'What is it we are going to do?'

'Make him feel welcome Miss,' the children replied.

'Thank you,' said Miss. Williams, 'but this time, shall we all try and say it together. I'm sure we can do it if we try hard enough.' The children complied.

Miss Williams (a small, slim woman with dark hair and a round face, whose thick-rimmed glasses slightly accentuated her cross-eyed eyes) put her cane away and ordered Alan to take up the only available seat next to the annoying Malcolm Smith.

Malcolm, who sat in the back row by the window, gave Miss Williams a sarcastic smile. He did not care tuppence for her. He smiled even more knowing that the school's nickname for her was 'Cock-leg.' Miss Williams, who seemed to love dishing out corporal punishment, would, when caning you, raise her right leg about twelve inches and would then stamp it down in sync with the cane – hence the name, 'Cock-leg.' Most of the school's senior children made fun of her in the playground by imitating her.

Opening the register-book, with pen in hand, Miss Williams began to call out the children's names. Those who answered were given a tick. Those who did not were marked absent with a cross. When the last name was called and the register book closed, Miss Williams addressed the class in a harsh tone. She informed them that they were still being let down by absenteeism, adding that she did not think they would ever reach 100% attendance and earn an early Friday afternoon finish.

Looking around the room with her beady eyes, she asked why form 2X could not be like form 4X, Mr Pritchard's class, which very often reached 100% attendance. She then asked if there was not a twinge of envy when they saw Form 4 going home at three-thirty instead of four o'clock most Fridays.

Knowing full well the children would not answer her next question honestly, if at all, Miss Williams nevertheless asked if any of the absentees played out after school. The children, as ever, refused to snitch, lowered their heads and began to fidget. Seeing she had failed yet again, Miss Williams instructed the class, whose first lesson of the day was English, to open their books.

Taking any one of the subjects on the blackboard, they were to write an essay of at least two full pages and in their best handwriting. The choice of subject was the 'Four Seasons'.

As the children began to write Alan's name was called out. 'Come here boy,' scowled Miss Williams, handing him a clean exercise book with instructions that it was to be taken home and covered with brown paper. Miss Williams, with full eye contact, said rather brutally that scribbling would not be tolerated and then asked if he understood her meaning.

When Alan replied, 'Yes, Miss,' he was ordered to sit down. Using his eenie, meanie, miny mo, ploy, Alan chose to write about winter.

Minutes into the lesson and checking to see what old misery guts, (Cock-leg) was doing, Malcolm nudged Alan's arm. Whispering he said, 'Hiya mate, I'm Malcolm but call me Twab. That's my nick-name.' Alan nodded, but was too nervous to answer, just in case.

Again making sure Miss Williams was not looking, and again whispering, Twab asked Alan what his nickname was? Alan shook his head to mean he did not have one.

'So where do you live?' Twab asked, again whispering. Not wanting to be caught talking in class, not on his first day, and in the lowest whisper he could manage, Alan said he and his family had moved into Heol Wen on Saturday. Twab's face lit up. 'Oh; so you're the new kid. Hey, pleased to meet you.' His enthusiastic response caused Miss Williams' ears to prick up. Failing to pin point the culprit, she reached for her cane. Quite sternly she ordered everyone to stop talking and get on with their work or she would keep them in for half-an-hour after school.

Using the boy in front as cover, Twab began to pull faces at Miss Williams. Suppressing a giggle, Alan could not decide if he was mad or stupid.

Two rows up from Twab, Brian Davies from Southsea stood up and informed Miss Williams that he needed to go to the lavatory.

'Sit down Brian.'

'Please Miss, its urgent.'

'Sit down Brian; get on with your work.'

'Please, Miss.' But before Brian could speak another word, Miss Williams slammed her cane down on her table and ordered him to sit down or else. Brian sat, but when he was convinced she was not looking, began to pull faces at her. Maureen 'Bacho' Roberts burst out laughing.

Slamming her book shut, Miss Williams stood up and ordered Brian to come to the front. 'Come here you horrible boy,' she yelled.

'Why Miss?' said Brian not realizing she had seen him pulling faces at her. Knowing what the outcome was going to be, the rest of the class watched and waited. They knew what Brian's fate was going to be.

'Come to the front,' yelled Miss Williams beginning to shake with anger, her blood-pressure rising.

'Why Miss? What have I done?' Brian doled out defiantly.

'You'd better do as you're told, my lad,' said Miss Williams whose face was turning red with anger.

Making sure his desk-lid was closed, there being things inside it that were for his eyes only, Brian approached Miss Williams. He was immediately ordered to hold out his left hand. 'Why am I having the cane miss, I haven't done anything?'

With her patience exhausted, Miss Williams took Brian's hand and forced it out. Brian was caned not once, but twice for being so insolent. She then ordered him to sit down and get on with his work. Again, a pin could have been heard had one been dropped.

Brian walked back to his desk with a slight grin on his face. Old misery-guts had cocked her leg as usual. Slamming her foot down in sync with the cane was always amusing. Miss Williams was always laughed at whenever she dished out corporal punishment. Nearly everyone in the class had to stifle a grin, apart from Alan and those in front. Those in front cowered. But, being new to the school, Alan did not know what to expect, even though Twab was grinning, as were a few other boys.

With his left hand tingling, Brian sat down and got on with his work. His plan had failed. He would have to wait until the eleven o'clock playtime for the smoke he felt he was in need of.

Those who feared Miss Williams got on with their work, especially when she patrolled the classroom, peering over their shoulders. The others, including Twab and most of the boys condemned her for being so sadistic. Sadism and corporal punishment seemed to go hand in hand with most teachers in this school.

With just ten minutes of the lesson remaining, Gordon Morris, a local farmer's lad, stood up. In his grouchy voice, he explained when Miss Williams allowed him to speak that his pencil needed sharpening.

'Then come to the front and use the waste paper basket,' she bellowed.

Gordon only pretended to sharpen his pencil. When he was sure that no one was watching, he reached into an inside pocket of his jacket and produced a rat that had been killed that morning by one of the cats that lived on the farm. He very carefully lowered it into the waste paper basket and covered it over. Then, convinced he had not been seen, he returned to his desk feeling rather pleased with himself. It was pay-back time.

Knowing Miss Williams would be emptying the basket sometime during the day, Gordon tried to visualise the chaos the dead rat would cause. He sat there wishing he could be a fly on the wall when the headless rodent was found.

Gordon watched her writing work for her next class on the lower half of the blackboard and hoped she wet herself when she found his little surprise which was revenge for an accident the previous Friday. Gordon had accidentally spilled a blob of ink on the cover of the English text book. He was not only given the cane, but was told off in front of the whole class. He and the rest of the children were again reminded that school books do not grow on trees. That saying about revenge being sweet was very relevant on Alan's first day.

With the lesson about to end, Miss Williams ordered the monitors to collect the books and place them on her table in a neat pile. A minute before the bell was due to ring, Miss Williams ordered everyone to form two lines as quickly and as quietly as they could – boys to the left, girls to the right. When the bell rang, the children were instructed to walk on quietly. As Gordon filed past the waste paper basket, he looked down and began to chuckle.

Form 2X's second lesson of the day was art with Mr Robinson in the adjacent room. Mr Robinson was of average height with blond hair that was beginning to thin. He was slightly overweight for someone who taught sport as well as art. He was the only teacher who had leather patches on the elbows of his jacket.

Form 2X lined up outside Mr Robinson's class and waited patiently on the left-hand side of the corridor while the previous class, form 5, filed out from their art lesson in single file. While waiting, Twab spotted his two best friends in the world walking across the school yard to their next lesson. He pointed them out to Alan and said he would introduce him to them come playtime. Waving his arms, trying to draw their attention, Twab explained that Sparrow and Golcho were members of a little gang he had formed. He then asked Alan if he would like to be in his gang seeing as he lived in Heol Wen. The truth was Twab had always wanted a gang of four and there had only been three because no one else in the village of their age came up to scratch. Sparrow and Golcho, who were fit for anything, were ideal gang members. The three of them with their rough and tumble attitude made the rest of the village kids look like wimps. Twab had been wishing for a fourth member for some time now. Being a gang of three was very often awkward, especially when playing games like Stroke the Bunny, or chasing, or when playing marbles, or having a conker competition, plus the fact that two against one while playing Robin Hood or Commandos never worked out.

Alan jumped at the invitation and thanked Twab most sincerely. He had been a gang member all his life and knew the benefits. He then remembered yesterday afternoon while standing in his gateway. He began to think it was Twab and his two mates (whose names he had already forgotten) whom he saw running down the road, just before he had to go upstairs and help with Jeannie's bed.

Now that Alan was in the gang, Twab began to wonder how Sparrow and Golcho were going to take it. He could not see any problem, but would they? He was told that he would have to be sworn in, and that the ceremony would take place during the eleven o'clock playtime period.

During the art lesson, Mr Robinson was called away, but not before he had chosen a monitor to stand out in front and take the names of those who misbehaved. The moment he left the room, down went the crayons and out came the little elastic catapults that fired little rolled up paper pellets. There were no rules as such, other than you did not fire at the girls – well, not deliberately. So, with that in mind, the lads of form 2X got on with the business of shooting pellets at each other, whether they had catapults or not. The lucky ones were those who sat in the back row as, up to a point, they could use their desk lids as shields.

Stan Woods, who was desperately trying to dodge the paper pellets fired at him, was the monitor. But, being one of the lads and refusing to be a target, he gave as good as he got. Bobby Pugh from Bwlchgwyn was just taking aim at Harold Edwards, also from Bwlchgwyn, when Stan let fly with a pellet. It caught Bobby just behind the ear. He yelled out and caused half of the class to burst out laughing.

Suddenly, as the battle raged on, Anita Roberts from New Broughton was accidentally hit in the face and began to cry. All those involved in the fracas, seeing what had just happened, quickly put their catapults away. While some began to pick up all the pellets off the floor before Mr Robinson came back, others went about bribing Anita. She was offered several penny-chews and sticks of liquorice not to report the incident. Now that a truce had been called, the art lesson resumed as if nothing had happened.

With a pocketful of pellets off the floor for next time, as battles often took place when the teacher left the room, Twab sat down. For once he had managed to avoid being hit. Alan had never seen anything like this in a classroom before. He thought the Chester lads were tough, but these Welsh lads could show them a thing or two.

When Twab sat down, Alan asked to see his catapult. Seeing it was two rubber bands tied together he asked Twab where he could get one. Producing a spare one Twab said, 'Here, you can have this one.'

Alan placed his newly acquired weapon over his thumb and index finger. Pinching where the two bands joined (where the pellet was placed) he pulled it back and let go. The swooshing sound it made excited him. He had in his hand a most powerful weapon. Had he not just seen it in action?

Ten minutes later, Mr Robinson returned. Everyone was relieved that all the pellets had been picked up off the floor as Mr Robinson was a much better caner than Cock-Leg. When Mr Robinson caned you, you knew you had been caned. Then the bell began to ring – it was eleven o'clock and playtime.

'Come on,' whispered Twab when permission to leave was given. 'Let's go and find Sparrow and Golcho. I know where they'll be.'

Outside they raced over to the boys' lavatory via the main playground, an area of some 30 x 50 yards. Some of the first-year boys were playing chase, some were playing tick, others had yo-yos, while a few played marbles. Some of the older boys just stood around doing nothing.

As for the girls, some of the younger ones were skipping individually, while others were in competition. A few were also playing tick or chasing. Several third-year girls were doing handstands up against the school building, their skirts tucked into their knickers while certain boys gawped at them.

Others were playing hopscotch, while some played ring-a-ring-of-roses. Just inside the bike shed, some fifth-year girls, Menna Roberts, Ada Goodwin, Jean Flitcroft and Eirwen Williams were demonstrating the hoola-hoop to a crowd of envious onlookers.

There was also a good game of football being played on the top half of the school field – whereas on the lower half, girls were playing rounders. There was so much activity going on in the fifteen minutes of playtime. How different it was to the pent up feelings of the classroom.

Sparrow and Golcho were in the lavatory, as was Brian, the boy who had tried to fool Miss Williams earlier and been given the cane for his trouble. When Twab, with Alan in tow, entered the lavatory, he greeted Sparrow and Golcho with his usual, 'Hiya.' Then, coming right out with it he said, 'Gang, this here is Alan from Heol Wen. He's the new kid from Chester who's been lucky enough to sit next to me in class.' He then went on to tell Sparrow and Golcho how Brian had been given the cane off Cock-leg for trying to get out of class for a quick smoke.

With his left hand still stinging slightly, Brian began to call Miss Williams names that could not be said in church or written down on paper. Everyone present began to laugh. When he showed the cane marks on his left hand, he began to brag that Cock-leg could not cane for toffee and that she had not hurt him. Then, impatient to be off, he flushed his fag-end down the lav, thus getting rid of the evidence. With a 'Cheerio, see you later,' he shot off for a game of football in what little time was left.

Meanwhile, having informed Sparrow and Golcho that he had

invited this new kid from Chester to be in their gang, Twab brought up the subject again. Somewhat shocked and speechless, Sparrow and Golcho gave their leader a long, bewildering look. They could not believe what he had just said. And yet, it has to be said that Twab never said anything that he did not mean. Both could recall him in the past saying how much better it would be if they were a gang of four. But why this new kid, what was so special about him?

'He's from Chester,' Twab reiterated, hoping that would do the trick. But when no answer was given, and not being known for his patience Twab added, 'He looks tough enough to me to be in our gang. And you should have seen him just now during our catty fight in class. He wasn't half giving them what for with the catty I gave him. And he's a good shot.'

Playtime was only fifteen minutes long and they still had to collect their free bottle of milk. Impatient for an answer, and tutting – Twab always tutted when he wanted them to hurry up – he said: 'Come on gang, you know I've always wanted a gang of four. Just think how much better it will be when we're down the woods. We could have two on each side instead of two against one. Now doesn't that make sense?'

So with Twab's little porky about Alan being a good shot with a catty accepted (had it not, he would have pulled rank on them, it being his gang and all that) Sparrow and Golcho ummed and ahhed for a few moments, but finally gave the thumbs up on condition that this new kid got himself a snake belt from Gracie's shop in Coedpoeth as soon as possible. When Alan asked what a snake belt was, Twab, Sparrow and Golcho showed him theirs. He was flabbergasted, as he had never seen one before, but so impressed that he knew he had to have one. A snake belt was a colourful, elasticated belt, about two-inches wide which has a metal ring at one end and a clasp, in the shape of a wriggling snake on the other. When the snake's head was slotted into the ring, *violà*, your trousers were guaranteed to stay up.

When Alan was asked how his trousers were being kept up, he showed them his braces. Not only was he laughed at, but there were a few snide remarks thrown in as well. Did he not know braces were old fashioned? So, with a promise that he got himself a snake belt as soon as possible, Alan was sworn in as the fourth and final member of the Shanghai Bombers. He suddenly remembered his mum's words not three hours ago. 'I shouldn't worry, you'll soon make friends.' Wow, this was unbelievable!

The swearing-in ceremony went as follows. With Sparrow and Golcho flanking him, Alan was told to make a fist with his right hand, place it on his heart and then throw it out in a salute the way Twab had seen the Romans do in some film where Charles Laughton was the Emperor Claudius. And, while saluting, he had to swear his allegiance to the Shanghai Bombers which meant he had to nod his head and agree to everything that Twab said regarding orders and such things, him being the boss. And this is exactly what he did.

When Twab, Sparrow and Golcho went to the local cinema to see the film *Treasure Island*, starring Robert Newton as Long John Silver (who was in charge of a gang of scallywags known as the Black Spot Gang), Twab knew at once that he had to have a good name for his little gang of three. His first thought was of calling it the Snake Belt Gang (or SBG for short), it sounding much better than the Black Spot Gang, plus the fact he did not like the idea of them having a black ink spot on the palm of their hands the way the Black Spot Gang had in the film. It would have caused too many problems both in school and at home.

When he read about the Shanghai Bombers from a school book he was reading, and realized they were a much tougher lot, he changed his mind and so they became the Shanghai Bombers. It may seem a little confusing but it made sense to Twab. And once he had made up his mind, there was no changing it.

So, while shaking arms the Roman way in compliance with the rules, Sparrow, sidled up to Alan and said, 'Hiya mate, I'm Robert Williams. I live on Heol Celyn, the street below you, but call me Sparrow, everyone else does.'

Golcho, who was several inches taller than Twab, Sparrow and now Alan, nudged Sparrow out of the way. Shaking Alan's arm the Roman way, he said, 'Hiya mate. I'm sorry we have the same name, but I'm Alan Jones and I live on the corner of Heol Wen. I saw you arriving last Saturday in that big van. I thought the slogan on the front and back of the van was great.'

'What slogan, what did it say?' Twab wanted to know.

'Here Come's Dodd. There Goes Dodd,' said Golcho. Turning to Alan, Golcho said that you could not miss my house, it being the one with the big diamond flower bed in the middle of the lawn. He then insisted that he be called Golcho.

With another round of arm shaking, the Roman way, and now knowing that Twab lived on Heol Islwyn, Alan asked where their fantastic nick-names had come from. He was so envious of them.

Golcho said he got his because of his grandfather. As a young man his grandad worked in the lead mines in Minera as a *golcho*, a lead washer.

Sparrow said he was given his nickname by a John Hughes, a slightly older lad of the village. It seems one day John started calling him Sparrow and it stuck. Twab also admitted that it was the same John Hughes who gave him his nickname. According to John, Malcolm was a dead ringer for the American singer Tab Hunter and somehow Tab had became Twab.

Suddenly, Sparrow disappeared into one of the lavatory cubicles. Moments later he re-emerged with a packet of five Woodbine and a few matches. If ever he needed a smoke it was now, having had the shock of being told that some kid from Chester was joining their little gang of three. He took a ciggy from the flimsy, open-ended packet and broke it in half, placed the two ends between his lips, lit them and, while inhaling what smoke was in his mouth, handed one over to Golcho.

Because Twab did not want to smoke at the moment, Sparrow returned the contraband to its hiding place, a carefully loosened brick that he'd inherited for a shilling from an older lad who had since left school.

Twab then explained to Alan why you do not carry ciggies on you. 'Not only will the bigger lads take them off you, but if the teachers find them, then you're in BIG trouble. Alan soon realized that the lavatory had two uses. One, it was somewhere you came to when nature called, and two; it was an ideal smoke den.

Suddenly, four mean looking fifth formers came in and caught Sparrow and Golcho in the act of smoking. Terry and Frank grabbed them by the scruff of the neck and taking their dog ends off them, began to smoke them.

Dave and Ernie, the other two ruffians shuffled everyone else out of the lavatory rather roughly. They then asked Sparrow and Golcho if they had any more ciggies on them, threatening them to tell the truth or else.

Terry and Frank were having a competition to see who could produce the best smoke-rings. After several attempts, Terry played his trump card and was deemed the outright winner when he blew one smoke ring through another, a feat that was admired by one and all, especially Sparrow. In fact Sparrow was so impressed he gave Terry a round of applause.

Not believing that Sparrow and Golcho did not have any ciggies on them, Dave ordered them to turn out their pockets, but none were found.

When Alan was approached by Terry, whose rule it was to suss out all new faces personally, three boys come in, saw what was going on, and scarpered out as quickly as they could. They knew what was going on.

Having taken no notice of them, Terry, who was clearly the boss, turned to Alan and asked if he was the new kid? Alan nodded to mean he was. Grabbing him by the scruff of the neck, Dave said, 'So what's your name kid?'

'Alan Fletcher.'

'Well, Alan Fletcher,' said Dave almost choking him, 'have you got any ciggies on you?'

Shaking his head while trying not to cough Alan said he did not smoke, but was still ordered to empty his pockets out. When it was seen that he was telling the truth, and grinning, Dave suggested he be taken to the stink pipe. Cursing the dreaded stink pipe, a fate worse than death, Twab, with fingers crossed asked that Alan be left alone, adding he had not done anything.

'So would you like to go instead of him?,' Frank asked grabbing Twab by the hair causing him to squirm. Determined not going to cry out, having had the stink pipe treatment, Twab said nothing. He knew he'd spoken out of turn and felt his best chance now was to say nothing and act dumb.

With his contorted face just inches from Alan's, making himself look tougher Frank said, 'We've got a little surprise for you kid, but not just yet, the bell's gonna go in a minute, there won't be enough time, so we'll see you dinnertime; won't we fellows.' With that he pushed Alan to one side. He then pushed Twab and Golcho to one side when he saw his pals leaving in search of another victim and went after them.

Everyone was glad to see the back of them. Wondering what the surprise could be, Alan asked what on earth could the stink pipe be? When no one answered Twab said, 'Come on we'll show you.'

From the lavatory Alan was taken to a set of black Victorian gates in what was the playground annex. The gates were open and in the supporting wall to their left for all to see was a large metal bowl. It was where all the unwanted milk was disposed of. And, coincidentally, it was just large enough to accommodate a human head.

Looking at it Twab told Alan to have a sniff. Looking at his three newly-acquired friends with suspicion, Alan lowered his head but quickly pulled it back. It stank terribly.

'It's blocked up with milk,' Sparrow informed him, adding that it was where the head went when they stink piped you. 'All first years and new kids to the school have their heads shoved in there,' he continued. 'And the teachers all know it goes on, but do nowt about it,' said Golcho adding, 'I'm sure they think we think it's all part of school life.'

'Golcho's right,' insisted Sparrow. 'They don't even try to stop it.' Then with his next breath he said rather excitedly, 'But hey, did you see Terry blowing that smoke ring through the first one. Cor, I wish I could do that.'

Alan asked if any of their heads had been shoved in the bowl.

'We all have,' said Twab. 'Like Sparrow said, all first years and new kids to the school are brought here and given the treatment.'

'Yea,' said Sparrow adding that it was something to do with tradition.

'Well, they'll have to catch me first,' said Alan rather confidently.

'Oh, they'll catch you,' said Golcho while trying to shove Sparrow's head in the bowl, 'you can be sure of that.' With his next breath and with Sparrow's head almost in the bowl, he explained how it was fun for Terry and his lot, that they loved to see someone kicking and screaming when they were brought there.

Having fought back, with Golcho's head almost in the bowl, Sparrow let him go when he promised to pack it in. The smell was terrible. Turning to Alan, Sparrow said he was here when they did John Roberts, adding that you could see on their faces how much they were enjoying John's squealing. He was trying to point out that Alan had no chance.

'He's right,' said Twab, 'you'll be done dinnertime, guaranteed.'

Confident that he would be able to out-run them, Alan suddenly remembered and threw up his hands. 'Oh no,' he cried, 'I'll have to go. I promised me mum I'd keep an eye on my sister.'

'Let's go with him gang,' said Twab. 'One for all an' all that.'

Shaking arms the Roman way; they put the stink pipe problem behind them for the time being, and went in search of Jeannie. They searched the school field first, but there was no sign of her.

Jeannie was eventually found by the middle cloakroom, playing skipping with her two new found friends, Wendy Pritchard and Hazel Jones, and other girls as well. 'Hiya Sis. How's it going?' Alan asked.

But Jeannie never answered. She was too busy trying to find the right moment to jump into the skipping rope. Suddenly and with perfect timing she jumped in, found her rhythm and sang out: 'I call in my very best friends.' With that Wendy then Hazel also with perfect timing jumped in and began to skip. All three girls found their rhythm and skipped their hearts out. Then, one by one, they jumped out and watched as three other girls jumped in.

Having retrieved four bottles of milk from the milk station, Sparrow handed them out. Twab, Sparrow and Alan removed the silver coloured milk tops with their thumbs and then drank the milk, intending to put the crumpled-up milk tops back in the bottle when finished. Causing litter got you the cane.

Golcho on the other hand removed his silver milk top by pressing down in the centre and then took it off very carefully. As planned, it came off whole. Drinking his milk, he then handed the empty bottle over to Sparrow. Telling everyone to watch, he placed the milk-top between his index and third finger. Smirking, he again told everyone to watch. When he had their full attention, he raised his hand and flicked his fingers. The silver-top whizzed away for several yards like a miniature Flying Saucer. He actually called it his flying saucer because it resembled the flying saucer that came to earth in the film, *The Day the Earth Stood Still*, staring Michael Rennie and a giant robot called Gort who could melt steel and destroy the world if it wanted to.

When he was asked who had shown him how to make flying

saucers, Golcho said he had seen it being done by one of the lads in Form 4.

Seeing Jeannie was okay and enjoying herself, Alan said he would see her at dinner time. Jeannie never answered as jumping back into the skipping rope was her priority now.

When the four empty milk bottles were returned to the milk station, Alan was just about to shoot a pellet into the air that Twab had gave him, but was ordered to put it away. A scuffle had broken out by the metalwork classroom. 'Come on,' said Sparrow somewhat cheered up by the fracas, 'let's go and see who's fighting.'

Within seconds, a crowd had gathered around the two combatants, but as the lads ran over the bell rang.

'Well, I'll go to the foot of our stairs,' said Golcho scrunching up his face 'That's a bit of bad luck. We haven't had a good scrap in ages and when we do, the bell goes.'

The fighting stopped immediately on the bell with the crowd quickly dispersing. Anyone involved in a playground disturbance, even as a spectator, would end up having the cane off Mr Samuels.

The two fourth-year combatants stood up and brushed themselves down. The incident was far from finished and was going to be resumed after school and, hopefully, in private. In 1953, to be called that word that meant you had been born out of wedlock was not the done thing. Had the law been involved, it would have meant someone in front of a judge and rightly so.

Within moments of the bell ringing, the playground was once again silent. Alan was about to meet Mr Ellis the maths teacher.

While the monitors were handing out Form 2X's exercise books, Alan was standing in front of Mr Ellis with his hands behind his back, more or less standing to attention. Sir was informing him that a quiet boy is a busy boy; a noisy boy, a nuisance. Alan was then asked which he was going to be.

'A quiet boy, Sir,' Alan shot back.

Mr Ellis, a short stocky man, whose brown hair was parted on the left, had huge hands but was noted for his sadistic smile. He glared at Alan and said he was pleased with his decision. Holding out a clean exercise book, he insisted that Alan's work be clean and readable.

'Yes Sir,' said Alan who was then told to sit down.

Turning the blackboard round to reveal the day's work, multiplication of fractions, the children were told to get on with it. While some struggled with the lesson (maths was not everyone's favourite subject) Alan, Twab and a few others found the lesson easy having grasped the idea of dividing things into portions.

Twenty minutes on, with most of the problems worked out and copied in his book, Alan nudged Twab's arm and whispering asked if he smoked? Twab nodded to mean he did, but whispered back, 'Not as much as Sparrow or Golcho! Why?'

'I'd like to try it?'

With Mr Ellis marking books; Twab scrunched his face up and said barely audible that he did not think he would like it.

But Alan was adamant, he wanted to try it.

'You go dizzy, green and cough your heart out.' Twab whispered.

Not to be put off, Alan said his all-time favourite film star smoked.

Again, checking on Mr Ellis, who was still marking books, Twab whispered who his all-time favourite film star was.

'Alan Ladd.'

Twab scrunched his nose up to mean he was okay, but said Errol Flynn was better. Seeing danger, Twab nudged Alan's arm to warn him that Mr Ellis was on walk-about to see how their work was coming along and both forgot all about film stars and smoking and concentrated on their work.

Leaning over Malcolm's shoulder, then across at Alan's work, Mr Ellis congratulated them both on there being no wrong answers thus far before completing his round and returning to his desk where he continued to mark the books from his previous class.

Going back to film stars, Twab explained as quietly as he could that there was a smashing picture house in Coedpoeth not two hundred yards from where they were sitting and that he was welcome to go with them if he wanted to, but was not to worry if he had no money to get in with. Winking, and again just audibly, Twab announced that they have a way of getting in free.

'How do you do that?' Alan grinned, adding that he loved the flicks.

'One of us pays to go in,' said Twab with an eye on Mr Ellis, 'then at 7.30, when the lights go down, who ever paid to go in opens the lavatory door for those of us who are waiting outside.'

'Does it work?'

Twab nodded.

Just then there was a disturbance. Two third-year girls having to pass through Mr Ellis' classroom in order to reach Mr Pritchard's classroom forgot to ask permission. Alan was horrified when Mr Ellis reached for his cane.

'He's not going to cane them, is he?'

'You watch,' whispered Twab, his face scrunched up in contempt of the man. 'E's nothing but a big bully just because he used to box for the army.' Both girls received the cane, and both girls burst out crying.

'You won't forget to ask in future,' Mr Ellis told them. Putting the cane away he told the girls to be on their way. Form 2X watched sympathetically as the girls, sobbing, entered Mr Pritchard's classroom.

Twab was horrified that the girls had been caned as hard as any boy and most of the class had shuddered when they saw the cane striking the girls' hands.

Sensing the children's animosity, Mr Ellis attracted their attention by slamming down an empty desk lid and ordering them to get on with their work. Some seven minutes later, and to everyone's delight, the bell rang. Mr Ellis ordered the class to put their books away and stack them on his table in a neat pile on their way out. It was twelve o'clock and dinner time.

Form 2X filed out of the classroom in an orderly fashion, their books stacked on Sir's table in two neat piles, boys on the right, girls on the left. As Twab and Alan went into the adjoining cloakroom, Sparrow and Golcho were already there waiting for them.

'We've got to find somewhere for Alan to hide,' Sparrow barked while Golcho added, 'Yea and quickly. You know who are coming for him.' Terry and Co were indeed coming for him. They had meant what they said about this new kid from Chester going to the stink pipe in the fifteen minutes before dinner. Looking at his new found friend from Chester and seeing no way out for him Golcho said, 'I'm afraid its stink pipe time for you, mate.'

Looking through the porch window, Alan could see Terry, Frank, Ernie and Dave coming their way, spread out blocking off any escape route. Alan was trapped or so it seemed.

'You could make a run for it,' Twab suggested, wishing there was something they could do for him, 'they're too big for us to be of any help, but I wouldn't go back through the classrooms if I was you. You saw what happened to those girls.'

'What girls, what's been happening?' Sparrow wanted to know.

'They're almost here,' warned Golcho panicking for Alan.

Calming Sparrow down, Twab said how old bully boy Ellis had been at it again with the cane – girls this time. He said he would explain in full, later. He was more interested in what Alan was going to do at the moment.

Confused and trying to think, Alan stepped outside to see if there was any way out? He began to believe he was going to have to take the stink pipe treatment like a man. Then he saw what he thought was a possible way out. To his left, and running three-quarters of the way across the playground, stood what was once a segregation wall. There was no other way, and his plan would have to work on his first attempt. There would be no time for a second try. He also knew his plan would only work if his timing was right, and time was running out. If it didn't work, well – he would find out what it was like to be stink piped.

Alan walked towards his tormenters to give them the impression that he was coming quietly. The schoolyard was filling up. That could be a problem. Reaching the distance he needed from the wall, he spun round and raced for the four-foot high barrier. Not only was the chase on, but it was also the moment of truth. Would his plan work? As he neared the wall, hoping his timing was right, he dived and landed perfectly flat on it, then slid down the other side and raced off.

All those who were watching, knowing what was going on, silently cheered for this new boy from Chester as did Twab, Sparrow and Golcho. But not to be outdone, Terry and Co, who were determined that this new kid from Chester was going to the stink pipe no matter what, gave chase.

Dave and Frank scampered over the wall after Alan, thinking he was going to run straight on. But Terry and Ernie, believing their victim would be heading for the playing field took a short cut through an entry that separated Miss Williams's class (Alan's class) from the bike shed.

Not knowing where he was running to, Alan ran past the bike shed and, seeing an open gateway, ran through it onto the school playing field. Not knowing which way to run for the best, and seeing his chasers were closing in on all sides, he joined in with the football, hoping they had not seen him. It worked for a while, but he was finally spotted by Dave and Frank who had run onto the pitch with him.

'He's here,' they informed Terry and Ernie who were also on the field.

Seeing which way Alan was running, Terry and Ernie tried to cut him off. Alan zig-zagged his way past them and ran like the devil, but as they were closing in on him, it was only a matter of time. In one last desperate attempt, he reached down for that special gear and hoped for the best. He raced on down the school field towards the canteen.

Twab, Sparrow and Golcho followed behind as did several children, knowing what was going on, but could do nothing about it. Feeling sorry for Alan, they began to cheer him on when he opened up a substantial gap between himself and his chasers. There being safety in numbers, some of the children began to shout for the new kid, but with fingers crossed that they were not taken to the stink pipe instead.

Reaching the canteen building, and with nowhere else to run, Alan was finally caught inside the doorway. He tried to struggle free, but it was useless. When he tried to implement a judo throw, Terry picked him up and told him to pack it in or he would throw him down the steps head first.

'Got ya, you little bugger,' said Terry puffing and panting. Moments later when he had got his breath back, he told Alan that he had taken some catching. In fact he said, 'That was the best chase we've had in a long time.'

As much as they too were puffing and panting from being smokers, Frank, Ernie, and Dave also agreed that it had been a riveting chase. As Alan was frog marched away, he noticed that the council men were still tarmacing the path. The smell of tar was quite strong now that they were up to the canteen, but there was no sign of the workmen.

As they led Alan away, Terry decided he liked this spunky kid from Chester. He was reminded of himself at that age and, turning to Alan while tightening his grip, he said, 'You did well kid. I'm impressed.'

'Yea, but was it good enough to be let off?' Alan asked hoping it was.

Laughing and coughing at the same time (from being a smoker) Terry shook his head. 'Fraid not kid.' But with his next breath he told him not to worry. Newcomers to the school only have the one visit, unless they do something silly like show-off or give Terry, or someone like him, cheek.

'We'd better get a move on,' said Ernie impatiently. 'The bells gonna go in a minute and it's already saved 'im once.'

'Yea, e's right,' Dave put in.

So Alan was frog-marched a little faster, with most of the school looking on, and suddenly he was staring at the dreaded stink pipe. While holding his breath he tried to break free, but they were too strong for him. He knew there was nothing he could do to stop them from shoving his head into that smelly bowl. If only they were his size, he could have implemented his judo, but they were too big for him, plus there were four of them.

The smell was horrible. But suddenly, the bell announcing dinner-time rang which was music to Alan's ears. He could not believe he had been saved by the bell yet again – nor could Terry and Co.

'Well if that don't beat all,' Terry cursed, as he slapped Alan across the head out of frustration. 'That's the second time the bell has saved you, kid.' Looking up, Terry wondered if there was anyone up there looking after him.

Alan was so pleased to hear the bell and, not wanting to antagonise them, stood perfectly still. Ruffling his hair, amazed at how some things can work out, Terry, with full eye contact said, 'Well kid, you've obviously got someone looking after you. I suppose we'll have to see you after dinner now. Go on,' he said, shaking his head in disbelief, 'go and get ya grub.'

Standing there watching their quarry run away, Ernie, turned to Frank and Dave, to imply that Terry was going soft in his old age. Meaning he would have done the business regardless of the bell and had done with it.

'Now, now, Ernie,' said Terry as he began to walk away thinking how lucky the new kid was, having the bell save him twice. 'Don't get ya knickers in a twist, we'll get him after dinner.'

Alan hurried out of the annex yard, past the lavatory and, seeing the canteen queue by the metalwork shop, was spotted by the lads and waved over. But seeing Jeannie in her queue Alan went over and asked if she was alright?

Knowing nothing of her brother's trouble, Jeannie said she was fine, but was awfully hungry. Arrangements were made to meet up after dinner.

Back in his own queue, Golcho asked whether he had been 'done'. Alan shook his head, wishing that he had been and it would have been all over now. He told them that the bell had saved him again and that they were going to get him after dinner.

'They will,' said Golcho emphatically. 'They won't let you get away with it. No new kid to the school gets away with it.'

Mr Ken Hughes, the metalwork teacher on canteen duty blew his whistle and waited while the children straightened their lines, boys to the left, girls to the right. When he was satisfied that all the fidgeting had ceased, he led them down the school path in an orderly manner. Approaching the canteen, he raised his right arm and brought the procession to a halt. Facing his charges he told them to smarten their lines up and look lively. He then instructed the girls to march off quietly and properly to their appropriate door on the right-hand side of the building with the mandatory one hundred lines for anyone who misbehaved. When the last set of girls passed him, the boys were told to smarten themselves up again. Satisfied, Mr Hughes led them to their appropriate door and brought them to a halt, where they were again told to smarten themselves up and look lively about it. Mr Hughes opened the canteen doors, stepped inside and walked down the middle as far as the serving hatches before allowing both sets of children to enter the canteen, sit at their appropriate tables and be still.

While Alan and Twab, who were in the middle of the queue, were waiting for their turn to enter the canteen, Alan spotted the council workmen. They had finished the tarmacing and were loading their lorry up with their tools. The freshly-laid tarmac by the canteen was still steaming, even though the steamroller had levelled it.

Stepping through the cloakroom into the canteen, Alan counted five tables on either side of the long room with benches that would sit ten people in all. He also saw the same set up for the girls at the far end of the building. Opposite the serving hatches, where Mr Hughes was directing the children, were the teachers sitting very smugly around a huge table that had been set with the appropriate cutlery, including jugs of water and a white tablecloth.

Form 2X sat around the table nearest the serving hatch. The smell of the day's menu was delicious. When everyone was perfectly still, Mr Hughes said grace then instructed the canteen staff to serve the teachers. He then pointed to the table on his left and ordered the boys to go and receive their food before immediately walking over to the girls' section where he ordered the first table to do likewise.

The menu was ponchmipe, sausage and peas, with cake and custard for pudding – Twab's all-time favourite school meal. Never having heard of ponchmipe, Alan asked what it was. Twab said it was mash potato and swede, and promised him that he would enjoy it, adding that if he didn't, then he would eat it for him.

With the queue down to the last five, Mr Hughes pointed at Alan's table and told them to quietly join on, then ordered the girls to do the same.

Picking up his plate off a large stack which was lovely and warm, Alan was amazed when a large spoonful of pomchmipe fell onto his plate. The question was would he like it? He hoped he did as he too was starving. While taking in the food's aromas, Twab's nod told Alan that he was going to enjoy his. Both smiled when they saw the size of today's sausages – they were huge. Moving along the counter, Alan had doubts whether cook was going to get all the peas she intended giving him onto his plate without spilling any, but she did, not one pea fell off the large spoon.

While waiting for his peas, and again taking in the wonderful aroma, Twab told the serving lady that this was his all-time favourite school meal and wished it was served up more at home. Smiling at the compliment, and making sure head cook was nowhere around, an extra sausage was placed on Twab's plate and quickly covered over with a spoonful of peas. Smiling back and winking, Twab said a silent but very sincere thank you. But before he could sit down, he had to shove the boy next to him up a little. When he was seated, he turned to Alan who was sitting opposite him, and nodding at his extra sausage said, 'Giving a compliment works every time.'

Several boys on the table, especially Gordon Morris and Bobby Pugh, teased Twab about it, making out he was cook's favourite. But Twab didn't care. He was starving and so got stuck in.

Half way through the meal, with the sound of clanking cutlery everywhere (a good sign that everyone was enjoying their food), Twab gave Alan the canteen rules which were: accept all you are given and then swap what you don't like for something you do like. Looking down the table, he pointed out a good example – John Kenyon was swapping his peas for Ivor Ellis's sausage. Alan was also informed that if you sit up straight and behave yourself you would be selected for seconds – if you were still hungry and wanted seconds.

While enjoying his meal, Alan was bonding with Twab, Sparrow, and Golcho. He never thought it possible so soon. It usually took Alan ages before he declared anyone a good friend. But he was in awe of these three Welsh lads and their fantastic nicknames. He had even forgotten all about Terry and Co (who were sitting on the table nearest the door) and what they were going to do to him. As a twelve-year-old Alan was incapable of explaining how he had become so friendly with these three Welsh lads in such a short time.

Meanwhile, while those in the canteen were enjoying their meal, an evil deed was taking place in Miss Griffiths' classroom. Two fourth-year boys had illegally entered her classroom. Three days later when they were found out, they said that all they had wanted was a closer look at the recently purchased violin. But things did not go according to plan. They were doomed from the start having been seen creeping into the classroom by a monitor. During their handling of the violin a string broke. In their panic to flee the scene of the crime, they knocked over the blackboard which in turn fell against a stack of shelves which then sent the tambourines, triangles, recorders and drums crashing to the floor. Basil Davies and Richard Trematick were later taken to Mr Samuels' study and given six of the best. The headmaster always caned you across both hands, at chest height, making sure your thumbs were also included in the punishment. You were always in great pain whenever you left Mr Samuels' study. Miss Griffiths wanted the two boys expelled, but later calmed down, not that she ever forgave them.

Meanwhile, back in the canteen, Alan looked at Twab and then across to where Sparrow and Golcho were sitting, (they too, from the look on their faces were enjoying their dinner) and knew he had found three fantastic friends in these three Welsh lads. While spooning up the last of his cake and custard, and wishing he hadn't eaten it so fast (it being delicious), Alan asked Twab why Mr Hughes was searching certain boys on leaving the canteen. Turning to have a look while licking his spoon clean, (cake and custard a favourite with him) Twab said, 'For fags.' Placing his spoon into his dish, feeling quite full, Twab went on to say that Mr Hughes and Mr Pritchard (whom Alan would be meeting first lesson that afternoon) often searched the older boys on their way out. They would be pulled over and asked to empty their pockets and any fags found, were taken off them. That was why Sparrow hid his in the lavvy.

Because licking your plate clean in the school canteen was frowned upon, Twab scooped up the very last of his custard with a finger then explained that with Mr Hughes and the other teachers it was the cane, but with Mr Pritchard you could either have the cane or write out five-hundred lines. The choice was yours. While trying to work out which was the lesser of the two evils, and amazed at Twab for the way he had just cleaned his plate (it was spotless), Alan just happened to look towards the window, 'Oh, oh,' he said causing Twab to look up. 'Look who's gawping in through the window.'

Terry and Co were waving at them to hurry up.

'Now what do I do?' Alan asked trying to ignore them.

'I don't know,' said Twab staring at the window. 'But I think you've had it, this time. There's only the one way out, the way we came in.'

Beckoning Sparrow and Golcho over, Twab asked if they could think of a way out of this mess. After several moments and as a last resort Sparrow suggested that Alan tell Mr Hughes what was going on and be done with it.

'No way,' said Alan sharply, adding that he was no snitcher. He then pointed out that they would be taking kids to the stink pipe in a couple of years, wouldn't they?

'Yeah, I suppose we will,' said Golcho trying to come up with an idea.

Pleased with Alan's answer, Twab said he had just passed a very important test as nobody likes a snitcher. A snitcher's life in school is not good. With his next breath Twab said. 'I tell you what, we'll go out and see if we can distract them long enough for you to make a run for it.' When nothing else came up, everyone thought that was a good idea.

'I know it wasn't funny,' said Sparrow, 'but when you know who was chasing you before dinner, half the school was on your side. We've had the stink pipe and know what it's like, and it's not nice, is it gang?'

'I'll tell you what though,' said Golcho, 'you certainly gave them a good run for their money.'

'Yea, you certainly did,' admitted Twab.

Cheered up a little and grinning, Alan agreed that he had given them a good run for their money. He then explained how he just loved to run. He was always in the sports back in his old school in Chester and had won several cups and shields for the school.

'Come along you lot,' said Mr Hughes, his deep voice causing the lads to jump. 'Let's have you out. They're waiting to clear up.'

Standing, not realizing they were the last to leave, the lads saw Terry and Co running towards the door ready to spring their trap.

'Looks like I've had it then,' said Alan as they walked towards the door. Being ushered out by Mr Hughes, Alan was captured the moment the door was closed. Grabbing him by the arm, Terry informed him that, having had a little think, there had been a change of plan. They were going to give him a chance to get away, meaning they were going to chase him.

'What,' said Alan not believing his ears?

'We gonna give you a chance kid,' said Terry. 'Because you gave us a good run earlier, and seeing as there's ten minutes before the bell goes, time enough to catch you and stink pipe you, we're going to let you go.

'If we fail to catch you, which we won't, then we'll let you go.'

'Honest,' said Alan looking at his mates in disbelief. Twab stared at him, Sparrow scrunched up his face. Golcho looked away. They did not know what to say or think. Nothing like this had ever happened before. Usually, if someone was going to the stink pipe, they were taken to the stink pipe and stink piped.

'Yep,' said Terry, 'that's the deal now, kid. You've got until I count to ten. One - two - three ...'

Alan raced off alongside the canteen and up the school path as fast as he could. He knew the odds of four to one were not good, but was determined they were not going to catch him. No way was he going to the stink pipe.

Suddenly Terry shouted ten. The chase was on. It was now or never. Guessing he had a twenty-five-yard start, Alan, as the adrenaline kicked in, knew it was enough. Now they would see someone who loved to run. Now they would see what he was made of and realise he was no push over.

Halfway up the school path, he had to change direction and ran onto the school field. There were too many obstacles (in the form of children) in his way to carry on up the path. Racing across the field he made for the bike shed. He knew the gates by the dreaded stink pipe were open and needed to reach them. Once on the open road not even Roger Banister would catch him. Staying on the school premises he knew would be his downfall. He had to reach the open road at all costs. He had to outrun Terry and Co for the next ten minutes or so or until the bell rang.

Alan reached the bike shed, but instead of turning left for the gates and the open road, decided to try his luck. He knew from Sparrow that there was another set of gates somewhere to his right and so raced for them which would mean reaching the open road that much sooner. But as he raced around the school building and saw the gates, he knew he had made a big mistake. The gates were there alright, but when he saw the huge padlock and chain, his heart sank. The gates were locked. Oh no!

Running up to them and rattling the chain hoping it would fall off, Alan could feel his tormentors closing in. Turning, he saw Terry, Frank, Ernie and Dave grinning at him with their arms outstretched. They walked slowly towards him knowing they had him. 'Got ya now you little bugger,' said Ernie smiling like a Cheshire cat.

Alan was desperate for a way out. On his left was a five-foot high wall with a three-foot high wire fence on top of it. There was no way out for him there. Besides it was the caretaker's residence. Alan had enough trouble on his plate without the caretaker chasing him as well.

On his right was a bank of coke wedged between the school building and the outside wall which fuelled the central heating. It was about six-feet wide and some three-feet high. Alan knew the open road and stink pipe were at the other end of this bank of coke – he could see them over the top of it. He also knew there was no other way out. Hoping it would work, he scrambled up the mound of coke and began to race along it as best he could. He had to reach those open gates.

Cursing, Terry ordered Frank and Dave to run back through the school yard and cut him off. Terry knew that if this kid from Chester did reach the gates and the open road their chances of catching him would be that much slimmer. Terry and Ernie scrambled up the wall of coke after him.

Running on top of loose coke is not recommended. Not only can you not run fast, but there is the possibility that you could at best end up with nasty scratches or at worst with a broken ankle. But Alan was as desperate to escape as Terry and Co were to catch him. They now only had eight minutes in which to catch him and stink pipe him.

Half way along the coke and cursing under his breath, Alan looked over his shoulder and wondered why there were only two chasing him. But for all his wondering, and cursing, they were gaining on him. He could hear their moans and groans now, and what they were going to do after they'd stink piped him. The thought of his head going down the lavvy and then flushed made Alan the more determined to keep going. He dug down deep for that extra gear, and *voilà*, the open gates were that much nearer; as was the stink pipe.

As he struggled to run over the coke, it suddenly dawned on him why there were only two chasing him. The other two were racing through the school yard to cut him off, which meant he had to reach the gates before Frank and Dave did. Still fumbling his way over the loose coke, and hearing real swear words from you know who, Alan spurred himself on yet again. At last, with aching and scratched ankles, he slid down the wall of coke on his heels and raced for the gates and open road believing he had made it.

When Ernie shouted how grateful he was that Alan had taken himself to the stink pipe, Terry, referring to him as a blockhead, informed him that they had not caught him yet.

Racing up to the gates, Alan's heart sank when Frank and Dave stepped out from behind the wall. They'd been waiting there for some time. With outstretched arms they blocked off Alan's escape route. This is it Alan thought. He could not go forward or back the way he had come. The only way open to him was to race back to the lavatory and possibly lock himself in one of the cubicles. But he knew that would not work as none of the cubicles had any bolts on them.

Without thinking, he decided to take a chance and ran towards Dave. At the very last moment he dropped down on all fours and scrambled through Dave's gaping legs. Even Frank's trying to grab him failed. Rising, he ran through the gates and turned left, then right, down a little hill that was known as Nant Square. Turning right at the bottom he ran for all his worth along Middle Road knowing no one would catch him now, not even Roger Banister or Chris Chattaway.

Not knowing the area, and for the moment not caring, Alan raced on knowing Terry and Co were on his tail. He raced up to, and past Edwards' Bakery, an outside lavatory, the Library, park, tennis courts and Cenotaph just up ahead. Turning right up a little side road that ran alongside the cinema (not that he knew it was the cinema) he reached what he later learned was a kissing gate and, rushing through it, turned left and raced on down Tabor Hill.

Knowing they were never going to catch him, Alan began to enjoy the chase. Did they now see how good a runner he was? Now all of a sudden, Terry and Co were not tigers chasing him, but just a bunch of thugs who had no chance of catching him. By using the tiger ploy, Alan often found the extra speed and stamina needed to outrun his attackers.

Reaching the main Wrexham to Ruthin road (the A525) Alan did not realise he was in the village of Coedpoeth, being too concerned with waiting for a break in the traffic to cross over. But then he thought he heard Terry shouting, telling him that the bell was ringing and that he was not to be afraid, he had won, fair and square and that it was best he got a move on. He thought they were trying to trick him, then heard the bell himself. As much as he did not trust them, he ran back up Tabor Hill slightly worried. Would they stink pipe him regardless of the bell ringing?

It has to be said that neither Terry, Frank, Ernie or Dave, wanted this new kid from Chester to be in trouble for being late in the afternoon. Rogues they might be, but their word was their bond. So, as promised, he was released from the stink pipe threat.

Terry and Co even waited for him while he raced up Tabor Hill. Ruffling Alan's hair, Terry said he had won fair and square, and to prove their word was good, they ran through the school gates as a team.

They may have run through the school gates as a team, but nevertheless, Alan had a sneaky peep at the dreaded stink pipe looming there looking innocent. Terry said he was not to worry about it as it was not for him. He had out run them and that was fair enough, but he was to sod off in case he changed his mind.

Alan's first lesson of the afternoon was geography. With permission given, form 2X marched through Mr Ellis's classroom and entered Mr Pritchard's domain. The teacher was in his chair, twiddling his fingers and looking quite stern. Alan thought he looked impressive watching everyone as they came in. He somehow had a feeling that this teacher was different. Well, he was about to find out.

It was more out of respect than fear that the children sat down quietly and waited for the lesson to begin. Mr Pritchard, although strict, was seen by the children as one of the better teachers. Even so, it was a well-known fact that if you were caught scrapping on the school premises by him, both you and your opponent ended up in the garden shed and, with the gloves on, were made to box three rounds under his supervision.

But, if on the other hand you were caught bullying, something entirely different, you were still taken to the garden shed, but this time you were met by someone much bigger than you. A fifth year would then give you a taste of your own medicine in the same said three rounds. It was Mr Pritchard's belief that it prevented a lot of bullying from taking place.

When everyone had settled down, Mr Pritchard stood up and enquired about certain absentees who were crucial to the school's football team. He then turned his attention to Alan. Sitting on the edge of his desk (while Twab and the rest of the class looked on) Mr Pritchard introduced himself as his Geography and PT teacher, and then added that he was pleased to meet him. He then extended his hand which Alan took, a little bemused; he was not expecting this level of civility. All he had experienced thus far was hostility.

'How are you coping on your first day?' Mr Pritchard asked.

'Okay, Sir,' Alan replied a little uneasy.

'Do you have any complaints?'

'No, Sir,' said Alan, wondering where this was leading.

Speaking more as a friend than a teacher, Mr Pritchard informed him that he and a few other teachers had noticed how he was being chased during the eleven o'clock playtime, and again just before lunch, by four fifth formers. Making full eye contact with him, Alan tried to assure him that the chasing was over now and that there were no complaints.

'You don't have to put up with that kind of treatment in this school,' said Mr Pritchard, adding that bullying would not be tolerated.

'I enjoyed the chase sir,' said Alan, which was true once he knew they were not going to catch him. 'I love to run sir. They never caught me even though there was four of 'em.'

'Even though there were four of *them*,' corrected Mr Pritchard.

'Yes sir, but I outran them. They never caught me. I don't mean to be a bragger Sir, but I can run faster than most boys my age. I just love to run sir. I saw them as tigers, not as ....' Alan nearly blurted out Terry and Co's names, for which he would never have forgiven himself. He was no snitcher. He then explained how every time he thought of chasers as tigers, he usually got away.

Astonished with the boy's answer, Mr Pritchard decided to leave well alone for the time being. He would wait and see how the situation developed. Seeing Alan was not going to say any more on the subject, he suggested that he show how good a runner he was by running for the school. If he was good enough, he could run in the school's sports in six weeks time.

'Yeees, Sir,' Alan replied enthusiastically. 'I'd like that.' With full eye contact with Mr Pritchard for the second time, he explained how he had won several cups and shields for his old school in Chester.

Mr Pritchard stood up and addressing the rest of the children said, 'Class we may have a champion amongst us.'

Twab's ears picked up. He could not believe it. He had only been pondering about it all morning. But Mr Pritchard had just solved the problem of what to call Alan (it being crucial he have a nickname). Twab squeezed Alan's arm and thought it was great that Mr Pritchard thought he might be a champion. Enjoying the moment and smiling, Alan decided he was right about Mr Pritchard being different.

'Right class,' said Sir. 'I want you to finish off page eight and then go onto the blackboard. It's time you learned how to draw Great Britain.'

Twenty minutes into the lesson, the door opened and in walked two third-year boys. Both had their hands tucked under their armpits. Twab pointed out that both lads were from their village, but just that little bit older.

'Sir,' said Eifion, 'Stan and I have been caught smoking. We've been told to report to every teacher by Mr Samuels.'

Realizing the boys had been crying, Mr Pritchard asked to see their hands. As expected, they were red and swollen. Asking the class to go on with the lesson, he escorted the boys out of the classroom.

The moment the door closed the children began to wonder what Mr Pritchard was going to do with them. Both Eifion and Stanley were taken to the nearest cloakroom where each bathed his hand in cold water. Mr Pritchard, who disagreed with corporal punishment, then gave the boys a severe dressing down with a lecture on the dangers of smoking. He emphasized how smoking makes you ill in later life. He then took them to the garden shed and asked then to tidy the place up as best they could. He said they were excused lessons for the remainder of the afternoon.

While Mr Pritchard was having a heated discussion with Mr Samuels about the boy's treatment, the bell rang. Anita Shaw, Form 2X's female monitor took charge and asked everyone to place their books on the table in a neat pile. Filing out into Mr Ellis' classroom, with no sign of him, both classes in passing began to discuss what they thought had happened to Eifion and Stanley. During the brief encounter, it was pointed out that both boys had been caned by Mr Ellis. Those who felt sympathy for the boys hoped they had been sent home to recover, but others thought differently.

Form 2X boys made their way over to their next lesson, woodwork, with Mr Lloyd. For the girls it was needlework with Miss Friedman. Halfway across the school yard, Twab informed Alan that, in his opinion, Mr Lloyd was a horrible man who everyone called '*Tarw*'. When Alan asked why that was, Twab said he did not know, but that was what everyone called him behind his back.

Half way up the spiral stairs that led up to Mr Lloyd's classroom, and grinning at the snide remark he was about to make, Twab said Mr Lloyd was called *Tarw* because he very often acted like a bull, adding that he certainly looked like one. On one occasion Mr Lloyd had thrown a piece of wood at a boy in a higher class and made his head bleed. That was the level of his temper. At the top of the stairs Twab explained to Alan that Mr Lloyd was a horrible man, as he was about to find out.

Alan, like all the boys of form 2X, pulled a face when he entered the workshop. The stench of glue on the boil just inside the doorway was horrendous. Mr Lloyd always had glue on the boil.

'Line up,' shouted the teacher while opening a huge cupboard that housed form 2X's unfinished work.

With everyone given their work (which was, at this early stage of their carpentry career, stools, candlestick holders, clothes maids, and book ends) each boy quickly found an empty bench and waited until he was given the appropriate tool or tools.

Twab, who was making a clothes maid for his mum, proudly showed Alan his work so far. He thought it was coming along nicely and was hoping to start on the mortice and tenon joints today. Impressed with his friend's woodwork skill Alan hoped he would be allowed to make a clothes maid for his mum. He knew she would love one.

Taking Alan over to an empty bench, Mr Lloyd, who was of average height with dark hair, glasses and boney hands, scribed a piece of scrap 2 x 2 wood to the depth of one quarter-of-an-inch. He then clamped it in the vice while looking at Alan to make sure he was taking notice. Picking up the wood plane, he showed Alan the cutting edge and then warned him that it was razor sharp. He was then shown how a wood plane should be correctly held and Mr Lloyd proceeded to plane down to the scribed line. Alan, with one eye on what Mr Lloyd was doing, watched as thin slivers of wood shavings fell to the floor. He was amazed they were so thin. The secret, according to Mr Lloyd was to keep the plane level. Failure to do so would end in disaster. When the task was completed, Alan was allowed to inspect the work. He noted the scribe lines were just visible. Mr Lloyd had not gone below them. Alan accepted that a good job had been done and handed it back. Mr Lloyd then applied two more scribe lines to the depth of a quarter-of-an-inch and told Alan to clamp it in the vice as he had been shown. Just as he was about to begin planning the wood, Mr Lloyd stopped him and rather sarcastically said, 'Before you begin to defile this piece of innocent wood, do you know what the judge says to a condemned man?'

'Yes, Sir,' said Alan puzzled, 'may the Lord have mercy on your soul.' Towering over Alan and straight faced Mr Lloyd said, 'And may the Lord have mercy on your soul, should you go below the lines I've scribed for you. They are there to tell you when to stop. So keep your eyes on them.'

Alan broke eye contact with Mr Lloyd and suddenly knew what Twab meant about this man being horrible. He was then left to get on with it as the teacher returned to his own workbench. With one eye on the class, he resumed polishing an astronomical mirror he was perfecting for his home made Newtonian telescope – he was apparently very interested in astronomy. And why shouldn't he be thought some of the children – was his image (Taurus the Bull) not up there in the night sky?

With care, Alan planed down to the scribed lines and nervously reported back to Mr Lloyd. Finding no fault with the work, and with a hint of a smile, he said. 'Well done lad. It seems I won't be handing you the death sentence after all.' Examining the work, he then asked whether he had been given any woodwork lessons in Chester.

'No, Sir,' replied Alan, 'this is my first attempt.' Seeing the benefits of woodwork, and with full eye contact with Mr Lloyd, he added, 'Please, Sir, I would like to learn woodwork,' wondering whether, like Malcolm and a few others, he could be allowed to make a clothes maid for his mum as she had nowhere to hang the wet clothes.

'We'll see,' said Mr Lloyd, adding that it all depended on how well he fared with the other tools needed.

For the next forty-five minutes, full of enthusiasm, Alan was shown how to use a scriber, a mallet and chisel, a tenon saw, and how to make a mortise and tenon joint. Because of his progress, Mr Lloyd said he could start making a clothes maid in his next lesson on Wednesday. Alan was elated, but sadly the lesson came to an end and, with all the tools and work safely put away, the class was made to stand to attention by the door next to the smelly glue pot that was bubbling away. It was three o'clock and playtime. As form 2X, scrambled down the spiral stairs pushing and shoving one another Twab said, 'Come on; let's go and find Sparrow and Golcho.'

While racing over towards the lavatory, Alan asked Twab why he always said Sparrow's name first and then Golcho? Shrugging his shoulders Twab said, 'Do I always say Sparrow first?'

'Every time.'

Twab shrugged his shoulders again and said he did not know why and left it at that. What a silly question that was.

As they entered the lavatory several lads were already there smoking, including Sparrow and Golcho. With the greetings over (the Roman way) Alan asked Sparrow if he could have a puff, but was politely told to 'Bugger off.' Sparrow was desperately trying to emulate Terry and so wanted to be able to blow a smoke ring through another, but suggested that Alan should ask Golcho for a puff as his dog-end was all he had at the moment.

'You could have had a puff of mine had you got here sooner,' said Golcho flushing what was left of his down the lavvy pan.

'Go on Sparrow,' said Twab, 'don't be so mean. Give the lad a puff. One puff won't hurt you.'

Sparrow, who was already holding his dog-end between his finger and thumb, took one last puff and grudgingly handed over what was left. He knew there would be nothing left of it once Alan had taken a puff. All three watched as Alan, whose fingers were burning slightly drew in a puff of smoke. Holding the smoke in his mouth, he gave the dog-end back to Sparrow who, seeing there nothing left, flushed it down the lavvy.

Now, with all the attention on him Alan mumbled, 'One, two, three,' then inhaled the smoke and immediately began to cough, choke and splutter. He coughed and coughed and, even though he knew he was being laughed at, tears began to roll down his face. Not only was he coughing and choking; but he was also going dizzy and he seriously thought he was dying. He tried to spit the taste from his mouth, but all that did was make everyone laugh all the more.

Suddenly, two third-year boys came in and, while seeing who could wee up the wall the highest, Dennis (who was losing) asked what all the laughing was about?

'It's his first fag,' said Twab laughing at the state Alan was in. He almost shouted out, 'I told you, but you wouldn't listen,' but thought better of it. Joining in the laughter, but concentrating more on the weeing up the wall competition, Tony (who was winning by a mile) said, 'Don't worry kid, you'll soon get used to it, you'll soon be a smoker.'

'Oh, no I won't,' spluttered Alan still coughing and choking and feeling giddy and wanting to die, 'This is my first and last attempt at it.' His mouth had never tasted so vile. No way was he ever going to smoke again. Later, while having a few minutes with Jeannie in the playground, Twab, having stopped wrestling with the problem he had been deliberating about for the last hour and three-quarters, turned to Alan (who was still having the occasional cough and splutter) and said, 'Well, I've finally decided on your nickname.'

'Oh,' said Alan not that interested, 'and what is it to be?'

'Well,' said Twab. 'If the truth be known, it was Mr Pritchard who gave me the idea, when he thought of you as a champion.' When Mr Pritchard's remark was explained to Sparrow and Golcho, Twab added, 'You certainly were one when you know who was chasing you; so I think your nickname will suit.'

Placing both hands on Alan's shoulders, and with Sparrow, Golcho, Jeannie and her two friends (Wendy and Hazel) looking on, Twab, with all the power invested in him, said, 'Alan Fletcher, from Chester, who is now living in Heol Wen, I hereby christen you.' Pausing for effect he said, 'Champ.'

Alan smiled ever so weakly. He was still trying to clean his mouth up. How Sparrow and Golcho could smoke all the time he thought was yuk. But, as the seconds ticked by and with all the congratulations he was receiving off his three new found friends and his sister, even though she did not know what was going on, the sound of his new name began to appeal to him. 'Champ' he said several times to himself and then out loud. 'Yea, I like it,' he said, 'it's great.'

With one last clear of his throat and turning to face everyone he said, 'Thanks for that fellows. I only hope I live up to my new name.'

Suddenly the bell began to ring. Sparrow and Golcho in the slightly higher class, Form 2, said they would see Twab and 'Champ' at home time, and shot off for their last lesson of the day which was English with Cock-leg.

Jeannie and her two friends' last lesson of the day was geography with Mr Pritchard. But before they ran off, Alan asked Jeannie not to mention that he had been smoking to their mum. Jeannie promised not to do so.

Alan, or 'Champ' as he was going to be known from now on by the lads, smiled when Twab said that their last lesson of the day was sports, thinking Mr Pritchard would be taking them. He was surprised therefore when they ended up in Mr Robinson's classroom. 'I thought he was the art teacher?' Champ said looking confused.

'He also does PT,' said Twab, 'I did tell you this morning.'

All the boys of 2X stripped down to their vests and placed their shirts and pullovers on the desk tops. Twab knew he was going to have to get his new friend a timetable or he was going to end up in the wrong classroom.

In less than a minute (PT being everyone's favourite lesson), most of 2X, including Twab and Champ, were on the school field and mingling with boys from the other two classes who were also having sports.

Champ noted that Mr Pritchard was in charge of a football game that was already in progress. Two sides had already been picked and had kicked off.

'I understand you like to run,' said Mr Robinson when he called Alan over. 'Is that right?'

'Yes, Sir,' said Alan rubbing his hands excitedly.

'Right then, let's see how you fare against these boys.'

Alan was taken over to a group of seven boys, some his age, others slightly older, all dressed in full PT kit – vest, shorts and plimsolls. Lining everyone up, after a brief introduction had been given (not that one was needed, the whole school had seen Alan's treatment of Terry and Co), Mr Robinson explained that they had to run on the outside of the field, stay well away from the football match that was in progress, run into the corners and around the posts with no cheating and may the best man win.

'Right lads,' said Mr Robinson lining them up, 'on my whistle.' With his left arm counting down, Mr Robinson blew the whistle. The race was on.

Running the first leg towards the canteen, Alan (or Champ) fell behind deliberately to see what the others would do. Two of the boys took up the lead and sped off. There would be no threat from them. They would soon burn themselves out. The other five, more sensibly ran as a pack. It was much too early to make a serious break.

All fired up and thoroughly enjoying himself, Champ tagged along for the time being. Having mentally measured the course, he drew up his plan.

Approaching the first corner post (down by the canteen and turning left) Champ saw an opening and decided it was time to show these people his running prowess. While racing through the gap, he was pushed and shoved several times which was to be expected, everyone was in this race to impress Mr Robinson and achieve a place in this year's sports which were only six weeks away. Champ knew he was running against the school's top runners in the under fifteen's class. Breaking clear, he accelerated away with the pack coming after him. It was felt they could not afford this new boy any leeway. Determined to impress, Champ accelerated again and overtook the two boys who had foolishly spent their energy. He was now in the lead with just under half of the race run. Now they would see what they were up against, he told himself. Digging deep for that extra gear, he opened up a gap with three of the pack coming after him.

Reaching the second corner post (the half-way stage) Champ had a quick look over his shoulder and saw there was no immediate threat coming up whatsoever. All he had to do was to keep on running at this pace. Somewhat impressed with Alan's race and wanting to see the outcome, Mr Pritchard blew the whistle and told the footballers to take an interest in the remaining race that was in progress. Knowing he was being watched, and loving every moment of it, and with the adrenaline having kicked in, Champ knew he was going to win.

Impressed with his new friend, Twab began to shout, 'Come on Champ, show um what you can do. Go, go, go!'

Alan reached the three-quarter stage and ran around the post. He knew he had opened up a substantial gap and that he was going to win this race in style. Simply winning, however, was no longer good enough. He accelerated down the home straight digging deep to find that certain something that makes champions. Willing himself on, and with the crowd's encouragement, he raced on towards the finish line. Everyone on the school field joined in, with Twab shouting encouragement, 'Come on Champ! Come on Champ!'

With both eyes on his stopwatch, Mr Robinson clocked Alan as he crossed the finishing line some fifteen yards in front of Derek, his only rival.

Smiling, Mr Robinson openly congratulated Alan then went straight back to timing the others as they came in. Finally, turning to Alan, Mr Robinson said that he had run a very good race, running the quarter mile in one minute, forty seconds, a good ten seconds faster than anyone else.

'Thank you, Sir,' said Alan pleased with the result.

While controlling his breathing, he informed Mr Robinson that it had gone to plan.

'You mean you planned your race?'

'Oh yes, Sir,' said Alan, adding that his Uncle Dave in Chester had taught him the importance of breath control while running.

'Would you like to run for the school?'

'Yes, Sir, very much,' said Alan gleefully.

Derek, who came in second, along with the other six runners, came over to congratulate Alan. They all said it had been a good clean race.

With the time approaching a quarter to four it was time to pack in as it was nearing home time. As Champ, Twab and a host of other boys walked back to the classroom, Mr Pritchard and Mr Robinson were already drawing up plans for this new boy from Chester. Both agreed he would be good for the school.

Alan, who was already dressed and thoroughly enjoying a drink of water, whilst waiting for Twab to do up his shoe laces, summed up his first day in his new school. He could not believe how he had not only made friends with three great lads and become a member of their gang, but also ended up being seen as a champion, and been given a nickname to correspond. He had also impressed a couple of teachers with his running and was going to be starting woodwork on Wednesday which he would really enjoy. To top it all, he had managed to avoid being taken to the stink pipe by out running Terry and Co. All in all, it added up to being a most fantastic day.

Moments after the four o'clock bell sounded, the playground was once again filled with the hustle and bustle of children. It was so alive. But this time the children were preparing to go home, school was over for the day.

Those who travelled by bus quickly made their way to the bus stop in the centre of Coedpoeth. Those who lived locally began to walk or run home in their little groups. While giving Jeannie all his news, Alan placed his English book (the one that was to be covered with brown paper) in her satchel and, accompanied by Jeannie's two friends Wendy and Hazel, they set off for home in the company of Twab, Sparrow and Golcho.

Hazel, who lived on Smithy Lane, was the first to leave the little group, followed by Wendy, who lived three houses up from the Grosvernor Arms. Jeannie wormed her way over to Sparrow whom she had already decided was so good looking. She loved his wavy hair and blue eyes and so for the rest of way home could not take her eyes off him.

When they entered Lloft Wen Lane it became a race to see who would be the first over the stile – Jeannie was the last – and then parting company, after arrangements had made to meet up after tea by the lamp post at the bottom of Heol Wen.

Twab said 'So long,' turned right and ran down a path that would one day be Heol Glyndŵr. A little further on, Golcho turned right and ran down another path that would one day become Heol y Gelli. Alan, Sparrow and Jeannie continued on down the path until they came to the hole in the hedge that Alan, Jeannie and their mum had slipped through that morning on their way to school. But the hedge was no longer there. It had been completely ripped out. Even the bulldozer that Allan had so admired was gone, but not the workmen. Like this morning, they could still be heard but not seen. The mixers were still pouring out mortar.

The path that everyone in the village was using at the moment would one day be known as Heol Cadfan, which was going to be a very prominent street in the village.

Sparrow said, 'So long,' and continued on down the path until he came to a set of three concrete posts that gave access to his street, Heol Celyn. The path continued on to a little farm which was run by one of Sparrow's neighbours, Mr Jones 'Top House' (also know as Arthur Tattoos).

When Alan and Jeannie entered their house, it was so different from that morning. Pictures were hanging from the picture rail that went all around the living room. Their dad's picture, the one Alan worried about last Saturday in the back of Dodd's removal van, was on the mantle piece. Both of them were so pleased about that and they said so. It looked lovely standing there in between their Coronation mugs. Their dad's big booming smile beamed out at them as always. 'Pride of place' said their mum.

Also on the mantle piece, standing ten inches high, was a pair of brass horses which Alan liked to draw. They were once his dad's and would one day be passed on to either him or Jeannie. Both also knew that their mum had not only been busy with the housework; there was a lovely aroma coming from the black-leaded oven. Actually, the aroma hit them the moment they opened the back door. As promised that morning, it was their favourite lob-scouse pie.

Kissing their mum and briefly telling her what a marvellous day it had been, Alan and Jeannie rushed up stairs and changed into their playing clothes. When two English books were placed on the table (Jeannie had also had an English lesson) Mrs Fletcher wondered where on earth she was going to find some brown paper for the morning? While trying to think, she asked Jeannie to help by laying the table and Alan was to see to it that there was enough coal and sticks in the bucket for the morning's fire – the coalman had delivered two bags of household coal.

Mrs Fletcher, still wondering where on earth she was going to find some brown paper, began to read Alan's English essay entitled 'Winter.' She loved the way he described how the trees first lost their leaves in the autumn, and then had to bear up to the hard frost and snow, and how hard it was for the animals and birds. Ironically, Jeannie wrote about spring. How she was going to enjoy seeing the daffodils, primroses and snowdrops.

With the table set, the next thirty minutes were spent on the sofa by the fire, with the children telling their mother all about their first day at school.

During their evening meal, Jeannie announced that her two friends, Wendy and Hazel were coming to visit her after their tea. They so wanted to see her doll's house and the way she had set it up.

After telling his stories, but leaving out the stink pipe saga, Alan asked for and was given permission to go out and meet up with his new friends, Twab, Sparrow and Golcho.

Alan thoroughly enjoyed telling his mum and sister how their nicknames were given them, and how they had formed their little gang called the 'Shanghai Bombers', how he had been sworn in, how they shook arms the Roman way, how Brian Davies had been given the cane, how someone had broken a violin string, how strict the teachers were and how a fight had broken out.

But she was not so pleased when she learned that he was going to be referred to as 'Champ', but realised that she was going to have to accept it. It was after all part of her son's growing up.

And what an evening was had. Twab, as leader, along with Sparrow and Golcho, decided it was crucial that Champ be given an extensive tour of the village. That night in bed, Champ decided that today, Monday, 8th June, 1953, was the best day of his life.

Part Two: Down the Woods, June, 1953

THE TWO JOBS THAT MRS FLETCHER DEEMED IMPORTANT in her weekly schedule, apart from the hundreds of other chores a widowed mum has to do, were big shop day (Saturday morning) and wash day (Monday morning). She set off with Jeannie in tow (it being time she began her domestic training in earnest, and seeing no reason for changing a well-established habit just because the locality had changed), having decided her big shop was going to be in the Co-op opposite Lloft Wen Lane.

Alan, enjoying his breakfast of toasted soldiers and runny egg was left in charge of the fire, with orders that he was not to let it go out. Clothes were going to be dried in front of the fire when the shopping was done.

Seeing there were only seconds to go before his mum's most precious clock chimed, Alan decided he was going to sing along with it (the clock had been bought by Alan's dad for one of their wedding anniversaries).

'Ding, dong, ding, dong,' he and the clock chimed out. 'Ding, dong, ding, dong.' There was a pause then they both chimed out, 'Dong.' It was 9.30 on Saturday morning, 13th June, 1953, and it was a lovely sunny morning.

Alan could not believe that he and his family had been in the Adwy for seven days, a whole week, and what a marvellous week it had been. So much had happened. Their lives had been turned upside down.

While chewing on a piece of toast, he thought back to last Saturday when Dodd's removal van had turned up outside his old house. Not only was the van huge, but bouncing on the tailboard was as good as jumping on the bed when his mum was not around. And what about the van's slogan! 'Here Comes Dodd. There Goes Dodd' Whoever thought that one up deserved a medal.

But even so, a week on, Alan still felt he had pulled his weight with the loading and unloading. Yes, he had been told to get out of the way several times, but who was it that carried all the boxes, rugs and knick-knacks to the van? And who was it that resolved the overcrowding problem in the cab? Alan was still pleased about that. Then he again tried to picture Billy Watts standing on the van's bumper to see inside the cab. What a lad he was.

He then began to wonder how his old mates in Chester were doing. Were they missing him? There was a twinge of guilt because he was not missing them. But how could he be missing them, when he had three great friends in Twab, Sparrow and Golcho? They were his three best friends in the world and he had bonded with them in record time and five days on that bond had strengthened. Were they not taking him down the woods this morning, a place they said was special? Was that not true friendship?

Then he remembered the long bumpy ride in the back of the van while being Dick Barton Special Agent, and how he had saved the world by shooting all the Russian and German spies. But, he would never forget his first glimpse of the village when the van finally pulled up outside their new house, Number 8, Heol Wen, with his arm resting on Jeannie's shoulder. He knew the memory would stay with him for ever and a day.

Chewing on another piece of toast, Alan also knew that standing in their gateway last Sunday afternoon, wondering what was beyond the hedge that was now no longer, would also never be forgotten. And how ironic it was that the three lads he saw for those few moments running down the road were Twab, Sparrow and Golcho who were going down the woods to play Robin Hood, the very woods they were taking him to that morning.

He looked at the clock. It was twenty-five to ten. He was going to have to get a move on. They were coming for him at ten o'clock. Thanks to the lads, Alan now knew that the Council was expanding the village, and that all the trees that were marked with a red cross apparently had to go to make way for houses.

Twab had heard on the school grapevine that, when all the building was finished (a couple of years from now), the Adwy and Coedpoeth would be one village. But Twab did not want to believe that. He said he hoped it would never happen. He said the Adwy was big enough as it was.

There was one oak tree though that was apparently safe; the one at the bottom of next-door's garden, the end house, Number 10. It was in fact going to be a garden feature for whoever came to live there as the house was still empty at the moment. It was a good subject for a budding artist like Alan to draw.

Then there was the novelty of flushing the lavatory. Not having had a flush toilet before, Alan thought he would never tire of seeing water filling the bowl and flushing everything away. But seven days on, the novelty was beginning to wear off.

Still hungry, Alan toasted his favourite part of the loaf, the crust, on the open fire with a toasting fork his dad had made. As in Chester, it hung on a nail on the right-hand side of the fireplace. With a good spreading of butter and marmalade, and a second cup of tea, Alan continued his breakfast.

While munching away, he began to curse himself for not wanting to go to school last Monday. Last Monday only turned out to be the best day of his life. How grateful he was to his mum for making him go that day. He was also grateful to her for allowing him to mark the event. She had given him permission to write last Monday's date, 8-6-53, in the top panel of his bedroom door, adding that it could always be painted over if they ever moved.

Alan swallowed another mouthful of tea and relived last Monday in school. He very much doubted he would ever have another day like that if he lived to be a hundred. He was so pleased he was competing in the sports for his new school in a few weeks time. That was something he was really looking forward to. Actually he could not wait for the event and was training very hard for it. Since last Monday, Alan, or Champ as he was now referred to by all but his mum and the teachers, was tested several times by Mr Robinson and was going to run in the 200 and 400 yards. He was also going to be the anchor man in the 4 x 100 relay. And to think, he mused to himself while looking out the window towards Aunty Jinni's house, because he had out-run Terry, (Aunty Jinni's lad, would you believe, and his lot) he was the only kid in the school that had not been stink piped by them.

But his three best mates on the other hand had other ideas. No way were they going to let him get away with it. The ruling was, every first year or new kid to the school goes to the stink pipe, no exceptions. After the deed was done, Alan wondered if the no exception rule would have applied had Prince Charles been a pupil of Penygelli Secondary Modern. Somehow he doubted it. But what a lark it would have been. Alan could see the headlines in the *News of the World*: 'Prince Charles dragged off and Stink Piped.' Would the Queen have made a fuss, or would she have gone along with the school tradition?

So with Twab, Sparrow and Golcho the main instigators, Champ, and not Prince Charles, had gone kicking and screaming to the stink pipe yesterday dinnertime (Friday) where he had been given the full treatment (two minutes of having to take in that horrible smell of sour milk). As if that was not enough, Twab had arranged that Terry, Frank, Ernie and Dave, and anyone else who wanted to see the show, could be there. Like in the days when heads were chopped off, it was done publicly, not that anyone did any knitting or heckled. But the smug smiles on Terry and Co's faces when Alan struggled, as Twab, Sparrow and Golcho forced his head into the bowl, was proof enough that they were happy that the school's tradition was being upheld.

Terry commented later that it was good that the books were straight. He even praised Twab, Sparrow and Golcho for seeing to it and, because the treatment was taken like a man, Champ was now one of the boys. Not that a second visit would not be given if he ever stepped out of line.

While chewing on his toast Alan suddenly remembered Mr Davies, the history teacher, and felt a little sorry for him. According to Twab, during one of the wars (he did not know which one) Mr Davies was apparently shot in the head and had a metal plate inside his skull. Mr Davies either had a wonderful sense of humour or was totally mad. He very often made Alan and the class laugh. For example, if anyone gave a wrong answer to an historical question, he threatened to have that person cooked on an open fire and then sent home on a plate, so that the idiot's family could at least feast on him or her, as that person was no good to the school. Nor did Mr Davies use the cane. Instead, he jabbed pupils in the ribs with a little stick he carried around, if and when they had been caught doing something wrong.

Then he remembered Mr Hughes, the metalwork teacher, who was a very tall man. In fact he was the tallest man in the school, but was a good teacher. Alan was in the process of making a poker, and never realized how slow filing a piece of metal could be, but did like to see the filings accumulate. At the end of the lesson when all the filings were collected, Alan wondered if anything could be done with them. It was a shame they had to be thrown away. But, unbeknown to him, they were used in the science lab. Mr Ellis, the maths teacher, who also taught science, often used them in little experiments.

Then there was Miss Griffiths, the music teacher, who clearly loved her subject. She was so enthusiastic. Alan loved it when she demon-strated how she wanted a piece of music sung, how she would hold onto a certain note and make that note quiver.

Then there was Miss Edwards, who taught religious instruction. She seemed to be a quiet woman who never shouted at you the way Cock-leg did. But she did sound her Ss funny, making them sound like Zs. She was often taken the micky out of in the playground by certain boys mimicking her, saying something like, 'Come here boy, I want to zee you.' But she obviously loved God because that's all she talked about all day.

But, there was one boy in year three who said he no longer wanted to learn any more religious instruction or history. Somebody said that when he was questioned by Mr Samuels, the boy stated that he no longer believed in either God or history. His argument was where was God when the explosion in Gresford Colliery took place, killing some 265 men, including his granddad. The other half of his argument was that he was no longer interested in all the kings and queens of British history who were ever so cruel and sadistic.

Mr Samuels not only hit the roof (how dare the boy make such a request), but promised him that his parent would be receiving an official letter, and then sent him back to his class – religious instruction.

Mrs Freudman, according to Jeannie was a lovely teacher. She taught domestic science (which included sewing, cooking, home management, washing up, doing the laundry, cleaning, as well as all the other jobs her mum has to do).

Suddenly Alan's reverie was over. His mum and Jeannie were back from the shop. With Jeannie's help, Mrs Fletcher put the shopping away. For the first time since their arrival in the Adwy, the pantry looked like a pantry. It was so nice to see all the different foods on their allotted shelves. His mum, having instructed Jeannie to fold and put away the two brown-paper carrier bags for further use, filled up the clothes maid (only brought home yesterday) with damp clothes and placed them in front of the fire to dry. The fact that his mum now had a clothes maid was wonderful. The fact that it cost half-a-crown was neither here nor there. Alan deemed it was money well spent when his mum said she loved it, adding that it was a God send.

Thanks to Twab, Sparrow and Golcho, Champ now had a good intimate knowledge of the village. Each evening after tea and chores (making sure there was enough coal and sticks in for the morning's fire, plus making sure his bedroom was tidy) he was introduced to the four corners of the village and beyond. He was, for example, shown all the best places for scrumping apples, pears, plums, damsons, and 'goosies' as the lads called gooseberries. They also divulged the best short cuts for when they being chased either by the owners of the fruit, or by certain residents whose doors were 'ran-tanned' on dark nights using a long length of cotton, a prank which Champ already knew always got a laugh. But it was not funny when the likes of Clifford Goodwin, Glyn Davies, Milton Clee, Ronald Stoker, Frank Flitcroft or Len Lewis chased you for giving them cheek. Nor was it funny when Terry and Co chased you for no apparent reason. You then had to try and out run them which was hard on account of their knowing the same short cuts as well. It was probably them who had made the short cuts in the first place.

But why did Terry and Co have to live in the village as well? It was not fair. What was that saying about nettles not welcome in a rose garden? Oh, if only!

Just for the record, that game of giving cheek to the young men of the village came about one Wednesday night, months before Champ arrived, because Sparrow was bored, saying he was in need of some excitement. Seeing Clifford Goodwin approaching, Sparrow, who was egged on by Golcho, called him 'Big Head,' adding that his ears looked like a monkey's. So Clifford gave chase but failed to catch them. Believing they would always get away with it, the lads improved their running skills by giving cheek to the other young men of the village. They deemed it to be good fun until Sparrow was caught a couple of nights later. Then it was not such a good game.

Champ was shown the best pubs and private houses for singing carols at Christmas time. Twab even pointed out four privately owned houses that paid sixpence whenever he shopped for them while shopping for his mum. That, and his early morning paper round with Jonah Lloyd's news agency in Coedpoeth, was how Twab made his money. His round was the Adwy. There were not many people in the village who did not know Twab (or Malcolm as they called him).

Knowing 'street cred' was vital in that day and age, nothing of importance was left out of Champ's initiation to the village. As the weeks went by, who was who among the other village kids was also pointed out him. There were only two characters that were not to be trusted, all the others were fine and dandy up to a point.

Had he had his way Champ would have increased the numbers in the gang, but Twab overruled him saying four was enough and that Champ would understand when he got to know the village kids better. They were in Twab's eyes what he called wimps. They would not do this; would not do that, so in the end he gave up on them, but not with Sparrow and Golcho who were just like him, rough and ready, and fit for anything, ideal gang members.

There were certain people in the village that you stayed well clear of on account of them not liking the younger generation. Those misery guts as they were called, sent you away if you as much as played around their gateways during the evening. So for revenge, it was their doors that were knocked on dark nights, along with those who told you to sing up, as they could not hear you singing your carols at Christmas time – and then, when you finished, told you to go away as they had already given once that evening. They were crooks.

Thinking he had been shown all the shops in the area (all handy for sweets, fags and things) Champ was shown another shop, Oswald's, tucked away between Lloft Wen Lane and Rhos Berse Road. Alan pointed it out to his mum, who never let on that she knew of it. Mr Williams, the shopkeeper, known affectionately as Oswald, had a delivery service for his customers. A slightly older boy, Richard Trematick, who, with Basil Davies, broke the violin string, who was fairly new to the village and living two doors up from Twab, was often seen after school delivering boxes around the village on a hand cart that looked like the hand carts that were used at railway stations. It was Oswald who gave you worn-out sacks for collecting leaves and old papers when it was time to start collecting for the bonfire.

One time Richard let it be known that Oswald had a card school going for those who wanted to play cards on the sly, gambling being illegal. He told Twab one day that he would have been more than surprised if he knew the names of all those who played cards, not that he was going to tell. There were some big names in the village on that list.

The two chippies, Roberts's (opposite Glyn's shop) and the one in Coedpoeth, were very handy, especially when leaving the cinema. Twab could not think of anything nicer than a chip supper with scratching to finish the night off. Both chippies would give you some scratchings if you asked nicely. It was also handy to know the whereabouts of the police station in Coedpoeth, which was situated in Bryn Clywedog. Panic set in among the local kids when a rumour was put out that the Adwy was going to be having its very own Bobby, and soon.

Now that he knew the rest of the Adwy children by name, some eight lads and six girls, Champ was beginning to feel he was part of the village. His memories of Chester and the lads he played with were beginning to fade. He hardly ever thought of Billy Watts any more, or Stan, Percy or Kenny.

When it came to all the roads and paths in and around the village, Champ was amazed. They all seemed to be connected to one another with their twists and turns, unlike Chester where roads and paths all seemed to go on for ever in a straight line. Alan blamed the Romans for that. According to the history books, the Romans made their roads straight so as to be able to transport their armies and machines easier. If that was true, then it would appear that they never conquered the Adwy or Coedpoeth.

And when it came to pubs, they were everywhere. There were eight between the Adwy, Coedpoeth and the Talwrn. Was everyone an alcoholic? It was the same with the churches and chapels. There were six to Champ's knowledge. Was everyone that religious? There was Harry Junk's shop on Smithy Lane which sold anything and everything. Harry was doing a roaring trade selling second-hand goods.

The only worry for Champ was Terry, Aunty Jinni's lad, who lived across the road from him, with Frank, Ernie and Dave just around the corner on Twab's street, Heol Islwyn. But thankfully, Terry and Co were not the bullies they were in school, well not quite. But even so, the lads, to be on the safe side, kept out of their way whenever possible.

Due to the Council building new houses on land that once belonged to Bryn Celyn and Pentwyn farms, at the top end of the village, Twab argued that the building sites were compensation for the loss of the fields that were once roamed over and played in. At every stage of their development, the village children (including Twab, Sparrow and Golcho) found them great places to play in, especially when the roofs were on and it was raining. But that pleasure was stopped. The Council in their wisdom hired a watchman who just happened to be a good runner and carried a stick and there were many tales the lads could have told about their relationship with the watchman. For instance, how he would sneak up on you and chase you all through the village. But in the end, a truce was called. It was ten times better being friends with him rather than being chased by him and while the truce lasted, they got to sit with him in his little cabin on cold, dark nights. His coke fire was very welcome on frosty evenings, and you could smoke if you wanted to, and he told you stories of when he was a youngster.

He had left school when he was twelve and his first job was down the Hafod mine, where the lads now sometimes played. It seemed he had to push tubs of coal for twelve hours a day and was paid something like four shillings a week. The clay pipe he smoked fascinated the lads. It had a long slim handle, and was filled with a foul smelling tobacco called shag. On one occasion, Sparrow apparently asked if he could have a smoke, but Mr Roberts said no.

Because it was Champ's first weekend in the village, and he being, according to Twab, a 'free spirit', it was decided on the Friday night just before Champ had to go home, that he was going to be taken down the woods first thing on Saturday morning, a place that was very special to the 'Gang'.

It was ten to ten on Saturday morning and the sun was shining but Alan had only ten more minutes in which to do something that was very important before the lads came calling. With his pots in the sink and his mum upstairs, he informed Jeannie (who was part of the conspiracy) that he was going into the wash house to do a little more work on 'You know what'. Thirty minutes later, Twab was pounding his very own special knock on Champ's back door – the one he used when out carol singing - Da-da- dada-da- da, da. Jeannie, who had gone upstairs to play with her dolls, nearly jumped out of her skin. She thought the door was being kicked in.

'Just a minute,' shouted Mrs Fletcher as she dried her hands in her pinny. She too had nearly jumped out of her skin. When she opened the door, Twab, rather bubbly said, 'Hello Mrs F. Is he in?'

There was a stick somehow attached to Malcolm's trousers which caused Mrs Fletcher to wonder what on earth it could be. But she had to smile. Ever since the previous Tuesday when she had been introduced to him and the other two, who also had funny nicknames, Doreen was unsure whether she liked the idea of being called Mrs F. By Thursday she had accepted it although she did not know anyone who was referred to by the initial of their surname. She now thought it unique.

Wondering where the other two were she said, 'He's around here somewhere Malcolm. Come on in.' Giving him a biscuit out of the tin, Mrs Fletcher went to the bottom of the stairs and shouted up, 'Jeannie, where's Alan? Malcolm's here for him?'

Not thinking she shouted down, 'He's in the washhouse Mum,' and then began to panic and there was no way she could warn Alan that she'd slipped up. Oh, dear.

'Did you hear that, Malcolm?'

'Sure did Mrs F. I'll go and get him.'

Jeannie let out a huge sigh of relief. Whew, that was close, she thought.

Unable to open the washhouse door (it being locked from the inside) Twab, when the door was finally opened, asked Champ why it was locked. Champ pulled him inside and, checking to see where his mum was (thankfully she was nowhere to be seen), explained that it was her birthday on Thursday, and that he was drawing a picture of their house and garden for Jeannie to make into a birthday card.

Showing his friend the drawing, which was nowhere near finished, Twab, very much impressed, said, 'Hey, I didn't know you could draw this good?' Smiling Champ assured him that drawing was all that was going on, hence the door being locked. But, before Champ could stop him, Twab stepped outside to compare the drawing to the house and garden. Yanking him back in and telling him off, Champ said it was supposed to be a surprise.

'Oops, sorry,' said Twab handing it back.

Checking that there were no dirty finger marks on it, Champ put the sketch back in its folder. For safe keeping he placed it and his pencil behind the boiler until Jeannie could take it and the pencil upstairs where she was hiding them in her school satchel.

Eager to show Champ his sword, (the stick that Mrs Fletcher saw dangling from his trousers) Twab unbuttoned his coat and slowly unsheathed it from the loop in his trousers (which was the scabbard.) Holding it out for him to see, and then handing it over he said, 'Well, what do you think?'

'Wow,' said Champ swishing it through the air the way he imagined Errol Flynn would have. 'It's fantastic. Did you make it?'

'Yeah,' said Twab who then explained that Sparrow and Golcho (who were waiting for them by the lamp post) also had one, and that he Champ would be having his when they reached the woods.

'So, when did you make them?'

'Last year sometime,' said Twab who then explained that it was made out of holly. The sword, some three feet in length, was slightly tapered. All the dark green bark from the handle down had been scraped off, giving the blade a dull white colour now that all the sap had dried out. The top four inches, the handle, was unscraped. It was that which gave the sword its character, strength and meaning. The sticking end was blunted in the hope of avoiding injury.

Champ (as Errol Flynn) fought off the evil Sheriff of Nottingham for a minute or so, then handing the sword back said he could not wait to have one.

'Right then,' said Twab, sheathing the weapon through the left hand loop of his trousers, 'let's go and get you one.'

Back in the house, and while putting on his jerkin, Alan winked at Jeannie to remind her that the picture was in its usual place in the wash house. He then let his mum (who was upstairs) know that he and the lads were going down the woods – a very special place according to Twab, Sparrow and Golcho.

Hearing the gate being closed (slammed actually), Mrs Fletcher opened Alan's bedroom window, and while shaking her duster told them to be careful as she did not want any accidents or the police calling.

'We'll be okay Mrs F.' Twab assured her.

Doreen watched them as they ran down the street to meet up with Sparrow and Golcho, the other two little horrors. In awe of their innocence she closed the bedroom window and suggested she and Jeannie have a break form the house work as it was time for a nice cup of tea and a digestive biscuit.

It was 10.30 on a beautiful sunny Saturday morning and Alan Fletcher, alias Champ, was about to be taken down the woods for the first time. A place which, if he was anything like the others, he would fall in love with immediately.

As they approached the lamp post, Champ began to admire the fencing skills of both Sparrow and Golcho. They were both very good. But after a few minutes of some stunning sword play, Golcho was jabbed in the stomach.

'*Touché* or whatever it is the French say,' Sparrow yelled out as he raised and kissed the hilt of his sword the way he had seen Stewart Granger do in the film *Scaramouch*. Sparrow loved his striped trousers, whereas Golcho thought he looked like a cissy.

But Golcho was angry with Sparrow. He had stuck him in the belly too hard. While rubbing his wound, he began to swipe the air with his sword in frustration. He thought about challenging Sparrow to another duel, for revenge, but instead greeted Twab and Champ, as did Sparrow. It was time to put away the swords. It was time to go down the woods.

Setting off, their stroll down Heol Islwyn suddenly became a race. Twab had developed a bad habit of announcing that their walk or stroll was now a race, with today's winning post being the green gates. As he sped off Twab also announced that the last one in was a smelly pig. Taken off guard by the sudden challenge, Champ, Sparrow and Golcho gave chase.

Suddenly, remembering where the green gates were, Champ over-took Sparrow and Golcho while running down Heol Celyn. Turning left into Heol Offa, Champ chased after and overtook Twab and then ran on until he finally came across a set of green gates on his left.

Moments later, Twab came in followed by Golcho. It was Sparrow who ended up as the smelly pig. All three were out of breath. During their puffing and panting, with a little wheezing going on, Twab was told off by Golcho – when the latter got his breath back – for being so sneaky. He added that he was glad that Champ had beaten him.

While Champ waited for them to recover, he said it was high time they learned how to control their breathing while running. A moment later he asked if anyone knew why there was barbed-wire on the top of the green gates.

For a while Champ began to think they were enjoying their coughing and spluttering. They looked a right mess keeled over coughing their hearts out.

Twab, who was clutching his knees, was a little red in the face as he was so out of condition. Sparrow and Golcho did not look that much better and were both clutching their sides and moaning. They probably had a stitch.

Champ did not think they were going to answer his question just yet, not the way they were coughing and spluttering. To amuse himself he began to look through a peephole in the gate that had once been a knot, but all he could see was a small section of field, an untidy hedgerow, and an old dilapidated building that looked as it was going to fall down any minute.

'I suppose,' said Sparrow the first to recover, 'the barbed wire's there to keep the likes of us from climbing over.'

Champ thanked him for that little piece of useless information. He had already guessed that. While waiting for the others to recover (they were still coughing and spluttering some) Champ began to study the surrounding area.

He already knew of the row of houses on their left that led up to the Talwrn Road, and the three empty houses on the corner where Terry, Frank and Dave used to live (it was a shame they now lived on Twab's street).

Champ walked across the road, and cast his eyes over the fields and hedgerows that belonged to Llidiart Fanny Farm in the direction of Southsea. He then leaned against the five-bar gate that he was going to draw one of these days, along with the lovely oak tree that accompanied it which was at the bottom of next door's garden, once he had learned how to draw. He scanned the area for some time and then focused on a huge bank of red shale known affectionately as Southsea Bank. Champ thought it was a mini mountain. A little further, to the left of Southsea Bank, was Tan y Fron Bank, another mini mountain which was the bank that Jeannie could see from her bedroom window. Both were the debris from the closed down pits which once produced thousands of tons of coal each week, providing jobs for a lot of the men in the area. Some people saw the two banks as monstrosities. For Champ, the fields and hedgerows and trees that belonged to Llidiart Fanny Farm on his left and Ty'n y Coed on his right were magical. He had never seen so much open space before coming to live in the Adwy.

Having regained his breath, Golcho, to get a laugh, suddenly raised his arms to shoulder height and making a Frankenstein's monster face caused everyone to burst out laughing.

When Champ rejoined them, Golcho, in a most exaggerated lisp in answer to Champ's earlier question about the barbed wire being on top of the gates, said, 'Perhapsh, theresh a monshter there that only comesh out on Shaturdaysh and Shundaysh – to keep the likshs of ush out.'

While the lads were laughing their heads off, Golcho finished his whacky sentence with a long ghostly, 'Oooh.'

While laughing at Golcho's terrible impression, the lads scragged him to the floor. Then they played out their version of a Frankenstein's monster, each claiming that their interpretation was the best. Suddenly and for devilment, Twab, again with no warning, ran off down the road with the lads cursing and then pursuing him. Reaching the Talwrn Road each gave their version of how a Frankenstein monster should cross a busy main road. Not only were they shouted at by several irate motorists, but Golcho ended up being scragged again – for being the funniest.

Turning left just this side of Llidiart Fanny Farm (owned by Mr Moss, the richest man in the world according to Twab), the lads, having calmed down began to walk along a stretch of road affectionately know as 'The Woods Road.'

The hazel hedge on their left being quite low gave a superb view of Minera Mountain in the distance. The mixed hedge of hawthorn and hazel on the opposite side was so high that it concealed most of the farm's out buildings, the shippons. Drawing his sword, Twab began to attack a giant hogweed flower and eventually decapitated it.

Not to be out done, Sparrow and Golcho, drawing their swords began to attack a large clump of nettles and between them they annihilated what they saw as the enemy. Champ could only stand there and watch in amazement as Porthos, Aramis and Athos displayed their sword skills. Their tactics included a lot of running in, swatting the plants (the enemy) and *touché*-ing when a kill was made.

The battle lasted for several minutes, but ended when the hogweed and nettle bed were scattered all over the embankment and road. All three would-be musketeers faced each other and kissed the hilts of their swords. 'All for one, and one for all,' they cried out in unison, while raising the handles of their swords to their foreheads as they had seen in some Roman film.

Just as they were about to set off, Twab remembered a funny incident relating to a wasp's nest and began to tell Champ the story. Pointing to the exact spot where the nest's entrance had been, he said they had been in the process of robbing it, and the plan was to run in with your swatter, swat the wasps a couple of times, and then run out. And all was going well for a while, until Golcho ran back and a bunch of wasps landed on his jumper and started to walk up his arms and chest. Insisting that he should tell the story, Golcho, who like the others was laughing his head off, said, 'Because the wasps were all over me, I began to panic and so ran towards these two so-called mates of mine, but instead of helping me, they ran away. So there I was screaming my head off with stinging wasps all over me and these two dozy sods were running away from me as fast as they could. Some friends.'

Because no one could stop laughing, the story was put on hold for several minutes, as no one could finish it. Finally, Golcho delivered the punch line. 'The funny thing was,' he said as Twab and Sparrow burst out laughing again. 'These two silly buggers were stung several times whereas I got away with it. Not one sting did I have.'

With that, the laughing started again and was uncontrollable, especially when one of them remembered something and told it, causing the others to burst out laughing again. Sides were splitting, jaws were aching and tears were rolling down faces, but still the laughter continued.

After several minutes, the laughing died down long enough for them to move on. While wiping the tears from his eyes, Champ said he would have given anything to have been there when it happened. The laughing more or less petered out by the time they had reached the top of the Woods hill, some eighty yards further on.

Now that they were serious again, they stood in the only gateway on this little stretch of road. The view of Minera Mountain, some three miles away, was an amazing sight. The only thing that separated the lads and the mountain were fields and hedgerows and nothing else. Twab very proudly proclaimed that this was the only spot he knew of where there were no houses or buildings to spoil the view. The mountain's only feature, apart from its bluish/brown colour, was a tree which, being so far away, reminded Champ of that obelisk thing in Egypt, but the others thought it was pear shaped. Sparrow thought Champ needed his eyes testing. Moving on, fed up with the view, the lads stepped back onto the road and began to walk down the Woods hill in full sunlight. The sloping bank to their left, with a holly hedge growing on it was something like fifteen-feet high and was very impressive. But the mixed hedge opposite, which consisted of holly, hawthorn and blackthorn, was nowhere higher than six feet.

Champ then heard what he thought was trickling water. When asked where it was coming from, he was told there was a ditch on the other side of the hedge. Insisting that he was shown it, Twab led them to the only place it could be reached, and they each in turn crawled through the tiniest of gaps.

It was much darker and cooler now that they were out of the sun. Between the tree branches and the hedge it looked like they were in a tunnel. Champ approached the trickling water with difficulty as it was very uneven underfoot. Then he listened as the water trickled along from one pool to another. It was amazing. There were miniature waterfalls no higher than three inches and little eddies, or as Golcho called them, whirlpools, all along the little stream. Then to his amazement, Champ spotted little shrimp like things swimming and scurrying about in the different pools. Very enthusiastically he searched a few of the pools and found other wriggly things that neither he nor his mates who took all this for granted could put names to. Apart from the wriggly things that lived in the water, there was one thing that looked like a spider that ran along the surface. Sparrow called it a boatman.

Twab then pointed out a spider which was stalking Sparrow's boatman. Everyone watched in amazement as the spider used a little piece of twig to run along and then pounced on its victim. The struggling Boatman soon ceased struggling as the spider dragged it up and out of the water.

Now that the drama was over, Twab suggested they move on. He was itching to be doing some serious sword fighting. With Sparrow the last one to crawl back through the gap in the hedge, they set off down the Woods hill and stepped into a long stretch of shade that went as far as the first curve in what was an S-bend. The shade was due to all the overhanging trees on either side of the road that also went as far as the bend. It being so hot, they appreciated not only the shade but also the gentle breeze that washed over them. Champ pointed out what he thought was a most fascinating phenomenon. The trees, being so close together, had created a tunnel effect over the entire road. He was so amazed at the spectacle that he could not take his eyes off it. He also noticed that, not only were trees abounding, but the grassy embankment on their left was home to different kinds of wild flowers. He as if he was walking through a picture book.

When they reached the S-bend, the sun, breaking through the canopy here and there, made lovely patterns of light and shade on the road. Twab said it was called dappled sunlight. Champ did not care what it was called, all he knew was that he had never known a situation like this before. In fact, he had never seen so many trees before, let alone dappled sunlight or grass-banks that were home to so many wild flowers. He was so excited he let out a long, 'Wow,' and again began to believe he was walking through a page in some picture book.

When he pointed out the tunnel effect the trees had made, the lads, slightly flabbergasted, said they had never noticed it before, but were fascinated by it. Champ broke everyone's reverie when he said rather dreamily that there was nothing like this in Chester. When he realised he was speaking dreamily and felt silly, he said the only thing they had in Chester was the park and that was too far away, adding that when you got there, the swings were either broken or taken up with the bigger lads. Golcho actually admitted that the more you looked at the shaded area, the more it resembled a tunnel. Having stared at it for some time, Golcho then explained why they had never seen it before – they always ran down the Woods hill.

Going into the S-bend the scenery changed, the high bank and hedge on their left petering out and becoming an integral part of the wood. The lie of the land was also completely altered. Champ could not believe his eyes. Before him on the grandest of scales was an even more magnificent sight. He was completely surrounded by trees. He had never been surrounded by trees. He was speechless. When he finally came back to reality, he noticed, not twenty yards away, a cute little bridge with crenulated walls. His instincts told him that this area was going to be a great place to play in.

While trying to take it all in, Champ was told that the river which flowed under the bridge was damned every summer and it was possible to swim in it. It was dammed at the moment said Sparrow. When Champ asked where it was, Sparrow pointed to his right and said over there, on the dump side. Champ confessed that this was indeed a very special place.

Gazing up at one of the big oak trees on his right (the dump side, so called because it was a land fill site) Champ saw a flash of movement. A squirrel ran frantically along the top branches with Sparrow wishing he had brought his catty along as they made good targets, as did certain birds.

Champ went over to look at all the different species of wild flowers some of which he could not name. All were living in harmony in the grass. There were fox-gloves, buttercups, common spotted orchid, speedwell, daisies, dandelions and herb bennett, whose flowers were beginning to lose their crispy, sharp yellowness. Sadly, Champ had missed the bluebells, the wood anemone, the celandine, the snow-drops and primroses. He was told they were dormant until the spring when they would reappear and, when they did, it was a sight you would never forget. The wood's floor Champ was promised would have carpets of white, then yellow then blue for several weeks in the spring.

Young saplings that lived for hundreds of years were sprouting up here and there. But there was one old, oak tree that looked to be in a spot of bother. It was leaning so bad that Twab predicted it would be blown over in a few months when the winter winds came.

Then there was all the bird song. If you could not see them, you could certainly hear them. In the distance, magpies were cackling, crows were cawing and nearby smaller birds were singing and twittering. There was a lovely cacophony of bird song. And there were white and coloured butterflies flitting over the embankment in search of nectar-rich flowers. Champ watched a lovely white butterfly with black spots on the tips of its wings unfold its long tongue into a flower and invited the others to come and see. He had never seen anything like it before, nor had the others. They all watched mesmerised as the cabbage white rolled up its long tongue and then sought out another flower. It was amazing.

Taking a deep breath, Champ asked why the air seemed to taste sweeter now that they were surrounded by all these trees? The reason was that every household in the village, including the privately owned houses, burned logs to help out with the coal. On bad days, wisps of sulphurous clouds hung over the village where you could actually taste the sulphur. But suddenly the enveloping silence was shattered with Golcho's sudden explosive rendition of the *Drinking Song* from the film *Student Prince* which starred Edmond Purdom miming to the voice of Mario Lanza. Everyone jumped as Golcho held onto his infamous top C, as Sparrow called it. His face began to turn red from holding onto the highest of all the high notes that Champ had ever heard.

Twab cursed himself under his breath. It was he who recommended that they see the film. Twab only wanted to see the film because his mum loved to hear Mario Lanza sing. He wanted to see and hear the man for himself. So off they went as a threesome to see the *Student Prince* in their beloved picture house in Coedpoeth. And that was when Golcho had became hooked on Mario Lanza. It was a mystery how he learned all the words to the *Drinking Song,* but he did and was always singing the damn thing. Being ordered to shut up, Golcho did, but not before he sang out, 'Oh let every true lover salute his sweetheart and drink.'

Telling Golcho off while trying to be serious about it, having already called him a 'Dozy plonker,' Twab pointed out that he had only frightened all the birds away. But suddenly, seeing the funny side of it and turning to Champ and chuckling he said, 'Don't worry mate, he often does this. I'm afraid you'll have to get used to it.'

'Yeah,' said Sparrow grinning, 'and if you think that was bad; you wait till you hear his David Whitfield's *Cara Mia Mine.*'

Because Golcho had shattered the peace and quiet, it was decreed by all that he be scragged. Knowing what was coming, Golcho tried to fight back even though he was being pushed and shoved from one to the other quite violently. Sparrow, for good measure gave him a sneaky dig in the ribs, thinking Golcho would not notice it. But it was noticed and memorised.

When Golcho promised on his grandmother's deathbed to behave himself (she had been dead for several years), the woods again fell silent to all but the birds and insects. Tranquility reigned once more.

Now that the wood could be seen on both sides of the road in all its glory (trees, trees and more trees), and it being what the lads had promised, 'very green and beautiful,' Champ took it all in for several moments, first looking at this tree then at that one; then as a budding artist he focused on the bridge. He loved its crenellated walls and saw a must-draw picture that he was going to draw one day when he knew the area better. The bridge with the fields, hedgerows and pylons in the background would make a stunning picture.

Champ was suddenly put on the spot. He was asked to choose. They could either enter the Hafod side of the woods, on their left, where all the best battles had taken place, or they could enter the Dump side, which contained the swing known as the 'monster' and the swimming pool.

The Dump side, with all the gas and toxic fumes spilling out of the ground, was a land fill site and had been for several years. But thirty yards beyond the rubbish, the woods were what the lads called normal again, that being trees, trees and more trees. Bubbling with excitement and feeling spoilt for choice, Champ asked the lads to choose for him. He was too overwhelmed.

'Well it is a sword we've come for, and the Hafod side is the best site for them,' said Golcho unsheathing his, hoping to entice Sparrow to take him on. He had a score to settle and wanted to return that jab in the belly and the dig in the ribs he had been given. They were still hurting.

'Okay then. The Hafod side it is,' said Twab, nodding to Golcho to sheath his sword. Now was not the time for settling scores.

Approaching the Woods entrance which was no wider than a gate, they each in turn stepped off the road and onto a mound of bare earth.

Led by Twab they entered the Hafod side of the woods in single file, and strolled down the three slopes that veered slightly to the right. Turning left at the bottom, the path levelled off but continued on through the first of several clearings. But because everyone was in short trousers, their legs were scratched on the second slope. A huge holly bush was part growing across the path. Golcho had promised several times to cut the blasted plant down, but as yet it was still standing. The lads were more or less surrounded by trees and bushes the moment they had started down the Woods hill, but being in the actual woods with yet more trees and bushes was tremendous. So too was the lush grass that was home to so many types of wild flowers, and then there were all the bird songs.

Champ was so exhilarated he likened it to the first time he saw Tarzan's tree-house with its fabulous dangling vines in the film where Boy was taught to swim, while Jane and Cheetah watched from the far bank. That was one of his all time favourite Tarzan films, not because it starred the best of the Tarzans (Johnnie Weissmuller), but because a young Johnnie Sheffield played Boy, and Maureen O'Hara, Jane. Champ loved Boy's curly hair and often wished he could be him. But this was no jungle movie, no play-acting, this little wood was real and it was fantastic. He could not explain it, but the environment was stirring up unknown emotions. There was a huge lump in his throat – a catch in his voice. As a twelve-year-old he was feeling things he could not explain, but knew they were important. Being completely surrounded by trees, bushes and bird song, awed him to the point where it made him feel small. It was another experience he had never known before, but my, he was going to love being in this wood. It was as the lads had promised, very green and very special.

They walked on with Champ mesmerised. Suddenly, as if he had not seen enough for one day, he heard something else that he had never heard before – running water as in a river. When he asked what the sound was and was told, he asked to be taken there. He wanted to see it for himself. It took some time to scamper down the bank having left the main path but, winding around a huge hazel bush, with Twab leading, they each in turn jumped onto a stony stretch of beach. Champ was mesmerized by the river's gurgling sound. It was so euphoric. He had never heard a river trickling over stones before and was awed by it. The river was never anywhere more than two-feet deep or ten-feet wide, but its musical overtones were very melodic. Champ realized that the different sounds this little river was making were being made by the water trickling over, or around stones of different size. The bigger ones, the ones that were jutting out of the water which could have been used as stepping stones, were giving off a kind of gurgling sound, while the ones that were being flowed over were giving off a trickling sound. It was the bigger stones that actually interfered with the river's natural flow. He also noticed that, due to the river's unevenness, there were miniature waterfalls and swirling eddies and little stretches of water which rippled over the myriads of stones that were whiter than white, which helped in making the river so melodic. All the stones and pebbles had been smoothed over eons ago. Some were even slimy.

While Champ listened to the river's sounds, he knew he would never forget them. In fact he did not want to ever forget them. They were the sounds that only a little river can make and now they were his for the rest of his life. He was speechless for some time. When he saw leaves and little twigs go floating by, he hoped they avoided all the hazards that could trap them. Some were already stranded in little eddies and held there spinning round and round. Those that managed to break free, continued on their journey to – who knows where? Several parts of the river's bank had been gouged away over the years, leaving pools of water deeper than the natural flow. There, stretches of mud were home to several kinds of water plants and tough looking grass. Some plants were growing in mid stream. One such plant was water drop wort, apparently very poisonous according to Sparrow, who could not remember how he knew that, but advised Champ to stay well clear of it.

Casting shadows over the river while making weird and wonderful shapes when the sun shone on them were the hazel bushes and the alder trees which, on days when the sun did not shine, gave character to the fields and hedgerows that belonged to a great farmer known simply as, Old Mr Williams.

Champ's eyes were everywhere trying to take all this nature in. Then something clicked in his head, he fell in love with nature, something that he knew would stay with him for ever. Seven days ago he did not know what nature was. But now all of a sudden he loved it. And it was all down to being in this little wood. There was no Cecil B De Mille extravaganza, no great flash in the sky like you see in the movies to announce the event, but this little wood, Champ knew, was going to be a very important place in his life from now on.

Golcho suddenly picked up a stone and threw it at one of the leaves that was trapped in an eddy. A moment later, Twab and Sparrow joined in. When Champ went to pick up a stone to join in, he noticed something glittering in the water. Stepping onto a stone while checking his balance he pulled out a piece of broken bottle. It was green and so smooth. He had never seen a piece of broken glass like this before. It was about the size of a penny. When he looked at it again and saw that it was heart shaped he decided he was going to keep it as a memento. As he went to straighten up he saw his reflection in a little pool and watched his face as it rippled back and to. When he began to move his head from side to side he was reminded of being at the fair one time, having paid sixpence to go in to the Hall of Mirrors where he was made to look tall, short, fat and thin. But after several minutes of throwing stones at the leaves and twigs and getting wet, Twab suggested they move on. They were here to get Champ a sword.

Back on the main path and some fifty yards into what was paradise, and still mesmerised by all that was going on, Champ found that he was tripping over roots that sprawled along the ground like giant snakes. Suddenly, the path, at the end of a long right hand curve, petered out and became two slightly lesser paths. One veered off to the left and higher ground, reaching Mr Moss's fields (who, according to Twab was the richest man in the world, owning Lloft Wen House and Llidiart Fanny Farm). The path that veered off to the right went back down to the river and good old Mr Williams's fields who was the undisputed best farmer in the world – again according to Twab.

Champ asked to be taken back down to the river. He wanted to see and hear it again. He could not get the sound or sight of it out of his head. After some disagreement (they were here to get him a sword after all), he got his wish.

Back on the stony beach, Champ stared at the gurgling water for ages. Finally he walked up to the edge and simply looked at it again. It was wonderful being able to see and hear the gurgling sounds first hand once again.

Kneeling down, he dipped his hand in the rather cold water and knew he would never forget the moment, or the melodious song this snake-like creature was making as it twisted its way along. He retrieved his piece of broken glass and rubbed it between his finger and thumb. It being so shiny and smooth, he could almost see through it. He suddenly remembered *King Solomon's Mines* with Stewart Granger and Deborah Kerr and pretended that his piece of broken glass was a diamond. But Twab was now impatient and insisted they move on. Actually he pulled rank on Champ, arguing that they were here to get him a sword or had he forgotten? So with that they made their way back up to the flimsy path that led up to Mr Moss's field, in search of a good holly bush.

All the trees on their way were pointed out to Champ. It was obvious that his mates really loved them. And why shouldn't they, they were magnificent in shape and height.

But suddenly, being told they were in Twab's favourite clearing, the one with the three oak trees in a dead straight line, on which he had carved his initials with his dad's jack-knife last year, Champ asked if they could sit a while. With their swords removed from their scabbards (their trousers loops) and rammed into the soft earth, as a stand-by, it was explained to Champ that sitting is always done cross legged, Red Indian style.

Having flopped down by a clump of holly bushes which had supplied Twab and his family with Christmas trees for the past two years, the lads simply sat there admiring their surroundings. Bird song, as always, was plentiful. Suddenly a blackbird perched on a branch not ten feet away and began to sing its most melodious love song, thus captivating the lads even more. Who taught the bird to sing like that? Champ wondered.

Pleased that he had asked Champ to join his little gang, and knowing how he must be feeling and breaking the silence, Twab explained that they spend a lot of time down here in this little wood in the summer.

Both Sparrow and Golcho nodded to mean they did. Golcho said a lot of fun could be had in this little wood, it would take him all day to count the amount of times they had played Robin Hood or whatever. Both Twab and Sparrow nodded their agreement. For several minutes the lads, for once, just sat there looking and listening, enjoying the moment. This was a rare moment indeed. The lads did not know what it was to be still.

When Golcho began to describe some game they had played here ages ago, Champ found he was more interested in all the bird song that was going on, especially that blackbird who was still singing its head off not ten feet away. He wished he could see it, but it was too well hidden in the bushes. As he listened to its song, he began to wonder how something so black could be so well hidden. His search failed to find it.

'Well,' said Sparrow at last (whose bum was wet from sitting on the grass, as was everyones), 'are we going to get this lad a sword or what?'

Because Twab had the only knife, his dad's jack-knife (the one used when rabbiting, for gutting them) they continued their search for a good holly bush. Having taken the path up to where the woods and fields belonging to Mr Moss met, they found an ideal bush. Knowing they would be chased if spotted, Twab put Champ, Sparrow and Golcho on red alert while he tried to reach the branch he was after. Again Twab struggled and openly complained with the number of scratches he was receiving as he climbed up the bush, but finally the branch he was after was cut down.

After showing everyone his scratches, one of which was bleeding, and after being told by Sparrow to get on with it as they did not have all day, the would-be sword was stripped of its branches, cut to length and scraped (barring the handle), with the sticking end blunted. While the others looked on, Twab admired the weapon he had just made. He would not have minded keeping it for himself, but after some fancy swordplay, as good as anything Errol Flynn could have done, he presented Champ with his first ever sword. The fact that it was not perfectly straight did not matter.

On receiving it, Champ ran his hand up and down it. The sap, slightly sticky, wet his fingers, but he was amazed at the power it generated inside him. He held the sword in both hands above his head the way he had seen Burt Lancaster do in the *Crimson Pirate*, and then he began to sword fight the holly bush from which the sword had just been taken. It felt like a real sword.

Because no one had any money on them they chose sides by

guessing which hand the stone was in. Twab and Golcho were taking on Sparrow and Champ.

'We'll go and hide and give you our secret call when we are ready,' said Twab. Watching them run off, Champ asked Sparrow what was all this about a secret call? His gang in Chester never had a secret call. With his eye on Twab and Golcho, who were now the enemy, and the direction they were taking, Sparrow explained that they made a squawking sound the way an Indian did one time in a western featuring Gary Cooper. 'You'll hear it when they're ready,' he said, again noting the way Twab and Golcho were taking. Suddenly they turned off the path and disappeared. But after some five minutes, while still waiting for the signal, Sparrow asked Champ how much sword fighting he had done in the past.

'None,' was the answer.

'Oh,' said Sparrow, 'in that case we'd better have a little practice in what time we've got left.' Facing Champ, Sparrow, very professionally drew his sword and lowering the tip to the ground, raised it and kissed the hilt. It was then that he noticed Champ was just standing there like a dummy. Disgusted, Sparrow insisted that he follow protocol. They were going into battle for goodness sake. Ashamed and red faced, Champ complied. Now they were ready for battle. Nodding, Sparrow yelled, 'On guard,' and lunged in with several brutal thrusts.

Taken off guard, Champ just managed to sidestep the attack. He then instinctively began to defend himself. Their clashing swords echoed in the silence as Sparrow continued his attack. While being driven back, parrying Sparrow's thrusts by sheer luck, Champ put the fact that he had not been killed down to his judo, because a judo man is always blocking, trying not to get caught out. But for someone who'd never held a sword until now, Sparrow was quite impressed with Champ's prowess, but never said anything. He was trying to kill him, metaphorically speaking. Even so, Champ was killed several times during the practice run, and hoped to do better when the real battle began, which could be any minute now according to Sparrow.

Suddenly the sound of a crow filled the air, 'Caw, caw, caw.'

Champ was flabbergasted. The only thing he could think of was, 'Wow.' He lowered his sword and stared in the direction the sound had come from. Lowering his sword and having pin pointed the direction,

Sparrow, identified the call and on red alert said, 'That was Twab. Come on. Just do your best.' He then put both hands to his mouth and gave a return call to let the enemy know that they were now being pursued, 'Caw, caw, caw.'

Moments later, Golcho's call filled the air as if daring them. The chase was on, meaning alertness at all time. With Sparrow leading, Champ was advised to be on guard and search every bush and tree in their path, as Twab and Golcho could be hiding behind any one of them. When Champ asked why they were heading in the opposite direction to where the calls were heard, he was told that was a false ploy to fool them, as Twab and Golcho would have moved on by now, adding that Twab is notorious for playing that move.

Moving deeper into the wood, Sparrow and Champ continued to search and thrust at the bushes in the hope of flushing out the enemy. Unbeknown to them, Twab and Golcho were watching their every move. Being on higher ground and looking down on them, Twab and Golcho, with swords in hand, were creeping along from tree to tree, following them the way Spencer Tracy and his men did in the film they saw on the Friday night prior to Champ's arrival on the fifth of June. It was a cracking good film. Twab could not remember what the film was called, other than it took place in the Everglades in Florida. It worked for Spencer Tracy, and it was working for Twab and Golcho right now which was fantastic. Twab motioned Golcho to be ready to attack.

Golcho, who was always ready when it came to a battle acknowledged. He could not wait for the fighting to begin and had a score to settle with Sparrow for jabbing him too hard in the belly by his house and for the dig in the ribs not twenty minutes ago. No, Golcho was ready and eager to do battle.

Suddenly Sparrow and Champ were in Golcho's favourite clearing – the one which has supplied him and his family with two very good holly Christmas trees, with at least another two remaining. There would have been a third, but it ended up as the sword he was fighting with this morning. It was perfectly straight.

Sparrow put Champ on red alert. 'Get ready,' he said, betting that the attack would begin at any moment. Then as a warning which was nothing to do with the on coming battle, he advised Champ to keep his beady eyes off the two Christmas trees that stood out very prominently, adding that they were Golcho's, and that he would go bonkers if he thought anyone had their eyes on them.

Champ looked at them and decided they were good Christmas trees but was sure he would find one somewhere else when the time came. At the moment, this being a first, he had battle tactics on his mind not Christmas trees.

With swords at the ready and convinced there was going to be an attack, Sparrow motioned Champ to come alongside him. They waited, and waited, and waited. But there was no attack. Anxious, Sparrow began to look around, even behind. He had known Twab to attack from behind before now. Twab could be a sneaky so and so when he chose to be. So, with his sword shaking due to the impending battle, Sparrow put Champ on red, red alert and then whispered that they were close by, as he could feel it in his bones, insisting that his bones had never been wrong before.

Then frustration kicked in. 'Come on you two,' he yelled, frightening several birds who were feeding nearby. 'Show ya-selves,' he demanded, 'Let's get this battle over and done with. I'm dying for a smoke.'

Giggling, both Twab and Golcho kept their cover. Drawing Twab's attention, Golcho suggested they throw stones at them as that would shake them up. With several pebbles each, Twab threw his to the left of Sparrow and Champ, whereas Golcho threw his to their right. 'That'll fool um,' Golcho giggled.

When the stones began to impact with the bushes, Sparrow jumped and alerted Champ that this was it, that he was to be ready to die for his country.

With their swords at the ready, Twab and Golcho prepared to charge. On Twab's order, the woods filled with their battle cries as they broke cover and charged down the slope on Sparrow and Champ whose eyes were wide from the noise Twab and Golcho were making. Champ swallowed, and looked at his companion. Sparrow tried to calm him down by telling him that they saw a film once about Bonny Prince Charlie, whose men, dressed in rags and with all sorts of weapons, charged the English in the same way as Twab and Golcho were charging down on them, and that he was not to worry as it was only for show.

In their enthusiasm, Twab and Golcho, who were doing exactly what Sparrow had just told Champ they would, disturbed a flock of rooks that had foolishly decided to have their rookery where this battle was about to take place. The petrified birds leapt from their nests and filled the air with so much squawking that Sparrow and Champ, after the initial shock, began to think that Twab and Golcho were competing with the crows to see who could make the most noise. You could hardly hear yourself think. But in less than two shakes of a lamb's tail, Twab and Golcho, having raced on down the slope yelling their heads off, were upon Sparrow and Champ with their swords at the ready.

With two sets of battle cries filling the air, each trying to out-do the other, as well as the fifty or so squawking rooks deafening the place, the battle commenced. Taking on Sparrow, Twab ordered Golcho to take on the inexperienced Champ so that the two of them could then take on Sparrow who was a pretty good sword fighter. Clack, clack, clack, their swords sounded as each side tried to annihilate the other. Realizing Golcho was very good with a sword, Champ knew he was going to be killed and out of the game if he faced him head on. He had to somehow think up a cunning plan. He had to duck and dive as it were. Surviving Golcho's initial thrusts, Champ ducked and dived around the trees and bushes, and began to notice a pattern in Golcho's attacks. While lunging in, he would pause then lunge in again. It was here Champ felt he had a chance of avoiding defeat. He did not want to be killed just yet.

Reading Champ's mind, Golcho played his trump card. In wanting to be at Sparrow for jabbing him too hard and digging him in the ribs, he lowered his sword and looking puzzled and ready to run, said in a somewhat serious tone, 'Aye-up Champ, who's that behind you?'

Not exactly believing him, thinking it was a trick, Champ, while facing him, stepped back a couple of paces but at the ready and peeped over his shoulder.

Knowing his plan had worked, Golcho screamed out his infamous top C from the *Student Prince* and, holding on to the note (causing Twab and Sparrow to jump, and the rooks to leap from their nests filling the air with their horrible squawking again), stepped in and stuck Champ in the belly, killing him. 'Got ya,' he yelled grinning like a Cheshire cat.

Realising he'd been well and truly caught, Champ accepted his fate and then performed his death throes the way he thought Alan Ladd would have done had he been killed in *Shane*. He very professionally fell to the ground while clutching his stomach and died.

Golcho stepped in, and with his right foot on Champ's chest – his sword inches from his throat and in a terrible Long John Silver accent, trying to mimic Robert Newton, he said, 'Ha, ha, me hearty, never trust an old sea-dog called Ali Golcho.' Then he again laughed like Robert Newton. Knowing his game was over, Champ sat up and watched as Golcho ran over with revenge in mind to assist his partner in arms.

On his own and fighting like fury, Sparrow knew it would be over the moment one of them came at him from behind. And that is what happened. Twab ordered Golcho to do just that. Sparrow fought long and hard, but as he tried to block one of Twab's thrusts, Golcho, seeing his chance, stepped in and, with revenge about to be administered, stuck Sparrow really hard in the belly. 'Got ya' he yelled out. When he saw Sparrow cringing and holding his stomach he said. 'That's for jabbing me too hard outside my house, and for digging me in the ribs earlier on ya bugger. It hurts, doesn't it?'

Sparrow spent a few moments rubbing where Golcho had stuck him. But not to be outdone by the way Champ had played out his death scene, he performed his the way Basil Rathbone did when he was killed in the castle by Errol Flynn at the end of *The Adventures of Robin Hood*, which was in colour. He actually somersaulted and landed flat on his back and lay still. All three were amazed at the way he had somersaulted.

When Twab and Golcho gave their swords a victory kiss the way the Romans did in *Ben Hur* (a great movie), the rooks put up with that. It did not bother them. It was when they began to inform Sparrow and Champ with loud shouts that they were 'rubbish' that the birds took to the air again and squawked the place down.

While shaking arms with Twab (again the Roman way) Golcho decided he was going to celebrate their victory with a well-earned smoke. Walking over to the still as yet dead body of Sparrow (the count of a hundred not yet reached, he was only on seventy-two) Golcho began to rummage through his pockets.

'Oi,' yelled Sparrow trying to get up, 'what the 'ell are you doing?'

'You're still dead aren't you?' said Golcho with one foot on

Sparrow's chest trying to keep him from getting up. 'You've still got some more counting to do yet before you're allowed up. Twab's rules not mine.'

Twab had devised a method, ages before, well before Champ came on the scene, whereby if you were killed while playing a game, any game, you could come back to life after counting up to a hundred to thus extend the game. He thought it was a brilliant idea at the time and still did.

'So,' said Sparrow pulling a face.

'So you'll not be wanting your fags until then so hand um over.'

Pushing Golcho away and getting up, deciding not to comply with Twab's silly rule of counting up to a hundred and then automatically coming back to life, Sparrow broke a woodbine in half, lit them and gave the smaller half, the one not much more than a dog-end really to Golcho for sticking him so hard. The larger half he gave to Twab. He then lit a whole Woodbine for himself. Golcho did not seem to notice that he had been given the smaller half, but nevertheless enjoyed his well-earned smoke having had his revenge. But when Twab inhaled his first puff he began to cough. Champ advised him to throw it away but was ignored. This was the first time Champ had seen his leader smoking. Twab tried to make out that the smoke went down the wrong way, but Champ knew different. He had seen it all before. Twab, like so many mates in Chester, was defending the weed. All smokers seem to think smoking is good for you even though it causes so much illness. But, in his bid to emulate Terry, and with all eyes on him, Sparrow blew a perfectly round smoke ring, then waited while it expanded some, and then blew another smaller ring towards it, hoping it would pass through. But alas, it caught the side yet again and distorted the both of them. He tried again and almost achieved his ambition. But his next three attempts, like the first one, went terribly wrong. The rings kept crashing into one another. He eventually gave up and instead blew out a series of miniature smoke rings from a small opening in his mouth. He achieved this by tapping the side of his cheek with his index finger. The rings, about a dozen of them popped out of his mouth ever so perfect, one after the other. But Sparrow's smug smile was short lived.

Golcho, realizing he'd been given the shorter end of the Woodbine, aimed a deliberately planned sneeze at Sparrow's so called work of art.

Seeing the look of rage on Sparrow's face, Golcho made out it was an accident.

'No it wasn't,' yelled Sparrow. Seeking revenge, he stubbed out his cigarette and grabbed Golcho around the neck and wrestled him to the ground.

'We may as well sit down Champ,' said Twab, 'this could go on for ages.'

Both watched as Sparrow and Golcho grappled with each other. One minute Sparrow was on top, then Golcho. They were evenly matched, but there was no order in what they were doing, they were just grappling for the sake of it. If they only knew what I know, Champ mused, but now was not the time to reveal his secret. Several minutes on, from the amount of laughing that Sparrow and Golcho were doing (it having become a comedy match), they gave up. Wiping the sweat from their faces with their coat sleeves, both Sparrow and Golcho sat down next to Twab and Champ (who had more or less ignored them) and joined in with the battle assessment that was being discussed.

Golcho had immense pleasure in telling Sparrow and Champ that their every move was seen by them from their hiding place, right up until the moment the battle began. 'We were watching your every move,' Golcho grinned. Twab then informed Sparrow that they used the same tactics that Spencer Tracy used while tracking those bad guys in the Everglades, but he still could not remember the film, nor could the others. Champ had not even seen it.

Ten minutes on, with the smoke, the battle assessment and the bickering over, Sparrow suggested they make themselves a bow and arrow. Saluting the Roman way, and sheathing their swords through their trouser loops, while trying not to make any dirt marks on their snake-belts, Champ was rather chuffed that he was also going to be the proud owner of a bow and arrow, as well as a sword. If only his mates in Chester could see him now.

So they set off in search of some good hazel coppice. Thirty minutes on, four bows had been cut down; cut to length with the outer bark stripped off, barring four inches in the middle (for the grip), and strung with string supplied by Twab.

Twenty minutes later they had two arrows apiece which had been nocked to fit snuggly in the string. They had also been pointed to stick in the ground and marked for identification purposes to prevent rows. In the past, there had been much arguing with claims that, 'My arrow went further or higher than yours.'

'Oh no it didn't'

'Oh yes it did.'

So, like four Roman soldiers, they set off for the river and Mr Williams' field, the one that was noted for its hazel hedge running the full length of the field which for several years had given a good crop of nuts. While making their way down to the field, Champ decided that the piece of broken glass he had picked out of the river earlier was going to be his lucky charm from now on. While waiting his turn to jump across the river, he wondered how a hole could be drilled through it to be able to wear it around his neck. Perhaps Mr Lloyd, the woodwork teacher would know how? Well, he was going to ask him. Then he had a better idea.

If Mr Lloyd said it could not be drilled, he was going to ask him if it could be stuck onto something and made into a brooch? If that could be done, he was going to give it to his mum as a birthday present this coming Thursday. It was almost heart-shaped and would look lovely pinned on her coat. Yes, that was what he was going to do, providing Mr Lloyd could stick it on something for him. He was looking forward to the party and had a feeling his grandparents from Chester would be attending. He certainly hoped so. He suddenly wanted to know all the news. Had his house and the row been knocked down? He thought about asking the lads if they would like to come along, but thought better of it. He would wait and see if Jeannie's friends were invited.

Suddenly, it was his turn to jump the river. By choosing Mr Williams' field, they knew they would not be chased away if spotted. Old Mr Williams was nothing like Alum, the old misery guts who owned the fields on the Dump side of the woods, who always chased them away every time he saw them on his land. He was nowhere near as friendly as Mr Williams.

Having jumped the river and scrambled up the embankment, the lads then waited for Twab to do the honours by lifting the top strand of the barbed-wire fence as high as he could, and the middle strand down with his boot, thus creating a space for them to pass through. When all three were safely in the field, Sparrow then created the gap for Twab to climb through.

With all the birdsong that was going on, and armed with their bows and arrows, the lads began to shoot at little clumps of grass. Unbeknown to Champ, he was being taken to the top of this rather steep field.

Twab wanted him to see the view that he thought was fantastic. Looking from right to left the view began with just a hint of Minera Mountain, where in the summer months, like then, winberries could be had. Then there was the village known as Talwrn, Old Mr Williams' farm and several fields, the whole of the Hafod side of the woods, including the bridge, and Mr Moss' farm, plus a good showing of Fron's two red banks, but not the black one.

But on their way up to the summit a two-day-old cow pat some twenty feet away became a target. Each in turn fired an arrow at it. Sparrow won, with Twab second. Golcho pointed out that archery was not his strong point today. His arrow was way off target – as was Champ's. Suddenly fed up with being in competition, the lads began to shoot at random targets, ranging from cow pats (fresh or stale) clumps of grass, sorrel stalks and a red admiral butterfly. Other butterflies that were also flying about in search of food were tortoise shells, cabbage whites, gate keepers, painted-ladies, meadow browns, peacocks, orange tips, and a host of others.

When Champ asked what the flies on the fresh cow-pats were, that looked like wasps, Golcho said they were horseflies and harmless, meaning they did not sting you the way wasps would. When the question was asked, why do they eat cow muck Golcho shrugged his shoulders.

When they foolishly shot their arrows into the air, the old argument broke out, ('Mine went higher than yours', 'Oh no it didn't') There being no way of knowing who the winner was, they all gave up.

When they were just yards from the summit, Golcho informed them that he wanted a wee. Turning right they ran part way down the field to a little bridge which was so narrow that people had to cross it one at a time and it also stopped the cows from roaming from one field to another. The little river below the bridge flowed into the woods' river when the rain came off the hillsides, but it was dried up at the moment. Having crossed the bridge and scrambled down the bank, and under the cover of a clump of trees, the lads, because Golcho was having a wee, joined in and had a competition to see who could wee up the bank the highest. There was no winner on account of Golcho nudging and shoving everyone and laughing when someone had an accident. The trick now was to avoid weeing down your leg.

Back on the field, Sparrow's choice of target (some stick thing poking out of the ground some fifty feet away) was chosen. Standing four abreast like four Roman centurions, they each nocked an arrow to their bow. With his eye on the target, Twab released his, and while retaining his stance, watched as it sailed away. All were impressed when it fell some six feet away from the target. Twab smugly congratulated himself.

Drawing his bow string back, Sparrow took aim slightly higher than Twab and released his arrow. It twanged away and landed a little nearer to the target. Pleased with himself for beating Twab, Sparrow began to tease him, until Twab threatened to punch him one on the nose if he did not pack it in.

Determined he was going to give it his best shot, Golcho, having confessed earlier that archery was not a strong point, spat on the tip of his arrow for luck. On release it too twanged as it set off towards the target. All eyes watched as it sailed through the air. It came down so close to Sparrow's arrow that, from where they were, it was difficult to see who the winner was between them.

Twab, who was sulking if the truth be known, said nothing, but was not happy with the fact that he was losing. Sparrow and Golcho were arguing so much as to who the winner was between them that they only stopped when Champ asked them to be quiet. He was waiting to shoot his arrow.

Seeing how the others had shot from the orthodox position, vertical and at chest height, and seeing it done in some movie, Champ fired his arrow horizontally from the waist. He could not remember the movie he had seen it done in, but remembered the arrow hitting its target, a cavalry soldier on guard duty. He also remembered how it thudded into his chest, killing him before he could warn the camp that the Indians were attacking. Then he remembered the film. It was *Cochise*, starring none other than Jeff Chandler.

Champ's arrow also twanged as it left his bow. All eyes were on it as it sailed through the air and came down so close to the target that everyone knew he had won the contest. Yelling out a long yahoo while pretending to be Cochise, Champ folded his arms and, mimicking Jeff Chandler said, 'I win white man, you lose.'

Racing over to retrieve their arrows, it turned out that Twab was the absolute loser with Golcho beating Sparrow by a finger's length. When Champ's arrow was measured, it was only half the length of his shoe from the target. He was congratulated, not with handshakes, but by being scragged to the ground with clumps of grass shoved down his pants. That done, and led by Sparrow, the lads finally raced up the field, but Twab, who was having a bad day, trod in a fresh cow-pat and went sprawling to the ground.

Laughing at their leader's misfortune, the others ran on, and reaching the summit with its fantastic view, sat down and waited for their leader to arrive. When Twab finally sat down next to Golcho, he was swearing real swear words. In his *cythrel* (which means temper in Welsh) Twab removed his shoe, and with clumps of grass began to wipe away the mess which turned out to be a somewhat smelly job, plus his fingers were covered in cow dung. Knowing it was dangerous to laugh at Twab when he was in his *cythrel*, him being a good scrapper and all that, but laughing nevertheless broke out again when Golcho moved away, accusing his leader of letting off. Twab, who was not one for swearing really, defending his honour yelled out 'It's not me that's smelling you dozy bugger, it's me shoe.'

To keep the joke going, Golcho (who could be ruthless in such matters) made a fart sound on his arm and moved away another couple of feet. The others, catching on, also moved away, complaining that there was a terrible smell in the air. The laughing increased, as did Twab's temper. He had to sit there on his own while being accused of letting off. But he saw red when Golcho again pegged his nose and moved a little further away, accusing Twab of 'shitting' himself. Now that he had an audience, Golcho made several more fart noises on his arm ending with a long drawn out fart which ended up with everyone laughing their heads off, bar Twab.

Fed up with having the mickey taken out of him, Twab put on his shoe, fastened his lace and gave chase. Catching Sparrow, who claimed he was innocent, Twab wrestled him to the ground and had his revenge by shoving the soiled grass he'd cleaned his shoe with, and a bit more down Sparrow's pants while Champ and Golcho (the cause of the trouble) looked on from a safe enough distance.

While Twab and Sparrow were fighting it out, Golcho, out of devilment screamed out his infamous top C, (causing some cows in the next field to look up), jumped on Champ's back and forced him to the ground. Moments later it was a free for all with everyone wrestling each another.

As the laughing, tangled up bodies wrestled each other, there were shouts of 'Hey, whoever it is, leave my willy alone' and, 'Stop that, that's not fair' and, 'Hey, you can go to gaol for that.' It was not long before a truce was called. With everyone laughing, flaked out and panting for breath, Champ began to watch the cows in the next field, the ones Golcho had startled when he blasted out his infamous top C, and wondered what else they do other than eat grass all day?

Twab was thinking about all the frog spawn he would be collecting come springtime, wondering how many tadpoles would end up as frogs. There were loads of frogs last year and the year before that.

Low on cigarettes, Sparrow was wondering where his next packet of Woodbine was coming from? He was down to his last four and Golcho never seemed to have any. The more Sparrow thought about that, the more he realized that Golcho never had any.

Golcho was thinking about the Queen's Coronation street parties. And what a day that was. Apart from all the fun and games, Golcho had never had so much tea, cakes and buns. Then he remembered a joke. 'Hey gang,' he said. 'Have you heard the one about Robin Hood being killed by the Sheriff?'

Everyone agreed that they had not.

'Well,' said Golcho as he sat up and began to chew on a stalk of grass. 'Robin Hood and Little John were walking through the forest one day, when the Sheriff stepped out from behind a tree and shot him in the back. Little John chased the Sheriff away, then carried poor old Robin back to camp. 'Quick Little John,' said Robin, 'I've had it; I'm dying, take me to my cave and tell the others that I want them.' When all the men and Maid Marion arrived, Robin said he wanted his bow. When it was given to him, Robin said, 'Wherever this arrow lands men, you are to bury me,' and then he died.' With that Golcho went quiet. After several moments Sparrow said, 'Well, where did they bury him?'

Golcho stood up, ready to run and then burst out laughing, 'In the roof.'

Twab, Sparrow and Champ looked at one another for a long moment then burst out laughing. They could all picture a grave stone and flowers in the roof. After several minutes of uncontrollable laughter, and while wiping the tears away, Twab said that was the best joke he had heard in a long time.

When the laughing petered out, someone decided it was time to move on and, while waiting for Twab and Sparrow to tidy themselves up (their shirts needed tucking in their pants), Golcho pointed out several village features to Champ. There was Llidiart Fanny Farm, with a stretch of its original and unique metal railings which curved over at the top and ended in Heol Offa, opposite the now empty houses where the Pritchard, Clee, and Price families lived before they were re-housed in Heol Islwyn, Twab's street.

While pointing out Maggie Johnson's bus-stop, Golcho explained that Maggie's bus did not go to Wrexham down the main road, the A525, but went through Southsea, New Broughton and Caego, passing the BRS depot, and then, turning right by the first set of crossroads, went past Wrexham's football ground. He also said that Maggie's trip to Wrexham was cheaper.

He then pointed at the row of privately owned houses that lead up to the green gates, then the oak tree and the five-barred gate opposite, then the twelve houses that made up Heol Offa, where Len Lewis lived.

Golcho told the story of when Len was given a mouthful of cheek and chased them, which had been part of the plan. But catching Sparrow by the Co-op, Len had kicked his backside for him, which was not part of the plan. When he was allowed to go, Len said he was not to take it to heart as he could remember playing the same game when he was Sparrow's age.

Golcho then pointed out both their houses. Finding his was easy, it being a corner house with its main feature, a big diamond-shaped flower bed in the lawn. He then pointed out Champ's chimney pots and part of next door's roof.

When Twab and Sparrow joined in what was now a game (who can find what) Sparrow found his house easily enough and part of the holly hedge and the short cut which led to the Talwrn road and Arthur

Tattoo's orchard at the bottom of his garden which was always scrumped. He also pointed out diggings where new houses would be standing in twelve months. But, because of some trees hiding most of Heol Islwyn (Twab's street), and still feeling wretched for having trod in that stupid cow-pat, Twab failed to find his house. He was truly having a bad day. So with their swords sheathed through their trouser loops, they carried their bows and arrows in their right hand as was seen in some western, and headed off across Mr Williams's field towards the Hafod Bridge. Golcho asked Champ what it was like living in Chester?

'Well it's nothing like this,' said Champ, as Sparrow broke a woodbine in half, lit both halves and passed one over to Golcho. Going on, Champ said he hated living there as it was noisy, dirty and smelly, with nowhere to play. Using all the surrounding greenery as an example of what he meant, he said there were trams and buses rushing around all day and if you went to the park, which was miles away, the swings were either broken or taken up by the bigger lads who thumped you if you said anything to them.

'Yea, it's like that here,' said Sparrow.

'Yea, but not as bad as Chester,' Champ insisted. He then said that this was the very first time he had ever seen a wood this size, let alone play in one. 'And these,' he said meaning his sword, bow and two arrows, 'are the first ones I've ever had. I wouldn't have known how to make them. You lads are lucky always having lived here. The only cows I ever saw were in books, and school books at that. Look over there, there must be at least twenty in that field. Oh, and all them birds singing when Twab was cutting our bows down was fantastic. Oh, and that blackbird singing; wow, you lads are so lucky having always lived here. I ain't ever leaving this place and that's a promise.'

'I like them birds that's got little blue heads the best,' said Golcho.

'He means the blue tits,' explained Twab.

'And we've got other places like this to show you yet,' boasted Golcho.

'Yea, it is good living here,' agreed Sparrow, 'except for school that is.'

Wanting to clear something up, Champ asked if he was pronouncing Adwy correctly.

'Yes you are,' said Sparrow grinning. Thinking he had one on them he said, 'Yea, but does anyone know what it means?' When no one did and looking chuffed because he had one on them he said, 'It's an old Welsh word which means gap, or opening, so me dad tells me.'

When Champ thought about it he said, 'So that gap over there in that hedge is an Adwy?'

'I suppose so,' said Sparrow trying to make out that he knew.

'But you're not sure?' said Twab believing he was telling a porky.

Golcho took the pressure off Sparrow for failing to give an answer when he asked Champ why he had not yet become a smoker?

'What! After last Monday! No way,' said Champ. 'I thought I was gonna die when I swallowed all that smoke. I've changed my mind as far as fags go, they're horrible, and anyway, Mr Robinson said smoking would interfere with my running, something to do with tar burning my lungs away.'

Not believing his ears and speaking slowly Sparrow said, 'Mr Robinson has talked to you about smoking?' He had a quick look at Golcho.

'He was giving us lads who are running for the school a pep talk the other day. He said anyone who smokes can forget about running as their lungs will be full of tar.'

'What tar?' said Golcho not believing his ears.

'The tar you get in your lungs from smoking. According to Mr Robinson is the same as what the council puts down on the roads.'

'I don't believe that,' said Sparrow adamantly, again looking at Golcho.

'Well, that's what the man said.' Champ insisted.

Defending his habit, Sparrow said that cigarettes are good for you because they make you breathe deeply and breathing deeply is good for you.'

'That's not what Mr Robinson said,' said Champ.

'Then why do you cough and go giddy when you first start to smoke?' was what Twab wanted to know, aiming his question at Sparrow.

'Well, I don't know,' Sparrow said shaking his head, not caring.

Putting his two-penny-worth in Golcho, also defending cigarettes, said that his mum and dad smoked all the time and they were alright.

'So, do any of you smoke in the house?' Champ asked. It turned out that no one did. 'Well then,' said Champ believing he had won the argument. 'If it was safe to smoke and all that, your parents would let you smoke in the house wouldn't they.' Champ rested his case when no one argued.

Listening to Champ's argument and seeing the sense it made, Twab said, 'Well gang, I've just made me a decision. I'm gonna be a non-smoker like Champ here from now on.'

Both Sparrow and Golcho could not believe their ears. They looked at one another and then shook their heads. Twice in less than a minute they had been stunned. Flabbergasted, and with Golcho's backing, Sparrow said, 'What do you mean you gonna be a non-smoker?'

'I'm gonna be a non-smoker,' said Twab in his, don't you dare talk to me in that tone of voice. Somewhat cheered up with his decision he said, 'I only have the occasional puff or dog end so why all the fuss?'

'Why all the fuss,' said an angry Sparrow. 'You're only letting me and Golcho down. That's why all the fuss.'

Golcho nodded his agreement. He was just as angry as Sparrow. Twab had always been a smoker.

Shaking arms with Champ (the Roman way) and pleased with his decision Twab said, 'The point is, me and Champ here are gonna be healthy, while you two are gonna be ill.' He scrunched his face up in such a way that both Sparrow and Golcho knew he meant what he had just said and that there was no point in arguing any further. His mind was made up.

Letting out a long sigh Sparrow, having given up on Twab, this being the umpteenth time he had packed up smoking said, 'Well I'm gonna be ill if I don't have something to eat.' A moment later he suggested they go home, have their dinner and then come back down the woods in the afternoon.

'Okay,' said Twab, 'but let's go through the Hafod and show Champ here our secret water.'

Sparrow grumbled for a while but fell in line when he saw the look on Twab's face. He was already upset from having trod in that cow-muck.

Heading for the Hafod bridge, with its little meandering river (the same river that was dammed on Alum's side of the woods and good for swimming in from time to time during the summer), and knowing that they could not take their bows and arrows home (deemed by their parents as too dangerous), the lads found a good hiding place in the bushes for them until they were next needed.

Stepping onto the bridge, Sparrow and Golcho had a competition to see who could spit down river the furthest. Twab and Champ (ignoring them) began to walk up a narrow path in single file towards Mr Williams's farm, enjoying the sun on their backs while keeping an eye on the bull. Okay, the bull was tethered to a big stake by the nose, but the last thing they wanted was for the bull to get loose and come a charging. But the huge animal ignored them, the grass being deemed more important.

Having finished their spitting competition Sparrow and Golcho caught up with Twab and Champ at the top of the path. They too had kept an eye on the bull, but they were also completely ignored. Sparrow claimed that he had won the spitting competition with Golcho arguing that he had won by a mile. They each in turn climbed over the stile into what was a right of way through Mr Williams's farm. Twab and Champ being the first two over, were spotted by Meg and Bess, the two black and white collie dogs belonging to the farm. Running across the uneven yard, dodging the cow-pats, and reaching their side of the gate, Meg and Bess began to bark and wag their tails. Just for the record , Meg and Bess were not barking at Twab and Champ because they were trespassing, but because they were pleased to see them even though Champ was a stranger to them. They knew Twab very well.

The right of way, it must be said was a God send to all those who lived in the Talwrn. It allowed them access to the Fron, Tan y Fron and Brymbo. This is what Champ had meant when he said on first meeting Champ how wonderful it was having all the roads and pathways connected. You could not get lost in the Adwy if you wanted to.

When Sparrow and Golcho approached the dogs they crouched down alongside Twab who began to stroke them through the bars of the gate making a big fuss of them. Champ just looked on. He did not like dogs. The only ones he knew in Chester were either big scruffy ones or little scruffy ones which were forever trying to bite you.

Looking up at Champ and grinning, Sparrow explained 'Meg and Bess are our friends.' Turning to Bess (the mother), who was sitting there accepting his attention, 'Aren't you girl?'. Playing with her ear while holding her chin, 'Y-esss, you are' he added.

With all the commotion that the dogs were making, Mr Williams came out of one of the shippons to see what was going on. Approaching the gate and telling the dogs to '*Cau dy gêg,*' which means be quiet in Welsh, and pleased to see the lads, he asked them in broken English what they had been up to that morning. Between them Twab, Sparrow and Golcho told him all about the morning's adventures and then Twab introduced Champ.

'*Bore da, bachgen*' (good morning young man), said Mr Williams shaking Alan's hand over the gate, while trying to suss him out. Turning to Twab he asked if the new boy would be helping out with the hay in about a week's time. Seeing the puzzled look on Champ's face, Twab told him to nod his head, saying he would explain later what he had just agreed to, but promised it would be great fun. If he did not believe him, he only had to ask Sparrow or Golcho.

Telling the dogs to go in, Mr Williams said there was no more time to waste as there was too much to do. With the dogs gone and Mr Williams disappearing through an old doorway that looked as if it was about to fall down, the lads moved on down the path towards their special water.

When Sparrow began to sulk, claiming he was so hungry that he could eat a horse and saddle, Twab told him off, saying he should have had a bigger breakfast as he was showing Champ their secret water before they went home for dinner no matter what.

While walking down the path, Golcho explained that they and a few other village lads helped Mr Williams when it was time to bring in the hay.

'You mean he pays you to bring the hay in?' Champ cut in.

'Yea,' said Twab, 'but not with money.'

Scrunching his face up Champ then asked how they were paid.

'With fruit in the autumn when it ripens,' said Golcho.

Champ was flabbergasted. If you helped anyone in Chester (which you did not) you got paid cash and no mistaking. Twab then went on to describe the pleasure (for him at least) of being in the orchard filling up his pockets and jumper with apples and plums and, when they were ripe, pears. The pleasure was not having the worry about being chased which Twab said was the real reward. For Golcho it was playing in the hay loft after the day's work (as well as filling up his pockets and jumper with fruit). Sparrow, who was still sulking after being told off, said nothing, all he could think of was his dinner. He said his stomach was not half rumbling. When he asked Golcho to have a listen, Golcho told him to bugger off.

Going on with the story for Champ's benefit, Golcho explained that once the hay was brought in for the day, Mr Williams allowed them to play in the hay loft for an hour or so. He said it was great fun playing King of the Castle.' Whether you were thrown off or fell off, you did not hurt yourself because all the loose hay cushioned you. And it was great scrapping with other lads from the surrounding villages.

'He seems a decent sort of fellow,' said Champ.

'He is,' said Twab adding that he does not mind you being on his land.

'Not like old misery guts,' Golcho intervened, 'Alum, him on the other side of the Woods bridge. He's a right pain in the backside. He always chases you. Even if he sees you on the road he tells you to keep off his land.'

Climbing over a five-bar gate, the lads were in awe of the view. The valley in front of them was ablaze with gorse. Champ said it was stunning. The others agreed. It was another picture in the making for Champ when he knew the area better. The area reeked of coconut.

Adding to the picturesque scene was the lovely meandering river Gwenfro, running through Mr Williams' fields: the same river that was dammed on the Dump side of the woods: the same river where Champ had found his smooth piece of broken glass earlier.

After a few moments of taking in the view, the lads turned immediately left and, not five yards away, was an old unused well which was partly hidden by all the overgrown vegetation. As they approached it, Champ's jaw suddenly dropped. He had never seen anything so beautiful. There were several butterflies fluttering about which were beautiful in themselves, but when he saw a small whitish one with orange tipped wings, he immediately fell in love with it. Seeing that butterfly, officially called an orange tip, was a turning point in his life and he later swore an allegiance to nature in this country.

Meanwhile, Twab, having approached the well, swept away all the surface debris. He knelt down and scooped up a handful of water, followed by Golcho, then Sparrow, who was feeling better now that he had stopped sulking – but insisted he was still in need of his dinner.

When Champ went to drink, he was warned to be careful as the well water was quite deep. It was at least up to their chests, its depth having being measured with a stick. Champ took a drink of the secret water and declared it was very cold.

As far as the lads were aware they were the only ones who knew of this water, hence it being secret. All agreed that it tasted lovely, cold but lovely. Now that he was no longer sulking, Sparrow let it be known that this water was always cold, even on hot days like today, and scorching hot days like the previous Thursday. The temperature, according to the man on Sparrow's radio, was 78° F and everyone was advised to drink plenty of water.

Now that Champ had seen and drunk the special water, the lads made for home as their dinners were calling them. Back in the village and to Sparrow's delight (he could almost taste his dinner), arrangements were made to meet up in about an hour's time by the lamp post at the bottom of Heol Wen.

It was just gone two when the lads set off for the woods again. Reaching the top of the Woods hill they suddenly heard the council bin lorry revving its engine, which meant it was tipping its load.

Champ was informed that if and when he ever came across the bin lorry, or a tractor or anything that had an engine on this little stretch of road, it was important he get out of the way quick. You could either scramble up the embankment or run back up to the safety of the only gateway on this little stretch of road at the top of the hill which gave you a fantastic view of Minera Mountain which had been mentioned earlier that morning.

Their first sight of the bin lorry was as it came up the hill in first gear with the engine screaming. The lads were half way down the hill and, on Twab's orders, ran back to the safety of the gate which was on their right and from there they watched as the lorry approached them, filling the whole width of the road, hence the reason for them having to get out of the way. When the lorry reached the top of the hill, and the driver changed gear, the boys were covered in a cloud of dust and exhaust fumes as it laboured past them. Moments later, it turned right by Llidiart Fanny Farm and was gone, as there were more bins to be emptied in the village.

'Let's go and see what we can find,' said Sparrow when the dust cleared and all their coughing and spluttering ceased.

Running down the Woods hill and then onto the council owned tip (the Dump) they walked up to the huge pile of rubbish to see if anything of value was to be had. The stench of sulphur was quite strong and when Champ asked how long this has been a landfill he was told it had been one for ages.

When nothing of value was found, it was explained to Champ that it was great fun being here when there were several loads of rubbish to be pushed over the edge. When that happened, a bulldozer would come along, usually on a Saturday, which would push the piles of rubbish over the edge in order to keep the place tidy. But not so today. It was great fun watching the piles of rubbish being pushed one by one up to and over the edge. The driver did not mind you watching, providing you kept out of the way, as the big wide blade pushed everything over the edge creating a huge cloud of dust in the process. Twab estimated that the way things were going; there would not be enough room for any more rubbish in a couple of years.

Today's delivery was mostly cinders and tin cans. Golcho pointed out that a lot of people from the village come to pick the cinders to help with what little coal they had, 'But we,' he emphasised, 'just see what we can find.'

Sliding down the thirty-foot wall of rubbish on their heels and bums to where it had compacted on the extreme right of the bank and was reasonably safe, the lads spread out and began to root through it. After some thirty minutes of fruitless searching, it was decided there was nothing of value to be had today, it being mostly cinders, tin cans and bottles. An old bike frame was found, but no one wanted it or the chain. Because of the strong smell of sulphur and the other noxious gasses spilling out of the ground from fissures here and there. Champ was more than happy when it was announced they were moving on. He did not understand why they would want to root about here taking in all these gasses that were pouring out of the ground but, saying nothing, he just went along with it.

As they clambered over the debris in order to reach the main path, which was no more than a foot wide, Champ was told of the time when a village girl (Bronwen Thomas) found a brass telescope in good working order in amongst the rubbish, but had to fight tooth and nail with a village lad, Malcolm Clee, to keep it. Malcolm said he wanted it and took it off her.

'Come on,' said Golcho eagerly, 'let's show Champ the swing.'

Racing along the main path (which was always muddy) Sparrow said that in no time at all they would be having the time of their lives on the Monster.

'Why is it called the Monster?' Champ asked a little apprehensively as they raced along the soggy path in single file.

'You'll find out in a minute,' Golcho said while grinning.

It was decided by all, that Champ had to find out for himself why this particular swing was called the Monster. It exhilarated and frightened you to death at the same time. And, even though several children had fallen off and broken something, they did not keep off it (he was later told that one poor soul, Philly Pritchard, actually broke his collar bone as soon as it had been put up and was off school for several weeks).

The clearing which housed the tree from which the Monster hung was on a steep slope, which meant that when you swung outwards you ended up well above the bushes and river, at an estimated forty feet, which is really high. When it was not is use, the hessian rope just hung there looking so innocent. On this occasion, the lads were in luck in that they were the only ones present. Normally at that time of day, gone dinnertime, particularly at the weekend, there were other groups of children from the village there, all trying to claim the Monster for themselves – including Terry, Frank, Ernie and Dave.

'Bags me first,' said Twab as he reached for the rope.

Hauling it up to the take off point (which, for maximum thrill, had been carefully measured out), Twab took a firm grip on the rope with both hands and with fingers crossed, launched himself off. Yahooing while sailing outwards and upwards, with the air brushing against his face, the ground rushing away from him, Twab immediately experienced the tummy tickles, that feeling that your stomach is rushing up into your mouth with you wishing you had stayed on the ground. But the truth is that it was for the tummy tickles that they rode the Monster. The higher they went, the greater the thrill. They also forgot that they were something like forty feet up in the air with the river rushing by below. At the highest point they got to see parts of the woods which they never saw from the ground, including the bridge and fields belonging to good old Mr Williams. Even though the swing was at times dangerous, it also had a mystery that no one could explain. While swinging backwards and forwards you somehow ended up facing the wrong way to the way you wanted to face, which could be a nuisance sometimes. It was always better to face the way you were going, if only for safety's sake. But there was a way in which you could rectify the situation. But as yet, none of the lads had worked it out. The secret of how to avoid spinning was, when they took off and felt that they were beginning to spin, they had to jerk their body, either to the left or right, until they were facing the right way. Simple really; all it took was a few jerks to get them facing the way they were travelling. But unfortunately the lads had not worked it out yet. So, with his feet back on the ground, having landed backwards, Twab ran up the slope several strides beyond the starting point and, yahooing loudly, swung out even higher on his second run. For his third and fourth run he simply allowed the rope to carry him backwards and forwards while listening to the groans the branch was making under his weight. Jumping off he handed the rope over to Sparrow.

Yahooing on take off, Sparrow too had the tummy tickles as he flew outwards and upwards. He also loved the wind blasting into his face. On his return flight, even though he had begun to spin, he wrapped his right leg around the rope the way he had seen Tony Curtis and Burt Lancaster do in the film *Trapeze*. Hanging upside down while swinging backwards and forwards, Sparrow hung on by his right leg for dear life. He actually believed he was Tony Curtis just after he had completed the triple somersault to the delight of the audience. For his second and third run he simply sailed outwards and upwards thoroughly enjoying himself and the imagined applause he had been given for his daring trick. For his final run he again allowed the rope to carry him backwards and forwards the way Twab had. Jumping off, he handed the rope to Golcho.

Not one for heights, Golcho took the rope and ran as fast as he could to his right. No way was he going outwards and upwards. When the ground gave out he launched himself into the air and screamed out his yahoo as he circumnavigated the deep chasm of holly bushes and the river in a wide arc. On touch down, for his second run he yahooed and ran even faster across the open ground, thus giving himself an even wider flight path. Yahooing as he sailed out across the abyss (well the river and holly bushes) he noticed that Twab and Sparrow were lining up as if they were going to jump on with him. Yelling at them to keep out of his way, for his third and fourth run he swung outwards and upwards, but reached nothing like the height of Twab and Sparrow. He did not like the tummy tickles that much. Jumping off, he handed the swing to Champ.

There was no way Champ was flying outwards and upwards on his first run. He rather liked the circular flight path that Golcho had taken. Even so, the experience of sailing over the chasm was exhilarating, although it was only for a few seconds. Except for the strain on the arms while supporting your weight it was like flying. You could feel the air rushing past you. If you looked down you could see the ground far below you go rushing past. It was great. And you could pretend you were Tarzan. For his second run he pretended he was Tarzan, swinging through the trees to rescue Jane and Boy. Reaching firm ground, and all fired up, he ran as fast as he could across the clearing and enjoyed his third run sailing across the abyss. For his final run, he decided he would try going outwards and upwards from the starting point. Launching himself into the air, and automatically yahooing with the tummy tickles, he thoroughly enjoyed the ride. Jumping off, he gave the swing back to Twab.

Sitting on a huge stone and watching the lads swinging backwards and forwards and having a great time, Champ began to realise just how lucky he was in having these three boys as friends. Would he be sitting here with them had he not gone to school last Monday, he wondered? He somehow did not think so. He was going to hug his mum when he went home at tea time, to thank her for making him go to school last Monday, which was only five days ago. Wow! How could so much happen in just five days?

Because Twab was hogging the swing, Sparrow and Golcho decided to teach him a lesson. They were going to spin him. As Twab was about to take off for the umpteenth time, Sparrow grabbed his ankles and spun him for all his worth. Twab spun like mad as he flew outwards and upwards. He was much too high to jump off. He had no choice but to hang on for dear life while he completed the ride. He hoped he did not fall into the bushes or river and possibly break a bone, or worse. While fighting the giddiness, he was already planning revenge of some kind. Having completed the flight and being so giddy, with everything spinning, he reached out and managed to grab Sparrow and, wanting nothing more than to lie down, wrestled him to the ground.

With Champ watching the fracas, Golcho, with all the cheek in the world, reached for the swing and enjoyed several runs at his own leisure.

Having smeared Sparrow's face with dirt, Twab rolled off him, quite satisfied now that he had paid for spinning him. Seeing Golcho coming in to land and feeling much better, Twab shouted for him to stay on.

Knowing what was coming, and not wanting to go outwards and upwards, Golcho, when his feet touched the ground, ran across the clearing with Twab chasing after him. Twab just managed to jump on as the ground gave way. Both he and Golcho began to yahoo as they sailed over the holly bushes and river. On landing they both ran across the clearing for a second run. Wanting a piece of the action, Sparrow jumped on. All three clung on to the rope. Half way through the flight, and above all the laughing and yahooing, Golcho gave champ his first rendition of David Whitfield's *Cara-Mia Mine*.

Champ just stood there with his hands on hips. He could not believe what he was hearing and seeing. Here they were, his friends, sailing through the air at a considerable height with the possibility of one or all of them falling off and seriously hurting themselves, laughing their heads off at Golcho's whacky singing. Never before had Golcho entertained them in such a precarious situation.

Reaching solid ground and racing across the clearing for another run, Sparrow shouted for Champ to be ready to jump on when they next came in to land. Because the landing was clumsy (meaning Sparrow slipped and fell, causing the others to slip and fall) there was plenty of time for Champ to jump on and the four of them ran across the clearing and threw themselves into the abyss and immediately began to spin out of control with Golcho still blurting out David Whitfield.

Everyone hung on for dear life, and I mean for dear life. With their hands beginning to burn, they completed their flight and landed with a mighty bump. All let go of the rope and fell about laughing. Blowing on their hands to cool them, all agreed it had been a great half hour on the Monster.

'Come on,' said Golcho standing up, 'let's go for a swim.'

Racing along the narrow muddy path with the tree canopy covering them and having to dodge hazel and holly bushes, Twab asked Champ if he could swim. 'Of course I can,' said Champ as he squelched along the muddy path trying to visualise the swimming pool. Some eighty yards on, having reached a certain batch of holly and hazel bushes, the lads turned left off the main path and began to scramble down a steep bank that led to the river. Using tree roots and clumps of grass to prevent themselves from sliding, they made their way down the steep slope. Sparrow suddenly missed a hand hold and slid all the way down and landed feet first in a pool of stagnant water which had a muddy bottom. The disturbed sediment created a terrible smell.

On reaching the river, the lads waited while Sparrow cleaned himself up. He was unhurt, and managed to clean most of the mud from his soaking-wet shoes and socks, and the seat of his pants. They then crossed the river by using stones that had been laid down by a previous generation of village boys who were now young men with families of their own.

On Alum's field and fully alert in case he was around, the lads followed the river downstream for thirty yards or so. Twab suddenly ordered everyone to hit the deck, quickly. 'Keep still everyone,' he insisted. Pointing at the river and whispering he said, 'Look, over there on that big stone. The one with all the bird muck on.'

Champ was the last one to see the bird, a dipper which was perched on the stone and was dipping the way that dippers do. Champ was amazed by it. He had never seen a dipper before and thought its brown feathers and white breast were lovely. He also noticed that it had a white protective covering over its eyes when it blinked and wondered why that was? All four watched the bird plunge into the water and then return a few moments later to its stony perch.

'What's it doing?' Champ asked in a low voice.

'It's looking for food,' said Sparrow. 'He feeds on things that live on the river bed.'

'You mean like fish and chips?' said Champ giggling.

Twab shook his head and tutted him for being silly. Suddenly, and without warning, the bird emerged from the water, soiled the stone, flew up river and was gone. With that the lads got up and raced on towards a hedge that ran up the full length of Alum's field. Squeezing through a gap, they again raced on. Moments later they caught sight of the pool.

Impressed, Champ could see that the river, in a most convenient spot had been dammed with large stones, tree branches and loads of grass clods. The resulting pool was some thirty feet long, about eight feet wide and by the dam some three feet deep, deep enough to dive in.

'Who made this?' Champ asked, but before an answer was given said it was certainly different to Chester baths.

'We made it,' said Sparrow.

'With the help of the bigger lads,' said Golcho.

'Yeah, but we did all the donkey work,' Sparrow insisted. 'It was us who dug out all the clods.' Several areas where clods had been dug up were visible. And it was those areas of dug-up clods that annoyed Alum.

Standing level with the dam and looking into the clear water, Champ was amazed that a group of boys could work together and make such a pool. Nothing like this was ever done in Chester. Guessing what his friend was thinking, and in a quiet voice, Twab said, ' It's good, isn't it,' but added, 'be ready to run if Alum the farmer shows himself. He's not like Old Mr Williams. He always chases you and usually comes from that direction.' Twab pointed up the field to his left.

'His farm,' put in Golcho, 'is just over that bump. But don't worry we usually see him in time. He's never once caught us.'

'And be ready to run if the bigger lads come along,' said Twab, 'especially Terry and his lot. They spoil it for everyone when they're here.'

While Twab was rabbiting on about Terry and Co, Sparrow and Golcho stripped off and went into the water and began splashing about. 'Oh, its bloody freezing,' said Golcho who then very bravely splashed himself all over. Sparrow (to beat the cold) took the bull by the horns and dived under, surfaced and shivering agreed with Golcho that it was bloody freezing.

Deciding to join them Twab stripped off and like the other two threw his clothes in a pile on the floor and made his way onto the three-foot-wide dam. Standing in the middle where it was very sturdy, and as naked as the day he was born, Twab dived in. When he surfaced he began to wrestle Sparrow. Golcho had not told a lie when he said the water was freezing. Getting out of Twab's way, Golcho splashed his way into the shallow end, lay face down in the clear incoming water and enjoyed the feel of the stones tickling his legs, stomach and chest. Seeing Champ was still fully clothed and looking at them in the water he said, 'Are you not coming in?'

'What do you think?' Champ asked.

'Get your kit off and get in,' said Golcho secretly having a wee. 'It's okay once you're in.'

In no time at all Champ was naked and on the dam. Looking at his friends enjoying themselves he dived in.

'That's the best belly flop I've ever seen,' said Golcho grinning like a Cheshire cat when Champ surfaced. The initial shock of diving in had taken Champ's breath away. Seeing Twab was still wrestling Sparrow and to get warm, Champ pulled Golcho up to his feet and began to grapple with him.

During the scuffle, Golcho never questioned why he was being flung over Champ's right hip. All he knew was it was good fun especially when hitting the water and going under. Champ never let on, but he was using his secret weapon, his judo.

Now that everyone was in the water and used to it, Twab, having had enough wrestling, suggested they submerge by the dam and see who could swim the furthest under water. Lining up, and on Twab's count of three, they submerged and kicked off the dam wall. They each swam furiously and emerged in the shallows all about the same time. The contest was deemed a dead heat. The winner was going to be the one who could dress the quickest, including his shoe laces fastened correctly.

Hoping to win, Twab ordered everyone to the far side of the pool where the water was up to their thighs and began to count down, 'Three, two, one, – go!'

Determined to win, they each began to splash out of the water while employing dirty tricks. It began with Twab grabbing Champ from behind and ducking him, with him then being ducked by Sparrow and so on. No one was making any headway except Golcho.

While the others were wrestling each another, Golcho slipped out of the water unnoticed, grabbed his shirt and began to dry himself off with it. Keep fighting lads he mused, while slipping his vest over his head. Seeing how far ahead Golcho was in the race the others splashed out of the water and pounced on him. While he was on the floor being dripped on by Sparrow and Champ, Twab threw his shoes in different directions. Sparrow then bunched his stockings up into a ball and threw them as far as he could up the field. Champ rolled up his trousers and threw them also across the field.

While Golcho raced after his things, Sparrow, determined he was going to win, began to dress while still wet, as did Twab and Champ when they saw what Sparrow was doing.

'You sods,' Golcho yelled as he retrieved his things, which was not easy trying to avoid the stones and prickly things, 'that wasn't fair.'

'Everything is fair in love and war Golch, so me dad tells me,' shouted Sparrow laughing and racing to put his shirt on. But it was not the shirt he was having trouble with, it was one of the buttons; it just would not fasten.

With so much laughing and pushing and shoving going on, it was several minutes before Twab declared himself the winner and with everyone dressed and tingling from being in the cold water, they began wrestling each other in a free for all. With Sparrow and Golcho on the ground, locked in battle, Champ waited for Twab to make his move. It was about time these Welsh lads were introduced to his secret weapon. Twab, as far as judo was concerned, made a fatal mistake. He ran at Champ in the hope of knocking him over so as to pin him down.

As much as Twab's ploy of running in was a traditional scrapping move, Champ was ready for him. He had been trained for such an event. As Twab ran in, Champ, as quick as a flash grabbed his right arm with his left hand, then spinning on his left heel threw his right arm up and under Twab's right armpit and before Twab knew what was happening, Champ threw him over his right hip, *ogoshi*. He then declared that the throw was *ipon*, meaning it was a good clean throw, one that his Uncle Dave in Chester would have been proud of.

Not realising what was going on, Twab got up and tried his luck again, but this time, again with *ogoshi*, Twab went over Champ's left hip. Still not realising what was happening, Twab stood up and managed to grab Champ around the neck, but moments later with his hold broken, went over Champ's right hip.

Sitting on the ground slightly puzzled and trying to work out where he was going wrong, Twab was suddenly pounced on by Champ and placed in a head lock that prevented him from getting up. No matter how much Twab struggled he could not get up. After several minutes of frantic struggling and still in control, Champ explained to Twab that he has to tap him twice before he can allow him to get up as that was the rules.

Tapping twice, Twab surrendered and was allowed up. But instead of rising he sat there scratching his head wondering where he had gone wrong. 'Wow, is that judo thing that the Japs do?' He finally asked.

'It sure is,' said Champ smiling, feeling chuffed.

'Where did you learn it?' Twab asked while trying to think where on earth he could have learned it.

'My Uncle Dave in Chester taught me. He's a black-belt instructor,' said Champ proudly.

'Wow,' said Twab who then shouted across to Sparrow and Golcho to stop what they were doing and to come and watch.

With their shirts shoved back in their trousers, Sparrow and Golcho watched as Twab tried to approach Champ. But seeing his chance Champ stepped in and threw Twab over his right hip so fast that they missed half of what had gone on. They stood there dumfounded for a moment with a wow expression on their faces. But because the move had been done so fast, Sparrow asked for another demonstration, only this time, slower.

So for demonstrational purposes, Twab simply stood there while Champ went through the moves as slowly as he could, pointing out each move in turn. There was the grabbing the wrist, the spinning on the heel of the foot while crouching, the right arm going up the inside of the opponent's right arm and then the throw. Champ demonstrated the sequence of moves several times and, when Sparrow and Golcho said they were satisfied, Twab went over Champ's right hip as near as damn it in slow motion.

Seeing Twab on the floor all sprawled out and seeing the advantage of this judo thing, Sparrow asked Champ if he would teach them.

'Of course I will,' said Champ gladly. 'It's the least I can do.'

Champ began the lesson using Twab as the guinea pig. He demonstrated in slow motion the hip throw he had already used, two leg trips, two wrist locks, an elbow lock and the head lock that prevented Twab from getting up, the one where you throw your opponent to the floor then spread your weight over his head, chest and shoulders, with your legs splayed out for balance. The difficulty in getting up from that particular head lock comes down to the fact that your head is the heaviest part of your body. So if you control your opponent's head, you control the rest of his body. Your opponent will find it very difficult getting up from that particular headlock regardless of his size or weight.

So for the next hour, having shown the lads how to break fall, very important in judo, Champ put them through their paces, sometimes demonstrating, sometimes advising. But, at the end of the lesson, Twab, Sparrow and Golcho, not being as fit as they should be, were sprawled out on the floor having learned a little judo – not that they ever used it.

Feeling hungry again, Sparrow mentioned he was ready for his tea. Twab agreed with him this time and suggested they finish the day off by climbing the Woods wall.

The Woods wall Twab was referring to is an extension of the Woods bridge. The crenulated wall was about eighty-yards long and twenty-five feet high. It was also the land of the farmer who always chased them. Climbing the wall was an old tradition with the Adwy lads, and certain girls. Champ was told the custom went back several generations. If Sparrow was to be believed, his dad was one of the first of his generation to climb the wall as a means of escape from Alum's granddad who was then the farmer. The wall was only ever climbed where it ended, as it had a fantastic buttress ramp that made for easy climbing. For the rest of the way up to the farm there was a holly hedge. Because the wall had been climbed for so long, the many hand and footholds were very prominent. According to Golcho it was like climbing a ladder. Apart from being a means of escaping Alum when he chased you, climbing the wall meant you did not always have to cross the river by the bridge to be back on the road which was sometimes very convenient. As for Alum, he never once ventured to climb the wall when he chased them. He would run after them as far as the wall and then quit chasing. Twab reckoned he was afraid of heights.

Sparrow reached the wall first and led off, followed by Golcho then Twab. On the road and looking down on Champ, Twab with Sparrow and Golcho, told him to take his time, that he would be alright.

Champ placed his right foot in the first foot hold about a foot off the ground and leapt up. He then caught hold of the first hand hold, a jutting out stone on his left, and climbed a little higher. Realising it was going to be easy, he climbed up the rest of the wall in that manner and at the top jumped off the wall onto the road. Looking down to see what he had just climbed, and feeling a bit cocky, he asked if there was not anything a little tougher to climb?

'Well as a matter of fact there is,' said Twab grinning and winking at the others. 'It's a place called Harry's Rock and for your cheek we'll take you there tomorrow and see what you make of it.'

'So what's so tough about Harry's Rock?' Champ asked.

Grinning, Sparrow said sarcastically, 'You'll find out tomorrow.'

Winking at Golcho, who did not much care for Harry's Rock, he said, 'Won't he Golch?' Golcho never answered but suggested they just go home and have their tea. As they made their way down to the bridge, Twab could see that Champ was admiring the overall view, the trees, fields and hedgerows. Suddenly everyone looked up. A screeching sound caught their attention. They could not believe what they were seeing – a pair of buzzards was giving a fantastic aerial display – which was an incredible sight.

Everyone was gob-smacked when they saw the higher of the two birds ducking and diving as it swooped in at great speed, and how the one below at the last moment turned upside down with its talons extended. No one knew what they were doing, but it was a superb aerial display. The lads were so enthralled by it all that it saddened them when the birds flew away in the direction of Mr Williams's farm. The buzzards were actually practising food exchange. When they have young, the male goes off hunting and, when it has caught something, it calls the female who flies out to meet him. As he swoops, she turns upside down to allow the food to be transferred by the male.

When everyone had calmed down, and hoping to take Champ's

mind off Harry's Rock, Twab explained that the woods on the Hafod side went up as far as Mr Williams's farm, but on the Dump side went down as far as Southsea, which he did not know. But because it was so boggy in that part of the woods they rarely ever went there.

Because Champ was still going on about Harry's Rock, Twab told him about the time, sometime last year, when Alum had chased them. The farmer was apparently breaking up the dam, angered by all the clods that were missing from the edge of his field, and was called some terrible names and Golcho was blamed for suggesting that he had been born out of wedlock. That day Alum had run after them as far as Southsea, past the playground and smithy, but he had failed to catch them. But their shoes and socks were in a terrible mess at the end of the chase and had to be cleaned up before they went home or they would have been in deep trouble with their mums. At that time, Golcho, like most twelve-year-olds, was of an age where he was using swear words more frequently, with one word in particular, the 'B' word, the one that insinuates that you were born out of wedlock.

Reaching the bridge, the lads had a competition to see who would be the first to drop a stone on a passing leaf as it floated down river. After a few minutes Champ, while the competition was still being played out, mentioned to the lads that what they had shown and given him was fantastic. He thanked them for that and said he was never ever going to leave the Adwy. The only way he was going to leave the Adwy was going to be in a pine box.

Golcho, who was just about to drop a stone on the target, a leaf, said, 'Yea, we also like living here. We come down the woods on most weekends. Come the school holidays we practically live in the woods.'

Remembering a funny story, Sparrow insisted Golcho tell Champ about the time his mum came down the woods looking for him. Chuckling Golcho said, 'We were playing Robin Hood on the Hafod side and, as we fought it out, these two onto me as usual, we heard someone shouting. When I realised it was me mam, we ran to see what she wanted and I was only told off in front of these two for not going home for me dinner.'

When the laughing and teasing died down, Sparrow said being down the woods is so great it makes you forget all about time, adding that you only need time for things like going to school or the pictures or catching a bus and things – otherwise who needed time?

'And it's not that long before the school holidays,' Twab intervened, adding that they were already half way through June, with something like four weeks to go. Then there would be no school for six whole weeks. Then they would be down the Woods all the time. Twab said that Champ ha d not seen anything until he saw the autumn leaves and their colours, adding, that was when this here wood of theirs was a knock out.

Sparrow agreed, but announced he was getting hungrier and with that they set off for home. Approaching Llidiart Fanny Farm Twab asked Champ to ask his mum if he could go with them to the pictures that night as *Shane,* starring none other than Alan Ladd, was showing. That was music to Champ's ears, Alan Ladd being his favourite film-star.

During the evening meal, both Jeannie and Alan excitedly told their mum of their day's exploits. How Jeannie was taken to the park in Coedpoeth by Wendy and Hazel where they watched a tennis match being played in one of the two courts, while a game of bowls was being played on a fabulous green. And she had been in the library as Wendy had to return a library book. It seems you can borrow a book for two weeks free of charge. She said she had never seen so many books.

When Alan began to describe the woods and how they were filled with birds and trees and things, both his mum and Jeannie listened intently. But Mrs Fletcher was concerned when Alan described the pool and the fact that he had swam in it. But Alan convinced her that it was perfectly safe, the only danger being Alum, the farmer, but there had been no sign of him.

It was while Jeannie and her mum were washing the pots that Mrs Fletcher had an idea. Calling Alan over, she suggested he start writing a diary as it would be a shame if in the future all these memories and antics of his were forgotten. He thought it was a brilliant idea and said he was going to start one. His mum suggested he start straight away as she had a book that would make a good diary. She rummaged through the top drawer of the dresser and gave it to him. It was quite a thick book, one that would last at least two years. He then sat down and began to write the date at the top of the first page Saturday, 13th June, 1953, but changed his mind and wrote the previous Saturday's date, the 6th June, as that was where he wanted to begin his diary.

When Doreen asked Jeannie if she wanted a book, Jeannie said she was not ready to start a diary yet as she was too involved with her dolls.

At twenty minutes to seven, Alan's diary was up to date with the week's events. He underlined several entries, including that butterfly which had orange-tipped wings, the pool, the buzzards and the fact that he had a sword and a bow and arrow that was hidden. Then, while he was looking to see what else he was going to underline, there was a knock on the back door. It was Twab's unmistakable, da, da, dada, da-da, da.

Grinning Alan said, 'I'll go; we all know who it is.'

'Are you ready Champ,' Twab asked when the door opened. Sparrow and Golcho were in the outside loo having a wee and frolicking about. 'We're going early to make sure we get a good seat.'

'Yea, I'm ready,' said Alan, 'but come in; I want to show you something I made after my tea.'

Stepping into the living room the lads began to tell Mrs F and Jeannie about that evening's film, *Shane*, while Alan raced upstairs. Moments later, and brandishing his sword he said, 'Well, how about this then?'

'Wow,' said all three simultaneously, 'that's fantastic.'

Alan had made a hand guard for his sword out of an old ostermilk tin that Aunty Mair next door was throwing away. Alan's sword now looked like a real sword. It looked and felt great when it was looped through the loop in his trousers, with his left hand placed on the hilt. All three said he looked like a real musketeer. Because Golcho had a habit of deliberately swiping your fingers whenever you crossed swords with him Alan said, 'That's you sorted out Golch.' Then admiring his invention he said, 'It's good isn't it.'

All three loved the feel of it when they held it, and all three asked if Alan would make one for them. His saying he would meant the lads were now on the look out for three ostermilk tins.

With the back door locked and the key in the outside loo for safe keeping (an old habit from Chester), Mrs Fletcher, Jeannie and the lads set off for the cinema in Coedpoeth. Convinced by Twab that *Shane* was going to be a great film, Doreen decided it would be a nice treat for her and Jeannie as well.

Walking behind and listening to the lads squabbling as they relived the day's events down the woods, caused both Doreen and Jeannie to smile. Reaching the main road with the old Co-op facing them and turning right, they hurried on, passing Glyn's shop and Roberts's and their chippy opposite, then the Three Mile Inn, with the Adwy chapel across the road, then the Grosvernor Arms with its row of houses.

But when they reached Ford's shop, Sparrow and Golcho announced that they needed to call in as they each had a pop bottle that had a tuppence deposit on them. Sparrow's bottle was a Tizer bottle, while Golcho was dandelion and burdock. Telling everyone they would catch them up, they entered the shop.

Mrs Fletcher and Co had only just crossed over Smithy Lane with Lingard's shop nearing when Sparrow and Golcho caught up with them. Sparrow's winking at Twab meant their evil deed had been successful. Sparrow had entered the shop, handed over the two pop bottles and received the four pence deposit. Golcho, outside and hiding waited for Mrs Ford to stack them outside where they were kept.

When she returned to see if Sparrow had made up his mind as to what he was going to buy with the deposit money, Golcho nicked the said bottles and with all the cheek in the world, walked in the shop where he too was given the four pence deposit. Deciding not to purchase anything this time, they left the shop and raced after the others with their picture money intact.

Having passed the infant and junior schools, another row of houses and shops, with Gracie's, a fine clothes shop in the middle, they turned left up Tabor Hill and joined the cinema queue. If the long queue was anything to go by, that night's showing of *Shane* was going to be a good film. All those who had seen the previous night's performance said it was a cracking film.

At seven o'clock precisely, the cinema doors opened and the queue began to shrink. Everyone's excitement was raised when they neared the pay kiosk. When at last the lads received their ticket, costing five pence, they went in search of four seats next to each other. Mrs Fletcher and Jeannie sat in the slightly dearer seats, costing nine pence, and while chatting quietly listened to the pleasant background music being played.

The lads having found four seats together watched as the cinema filled up. For them and a few grown ups, the cinema was where you could lose yourself and become a hero for a while. And there would be a few heroes leaving the cinema tonight.

When Mantovani's *Charmaine* was played, Champ quietly listened and declared he liked it tremendously. Then, as the music began to fade and the big red curtains in front of the screen began to slide apart, the lights dimmed and went out. It was time for the evening's programme to begin. It began with a Joe McDokes comedy, followed by a Tom and Jerry cartoon. Next was an episode of Jungle Jim, then the Pathé news. When the news ended, the big red curtains closed, the house lights came on and, while the ice-cream lady sold her wares, several adverts were shown.

Suddenly, while the last three customers were buying ice-cream, the house lights began to dim. Moments later the big red curtains re-opened. It was time for the main feature.

Because everyone was eager for the film to start, you could have heard a pin drop, which was good news for the usherettes, especially the Grangers from Brymbo who ran the cinema.

The opening scene was of Shane riding towards some homesteaders place. The little boy (Joey), who was pretending to shoot his rifle, spotted Shane. When he informed his father that someone was coming, the father, played by Van Heflin, said, 'Let him. It's a free country.' Shane rode up and said, 'I hope you don't mind me riding through your place?' whereas Stark (Van Heflin) asked where he was headed. Shane told him 'Somewhere I've never been,' and then turned his attention to Joey and said, 'You were watching me, son.'

And so the film proved to be a big success. There were boos and hisses whenever Jack Palance came on screen (he being the baddie) and shouts of hooray and hand clapping when Shane appeared on screen.

During the fight scene in the bar, when Shane returned a soda pop bottle, everyone in the cinema was as quiet as a mouse. The children, worrying for Shane bit their nails and held their breath, but when he shot and killed Jack Palance at the end of the film, the children went wild. They shouted their hoorays, clapped their hands and stomped their feet so much that the usherettes and Mr Granger himself came around shining their torches asking them to be quiet. Several children were so rowdy that Mr Granger threatened to ban them for a week unless they calmed down.

When the film ended, with Shane riding off into the night, wounded slightly, with Joey shouting for him to come back, all the children rushed out to avoid standing for the Queen, but once outside and in their little groups, including Champ and Co, they began to re-enact the movie.

Knowing her lot would be playing at cowboys, Mrs Fletcher said she and Jeannie would meet them in Roberts's chippy. And knowing they would reach there first she asked that one of them stand in the queue.

Mrs Fletcher treated one and all to a bag of chips which were thoroughly enjoyed by everyone as they made their way home. Entering Lloft Wen Lane, Twab, Sparrow and Golcho personally thanked Mrs F for the unexpected treat and said they would repay her come November when the hazel nuts and chestnuts were ready. Back in the village, with Twab saying his goodnights, he nudged Champ to remind him that it was Harry's Rock for him in the morning. Before they reached Heol Wen, Champ tried to get more information out of Sparrow and Golcho regarding Harry's Rock but their lips were sealed. While Golcho walked up his yard, Sparrow, with one last good night, ran down Heol Islwyn and home.

When the Fletcher's reached home, Doreen reached up behind the toilet cistern and retrieved the backdoor key. Jeannie, after her cup of Oxo, went straight to bed. Alan, with his mum's permission, stayed down a few minutes longer. He wanted to add to his diary that he and his family, accompanied by Twab, Sparrow and Golcho, had been to the pictures in Coedpoeth to see *Shane*, and that his mum treated one and all to a bag of chips on their way home.

Part Three: Harry's Rock, June, 1953

SUNDAY MORNING SAW CHAMP ALL SNUGGLED UP IN BED thinking about the previous night's film, *Shane*. It was great seeing Alan Ladd up there on the big screen with Van Heflin and Jean Arthur and the baddie, Jack Palance. Champ was re-living the fight scene in the bar between Shane and Chris, one of Ryker's men, when Jeannie entered his bedroom with an envelope. Having crawled under the bedclothes and making herself comfortable, she opened the envelope and gave Alan their mum's finished birthday card.

It was roughly 6 x 4 inches and depicted their house and back garden as seen from the bottom of the garden. Alan had accurately drawn the house, washhouse and backyard. The garden was from Alan's imagination, how it might look one day. There were numerous flowers in three diamond-shaped beds, surrounded by lawn which made up most of the garden. There was a washing line, a prop, a path and a vegetable patch on the right hand side of the lawn. It looked very picturesque. Alan was going to do some gardening, a little bit at a time. The previous evening, while waiting for his tea and making the guard for his sword, Alan had suddenly remembered that there were some finishing touches he needed to put to the card. He had wanted to slightly improve the garden and he extended the lawn up the side of the house, finishing just in the nick of time. As the card was being placed in Jeannie's school satchel for safe keeping, his mum was at the bottom of the stairs insisting that he come to the table that minute as his tea was going cold.

He was pleased Jeannie had made it into a stand-up card. Her inscription read, 'Happy birthday to the best mum in the world. Hope you have a lovely day and lots of presents.' She signed it with her name and three large kisses. Alan thought for a moment then wrote a well known poem.

'Roses are red – violets are blue – sugar is sweet – and so are you.'

He then signed it and, like Jeannie, drew three large crosses. Pleased with his poem, Alan gave the card to Jeannie to read. While she was reading it, Alan complimented her on her card-making skill. 'You've done a good job with Mum's card our Jeannie.'

Smiling at her brother's compliment, and with a puzzled look on her face, Jeannie asked him if he knew how old their mother was. He shook his head saying that he did not think she was forty, which for him was a colossal age. He could not imagine being twenty let alone forty.

Jeannie then began to wonder how old their grandparents were, but gave up and put the card back in the envelope. Suddenly, there was a twinkle in her eyes. Sitting up she said, 'You won't tell him if I tell you, will you?'

'I won't tell who, what,' said a rather confused Alan.

Jeannie began to giggle when she thought about last night. She had only walked alongside the love of her life while walking home from the chippy. Giggling again she said, 'I think one of your friends is lovely.'

'Oh,' said Alan grabbing her and tickling her, 'which one?'

'Promise you won't tell him.'

'I promise,' said Alan dying to know.

'Promise and hope to die?'

'I promise and hope to die, now who is it?'

With glazed eyes and sighing Jeannie said, 'Sparrow! I think he's lovely and he's my boyfriend. I just love his wavy hair.'

'Oh, and does he know he's your boyfriend?' Alan asked.

'Not yet,' said Jeannie drooling over last night.

She did not think she would ever forget how close they were while walking home from the chippie. Sparrow had even spoken the odd word to her about the film and that was enough to cause Jeannie's heart to flutter. Their touching of hands when Sparrow gave her his empty chip bag to dispose of also caused her heart to flutter. She thought it was so romantic. Blushing she said, 'But you mustn't go telling him now. Remember, you promised.'

'Well, he is coming to call for me later,' said Alan trying to think up ways to embarrass her. 'They are taking me somewhere called Harry's Rock.'

'Harry's Rock, never heard of it. Where's that?' said Jeannie with a twinkle in her eye, knowing Sparrow was calling later. She was going to see to it that she was around when he arrived.

'I don't know where it is,' said Alan trying to suppress a yawn, 'they won't tell me, but it seems I have to perform a death defying feat.'

'Oh, like what?'

'I don't know that either,' said Alan. 'All they've said is, I'll find out.' While he was trying to imagine what they had in store for him, Jeannie, with Sparrow in mind, jumped out of Alan's bed and said she was going to dress. On the landing, and seeing her mum on her way up the stairs, Jeannie quickly opened her bedroom door and put the birthday card in her school satchel just in time.

Climbing up or down stairs was much quieter now that lino had been put down. But you still had to watch your step when in stocking feet. The lino being new was a little on the slippery side. Doreen entered Jeannie's bedroom with clean sheets and pillow cases. Seeing her daughter was dressing, she began to strip the bed. 'Morning love, I thought I heard you walking about.'

Jeannie said she had been talking to Alan and then began to brush her hair. Her mum took the brush from her and began to do it for her. Jeannie's shoulder-length auburn hair was always a pleasure to brush.

Seeing how much her daughter was growing up, and how much she was in need of a decent mirror, Doreen was going to call in Harry's junk shop to see if there was one for sale, like the one she had when she was Jeannie's age.

Jeannie's mirror had an annoying crack down the middle. While brushing her daughter's hair, Doreen mentioned that breakfast was on the go.

'Oh, thanks Mum,' said Jeannie applying several clips to keep her hair in place. 'I'll only be a few more minutes, I'm starving.'

In the doorway Doreen looked back at her daughter. My, how she was growing up. She was so proud of her. She thought back to when she was her daddy's little princess. 'If you could only see her now, my love!' Doreen sighed.

Whereas Alan looked like her, Jeannie was the image of her dad. Doreen spent a few moments thinking of Dave and the short life they had together. He was a lovely man. Snapping out of it she entered

Alan's room and seeing he was still under the clothes said, 'Come on, lazy bones, out of bed or you're going to miss this lovely sunny Sunday morning.'

Alan jumped out of bed and opening the curtains began to giggle.

'Oh, and what's so funny,' asked his mum.

'Well, every time I see Aunty Mair,' said Alan wiping his breath away from the window, 'she's talking to someone. She never seems to stop talking.'

Alan was told to mind his manners. Doreen said Aunty Mair was becoming a good friend and that she enjoyed their elevenses together.

Just then, Mrs Thomas, from number 7, opposite, came out and began to sweep up the yard. Watching her for several moments, and knowing her front door step was her pride and joy, Alan asked if she had red-leaded it yet?

'She was doing that while you were snoring your head off,' said Doreen.

Mr Evans at number five was in the front garden cutting roses from his lovely rose bush which was growing up against the outside lavatory wall. Mrs Evans, hearing her husband's call; came out and took the flowers off him, sniffed them and then re-entered the house via the front door. Alan could not wait for the day when his mum would be able to have flowers from their garden.

Ken, Mr Evans' 21-year-old son, was busy cleaning his fantastic 650cc BSA Gold Flash motor bike on their path. It was gleaming in the morning sun. Alan could not wait for the day when he too would have one exactly the same. He loved the bike's colour combination of green and chrome, but loved the engine's deep throaty sound more. He loved it when Ken rode into their street and revved the engine just prior to switching it off. That was when the throaty sound sounded best. To avoid damaging the front wheel, Ken had placed two house bricks at the kerb to lessen the jolt up off the road onto the garden path.

Roger, their all-black Alsatian dog, whom the postman was frightened to death of, was lying face down on the lawn apparently asleep.

There was a story going around the village that it was Ken who installed the Monster swing on the Dump side. How he had managed to climb the tree which housed the Monster was a mystery to Alan and a few others, but being that much older meant there was not much the likes of Ken and the other young men of the village could not do once their minds were set. But everyone said they were glad the Monster had been installed.

Looking out of the window, Alan could see no sign of life at all from number three, the Griffiths' house. When he pushed his face into the far corner of the window, and wiped away his breath from the pane, he could just make out Mr Jones, Golcho's dad, in his gateway on the corner. He was talking to someone that Alan had not seen before, Golcho's Uncle Albert.

'I like living here Mum,' said Alan as he continued to stare out of the window. 'It's a hundred times better than Chester.'

Pulling him to her Doreen said, 'Yes, I agree with you love. There's no trams, no buses, no smells, no dogs running loose. It's ever so quiet.'

It was agreed by all that it was a lovely sunny Sunday morning and that the weather was far better there than in Chester. It did not seem to rain as much in the Adwy as it did in Chester. It was much quieter by far. Jeannie, having finished clipping her hair and tidied up her dressing table, heard the conversation in Alan's bedroom and came to join in the discussion on the weather. Standing on tip toes she could just see out of the window. When she was asked what she thought of her new home, now that she was no longer missing her old friends in Chester, she replied that living in the Adwy was much better. She did not wish to go back.

'You two have certainly settled in alright,' said Doreen hugging them. 'What with you Alan out all day with your friends, and you Jeannie either in Wendy's or Hazel's, I don't get to see much of you at the weekends.'

Staring out the window, Doreen knew she was going to have to come to terms with the fact that her children were growing up and there were going to be many changes along the way that she might not agree with. But one thing she was sure of, she would always be there for them.

Opening the window and leaning out, Alan could just make out Mr Jones at number 4, two houses down on their side. He was leaning on his gate, apparently watching the world go by. Because of some dog barking in the distance, Alan could not quite make out the tune he was humming but, whatever it was, he appeared to be enjoying himself. Suddenly, Jimmy, Mr Jones' eldest lad, passed through the gate with his push-bike, said something to his dad, and then rode off. Watching him disappearing around the corner, peddling like mad, Alan guessed he was well over fifteen and had left school.

'How many friends have you made Mum?' Alan asked.

'There's only Mair next door and Sally who works in the Co-op. I'm chatty with most of the women of the village, but there's only them two I can call friends. But I'm alright the way things are. Don't you go worrying about me.'

'Who's Sally?' Jeannie asked.

'She's the lady behind the bacon counter who lives three houses up by the bus-stop. It's her garden wall that people sit on while waiting for the bus.' Smiling she said, 'She's asked me to go out with her sometime, her being a widow as well.'

'What's a widow?' Jeannie asked.

'Someone, whose husband has died,'

'Oh,' said Jeannie and left it at that.

'So are you going to go out with her?' Alan asked.

'Oh, we'll see,' said Doreen. With her next breath she said, 'It's a pity Bryn next door wasn't a bit older Alan. He'd love to be your friend. He loves it when you play with him in the garden.'

'Ooh, I'm sorry Mum,' said Alan sharply. 'I'm already in a gang and Twab has made it clear that we remain as a gang of four. I do play with Bryn sometimes when I'm not out with the lads. He plays football quite well.'

'Oh, so I take it then that Twab's the boss?' said Doreen.

'He certainly is,' said Alan defending his leader. 'He makes all the decisions and tells us what to do.'

'How boring,' said Jeannie pulling a face. 'Wendy and Hazel and I do our own things which I think is much better.'

Doreen began to giggle. The difference between boys and girls growing up was still evident. Boys do their war things while girls appear to be more domesticated. She then found herself giggling the way Malcolm insisted in calling her 'Mrs F'. What a funny lad he was, she thought. Then she said 'Ah well, enough of this idle chit chat,' then she remembered, 'Oh my goodness, your eggs are going to be as hard as bullets.' Rushing out of the room and down the stairs she said, 'Two minutes you two.'

Alan ordered Jeannie out of his room, but as he was about to close his window, saw Terry coming out of his front door. He could not quite hear what his mum, Aunty Jinni, was saying to him, but to avoid him he quickly closed the window and, hoping he had not been spotted, began to dress.

When Jeannie sat at the table she did not fancy her egg. It was too hard. So instead, she had a bowl of Shredded Wheat. Alan had Jeannie's egg and thoroughly enjoyed it. He had never had two eggs with toasted soldiers before and felt extra full.

With breakfast over, Jeannie placed her pots in the sink, ran some hot water, and washed them along with the others in the bowl, then dried them and put them away in the pantry. How different to Chester. In Chester you had to boil water before you could wash the pots or anything. Here all you had to do was turn on the hot water tap. It was lovely having hot water 'on tap'.

Placing the tea-towel on the clothes maid to dry, Jeannie announced that she was going upstairs to play with her doll's house. Actually, she was making sure she was around when Sparrow called.

Doreen asked Alan if, before going out, he would set a fire in the washhouse ready for the following day. Monday, being wash-day, was always busy, what with the washing, drying and ironing. Then there was the shopping. She was also hoping there was time enough to make a lob scouse pie for their tea.

With his breakfast over, Alan went about setting the fire in the washhouse. He scooped out all the ash with a scraper that his dad used when he was a lad, then picked out all the cinders by hand as they were going back on the fire. He not only set the fire and tidied up, but also placed the dolly peg and tongs at the ready, and filled up the coal bucket to feed the fire.

With his dad's trusty old axe, he then set about building up his stockpile of sticks from the hawthorn hedge at the bottom of the garden. He did not think his supply would ever run out as there was so much dead wood to be had.

Having started a conversation with Bryn, Aunty Mair's lad, and watching his two sisters playing on the see-saw that Bryn had made for them by placing a plank over a five gallon drum, Alan said he would have a game of footy with him sometime today, which cheered Bryn up no end.

A few minutes later, seeing Sparrow and Golcho approaching, Alan gathered up his sticks and, telling Bryn he would see him later, stored them in the washhouse in the old tea chest under the draining board. Rushing indoors for his sword, and with Bryn watching, he waited by the corner of the house. Hearing his friend's footsteps and mumblings while coming down the path, he motioned Bryn to be quiet, then stepped out and, seeing they were unarmed, held them at bay with his sword. He said they were going to be robbed the way he had seen it done in some film in which he could not recall the actor's name. He tried to remember the name as he waggled the point of his sword in their faces as he had seen it done in the film.

Bryn looked on with envy and wished he could play with them. Alan suddenly remembered who the swashbuckling someone was. It was none other than Burt Lancaster in *The Crimson Pirate*. Still waggling his sword inches from their faces, his hand guard glinting in the sun, Champ quoted Burt Lancaster's great speech of, 'Gather round Lads and Lassies, gather round. I have a tale to tell.' Burt was dressed in a pair of striped trousers, showing off his hairy chest, while clinging onto a rope ladder at the time. But Alan thought his speech very impressive.

But how different Golcho's speech was? He greeted Champ by pushing his sword away and saying, 'Sod off you silly bugger.' He then informed him that he was in the wrong film. 'The film you want,' said Golcho trying to think, 'is- um, um ...' Failing to remember he asked Sparrow what the film was called.

'It's you that's in the wrong film, Golch,' Sparrow informed him. 'You're thinking of um, – oh, what's his name, him who was in that film where – um ...'

Winking at Bryn while waiting for Sparrow to remember the film he was trying to remember, Champ, putting him out of his misery said it did not matter and greeted his two friends and asked them if his sword was needed today.

'No,' said Sparrow having already given up trying to remember the film he was trying to remember. Winking at Bryn and knowing Champ was going to be wetting himself shortly, Sparrow said, 'No Champ, no sword today. Today is for climbing.' Turning to Golcho he said, 'Isn't it?'

Knowing there were to be no clues given, Champ said, 'Ah, well, come in for a minute while I put my sword away. I want to show you something.'

Having said so-long to Bryn and entered the house via the back door, Alan pushed Sparrow into the front room where, seeing Jeannie starting to blush, said, 'Look who's here Jeannie.'

Mrs Fletcher said hello to the lads, then stepped outside hoping to catch Mair next door. Knowing she was blushing, Jeannie started to get up from her chair, but quick off the mark Alan said, 'Say hello to my sister, Sparrow.'

But before Sparrow could comply, Jeannie stomped passed them and ran upstairs yelling what a horrible brother she had.

Seeing the puzzled look on Sparrow and Golcho's face, Alan said he could not explain, as it was a private joke. He ran upstairs two at a time and put his sword away, then popped his head in Jeannie's bedroom doorway, and to keep the tease going, said, 'Aren't you going to say hello to him after he's come all this way to see you?'

Neither Sparrow nor Golcho nor Mrs Fletcher having returned could make out why Jeannie was shouting so much at Alan upstairs.

Realising he'd gone too far and hugging her, Alan said he was very sorry and that her secret was safe with him.

Back downstairs he asked what time dinner was going to be and, when told, said he would not be late. Saying 'Ta-ra' to his mum and Jeannie from the bottom of the stairs, he, Sparrow and Golcho set off for Harry's Rock, but not before calling for their leader.

Knocking on Twab's back door, they heard Mrs Smith shout for them to come in. Stepping into the living room, and knowing Mrs Smith did not like them calling Malcolm, Twab, Sparrow asked where Malcolm was. Mrs Smith was sitting in her favourite chair by the window with her legs tucked underneath her. She said hello to Robert, then to Alan, but not recognising the other boy asked who he was. Blushing slightly, he said his name was also Alan and that he and his family had just moved into Heol Wen.

'Oh, so you're the new people,' said Mrs Smith, happy now that she knew who he was. 'I see your mam passing sometimes. She's a lovely woman your mam. Our Malcolm has told me all about you.'

Sparrow and Golcho began to giggle.

Not sure why they were giggling, Mrs Smith nevertheless went on. 'You've come from Chester haven't you?' But before Alan could answer, Mrs Smith said, 'Didn't you like Chester? How do you like your new house and school? Our Malcolm tells me you sit with him in class, is that right?'

'Is Malcolm in, Mrs Smith?' Sparrow intervened to Golcho's delight. Twab's mum (according to Golcho) is a lovely lady and all that, very often she'll hand out biscuits. But oh my, she never knew when to stop talking. 'Um, he does know we're calling for him?'

'Well he shouldn't be long. He's gone rabbiting with his dad and Queenie. They went out about six o'clock this morning.' Looking through the window Mrs Smith with a lovely smile said, 'Ah, here they are now.'

With a quick 'Ta-ra', the lads went out to meet their leader.

'Where've you been,' Sparrow asked somewhat aggressively. 'Do ya know what time it is?'

While Sparrow was having a go at Twab, Champ looked at Mr Smith for a moment. He looked a funny shape around the waist. He then joined Golcho in making a fuss of Queenie, their rabbiting dog.

Having accepted Sparrow's telling off for being late, Twab introduced Champ. 'Dad,' he said, 'this here is Alan, who we call Champ. He's our newest gang member and has come from Chester.'

'Hello, son,' said Mr Smith. 'How are you?'

'I'm fine thank you,' answered Alan who then asked if they had caught any rabbits?' Mr Smith opened his jacket and showed Champ three dead rabbits hanging from his belt. Feeling sorry for them, Champ asked if he could touch one.

Untying the middle one Mr Smith handed it to Alan. Seeing the look on the boy's face he asked if he had ever seen a dead one before.

'No,' said Champ cuddling and stroking the poor thing.

'Have you ever tasted one?'

Champ shook his head. The rabbit was so cold.

Ruffling Champ's hair and grinning Mr Smith said, 'Ah well, we'll have to remedy that for you, son. Come for dinner sometime. Would you like that?'

Champ shrugged his shoulders. He did not know what to say. While holding the animal to his chest, he remembered how lovely and cuddly his friend's rabbits were in Chester. How anyone could kill and eat a rabbit was beyond him. This was a little piece of country life that he had no knowledge of. His meat was always given to him on a plate with no hunting or killing involved, but at least Mr Smith's funny shape had been explained.

Taking the rabbit back, Mr Smith entered the house and began to prepare the rabbits for the pot. Having already been gutted, the three were skinned and boiled.

Twab in the meantime was in the washhouse rubbing Queenie down with an old towel while making a big fuss of her, telling her what a good girl she was. 'I'm almost ready,' he shouted, giving Queenie some fresh water and a clean bed.

Queenie strolled into the yard and wagged her tail in appreciation of all the attention she was receiving from Sparrow and Golcho.

'What kind of dog is it?' Champ asked.

'She's a greyhound,' said Twab, 'and a good one,' he insisted.

'Does she actually kill the rabbits when she catches them?' Champ asked, not liking the idea.

'Course she does,' Golcho informed him, adding that they had seen her chasing and catching them lots of times and how, with one bite to the head, it was all over for the poor rabbit.

Sparrow, who was kissing Queenie' nose and petting her said, 'She can run ever so fast,' then speaking gibberishly said, 'Can't you girl?'

With his chores completed Twab opened the back door and, shoving Queenie inside, shouted to say he was going with the lads to Harry's Rock.

'Before we go, let's show Champ the frog bath,' said Golcho.

Hanging on a huge nail behind the washhouse door was an old tin bath that the lads had found one time while rooting on the Dump side of the woods. As there were no holes in it, they carried it home between them for the sole purpose of watching frog spawn turn into frogs in the springtime. All three began to laugh at the puzzled look on Champ's face for never having seen frog spawn. Their laughing increased while telling him that frog spawn looked very much like sago pudding, only a different colour. Being a lover of sago pudding, Champ hoped they were only pulling his leg.

'In the spring,' said Twab, 'we take the bath down and let it fill with rain water because tap water will kill the frog spawn which we get from the big pond on Clay Hill where we haven't taken you yet, and then we watch and wait while all the little black dots turn into tadpoles and then into baby frogs. We've being doing this for a couple of years now and I've noticed that when there's no other food for the taddie's, they start to eat one another.'

Champ had a funny look on his face, not because of the tadpoles eating one another, but because frog spawn and sago pudding looked the same. Unable to get his head around it, he decided he was not going to believe it. But, still referring to the tadpoles eating one another, Twab said, 'Oh yea, we've seem um doing it. A big one will chase a little one, catch it and eat it. Although you start off with hundreds of taddie's, you end up with only a few frogs.'

'What I like best,' said Sparrow 'is when they start to grow their front legs. They're only tiny at first, but they soon grow.'

'So what do you do with them when they're fully grown?' Champ asked.

'We take them back to Clay Hill in a bucket and let um go,' said Twab closing the washhouse door. Reaching the gate and being the last one through, he made doubly sure that the gate was closed properly with the metal loop pulled down over the gate post. Mr Smith had gone to a lot of trouble to make sure Queenie did not roam the streets, she being a working dog.

So, with the time at half-past-ten, Champ and Co set out for Harry's Rock. Leaving Twab's gateway they strolled on past the last two occupied houses on Heol Islwyn, but saw no one.

Not even Richard, Oswald's delivery boy, but then it was Sunday, a day of rest. Richard was most likely in bed resting, because from Monday to Saturday; he was often seen delivering food parcels on his little two-wheeler truck after school, as late as eight o'clock. He was always on the go.

While strolling along the unfinished road, an extension of Heol Islwyn, the lads commented on how the four houses on either side of the road up to the T-junction were nearing completion. When you see the roofs going on and the windows being put in, Champ was told, it would not be long until families moved in. Because it was Sunday, and the watchman's day off, Golcho suggested they show Champ how it was when they played in the empty houses when there was no one there to chase them away.

They entered the last house on their side, a corner house with its roof on, but as yet no doors. Following on was another block of two that were only half built that led on to Heol Offa, an original road with its houses made with Ruabon red brick. Entering the house, and disregarding the fact that the floor was littered with bits of plaster board, broken bricks, strips of wood, broken glass and the electrical wiring dangling from the ceilings in all the downstairs rooms they headed for the stairs and Champ climbed the bare steps up to the upper floor where he was reminded of how his house had been when they first moved in, sounding very hollow. This one sounded just the same. But when he began to stomp on the stairs, Twab told him off. They were trespassing for goodness sake.

Looking out of a front bedroom window frame that as yet had no glass in, Champ was told how great it was when they played in houses like this, especially on rainy days. But then the watchman usually came along and put a stop to it which was sad for everyone, including the other village kids, as many a good game of hide and seek could be played when there was no watchman.

It seemed that everyone in the village, barring Twab, was glad to see the village expanding. Twab said he did not want the village to expand and was happy with it the way it was. But when Champ said it was progress, Twab said progress was not always a good thing, and meant it.

When Sparrow, who was backing Champ up, said that he did not fancy having to go back to gas lamps, pointing out the smell. Twab said that was different and not what he was talking about. Of course, electric lights were better than gas lamps, but who wanted to live in a village with millions of people.

When Golcho mentioned that his granddad used to go to Wrexham in a horse and buggy, Twab again said that was different, but that was not what he had been talking about. Of course it was better riding in a bus.

'So what is it you don't like about the village expanding?' Champ asked.

'The fact that there won't be any fields left. Where will the taddie's come from if they build on Clay Hill? Where will the bonfire be held if they build top side of Champ's house?'

That caused everyone to have a little think. And it was Champ who, having started the argument, said that Twab could be right. Now that the mood was more serious, they stomped back down the stairs, out of the house and began to walk up a road which was Heol Glyndŵr in the making. The houses to be were only footings at the moment, but the lads, encouraged by Twab, began to play follow my leader over a line of kerb stones that had been put down where they were going to be laid. While part of the game was trying to keep your balance, Twab was thinking about how much money they would be earning from carol singing when these houses had people in them, which was a contradiction really. A few minutes ago Twab did not want the village to expand, but did like the idea of making lots of dosh come Christmas time.

With the game played out, having reached the top of the would-be road which looked as if a bomb had hit it, they looked to their right towards the Fron Bank some two miles away as the crow flies. Even the path which led up to Lloft Wen Lane that was in everyday use, was showing signs that more houses were going to be built, particularly on the side road that was going to be facing Twab's house on Heol Islwyn. All this expansion was going ahead whether Twab liked it or not. You could not stop progress. The path they were on at the moment was going to be Heol Cadfan, and the side road Heol y Gelli. It was obvious to everyone that the Adwy was going to be a much bigger place when all the building was finished. The lads began to think that Twab was not a full shilling for not wanting the village to expand. To avoid a row, they entered Lloft Wen Lane and raced along the dirt path, scragging each other to be the first over the still brand new-looking stile, which was only three months old. But when the last of them was over the stile, they raced along the original tarmaced Lloft Wen Lane and, before you could say Jack Robinson, were at the main Wrexham to Ruthin road, the A525.

Crossing over and wishing the Co-op was open, the lads spent a few minutes drooling over the different sweets they could have bought. Between them they had over a shilling, but like every other shop in the

Adwy, it was closed on a Sunday. Moving on, they ran down the wide, red-shale path which gave access to seven, privately-owned houses. Champ was told the people there were good payers at Christmas time. Most of them paid out as much as sixpence.

Reaching the end of the path, they climbed over another stile to where there were fields and hedgerows as far as the eye could see. They entered the first of the two fields they had to cross, with Harry's Rock looming in the distance to their right. Staying close to the hedge, they raced up to yet another stile which was of a completely different kind. In fact this was the only one of its kind in the area and entailed them walking up a set of steps, stepping over a wedge of stone, and then descending down nine much wider and steeper steps into a much lower field. While waiting for Sparrow and Golcho to stop their messing about and get a move on (they were scragging each other to see who was going to be first over the stile), Twab told Champ that the wood he could see in the distance, on the other side of Rhos Berse Road, was called the Adwy Wood, which was alongside the main road and was only ever visited when the goosies were ready towards the end of May. Champ was told that if he carried on along the path they were standing on (it being a right of way) he would end up at Nant Mill from where he could go on to Bersham one way, or to the Nant, with its little bridge, the other way. If he then crossed over the bridge and went up the Stryd, a little winding road, he could go to Minera Mountain. He then explained that *stryd* was Welsh for street. When he had been five-years-old Twab had lived by that little bridge and its lovely meandering river and had loved living there. He had played alongside the bridge and very often splashed and paddled in the river and would never forget the fun that was had. He would have told Champ a lot more had Sparrow and Golcho not just then sorted themselves out and were now ready for off.

Mr Kynaston's land which they were on, had a public right of way across it and, now that Sparrow and Golcho had stopped their messing about, they all turned right and raced along a well-used tractor path towards Harry's Rock. On their right, and running the full length of the field, was a mixed hedge of holly and blackthorn whose dainty little white flowers had finished and in their place little green berries were growing that, when turned blue, would be used by a lot of people for making gin. The holly berries were left for the birds. On their left were fields with black and white Friesian cows grazing away, with little clumps of trees and hedgerows as far as the eye could see. Up ahead, and waiting for them, was Harry's Rock and their race along the tractor path ended up as a walk because Champ wanted to take in all the wonderful scenery.

Seeing all these open fields was still new to him. He still could not get his head around the fact that the countryside was like this, fields, cows, trees and hedgerows, and, if you were lucky enough to see them, rabbits and squirrels.

When they were some 200 yards from Harry's Rock (a long abandoned quarry, stones from which were evident in many parts of Coedpoeth and elsewhere, and which was completely wooded over) Champ could see it was nothing like their little woods whinch had proper trees. Harry's Rock appeared to be made up of trees which he later learned were silver birches. But it was not the trees they were there to see on that lovely Sunday morning. They were there to see if Champ would accept the death-defying challenge that they had in store for him and which they still insisted remained a mystery until the last moment. They wanted him to be nervous.

In a bid to beat Champ in a race, if only the once, Twab ran off announcing that the winning post was a burnt-out old oak tree. Champ won. Sparrow and Golcho did not even bother to race, but walked in complaining why everything had to be a race. What ever happened to the good old days where they walked everywhere?

Seeing the condition of the oak tree, Champ asked for an explanation.

'It was sometime last year,' said Twab. 'Some bigger lads from the village came out here rather drunk. A dare was made and this poor old tree was set on fire as you can see, but don't ask me how it was done.' Golcho suggested they must have used petrol or paraffin. Walking on, Champ was given the rest of the story. But, however, the tree was set on fire, no one came to its rescue and the fire simply burned itself out leaving the poor old tree in a terrible condition. Fortunately, it did not die and still produced acorns every year by the barrow load.

Realising that he had never seen so many cows in one field, Champ counted thirty-three of the black and white Friesians all grazing away and swishing their tails. He wondered why none of them had any horns. But it was their udders that really amazed him; they were so swollen they were almost touching the ground. Passing close to one of the cows and staring at its udder, Champ could suddenly smell the animal. His comment of, 'Phew they stink,' was shrugged off by the others. Being country lads they were used to the smell of cows from working on Mr Williams's farm. They were very often in the shippon, slushing out when Mr Williams was hand-milking one of the cows.

All animals smell, Champ was told, although some smelled more than others. When Sparrow said it was in the cow's udder that milk was made, Champ did not believe him for one minute. But he had second thoughts when Golcho told of the time when Mr Williams, for a joke, splashed Sparrow all over with milk from one of the cow's teats. Champ ended up a little embarrassed when Golcho referred to the cow's teats as little 'willies'. To show that Sparrow was not telling porkies, Golcho chose an animal and crouched down beside it. The cow did not seem to mind. Nor did it mind when he began to milk it. Moments later and to Champ's amazement, a white liquid began to dribble onto the grass. 'Look Champ,' said Golcho laughing, 'it's milk, do you want some. It's going cheap. It's yours if you want some.' Champ stood there gobsmacked. He could not think of anything to say. Up till now he had only ever seen milk in glass bottles that had a silver top.

Not to be outdone, Sparrow approached another animal and crouching alongside it, began to milk it. Moments later he too was producing milk. As it spilled onto the grass he told Champ to come and have a closer look. Not wanting to, but knowing he did not dare refuse, and cringing with the thought of having to touch what Golcho referred to as a 'little willy,' Champ put on a brave face and stepped in. But the moment he did, Sparrow aimed the cow's teat at him and splashed him with milk. Sparrow could not have timed it any better. The flow of milk hit Champ in the chest and began to run down his jerkin. The sudden outburst of laughter and movement caused the animal to thrash its tail and move away, as did several other cows.

Champ wiped himself down amidst hysterical laughter. But no way was he going to allow Sparrow to get away with it. No sir. Picking up a handful of fresh dung, he gave chase, causing everyone to scarper.

Believing he was the target, Golcho ran away as fast as he could. Sparrow and Twab, believing the same, hung back so as not to miss any of the fun. But when Sparrow saw the look on Champ's face and realised his mistake, he too scarpered away as fast as he could.

Twab and Golcho gave out a long sigh of relief, but wanting it confirmed that it was Sparrow that Champ was after they veered to their right and, with fingers crossed, hoped for the best. Their faces beamed when they saw it really was Sparrow that Champ was after. Twab suggested they should follow at a distance as this was going to be something to see. Would Champ really douse Sparrow in cow dung?

'Who's going to be all smelly when I catch him?' Champ teased.

No matter how fast Sparrow ran, Champ kept up with him. He was deliberately teasing him with the cow dung. Knowing it was useless trying to out run Champ, Sparrow stopped and tried to buy his way out. But his two shilling offer was refused. Champ said he wanted revenge. Pulling faces to wind him up, while again threatening him with the dung, Champ moved in waving the green goo under his nose. 'Um, doesn't it smell nice?' Champ teased as he moved in for the kill.

Panicking, Sparrow tried to waffle his way out by telling Champ how good he was at running, how good he was at drawing, how good he was at everything. When he saw it was not working, he upped his bribe to two shillings and sixpence, to be paid within the next few days. But the look on Champ's face told Sparrow that he was wasting his time.

During the chase most of the dung had slipped through Champ's fingers, but there was enough for what he wanted. 'Ah, ha,' said Champ, 'here it comes.' Sparrow, who had never begged for mercy in his life thought he would give it a try. It just might work, but all it did was make Champ more determined. So, when Champ moved in for the kill, both Twab and Golcho looked at one another and wondered if Champ would really carry out his threat.

Champ flicked his left fist in Sparrow's face to throw him off his guard then, grabbing his left wrist, applied a wrist lock. Sparrow was forced onto his back. Jumping on him, pinning him down with his knees thus trapping his arms, and grinning like a Cheshire cat, with Sparrow now at his mercy, he said, 'I hereby christen you 'Smelly Wellie'.' Champ had no intention of smearing his friend with the dung and leaned over and wiped his hand in the grass. Then he ran off laughing.

Thanking his lucky stars, Sparrow got up and chased after him. Both went over to the animals' water trough alongside the far hedge where, while Champ washed his hands at one end, Sparrow took a drink at the other. With peace restored the lads approached Harry's Rock.

Climbing over the broken-down gate, the lads, except for Champ, were quickly reminded why Harry's Rock was seldom visited. The ever increasing nettle beds and briar patches made life unbearable, but they battled on. With stings and scratches received by one and all (they were wearing short trousers) they entered a clearing where, some twenty yards in front of them, was the reason for today's visit. When Champ was ushered to the front they walked up to an enormous hole in the ground. They all stopped some four feet from the edge.

The hole was about thirty feet in diameter. While he walked up to the edge for a nervous look down, Champ spotted an old broken down sign in the bushes which he could not read. It had once said, in bright red, painted capital letters 'DANGER THIS SHAFT IS DANGEROUS.' When he asked how deep it was Twab said he did not know, but climbing down was why they were here.

Peering down what appeared to be a bottomless pit Champ began to panic a little and asked a second time how deep it was. It was some time before anyone answered. 'We don't know,' reiterated Twab, adding that it was not that deep or dangerous that they could not climb down. 'When you reach that shadow,' he said pointing down, 'you're more or less on the bottom.'

Trying to see beyond the shadow and still convinced it was a bottomless pit; Champ began to think very hard about climbing down. 'Isn't it dangerous?'

'We've all done it many times,' said Twab.

'To prove it's not dangerous, we'll do it with you,' said Sparrow, adding that if Champ thought his voice was echoey in that empty house they were in earlier, it was nothing compared to being down there. He pointed at the shaft.

Golcho's ears pricked up. What did Sparrow mean 'We'll do it with you'? Golcho was under the impression that it was Champ who was being dared to climb down the shaft for being so cocky yesterday while climbing up the Woods wall. Why should he have to climb down just to prove it was not dangerous? He had never liked climbing down the stupid shaft. He had a plan and went in search of a stone about the size of a tennis ball. Standing over the hole, he extended his right arm and, looking at Champ, let the stone fall. Moments later there was a hollow-sounding crash as the stone smashed into all the other stones that had been thrown down on previous visits. 'There,' said Golcho hoping it was enough to frighten Champ into changing his mind about climbing down, 'that's how deep it is.'

No one said anything for a moment. Then Champ said, 'Let's throw another one down and count how long it takes to reach the bottom.'

Sparrow found a small rock about the size of a football and, with an effort, rolled it over the edge. He began to count, '1 and 2 and 3 and …' The stone hit the bottom giving off a tremendous hollow-sounding crash.

'It's quite deep,' said Champ with everyone agreeing.

But eager to be getting on with it, now that Sparrow had committed them, Twab said, 'Well, who's going first?'

'Let's draw straws,' suggested Sparrow.

'Well, you can count me out,' said Golcho adamantly. 'I'm not climbing down. We came here to see Champ climbing down. How can we judge him, if we all climb down with him?'

'Well you can blame Sparrow for that Golch,' said Twab. 'He's the one who committed us. You know the rules, one for all and all that.'

Taking a stalk of grass, Twab broke it into four pieces. Golcho was asked, and then ordered to take one. Being the loser, Sparrow approached the shaft on his hands and knees and peered over the edge into the gaping hole. He then took hold of an old, thick, rusty chain which was embedded in a thick concrete cap that someone had forgotten to put back over the shaft. When ready, he lowered his right leg over the side and found the first of the footholds. With confidence he lowered his left leg. Letting go of the chain with his left hand and reaching down the shaft a little, he took a firm hold of a jutting-out stone, and feeling confident to the point of showing off, lowered his right hand and leg, and found the next foothold and hand grip. He then began to climb down Harry's Rock. To him it was as easy as climbing up or down the Woods wall.

Twab, Golcho and Champ crawled over to the edge and watched as Sparrow descended down the shaft. As confident as he was, Sparrow still took his time. He was aware of the danger of falling. At the half-way mark, and for Champ's benefit, Sparrow shouted up to say how easy it was. But Champ noticed a change in Sparrow's voice. Just like the stones and in that empty house earlier, his voice sounded echoey. Shouting down, he pointed this out to him, but Sparrow being Sparrow and wanting to wind Golcho up for jabbing him too hard with his sword yesterday, began to mimic the devil's voice, 'Oooh, Mr Golcho,' he teased, 'are you coming down here-e-e-?'

Golcho was always nervous at Harry's Rock and told Sparrow in no uncertain terms to pack it in or he would drop a stone on his head if he thought it would not damage the stone. As if looking for one, he moved away from the edge. Suddenly, Twab began to laugh at Golcho for the way he had acted once when climbing down Harry's Rock. He had appeared nervous as if he did not like being in the dark.

Having reached the bottom and almost completely hidden from view, Sparrow waited while his eyes adjusted. Then with his voice sounding echoey and eerie, he shouted up the shaft to let them know that he was on the bottom and wanted to know who was coming down next.

Knowing he would not be allowed to stay behind and wait for them while they did their silly things down there, Golcho decided to get it over with and go next. Bravely, and like Sparrow, he too used the rusty chain to help him over the edge. When he was ready he began his descent down the shaft. Some five minutes later he too was safely on the bottom.

'Okay Champ,' Golcho's voice boomed up the shaft, 'your turn.'

Looking at Twab, hoping he would call the whole thing off, Champ, after some encouragement from his leader, reached for the old rusty chain. Looking down the shaft to see if he could see his mates, which he could not, they being hidden in the shadow, Champ shouted to let them know he was on his way. Golcho's voice, sounding slightly jumbled up said, 'Don't worry too much Champ, I'll talk you down.' Champ only understood some of it. Knowing how Champ would be feeling and determined he was going to make it as easy as he could for him, Golcho said, 'Just think of it as the Woods wall, Champ and don't look down.'

Grasping the chain the way Sparrow and Golcho had, Champ lowered his right leg over the side, and like them, after a quick look down, found the first of the footholds. With both feet safely on protruding stones, he let go of the chain and slowly made his way down the shaft with Golcho's help. The further down he climbed, the more he began to understand the instructions. Then, realising it was not all that difficult, he began to relax. Half way down, he looked up the shaft at Twab, who, lying on his stomach, was leaning over the edge watching his every move. Champ mentioned how cold it was, but Twab never answered. He knew it was cold.

With Golcho's encouragement, Champ continued on down and moments later two pairs of hands were grabbing his legs. He was on the bottom. He immediately shook arms with Sparrow and Golcho, the Roman way, then began to look around (not that there was much to see, just two tunnels) Looking back up the shaft he told Twab to come on down.

They all watched as Twab lowered himself over the side and found the first of the footholds. Twab was in a circle of sunshine. Champ began to calm down a little, now that he was on the bottom, but mentioned how cold it was and asked what that funny smell was?

'Well it's not me,' said Sparrow laughing out.

Not knowing what the smell was, but knowing of it, Golcho said the smell was always there but did not think it was dangerous. If it was, he said they would have been dead ages ago. Champ said it smelled like bad eggs. Sparrow told him to ignore it and concentrate on getting his eyes used to the dark.

When Twab was on the bottom, Champ mentioned that their voices seemed to go on and on. Everyone began to shout just for the sake of it. There were several 'Ois' and 'Hellos,' which got jumbled up. It was impossible to tell who was who. As much as it was chaos, it was fantastic chaos. Then, asking for silence as he wanted to see how far his voice would carry, Champ shouted a long 'Hellowww,' which carried down the tunnel for ages. When it finally petered out and knowing Golcho was unhappy down here and determined to wind him up, Sparrow yelled out a long 'Oooh,' in his bid to sound like the Devil.

Trying to be brave, Golcho listened as Sparrow's eerie voice made its way down the tunnel, but said nothing knowing how Sparrow would be if he did.

Not bothered about the smell, but coming at Golcho from another angle, Sparrow said that this used to be a pit years ago even though he knew it had never been anything other than a quarry, adding that they might have had an explosion down there like the one they had in Gresford all those years ago.

'Yea, that would account for the smell,' said Twab who then informed everyone that Gresford's explosion in 1934 had killed 265 men. He then went on to say that the rescue team found a lot of men had been killed by the very gas that caused the explosion. Some of the miners, according to his granddad, were fourteen-year-old boys.

Champ blanked his mind off for a moment and tried to imagine what working down a mine as a fourteen-year-old would have been like. Had he been born in an earlier time, he might have been working down a mine in two years time. He ended up thinking how lucky he was to have been born in 1941. He then remembered the story the lads told him about the watchman who had to push tubs of coal all day when he worked as a fourteen-year-old boy down the Hafod Mine. And he would have been in the dark for most of the time. What a horrible thought.

Knowing full well that Golcho was starting to bite, even though he was trying to put on a brave face, Sparrow said, 'Well I hope they got all the bodies out. Hey, I hope there aren't any skeletons down here.'

'Now stop that Sparrow,' said Golcho, not realising his words were all jumbled up because of the echo. Speaking them was easy enough, but receiving them was something else entirely. All the words were being overlapped. What sounded like Chinese to everyone was in fact, 'I'm nervous enough as it is without you making it worse.'

So when Sparrow finally gave up trying to wind Golcho up, Champ asked how far in the tunnels went?

'Well this one behind us only goes in a few yards,' said Twab answering for Sparrow, 'but this one in front goes in a long way.' Speaking slowly so as to be understood he said, 'We've only ever been up to a bend before on account of it being so dark. But you can go further. So who's for seeing how far it does go?'

'I'm game,' said Sparrow his words mixing with Twab's

'Me too,' said Champ, his words mixing with Twab's and Sparrow's.

'Well, you can count me out,' Golcho's words bounded out. 'I'm not moving from here.'

'Now, now, Golcho,' said Twab. 'You know the rules, 'All for one and one for all'. It's three against one so you'll have to put up with it.'

Golcho was very nervous, but what could he do? He had been under the impression that it was Champ who was being tested, not him.

Striking a match, Sparrow asked everyone to see if there was any paper to be had. Champ found a strip of thick cardboard on the floor and held it up while Sparrow tried to light it. When the flame was bright enough, Sparrow, with Golcho and Champ in the middle, with Twab as tail-end-Charlie, led off into the tunnel. They slowly made their way along the passageway which, as Twab predicted, was dark. What little light they had barely showed Sparrow's face. Golcho felt the dark was beginning to swallow him up. He had never liked being down there in that stupid tunnel. Not only were they constantly tripping over stones that littered the floor, but there was the constant fear of bumping their heads in the low ceiling. Reaching the bend they moved on. No one had ever been beyond this point before. They were, as Twab would have said, in new territory. Their pace was slow, but in single file with their little cardboard flame their only light source, they marched on in silence. Well not exactly – that last statement is not exactly true because there was the eerie sound of their shuffling footsteps as well as Golcho's heavy breathing through his nostrils. Oh, and some water that was dripping somewhere up ahead.

Sparrow suddenly brought the procession to a halt and felt around with his right foot. He spoke slowly to be understood, knowing each word would be distorted and jumbled up. He announced that he had come to the end of the stones that littered the floor. But because of the echo, he was not fully understood.

Moving on, they made good progress now that the passageway was clear but the smell of bad eggs which they had joked about earlier was getting stronger. They walked on engulfed in the tunnel's silence and eerie blackness. Even the shuffling sound of their shoes was sounding eerier by the minute because of the echo, as were the noises that they themselves were making, like someone clearing his throat, or someone sniffing. Each and every sound was being stretched out until it became unrecognisable. Golcho, who was so glad he was in the middle of the group, thought he was quietly having a heart attack. Having seen Bud

Abbott and Lou Costello's film *Meet the Mummy*, starring Boris Karloff as the mummy, was not helping, especially as the duo had been walking along a tunnel very similar to this one. They too were unable to see much. But how funny it had been in the cinema, and how unfunny it was now. Golcho decided he was never, ever going to climb down Harry's Rock again.

Suddenly, what little flame they had was about to go out. Speaking as slowly as he could, hoping to be understood, Sparrow asked if anyone had anything that would burn. With a quick search through their pockets, no one did. Because his fingers were beginning to burn, Sparrow said he was sorry then plunged them into total darkness. For about ten seconds no one moved or said anything. But in those ten seconds, Sparrow blew on his fingers: Twab said 'Oh, oh:' Champ thought what a mess they were in, and Golcho, poor old Golcho, was having a heart attack.

A few moments later, they slowly became aware of the water they had heard dripping. Plip-plop, plip-plop, plip-plop. It sounded so eerie. Golcho gripped Twab's left arm so tight that Twab bumped his head on the low ceiling. Golcho, while Twab was rubbing his head, shrieked out a jumble of words that no one understood. The echo was ten times worse now. Golcho's words, had they been understood were, 'Oh shit, that's all I need.' Seeing the funny side, Sparrow began to chuckle knowing he should not do so. He also felt a wind-up coming on.

'Don't hold my arm so tight Golch,' said Twab, not that he was understood. With a jolt he broke free of Golcho's vice-like grip. Rubbing his arm Twab said, 'You were hurting me.'

'Let's go back before it's too late,' replied Golcho, not that he was understood.

But speaking ever so slowly Sparrow chirped in with, 'Let's go on.'

When everyone fell silent, Sparrow said while listening to the water that was plip-plopping up ahead somewhere, 'We've never been in this far before. There just might be some light up ahead, who knows?' Not that he was understood either.

Wanting desperately to go back and speaking much too fast Golcho blurted out that he was not going on, adding that they could not see a bloody thing, with 'bloody thing' being the only words that were understood. Deciding to play the sympathy card he blurted out, 'I've already bumped my head and it's bleeding. Again, all that was understood was, 'I've,' and 'bleeding'.

Twab was becoming irritable and needed to re-establish order. Guessing what Golcho had just said, and speaking as slowly as he could, he said, 'You haven't bumped your head Golch, and nor is it bleeding.' He then shouted at everyone to be quiet as he was trying to think. But, because he had shouted, the only words that were understood, which went racing down the tunnel like a pair of race horses were, 'to think' which seemed to go on and on. Then, after another think, he agreed with Sparrow that they should go on. Who knew what might be found up ahead?

When the echo dissipated, Twab, speaking one word at a time, reiterated that although they had never been in this far before he also wanted to see what was up ahead. In other words they were going on, and that was an end to it.

Because the echo was now so bad (the only words that could be understood were 'end of it'), they all fell into an eerie silence, so much so that the dripping water, wherever it was, was all they could hear, apart from their breathing and the odd clearing of someone's throat.

Guessing their leader was angry, the silence continued with every-one just standing around waiting to see if they were going on or going back. But Golcho's heart sunk. He had heard most of Twab's words, especially those that said he wanted to see what was up ahead. He had felt sure that Twab of all people would have sided with him and decided to go back, but they were going on.

Giving Golcho what comfort they could, and with Sparrow suggest-ing they raise their right arm to touch the ceiling to prevent them bumping their heads, and keeping contact with the person in front with the other arm, they plodded on with Sparrow leading as best he could. Because he was usually tail-end-Charlie, Sparrow was beginning to wish he was not leading the expedition. He was not afraid of the dark, well, not normal dark, but this was not normal dark. You could feel it. It was like a vice clamping you. He led them on by feeling his way along the tunnel having decided that he was not going to use up his last two matches as they would be wanting a smoke when it was over.

After several yards they realised that the dripping water was becoming much more distinct and that they were walking in puddles of at least an inch deep. And the smell of bad eggs was getting stronger. They stopped and the silence that far in the tunnel was very eerie. No one had ever experienced anything like it before – it was deafening. As for the darkness, Golcho felt as if a sack had been placed over his head. None of them had ever been in such an environment before where you were not only in total darkness, as blind as bats as Golcho would have said, but one where it was so hard to understand the person next to you speaking. Champ's only comparison to anything like this was when he had played in the air-raid shelter in Chester. But it was not really like this. In the tunnel each sentence just carried on and on, only the first and last words of each sentence being understood and even then not all the time. With Golcho having to be reassured by the minute that they were not in any immediate danger and that nothing was going to happen, they listened to the dripping water up ahead which was amazing.

Gripping Twab's arm again, Golcho asked if they could go back. Twab, at the back, explained that the dripping water was not going to suddenly come rushing down and drown them. It was just water dripping off the roof and plip-plopping onto the floor, creating the little pools they were now walking through. But he was not understood.

Trying hard to overcome his fear Golcho managed to quieten down and listened to the drips of water plip, plopping, but it was no good, his fear was rising. Speaking as slowly as he could, hoping to be understood, Golcho said he accepted the explanation but felt it was not safe to go on, but his request to go back was again turned down. Speaking one word at a time, Twab insisted that they just listen a while as he was finding the dripping water fascinating as was Sparrow.

In the darkness, with Golcho only a little pacified, the dripping water began to sound like musical notes. Twab, who was learning to play the piano, appreciated it, as did Sparrow and Champ, up to a point. But poor old Golcho was at breaking point. This place was so claustrophobic and he felt it was closing in on him. Between the dark (which he hated), the dripping water (which he hated) and the lads not taking any notice of him (which he hated), it was just a matter of time before he snapped. So, as calmly and as slowly as he could, he again asked if they could go back having had enough now. As they could neither see nor understand what was being said, he felt he was not asking too much? He omitted to mention the fact that he was afraid of the dark. That was his business. All he was asking for was a little common sense.

At last, Twab listened to reason and decided it was silly to go on. It was no longer a novelty having to feel your way along, unable to understand anything that was being said, and the smell of bad eggs was getting stronger. To Golcho's delight, Twab gave the order to about turn. As they set off, Twab could not decide whether it was Golcho's elation or panic that caused him to grip his arm so tight, but whatever it was, Twab's arm felt like it was in a vice. Somewhat angry he asked his friend not to grip his arm so tight as he was hurting him. But the only words anyone understood were 'Don't' and 'Me.' Seeing the funny side, Sparrow began to giggle. Golcho's fear of the dark was once more funny, so much so that he was going to wind him up again.

Speaking as slowly as he could, Sparrow said, 'Hey, wouldn't it be a bugger if we couldn't get out of here and they found us all dead in about a week's time?'

Speaking as slowly as he could Golcho, who had understood the gist of what Sparrow had said, threatened him with a bunch of fives if he did not pack it in. The others then burst out laughing as Golcho could not see Sparrow let alone hit him. The laughter not only filled the tunnel, but gave Sparrow time enough to crouch down and search for a stone. Finding one, he began to scratch the wall. His order to be quiet lasted for ages. Then his 'What's that noise,' mingled with his, 'Quiet.'

Golcho's 'What noise?' also mingled with Sparrow's, 'Quiet' and 'What's that noise.' Scratching the wall again Sparrow's, 'There it is again' seemed to over ride Golcho's, 'What noise' and Sparrow's earlier 'Quiet.'

Standing there in the dark with only Golcho's heavy breathing and the dripping water dripping in the distance, everyone listened to the mysterious scratching which seemed to be coming at them from all sides. Wishing he could see Golcho's face, Sparrow said it sounded like it was coming through the wall, and then scratched the wall again. It sounded very much like when someone scratched a blackboard with their nails. Twab ordered everyone to listen, adding, 'There it is again.'

No one realised it was Sparrow playing a joke, but sure enough the scratching was there, and yes, it did seem to be coming through the wall. Knowing where everyone was in the tunnel, Sparrow nudged Twab and then Champ in such a way that they suddenly realized it was him who was making the noise, thus getting at Golcho. Twab, a strong believer in ghosts, was rather pleased that it was only a joke and for a moment began to wonder what in blue blazes was going on.

Champ on the other hand, a non believer in such things had already twigged that it was someone fooling around. But to keep the joke going they all went along with it at Golcho's expense. Winding him up again, Sparrow began to breathe like the devil and it was a very good impersonation. He only had to do it a couple of times. That's how good it was.

Convinced it was the devil Golcho gripped Twab's arm even tighter. Twab was so convinced that there wasn't any blood reaching his fingers he told Golcho to ease off, adding that his fingers were going numb. But because Twab had spoken quickly his words were all jumbled up.

So too were Golcho's plea, 'Come on fellows, let's get out of here.'

Again speaking and not being understood, Twab said he thought they'd better move on as he could definitely hear something.

Picking out Twab's, 'move on,' was music to Golcho's ears. In his elation he slackened his grip on his leader's arm. Twab could suddenly feel blood flowing again. In fact he had pins and needles for a while, but still going along with the joke while rubbing his arm he said he thought this place was haunted with spirits that couldn't rest.

That did it. Poor old Golcho couldn't stand it any longer and so yelled out his fear and frustration and deafened everyone. His yells filled up the tunnel with even more chaos (as if that were possible). He was so nervous he began to break wind rather loudly. Everyone wished they could see his face but when they realized just how much he was farting, everyone became hysterical.

With tears running down his cheeks and remembering last weekend when Golcho was taking the mickey out of him for treading in that cowpat down the Hafod, Twab said he thought Golcho was shitting himself. Not that he was understood.

Because he was panicking Golcho began to feel his way along the tunnel wall. He was, I suppose abandoning ship. He'd had enough. He was going to find his own way to the shaft bottom come hell or high water.

Golcho's uncontrollable farting, in echo, caused the lads to fall about. Not only were Twab's ribs hurting, but his nose was running. Sparrow found he was wetting himself, while Champ leaned on the tunnel wall helpless with laughter while trying to wipe his eyes. In need of a wee, Sparrow undid his fly and in the dark began to urinate, down Champ's leg.

Realizing what was happening, Champ stepped out of the flow and banged his head on the wall. Rubbing it he began to howl with laughter. The tunnel suddenly reverberated with their laughter because of Golcho's farting.

Having reached the shaft bottom and somewhat angry with his mates, Golcho could only listen to their hysterical laughter coming at him from within the tunnel. Never again he told himself would he be climbing down this stupid shaft. Today's teasing was the last straw.

Some fifteen minutes later when the others came into view, Golcho stubbed out his fag end and not one for holding a grudge (well not for too long) asked if they were ready to climb out of this stupid place.

Watching Golcho climb the shaft wall and still laughing, Twab and the others in their turn tried to explain that it was only a joke and that it was high time he grew up and stopped being afraid of the dark.

'You're twelve years old for goodness sake,' Sparrow scowled.

But Golcho ignored him. He wasn't even amused when told that Sparrow had weed down Champ's leg. But at the top of the shaft and back in the glorious sunshine, he began to see the funny side and started to chuckle to himself. But not before telling the lads off for not showing him any regard while they were down in the stupid tunnel, the one that he was never going to step foot in ever again. Knowing Golcho was still vexed with them, Twab was the first to admit that they may have gone too far with him that time.

Still giggling and unrepentant, it was after all only a joke, Sparrow began to climb the wall, followed by Champ. Twab as leader was the last man up. He would not have had it any other way. But when he peered over the lip of the shaft and saw Sparrow and Champ sitting by Golcho trying to cheer him up, he smiled. Golcho was taking full advantage of the fuss he was being given and Twab, when he sat down in the long grass, asked him if he was alright and put his arm around him and gave him a squeeze. Winking at the others he said, 'Didn't realize you was that afraid of the dark, Golch.'

For the next ten minutes Golcho sat there with his mates taking the Mickey out of him for being afraid of the dark. There was no point in fighting back. He was not bothered, now that he was back in the sunshine. They could take the mickey all they wanted.

They all commented on the echo and how it seemed to get worse the further they went into the tunnel. Twab said he wished they had stayed down there a little longer, if only to listen to the dripping water. He had found the sound fascinating (he was, after all, learning to play the piano). Every plop had sounded like a musical note. Both Champ and Sparrow agreed with him.

When Champ asked about the explosion down Gresford, Sparrow said it happened in 1934, at about half-past one in the morning. According to his dad, who was a miner, the explosion happened on a Friday night and that 265 men who worked 'Down the Slant', the district where the explosion had occurred, were killed. There was, apparently, a football match being played on the Saturday afternoon, Wrexham, versus … but Sparrow could not remember who. Some of the men wanting to see the match worked a double shift on the Friday night hoping to cheer Wrexham on, but were killed instead. He then added that all the men they could not get out were still down underground. The area of the explosion had been sealed off and, if you could somehow get behind the wall, it would be possible to see the men who died. Sparrow then said they would look as if they were asleep. Apparently the rescue team had come across a fourteen-year-old boy, sat at the engine he was in charge of, his snapping tin open – but the gas had got him.

Because the story was so depressing, Sparrow tried to impress everyone by trying to blow a smoke ring through another. He was determined he would do it one day, but after several failed attempts, he gave up.

Suddenly, not that he was expecting anything, Champ was congratulated for climbing down Harry's Rock. His hand was not only shaken the Roman way, but for the first time, the English way. Twab then suggested they go home, have dinner and meet up by the lamp post outside his house at two o'clock. They never knew that, had they gone three strides further along the tunnel from where Twab made the decision to about turn, a very serious accident could have occurred. All the drips of water which they thought sounded like musical notes, had filled up a depression. Had they struggled one of them would have fallen into water way over his head, the consequences of which could only be imagined. Golcho's fear of the dark had probably saved their lives.

At ten past two, the lads met up by Twab's gate. Sparrow was ticked off by Twab for being late, to reciprocate for Sparrow having ticked him off that morning for being late. What goes around comes around, was Twab's thinking. When it was suggested that Champ be taken to Nant Mill Woods, seeing as he's never been there, they all agreed and set off.

Reaching the end of Twab's street, Heol Islwyn, they turned left and were soon on the bottom road, Heol Offa, with Ty'n y Coed Farm facing them. When Champ had been told about the best scrumping places in the village, Ty'n y Coed's orchard had been one of them. There was a high wall to climb, but the climb was well worth it. Here they turned right and fifty yards on came to a crossroads. Twab brought the procession to a halt. Looking up New Road, a little side street, he informed Champ that years ago, when everyone wore rags, there were stocks here. According to a library book from which he had gathered this information, people were actually put in them for a day or two for being drunk and disorderly and other such crimes, including stealing and petty theft. Champ thought that throwing rotten fruit at those in the stocks would have been great fun. So too did Sparrow and Golcho.

Opposite New Road was Tan Lan, a little B-road that took you to the village of Southsea which had a park with swings, slides and a great roundabout. Champ said he would not mind being taken there one day. It was then pointed out that New Road was where they had finally felt safe the day Alum chased them through Southsea, the day Golcho suggested that Alum was born out of wedlock.

Moving on, they passed a row of houses set back off the road where Big Bill, the local milkman lived. They then came across Harold Rogers' house. Harold, a very clever lad who everyone knew was going to end up in Wrexham's Grove Park School, had a fantastic pile of American comics. Opposite his house were fields that extended as far as the eye could see, and a very famous mound of earth. Scrambling onto the mound which was about five-feet high and sixty-feet long, with its accompanying ditch, Champ was told that he was actually standing on the dyke built by King Offa who, Champ was told, was the king of Mercia (Hereford, Shropshire, Cheshire, Worcestershire and Gloucestershire) from 757 AD to 796 AD which, according to Twab was the Dark Ages. Twab decreed that the dyke was built not to keep the English out, but to keep the Welsh in. When Sparrow mentioned the Great Wall of China, Twab agreed that the dyke was nowhere near as long, or as great, but added that it was very impressive in some other parts of Wales. Champ had to admit that he had never heard of Offa's Dyke, or the king, but was impressed with Twab's knowledge of the old fellow. How he had kept the peace with his law and order was a mystery but he seemed a decent bloke. When the history lesson was over, Champ asked what it was in the distance that he was pointing at and was told it was Wrexham Parish Church, three miles away. Golcho declared that his uncle, had a pair of German binoculars that, on a clear day, would show them the time on the church's clock.

Sliding down the dyke onto the road, the lads moved on towards the main Wrexham to Ruthin road, the A525, a mere 200 yards down from Lloft Wen Lane, and they were suddenly facing Rhos Berse Road.

As they approached the main road, some singing which they had heard while standing on the dyke became much louder. When they reached the little chapel it was coming from, Champ asked if they could listen for a while. The little sandstone chapel was the very last building on Heol Offa, but, never having heard Welsh singing before, Champ was very much impressed and said so. He thought the harmonies were fantastic, not that he understood the words, being in Welsh. According to Twab, Sparrow and Golcho, the congregation was singing *Calon Lan*, a lovely Welsh hymn. All three of them knew the words and, on Twab's nod, they joined in with the singing while Champ listened. They were all good singers thought Champ who, using his hand as a baton, conducted them through the last verse.

Moving on, they crossed over the main road and began to walk along Rhos Berse Road with its fantastic sandstone, crenellated wall on their left, which was at least twelve feet high. On the other side of the wall was the Adwy Wood, which (as he had heard before) was only ever visited when the goosies were ready sometime in May. The goosies were had by either climbing up and over the wall or going through an entrance just a little way down the main road. The only other good thing about Adwy Wood was the big ditch that had a large, bushy plant that no one knew what it was called, but which made excellent pea-shooters in the autumn when the Hawthorn berries were ripe.

Still wanting to beat Champ in a race, if only the once, Twab raced away and announced that the farm gate on the bend up ahead was the winning post.

'You sneaky sod,' yelled Sparrow as he and the others gave chase.

With the winning post in sight and determined he was going to win, Champ dug down for that extra gear and overtook Golcho, then Sparrow, and chased after Twab. Catching up level with him and knowing it was annoying him, Champ pulled faces before racing away. Twenty yards on, leaning smugly against the winning post, he waited for them to come in.

Puffing somewhat, and aiming his anger at Twab for being so sneaky, yet again, Golcho said he could not understand why Twab wanted to beat Champ. Why was it so important? He was like a bloody racehorse when he got going. Doubled over, with hands on knees and puffing like mad, Sparrow bet a shilling that Champ could run faster than Queenie. Smiling at the compliment, Champ repeated that it was seeing them as tigers that gave him that extra gear needed to outrun them, plus the fact he was a non smoker.

With their breath back, Twab suggested their next stop be the turnstile some thirty yards on. As they strolled past the last of the five houses on their right, houses that were once farm buildings, an apple tree, standing proud in the middle of the back garden of the last house, was pointed out to champ with the comment that the tree would be visited when the fruit (which was coming on very nicely) was ripe, as it had been for the last two years.

The turnstile which was built into Rhos Berse Road's most magnificent sandstone wall signified another public right of way. By taking the short cut, you would end up in the village of Bersham, some three miles away, having experienced some lovely countryside. Everyone in the Adwy, young and old alike, was very fond of the turnstile and it was often heard in conversation that 'They don't make um like that anymore'. Twab himself was very interested in its history and Mr Davies, the history teacher in school, was in fact trying to find out when exactly it was built, but as yet had not come up with any dates.

The wall, at least a mile long, ran the full length of Rhos Berse Road and ended at Nant Mill bridge. All this prime land belonged to Colonel FitzHugh and was being farmed on a large scale. At potato picking time, people from the Adwy were hired to help.

Having reached the turnstile and jumped on the bottom rung, Twab, Sparrow and Golcho insisted that Champ push them round and round. The turnstile, in dire need of some grease, squeaked like mad as he spun the lads. Then, one by one, they jumped off field side. Golcho then spun Champ round and round for several minutes until he had had enough. The moment Champ jumped off, the turnstile screeched to a stop.

With their backs to the wall, the lads sat there looking out across Colonel FitzHugh's land very much enjoying the view. There was not one house or building to be seen, just fields, fields and more fields.

A Woodbine cigarette was broke in half with Sparrow and Golcho enjoying a smoke. In his determination to emulate Terry, Sparrow made several attempts at blowing one smoke ring through another, but gave up because of Twab's grinning and boasting that he was no longer a smoker. Twab was deliberately blowing the rings out of shape so as to upset Sparrow.

Soaking up the sunshine, while chewing on a stalk of grass, Twab told them that just a few weeks earlier he and his sisters, Hilary and Brenda and another fifty or so people from the village, were paid 2/6 for picking potatoes. Twab explained how you had to stand to one side while the tractor ran down the field exposing the potatoes, with you then picking them all up from your little patch and delivering them in sacks to one of the stations before the tractor returned. Then, back at your post, you did it all over again. Twab said it was alright in the morning, but by the afternoon, he had found it boring. He also said it was no wonder his back ached, having picked about a million spuds.

With the story and smoke break over, and with Champ pushing them for one last pirouetting session on the turnstile, the lads jumped off one by one onto the roadside. As they walked along, it was explained to Champ that the apple tree they had just passed was scrumped. It was simply a question of coming across the fields in the dark and sneaking into the garden. While one acted as look-out, the others filled their pockets, making sure there was enough to give the lookout his fair share.

The high hawthorn hedge on their right, which up till now had hidden the wall and blocked out a most fantastic view, petered out and gave access to the low stone crenulated wall, plus acres of open farm land with Minera Mountain dominating the view. Climbing onto the wall, Twab led the lads along or rather skipped along what he always called the castle wall.

'Look Champ,' said Sparrow pointing to a wooded area in the distance to their right, 'That's Harry's Rock over there.' Golcho kept a low profile when Sparrow, trying to wind him up, asked him if he wanted to go there. As Golcho skipped along the wall he told himself that he was never, ever going to Harry's Rock again – and meant it.

Reaching the end of the wall they came across a five-bar gate that ran across the entrance to Kynaston's Farm. It was Kynaston's land they had crossed that morning on their way to Harry's Rock. Champ judged that the path which led up to the farm was about 200 yards long and he did not fancy being their paper boy. But, looking at the gate, Twab announced that he was going to attempt to walk across the top rung like a tight-rope walker. There was a lot of tight-rope walking in a circus film he had seen with James Stewart playing the part of a clown. 'Watch this you lot,' he said, as he placed his right foot on the gate which was about a foot higher than the wall. With his arms outstretched for balance, he placed his right foot on the top rung then very carefully brought up his left foot and, feeling confident, set off very carefully, placing one foot in front of the other while at all times looking ahead. When he made it across and stepped onto the far wall, he was given some tremendous applause. Turning to face his audience, Twab gave them a big smile and a bow that any Japanese would have been proud of before jumping down onto the grass verge.

Looking up at Sparrow, who was next in line, Twab dared him to see if he could do it? Thinking it would be easy, Sparrow placed his right foot on the gate, but as he brought his left leg up, began to wobble and fell off. While being booed and laughed at, Twab assured him that he had fallen because he had not used his arms for balance. Sparrow huffed and said it was a stupid game.

Next to go was Golcho. Taking his time, and with Twab's advice, he raised his arms for balance, set off and slowly but surely made his way across by very carefully putting one foot in front of the other while trying not to look down. With just three strides to go and feeling confident, he gave his audience a bow which caused him to wobble and fall off. Among the booing and applause he received, Golcho, in a most terrible French accent said, 'And now, Monsieur Chemp Fletchure, it is yew tern.'

When all the laughing died down, Champ gave a bow and stepping onto the gate pretended to wobble causing the lads to burst out laughing. But being serious, he raised his arms for balance and set off very carefully. When he was half way, and thinking Champ was going to make it, but wanting him to fail, wanting to be the only winner, Twab began to shake the gate ever so slightly. Seeing what he was up to, Sparrow and Golcho both wondered if Champ was going to fall off or what?

'Oi, whoever it is, pack it in,' Champ yelled as he struggled to keep his balance. 'You're gonna make me fall.' Moments later he did fall, on the inside of the gate. 'That's it,' he yelled, 'now you're for it.' Laughing the lads ran off. Climbing over the gate and seeing that one of his shoe laces was undone, Champ fastened it while watching the lads running down the hill. The moment his lace was done up he set off after them at full pelt. Running down the hill as far as the bend, Twab and Golcho stopped when they realised that Sparrow was not with them. Looking back, there was no sign of him. Sparrow had scrambled up the embankment and was hiding in the bushes that ran parallel with the road.

Running past Sparrow, Champ caught up with Twab and Golcho who were now waiting for him. When he heard their plan, Champ joined in with them. They were going to play a joke on Sparrow. Running to the bottom of the hill and turning left at the junction, they began to look for somewhere to hide. In desperation they climbed up and over the high wall on their left and huddled together.

Realising his plan had gone wrong and after a good old swear for not having stayed with the others, Sparrow slid down the embankment and went after them. Turning left at the junction with Nant Mill Bridge some 200 yards away and with no one in sight, he twigged that they were playing a joke on him. Picking up a handful of stones he began to throw them at the bushes he suspected them to be hiding behind. Hearing their friend's cursing and suppressing their giggles, Twab, Golcho and Champ peeped over the wall and watched Sparrow sneaking up to a bush and cursing when no one was there.

Suddenly realising where they had to be hiding, Sparrow climbed up the wall and saw his chums all huddled together and began to pelt them with what stones he had. Realising there was nowhere for them to run, all three raised their hands and surrendered. Back on the road, Sparrow was teased something rotten. Had he obeyed orders, they would have been teasing Champ instead of him.

Now that they were friends again, Champ was shown a clump of sweet chestnut trees and Golcho asked him if he liked chestnuts. Champ said he did not know, never having tasted any.

'They are delicious,' said Sparrow. Pointing the trees out he said, 'You see all those green prickly looking things that look like conkers, well, there's two nuts inside every one of them casings.'

The clump of five trees was heavily cropped, but because they were so out of reach, Champ asked how they were reached?

'Well, you can either wait for them to fall,' said Sparrow, 'or you can do what we do; throw sticks at them. Very often you hit one or two of them.'

'The nuts look like baby conkers,' said Twab, adding that once they had scraped all the fluffy hair off, they tasted lovely and crunchy.

'Sadly though,' Golcho put in, 'they won't be ready until the end of October, which means they're not ready yet, it being only June.'

Walking on, Champ noticed a rather large stone jutting out of the wall which he thought would make a good seat. That seat Twab told him was supposed to be magic. According to his Taid, the stone belonged to the fairies of those ancient woods who would give 'those who hath been good a wish.'

'Don't you mean those who have been good,' Champ corrected him.

'No, I don't,' said Twab, adding that was how his grandad spoke.

'How he spoke?' Champ queried.

'Well, he died two years ago of a heart attack, and Taid didn't talk like you or me,' Going on with his wind up, Twab asked Champ if he wanted a demonstration on how he used to talk? Nodding, Champ said he would.

'Well,' said Twab, 'he caught me one day looking for birds' nests in the hedgerows and because he did not like me doing that he said, speaking like this, 'Oi seed ya looking for burr's nesses in yonder hedgerows. But when oi shakes me fisses at ya to heed ya to stop, ya no seed me.'

Not sure if his leg was being pulled, Champ looked at the others for some kind of confirmation but none was given.

'And that's how he used to talk?' Champ asked not quite believing it.

'Yea,' said Twab who then crossed his heart and hoped to die. For the record, Champ believed that story all through his life. In fact he told his children about it when they were young.

Meanwhile, and referring to the stone, Golcho said it was true about the fairies giving those who had been good a wish. He firmly believed it. Pushing everyone aside he said, 'Let me show you how it's done, Champ.' Sitting on the stone he closed his eyes and made a wish.

'So what did you wish for?' Champ asked when Golcho opened his eyes.

'You don't tell anyone,' said Golcho, tutting him, 'it doesn't work if you do. Your wish is between you and the fairies.'

Champ sat on the stone, closed his eyes and, half expecting the lads to run off laughing, made a wish. When he opened his eyes and feeling a little silly he said he did not think an ordinary looking stone like this could give wishes. It was ages before anyone answered. Finally Golcho said he was given an air rifle last Christmas having wished for one. But Sparrow contradicted him, saying it had never worked for him. Nothing that he had wished for had ever been granted.

'I don't think it works either,' said Twab. 'Oh, and while we're on the subject of Christmas .... '

'Who mentioned Christmas?' interrupted Sparrow.

'He did,' said Twab pointing at Golcho, 'When he mentioned his air rifle. The thing is, I'm not sure I believe in Father Christmas any more.'

'What!!!' said Golcho not believing his ears? 'What did you say?'

'I said, I'm not sure I believe in Father Christmas anymore.' Looking at everyone in turn Twab said, 'I haven't told anyone, but last

Christmas I actually saw my mam and dad putting my presents on the bottom of my bed and when I asked them about it during Christmas dinner they said I must have been dreaming, insisting that there really is a Father Christmas.'

'Well, I think he's real,' said Golcho most emphatically. Turning to Sparrow and Champ he asked what their thoughts were on the subject.

After what seemed like ages Champ said, 'Well I think I'm with Twab on this one. I only go along with it now for Jeannie's sake.'

Golcho could not believe what Champ had just said. Turning to Sparrow he said, 'Well, what about you? Do you think he's real?'

Just as Sparrow was about to answer, and wishing he had kept his mouth shut, Twab said, 'Just think about it Golch. How on earth can one man …'

'He's not a man,' interrupted Golcho irritably kicking at a clump of grass. 'He's Father bloody Christmas and he's real. I don't care what you say; he's real, so there.'

'Okay then,' said Twab, slightly angered and determined to go on with it. 'Tell me this, how can one Father Christmas deliver presents all over the world in one night, huh. Go on clever clogs, tell me that, then?'

'He gets all the elves and fairies to help out, doesn't he,' said Golcho beginning to see his backside with Twab and this conversation.

'Well, if that was true,' said Twab, all fired up now, 'there'd be thousands of them up there in Lapland, but you never hear about them on the radio or in the papers at Christmas time, do you.' Refusing to comment Golcho began to kick the grass again.

'The fact is Golch,' said Twab, 'he's not real, and the sooner you realise it, the sooner you'll grow up. You have to grow up sometime you know. You'll be thirteen and a teenager next birthday.'

Golcho again failed to answer but just kept on kicking the grass.

Sparrow said he had heard Norman Williams say that it is your mam and dad who put any presents you were having on the bed. 'What I'd like to know is,' Sparrow went on, 'how does he get down a dirty chimney all nice and clean? And what does he do if the fire's still in?'

'He's much too fat to get down a chimney,' insisted Twab.

'And another thing,' Sparrow went on, 'How does he manage to stay sober with all that port and sherry that's left out for him?'

Golcho, who was about to explode, yelled out, 'Shut up, the lot of you! You're doing my head in!' With his arms flailing he went on, 'He's real and that's all there is to it. If you lot don't want to believe in him that's fine with me, but I, Golcho Jones, of 1 Heol Wen, Adwy, Coedpoeth, near Wrexham, still happen to believe in him, so there, and sod the lot of you!' With that he stormed off towards the bridge with his head all mixed up. Turning back he yelled, 'We'll see whether he's real or not on Christmas morning won't we, when you lot have been left a load of old cinders, errrr.'

Twab stood there wishing he had never started the conversation. He was all fidgety and regretted all he had said. So for the sake of tempers being lost, he decided he was never ever going to mention Father Christmas again while Golcho was around. Each one was entitled to his own opinion, was going to be the policy from now on when it came to Golcho and Father bloody Christmas.

It was not a pretty sight seeing Golcho slumping down the road towards the bridge with his hands stuffed in his pockets; not that Golcho ever held a grudge for long. He usually came bouncing back after a few minutes.

So, instructing the others to tread carefully, Twab suggested they go after their old mate and make it up with him. They met up with Golcho on the bridge where all appeared to be well. He was simply staring over the parapet, at what, nobody knew.

Having to reach up on their tip toes to see over this much larger crenellated wall (something Golcho did not have to do as he was several inches taller), Twab apologised and said he was sorry, as did Sparrow and Champ. Now that peace had been restored it was the look on Champ's face, staring down the forty-foot drop to the river below that got things moving again. Champ was amazed with the river Clywedog's white water as it went rushing by. This river was much more alive than their little woods river.

On Twab's order they began to spit at the river to see who could spit the furthest. During the contest several wood pigeons, disturbed by all the shouting that accompanied the spitting, flew into the air and disappeared deeper into the wood. Other birds were heard but not seen.

It was the river's torrent that held Champ in awe for several minutes. It reminded him of the film, *Winchester 73*, where James Stewart and his on-screen brother were shooting at each other on some rocks with the river rushing by.

In places, the Clywedog's white water looked dangerous. Champ was also amazed at how much more densely packed this wood was than their little wood. But suddenly fed up with the spitting competition and wanting to liven things up, Twab went in search of what he and the lads called helicopters.

Seeing what Twab was doing, Sparrow, and Golcho, who was back to his old self again, went after him. Champ was left on the bridge admiring the view and pondering why there was an old worn-away tree trunk lying directly below him in a deep pool of water which had apparently been there for more years than anyone could remember. But when he saw the lads picking things up off the road he slid off the bridge wall and went over to them and asked what they were doing?

'Well, these funny looking things,' said Twab showing Champ what they were picking up, 'are Sycamore seeds from those trees over there.' Twab pointed at the trees and explained that not only had the seeds floated down this far, which was a long way, but if you followed the road you would end up in the village of Bersham about two miles away. When Champ asked if it was the same Bersham as the one that was pointed out to him earlier when they were pirouetting on the turnstile, he was told it was. Placing one of the seeds in Champ's hand, as they made their way back to the bridge, Twab said, 'Come and see what we do with them.'

Jumping up and leaning over the bridge's parapet, Twab gave a set of orders, 'Extend right arm. Be ready to drop.' With that, three arms extended over the abyss and on Twab's order, three Sycamore seeds were released and were watched as they began to spin their way down to the river like helicopters.

Champ was flabbergasted and yelled out a long 'Wow!' He then admitted that they were fantastic helicopters. He watched, mesmerized, as the three seeds floated down and away from the bridge ever so gracefully. It was magical.

'On my mark,' said Twab and three more seeds were released which immediately began to spin. Then three more were dropped, followed by three more. It was a fantastic spectacle. All eyes were glued onto the spinning helicopters as they coasted gently away from the bridge. On reaching the river, they each in turn were swept away by the current. Agreeing with Champ that it was a fantastic sight, the lads raced off the bridge to find more seeds when their supply ran out.

After some ten minutes and wanting to go on, and a little fed up with the game now, Twab ordered the lads to follow him. Champ while following tried to work out why the seeds spun the way they did. He noted that the seed itself, about the size of a pea, was attached to a wing which was about an inch long that had been very cleverly designed to catch the wind. While marvelling at this, and because he was falling behind, he was told by Twab to get a move on, he could study the seed later. The seed was designed to catch the wind and float away from the parent tree. If it fell like a stone, the seed could be damaged and would therefore not germinate, and it would not be allowed to germinate close to the parent tree.

Climbing over the bridge parapet, the lads slid down the forty-foot steep bank on their heels and bums and, reaching the bottom, stood on the stony beach some ten feet away from the river's edge.

Looking up at the bridge and mesmerised by the excitement of being there, Champ was amazed at how much bigger and different the bridge looked from down here. He admired its shape, especially the arch, and wondered how a bridge of this size and shape was built in the first place? He wondered if Mr Davies, the history teacher would be able to tell him.

Nudging Champ and having to shout over the rush of water, and pointing to the old tree trunk that had lain there for as long as anyone could remember, Sparrow said that his dad and his mates had used it as a diving board when they were young and swam in the pool. He then said it was still deep enough to swim in, but was very cold.

Also having to shout above the roar of water, Twab told Champ his all-time favourite story of last year when they were frog hunting. Knowing there are frogs in the area, Twab, on seeing this lovely green one sitting on the tree trunk, raced over hoping to catch it, but as he approached, it spotted him and dived head-first into the water.

'And guess what the silly bugger did,' yelled Golcho pointing at Twab who was grinning like a Cheshire cat. But before Champ could ask, Golcho said, 'He only waded in after the bloody thing.'

Looking at Twab, and having to shout, Champ asked if he had caught it?

'I certainly did,' Twab yelled over the rush of water, adding that the clout he had off his mam for going in wet was well worth it. The lads had never seen a frog so green before.

Turning to Sparrow and Golcho and frowning, Twab said he had that frog for ages until next door's cat got through the fence.

'Why, what happened?' Champ asked.

'He only ate it,' said Golcho trying not to laugh.

When the laughing and trying to wind Twab up had died down, and wondering how deep the pool was, Champ asked that very question. Twab motioned with his hand that it was chest deep, but emphasised it was very cold. 'As you can see,' he said pointing, 'because of the bridge being so high it never gets the sun. It's more than cold, its freezing.'

With several large stones thrown in for the splash, the lads moved on. Scrambling over the rocks and stones at the river's edge, they wormed their way along and eventually reached a second stony beach some fifty yards down river.

All four had wet feet. While the others were gathering stones to throw in the water, Champ looked back the way they had come and began to feel an excitement far stronger than when in their little woods. He decided this wood was a forest. The trees, being much closer together than those in their little wood, was not only fantastic, but was – somehow primeval. His overall feeling was of being swallowed up. How little man is in the scheme of things he thought?

Champ suddenly knew how Tarzan must have felt living in the jungle, at one with it. He then began to question what the attraction was in being in a forest of this size and this close to a river of this magnitude. His life has been so enriched from living in the Adwy and he would have to do a lot of serious thinking about these matters one day. He was so excited at being in these surroundings that he suddenly realised that he could no longer see the bridge, although it was only fifty yards away. His mind was so taken up with the roar of the river, and the environment in general. He felt he was in a primeval landscape and loved it.

The bird song was clear but the birds themselves could not be seen due to the foliage and density of the trees, bushes and scrub. This environment was giving Champ a picture of how it may have been when the Romans first came to this country. Prodding Twab on the shoulder he said, 'As much as I love our little woods, they are nothing when compared to this. You couldn't play here the way we do in our woods. You can't move for all the trees and things.'

'Yea, it's not only denser, it's also longer and wider than our little wood,' said Twab. Nodding to his left he said, 'It goes all the way to Bersham that way, and Minera that way. But you have to be careful in here because it's a privately-owned wood. If they catch you in here you could be taken to Wrexham and fined.'

Having reached calmer water, Golcho suggested they show Champ how they bomb German warships. With the rules explained, the first German warship (in the form of a twig) came within range. The intention was to blast it out of the water. Champ was allowed to throw first, but was too slow. As he took aim, the river was suddenly peppered with stones of various sizes all trying to hit the target. When the bombing stopped there was no sign of the enemy warship, but another one was quickly found in the form of a leaf and was attacked. After some twenty minutes of sorting out the Germans, and getting wetter by the minute from going too close to the water in order to cheat, Sparrow suggested they move on to the first of the two waterfalls.

Scrambling up the steep bank by grabbing tree roots and clumps of grass, with quite a lot of slipping and sliding going on, the lads reached the top and began to run through the ancient forest with the river Clywedog on their left. Champ was amazed there were no paths or trails as such to run along. The forest, according to Twab, was virginal, not that Champ knew what that meant. But ten minutes on, the first of the two waterfalls was heard in the distance and several minutes later they reached their destination.

Standing on a flat, stony overhang that had been created by nature thousands of years ago, Champ (while the others gathered stones for throwing in the deep water) inched his way to the edge and looked down at the icy cold water some twenty-feet below. It looked so cold and forbidding and the volume of water going over the fall, and the splash it made in the pool below, was very impressive. Fear of falling in was so great that Champ stepped back a few paces. But wherever he looked, he thought his surroundings were magical. He imagined it must have been like this when men first went out with spears and clubs to hunt game while dressed in animal skins. Shouting over the waterfall's roar, breaking Champ's reverie, Sparrow warned everyone that a tree branch was about to go over the edge. All eyes watched as it toppled over and plunged into the pool below, making hardly a splash which was most disappointing. When it surfaced, it remained trapped for several moments then suddenly it freed itself and continued on its journey.

They each in turn threw the biggest stones they could find off the ledge into the icy cold water for the sheer pleasure of seeing the splash it made. They then scrambled down the steep slope, again using tree roots and clumps of grass, with a lot of slipping and sliding.

Standing on the muddy beach they all stared into what they knew was icy cold water on account of it never seeing the sun. This water Champ was told was much colder than the water by the bridge. When Twab knelt and took a drink, Champ followed suit and commented on how cold it was. Instead of quenching his thirst it burned his throat. But Golcho insisted it was not as cold as their secret water in the Hafod.

'I swam in there last year,' Sparrow announced while pointing at the pool 'but only for a minute as it was too cold. All my muscles began to tighten up the moment I waded in. I was out like a shot.'

'I don't think I'd like to swim in there,' said Champ, 'it's too scary for me.' He then asked if Twab or Golcho had ever swum in it? Both shook their heads indicating that they had not.

'Shall we go on to Bersham waterfall?' Twab suddenly asked.

'I'm game,' said Sparrow enthusiastically.

'Me too,' said Golcho.

'What about you Champ, would you like to see Bersham waterfall with its concrete steps?' Twab asked.

'Yea, I would,' said Champ, nodding.

'It's down that way,' said Twab, pointing, adding that if they got their skates on it would not take them long. Everyone threw one last stone into the pool to see who could make the biggest splash. Then they scrambled up the bank which proved a little tricky owing to the slipping and sliding, but they eventually reached the top where they once again ran through the ancient forest in the direction of Bersham waterfall.

All four commented on how nice it was being back in the sunshine, albeit broken sunshine due to the overhead canopy. Champ once again pointed out the dappled sunshine and thought it was so picturesque. One minute you were in sunshine, the next in shadow. He loved this ancient forest with its ancient trees standing majestically to attention with the sun's rays beaming down on them, sprinkling them and everything else with its life-giving force. As they raced on through the wonderful environment, they made a game of it by jumping over things like tree trunks that were breaking down, low branches and the like, and the plants that had gone to seed. It was great fun, but no one gave a thought to the fact that there were no nettles or brambles. There was so much enthusiasm given to their game of being in a time when dinosaurs ruled the world that they even imagined they were being chased by a very large, meat-eating dinosaur that no one could pronounce. Not one of them knew how to pronounce Tyrannosaurus Rex. Golcho brought the game to an end by mimicking a cave man.

'Ug, ug,' he grunted, while hiding behind a bush, causing everyone to laugh. Stepping into the open he began to wave his arms about like a monkey, but it was the jumping up and down with the monkey face he made by pulling his ears forward and pushing his lower lip out with his tongue that caused the others to fall about laughing.

'He thinks he's a cave man,' Sparrow laughed.

'He looks more like Cheeta than Cheeta,' said Champ, also laughing.

When they began to run again, there were more outbursts of laughter whenever one of them slipped or fell. And because of the many hidden and not so hidden obstacles, tree roots and the like, each in turn gave the others something to laugh about. But some twenty minutes on their running slowed down to a walk. Being in short trousers, their legs, having been lashed by all the vegetation they had run through, were now red and stinging. When Champ complained, (having never done this sort of thing before) he was told to stop whinging. He was a Shanghai Bomber for goodness sake, and Shanghai Bombers were supposed to be tough. So Champ stopped whinging and just got on with it.

Reaching a stretch of river where they always crossed over whenever they came to Bersham Waterfall, Twab, Sparrow and Golcho began to roll their trousers up as high as they could, although they were all wearing short trousers as was the norm in 1953. But when Twab saw Champ just standing there like a dummy he told him to do likewise. When Champ tried to protest, he was ordered to roll his trousers up and they all sat on the bank and lowered their feet into the water which came up to their knees. So with their shoes and stockings on, they each in turn began to paddle across the river very carefully. Champ finally entered the water and paddled across. But while being helped up the little bank on the other side, he knew his mum would have a fit if she ever found out that he had paddled across a river with his shoes and socks on. He could see her now, ranting on about how much shoes cost, adding that money did not grow on trees but, like Twab said, he was a Shanghai Bomber.

While padding across he was amazed at the stones that made up the river bed. They were of different sizes of course, but what surprised him was the fact that every one of them, regardless of its size, was so smooth, white and rounded, just like some of the stones in their little river down the woods.

When he asked why that was, no one could tell him, but Champ finally accepted Golcho's theory that it was because they had been in the water for hundreds of years. When he moaned that his feet were wet, Twab pointed out that it was a small price to pay for what they had achieved and, when he saw the worried look on his face, assured him that a fire would be made before they went home to dry out their shoes and socks.

Champ was told to think of it this way – they were on the side of the river that they wanted to be on. How difficult was that? Plus, it was the shallowest part of the river in this area.

The river was in shade now and was flowing very slowly. But a few minutes later, the sound of water crashing down concrete steps could be heard.

Wanting to throw something at the moving objects that were floating down this tranquil stretch of river, the lads began scraping the mulchy remains of last year's leaves with the soaking wet shoes, hoping to find any stones that were lurking around. When one was dug up, a target was found and the stone thrown at it. Suddenly an adder, disturbed by the lads noise and movements, uncoiled itself and slithered out of their path into the bushes. As fast as it moved, Sparrow saw it and called out,' Snake, snake!'

Rushing over to where the snake had been basking, they strained their eyes and ears trying to locate the reptile. Minutes later they began prodding the bushes with sticks to drive it out, but the snake was long gone. Realising they had lost it, they gave up the search and moved on, looking back every so often in case it had re-emerged. It was agreed by all that the snake was at least four feet long and that no one had ever seen a snake of that size before.

'Wow, if only we could have caught it,' said Sparrow 'we could have had a good look at it before letting it go.' He then explained to Champ that it was either a viper or an adder, but he was not sure which.

Then the lure of the waterfall was the only thing on their minds and in less that a minute they were standing at the top of Bersham Waterfall which was so picturesque in the afternoon sun and was made up of fifteen slightly curved steps, some thirty feet in length with a drop of twenty feet. The steps, originally straight, had been worn away over the years. Sparrow said his dad had a photograph of the waterfall which had been taken in the 1890s when the steps were straight. Golcho saw the steps as banana shaped.

Even though the flow of water was low at that time of year, it nevertheless cascaded very gracefully over the top and down the central aisle of the now worn-away steps, with the outer edges being bone dry.

Even so, it was a spectacular sight. Twab said 'In winter, when the river is in flood, this tranquil scene is fantastic. The water, gushing over and down the steps is as white as snow and seems to stand out.' Champ knew he was going to be drawing this waterfall one day.

The pool, some eighty feet in length, petered out by the bridge to become the river once again. The depth of water for half of the pool's length was something like ten feet, ideal for swimming in. Champ was told that not very long before, the river, before going over the steps, had turned a huge wooden wheel which ground grain for making bread. The mill, now derelict, still had one piece of evidence to prove that men once worked there – a sluice gate which was always an attraction to any visiting children. Several minutes were spent opening and closing the sluice gate, thereby controlling the flow of water.

Moving on, the lads slid on their heels and bums down the three-foot-wide sloping wall that housed the fifteen steps. Reaching the bottom, they jumped off onto the embankment and began to do their own thing. Twab and Golcho found some stones and had a competition to see who could skim them the furthest. Sparrow threw what stones he found at some wood pigeons that were having a drink at the top of the steps. He had forgotten his catty again and said he was glad his head was screwed on because of his forgetfulness.

Champ was by the bridge watching and listening to the river's whooshing sound and the white water as it continued on its journey. He so admired the bridge's structure. It was identical, but on a smaller scale, to Nant Mill Bridge and again wondered how bridges were built? What puzzled him was why they did not collapse in the middle? What was holding them up? Turning back to the waterfall, he stood in awe of the view. How the water gushed over and down the steps, how it crashed into the pool at the bottom and how the trees on either side of the steps and in the background lent a hand in making this a picture that he knew he was going to draw one day.

But his thoughts of coming here next weekend to draw the bridge were interrupted as he was invited to join in with Twab and Golcho in their skimming stones competition, now that Sparrow had also joined them.

While throwing the flattest pebbles he could find across the pool, quite successfully, never having skimmed stones before, Champ was told that the big rock formation at the bottom of the steps was in fact a cave, and if you swam into it, the water cascaded over your head with such force (which was great) that you could feel your neck being pushed into your shoulders. And then, if you wanted to, you could climb out of it and be on the bottom step of the waterfall. 'Wow!' was the only thing Champ could think of to say.

'So, who's for a swim, then?' Sparrow asked.

Champ thought it would be too cold.

'No, it won't,' Sparrow said as he began to strip off, 'it's been in the sun all day. It'll be lovely and warm. Come on, last one in stinks.' Sparrow ran down to the bridge and jumped onto the stony beach, then waded into the water naked and, stumbling along from stepping on sharp stones with the occasional 'Ouch!' prompted the others to follow suit. Moments later, they too were naked and stumbling along the stony bottom, blurting out their cries of 'Ouch!' as the water crept up their bodies.

'Oh, it's bloody freezing,' Golcho remarked when they were level with Sparrow who was now waist deep with his hands around his face and shivering. But on his command, having decided it would be warmer in the water, they took the plunge. It was so exhilarating being under the water and the cold encouraged them to swim as fast as they could. Surfacing, they trod water. Sparrow sucked in a mouthful of water and showered Golcho with it then suggested they duck-dive and swim into the cave. On his count, they submerged and swam toward the cave's entrance. Sparrow entered first, followed by Twab, then Golcho and then Champ. When Sparrow surfaced, he took a deep breath and made room for Twab, who in turn made room for Golcho, who in turn made room for Champ. The little cave had never been so cramped. Treading water, and giggling even though they were all squashed together, the lads enjoyed the cold water cascading over their heads. It was so invigorating, and yes, they each felt their necks being forced into their shoulders. Sparrow's wavy hair that Jeannie was in love with was as flat as a pancake and was no different to that of the other three, until it was dry. Then the waves would return. Champ had a quick flash of Jeannie's face seeing Sparrow's hair like this and wondered if he would still be the love of her life.

Yahooing, Sparrow asked Champ what he thought of their little cave?

'It's fantastic!' he yelled out forgetting all about Jeannie. Eager to move on, Sparrow climbed up through the opening above their heads and came out on the bottom step of the waterfall. He then performed his favourite dive by taking a few strides and then diving in head first, the way Tarzan did in all his movies. Minutes later, he was back in the cave and giving orders. 'Come on,' he said ticking Twab's shoulder and then shoving his head under the water to give them time to scarper, 'let's play tick. Twab's on.'

In the time it took Twab to realise what was going on, the others had all skedaddled, Sparrow ending up back on the bottom step of the waterfall, with Champ and Golcho swimming towards the shallows.

Twab went after Champ and Golcho. Swimming hard and catching them up, even though Sparrow was shouting at them to get a move on,

Twab ticked Golcho on the foot and swam away as fast as he could. He submerged, entered the cave and moments later was standing on the bottom step with Sparrow congratulating him. Golcho in the meantime having caught up with Champ and was fighting it out with him. They were both ticking each other in the hope of making their escape. Champ was doing fine, until he stepped on a sharp stone and stumbled. Seeing his chance, Golcho rushed in, ticked him on the head, ducked him and swam away knowing he was safe. Moments later he too was standing on the bottom step of the waterfall being congratulated by Twab and Sparrow for his Shanghai tactics. When Champ duck dived and made for the cave's entrance, the lads ran up the dried steps and hid in the surrounding bushes. Following their wet footprints, Champ quickly found them and managed to tick Twab who in turn ticked Sparrow. While Twab and Sparrow, as naked as the day they were born, were fighting it out, Golcho and Champ made their escape down the sloping wall and diving in, made for the other side of the pool. Treading water they took bets as to who would be the next chaser. Ticking Sparrow, who stumbled, Twab scampered down the steps and dived head first into the water.

Telling Champ to follow him, Golcho swam to the shallows and climbing out of the water hid behind some nearby bushes. Not only was he covered in mud from scrambling up the muddy bank, but he was so cold being out of the water that he began to shiver.

Champ too was covered in mud from climbing out of the water, there being nothing to hang onto. He also began to shiver.

Sparrow, now the chaser, having used his favourite dive, came up alongside Twab and ticking him on the leg, made his escape. Slightly out of breath and treading water, Twab watched as Sparrow swam into the cave and emerged on the bottom step. Realising Twab had not pursued him, Sparrow began to taunt him by telling him how hopeless he was. But Twab was fed up with the game and began to swim for pleasure which did not go down too well with Golcho.

'Oi, Esther Williams,' he shouted from behind the bush that he and Champ were hiding, 'is the game over or what? It's bloody freezing out here.' Twab, who was going to make them suffer a mite longer ignored him and kept on swimming.

'Oi, bugger,' Golcho shouted. 'Is the game over or what? It's bloody freezing out here.'

Grinning and enjoying the moment, Twab duck dived and swam into the cave. Moments later he was standing on the bottom step trying to see where his pals were. But, failing to find them, declared the game over.

A loud, 'Thank God for that,' was heard coming from the bushes.

Tip toeing and trying to avoid the stones and holly leaves (especially the holly leaves that were everywhere) Champ and Golcho finally reached the bottom step on their side of the waterfall. Stepping on it and still covered in mud they both dived in head first and came up alongside their leader. With a big grin, Golcho announced how much warmer it was in the water and then to liven things up burst out into song. When Champ and Twab joined in, there was a terrible rendition of the *Drinking Song*. 'Let every true lover salute his sweetheart. Let's drink,' they screeched out. For a laugh, Golcho half filled his mouth with water and began to gurgle David Whitfield's *Cara Mia*. Wanting a piece of the action, Sparrow left his cover and, diving in, came up alongside his mates. Half filling his mouth with water he joined in with the others as they gurgled out David Whitfield's most famous song.

When all the laughing and pushing and trying to duck one another had died down, Champ suggested they see who could stay under water the longest. Champ won because, according to him, he was a non smoker. But to show how they felt about being lectured yet again on the dangers of smoking, Sparrow and Golcho jumped on him and shoved his head under the water, not once but several times, until he promised to stop preaching.

Breaking free, Champ swam away and called a truce, and suggested they play one of his favourite games, where you let most of the air out of your lungs and see how long you can sit on the bottom. It took several attempts before the lads got the hang of it, but once it was learned it was deemed good fun. Each in turn, while in the deepest part of the pool by the steps, exhaled their air and sank to the bottom and sat there for as long as they could. On account of the water being so clear, those who were brave enough to open their eyes saw several fish swimming about.

Golcho was one of the brave ones. He not only saw the fish, but rose to the surface by climbing up the vertical wall face which was hard to see on land. He likened it to climbing up the Woods wall which he thought was easy. An extension of the game, which Champ called flying, was then introduced. You now had to stand on the bottom, bend your knees, kick off at an angle and gently float up to the surface. For the next hour the lads thoroughly enjoyed this new water game. If they had enough air they could kick off at a lower angle and have a longer glide up to the surface.

But it was Golcho who brought the game to a close. He had enough of being naked in the water and the tips of his fingers were wrinkled. He also wanted a smoke. He left the pool, and shaking and rubbing most of the water off himself, Golcho jumped up and down until he was dry enough to begin getting dressed. Ten minutes later, while waiting for Twab and Sparrow to fasten their laces, Champ asked if anyone else had seen the fish. Sparrow who pointed out that the Clywedog was a good trout river and Golcho said he had seen one, this big, indicating two feet, which was a porky. Twab, who was ready for home and getting hungry, suggested they make a fire to dry off their shoes and socks.

Sparrow, who was also getting hungry, said it was a good idea and immediately began to gather dead leaves and ordered the others to start looking for sticks that were dry. While waiting, he broke a Woodbine in half and threw half to Golcho whilst keeping the flame going with more dead leaves. There was a lovely plume of blue smoke rising up into the late afternoon sky.

Within minutes, all four were sitting around the fire drying their shoes and socks while at the same time trying to avoid the smoke that seemed to follow them. It was Golcho who said how much he appreciated the fire. He at least was happy with it. His shoes and socks were drying nicely and he was enjoying his smoke while being lovely and warm. What more could anyone ask for, he thought? When he showed the lads his wrinkled fingers (from being in the water too long), they each looked at their own and began to compare their condition. Sparrow argued that his looked the worst, but Golcho showed him his and said Sparrow needed glasses as his were the worst. Twab thought his wrinkled fingers looked like his Granny's face. Champ just looked at his. He had never seen wrinkled fingers before.

One by one they put their almost dry shoes on top of their nicely dried socks. It was time to go. The fire was doused by everyone weeing on it. Mimicking a grown up, Twab used his hands to hide his 'thing' which caused the others to burst out laughing.

'Ugh, look at him,' Golcho teased, while falling about laughing. Asking where he had seen it done, Twab said this is what grown men do when they have a wee. It was what his dad did. Golcho then caused a riot when he dangled his thing in front of them while dousing the fire and said, 'And this is what a twelve-year-old does.'

When all the laughing died out and the ashes were scattered (it being their policy to leave a place as they found it), the lads wriggled through a gap in the railings and, with one last look at the waterfall, set off for home.

As they walked along the road, Champ again noticed that the trees they were walking under made a tunnel effect and was intrigued by it. Like yesterday, when he was taken down the woods for the first time, the sun was making lovely patterns of light and shade on the road. He wondered if he would ever be able to draw a picture showing the sun shining through the trees. But his reverie was broken when Twab said there was another waterfall about half-a-mile away where the water just flowed over the top and down a slope adding that it too was a great place to swim. Twab promised Champ that he would be taken there one day, with the promise that he would not be disappointed.

Some eighty yards on, approaching the Foresters Lodge, Champ was told to run as the big black dog behind the huge gates, even though tied up, would bark at them. Sparrow very often made things worse by throwing a stick at it. Suddenly, the dog was barking its head off. Thinking the Forester would be after them, they ran past the gates and up the little hill puffing and panting. With no sign of the Forester, and while strolling along the road, it was pointed out to Champ that in a few weeks time this area would be great for conkers.

Golcho then told the story of how three boys in his class were caught playing truant by none other that Mr Carrington, the truant officer. It seemed that the boys had decided that coming to Bersham for conkers was more important than having lessons and had sneaked out during the eleven o'clock playtime period. When they were ready for home they decided to walk along the road rather than go through the wood. When they saw a car coming along they thought it might stop and give them a lift, so one of them stuck his thumb out and hoped for the best.

Well, the car stopped alright, and when they saw who the driver was they nearly died.

Ordering them to get in the car, Mr Carrington drove them straight through the school gates and marched them to Mr Samuels' office. Not only where they given six of the best, with a lecture on how truancy would not be tolerated, but their conkers were also confiscated.

Champ was amazed with the story. He had never heard anything like it. When he asked if it was true, Sparrow confirmed it was. He said, 'You should have seen their hands after Sammy had finished with them.'

Coming up to a gap in the hedge, Sparrow pointed to a path that took you back into the wood to the first waterfall. But they plodded on with Champ noticing that the trees on their right were thinning out. Coming out of an S-bend, and taking a breather, the lads leaned on a five-bar gate and watched what appeared to be hundreds of crows feeding on the ground at the far end of the field. Twab yelled to frighten them off and everyone watched as the birds took to the air. 'There must have been hundreds of them,' Champ said, never having seen so many of the same bird before. They watched fascinated as the birds circled overhead. Their numbers were such that they looked like a huge, black, swirling cloud. And the noise they were making was deafening. They were much noisier than the rooks they disturbed yesterday while sword fighting down the woods. Fascinated by the spectacle, the lads watched how some birds landed in the trees, while others, the more experienced ones, fell back to the ground and resumed feeding. Champ thought it was a fantastic spectacle.

Moving on they puffed and panted up the steep hill and passed the only house en route which had a well-kept garden. Rounding a bend in the road, the lads came across a section of iron railings lying on the ground. Picking up a loose railing, Twab threw it at a clump of grass and realized it made a fantastic spear. Not realising it was theft, they each took one.

Approaching Nant Mill bridge (having come full circle) Twab came up with a brilliant idea. While on the bridge, he explained his plan. Of the three trees that loomed up from behind the bridge's wall, the nearest one, an old sycamore, was to be the target. The plan was to throw your spear and hopefully make it stick in the tree. Twab, as leader, lined himself up on the far side of the bridge, ran and threw his spear. All eyes watched as it sailed through the air. There was a dull thud as it found its target, sticking into the trunk with such force that it twanged for several moments. Twab was congratulated by all.

Sparrow threw next. Lining up and telling himself he could do this, he ran the short distance and threw his spear. There was another deep thud as his spear also became stuck in the trunk and twanged, some two feet below that of Twab.

Golcho walked the width of the road, turned and after yelling out his infamous Top C, ran the short distance and threw his spear. Again there was a thud. His spear landed just inches away from Sparrow's where it too twanged.

Determined he was not going to let the side down, Champ walked across the road, turned, and finding the spear's balance (as the others had done) ran and threw his spear. Not only were there four sets of eyes glued on the spear as it sailed through the air, but there were also eight pairs of fingers crossed. With a thud, Champ's spear landed about an inch away from Sparrow's and Golcho's, forming a triangle. It too twanged. When all the congratulations and arm shaking (the Roman way) had died down, Twab said. 'Gang, what we've just done, being Sunday whose date I can't remember, will always remind us of the day we took Champ to Harry's Rock and then onto Bersham Waterfall.' The date was the thirteenth.

As they made their way up the hill, past the fairies' stone that had caused so much trouble earlier, no one as much as looked at it or mentioned it. They did not want Golcho upset again. He and his bloody Father Christmas – but a problem did occur when they started to walk across Kynaston's fields. It began when Golcho asked how old everyone was?

It turned out that Twab and Champ were both born in March, 1941, Champ on the 6th, Twab on the 15th. Sparrow was born on the 24th of April, 1941 and Golcho on the 5th of May, 1941. But, not liking the idea of being the gang's baby, Golcho said he had made a mistake and insisted he was older than Sparrow. Of course, Sparrow argued the toss, and between them (one arguing this, the other arguing that) the rest of the walk home was most rowdy.

After tea, when the lads met up by the lamppost at the bottom of Heol Wen, Champ, having promised himself that he was going to make certain drawings, said he was going down the woods as he wanted to draw the Woods bridge. Because it was a case of one for all and all that, they all went. So, as Champ made his first drawing of the bridge, as seen from the road, the lads watched as it slowly came to life. But when Champ said he wanted to draw it and the river, they all scrambled down the concrete strut on the side of the bridge and, while Champ drew his second drawing, showing the river and a portion of Mr Williams's field, the lads made their way over to the Monster and had half-an-hour's fun on the swing.

As Champ drew, he had to stop several times as one of the lads either burst out laughing or cursed one of the others, for what Champ could only guess. But when he was ready, he shouted to say he had finished. As they walked up the Woods hill, the others told him that both his drawings were very good. But when they reached Llidiart Fanny Farm, the sky, which was getting darker by the minute, suddenly released a few drops of rain, then poured down. As they approached the green gates, a flash of lightning lit up the sky followed by a very loud clap of thunder. 'It's as black as your father's hat,' said Sparrow wallowing in the spectacle. He loved thunderstorms. As they were already soaked to the skin, they huddled together by the Green - Gates and waited for the next flash. It arrived several minutes later, followed by another equally bright flash. The deep roll of thunder that followed was like nothing anyone had heard. They all cheered and decided to see if there were going to be any more flashes – and there were.

Twab who said the storm was right above them and, when he was asked how he knew that, replied that you can always tell how far away a storm is by counting after the flash. If there was a five second count after the flash before the thunder, then the storm was five miles away.

'So that means the storm is right above us, then?' said Golcho.

Twab nodded, to mean it was, just as another flash lit up the whole sky, followed by an almighty clap of thunder. The sky was so dark now. Golcho said that when he was young; he and his dad, in their old house, used to stand in the front doorway and watch the storm. His dad said that the thunder was Father Christmas knocking nails in the toys he was making, and the lightning was when he put the light on to be able see what he was doing. When Sparrow told a similar story, he too was believed, but whereas Golcho was telling the truth, Sparrow was telling a porky. Sparrow had not liked thunder and lightning when he was younger. Neither Twab nor Champ had anything to say on the matter. To them it was just a storm. But, some thirty minutes later, when the rain eased off, the lads made a run for home. Sparrow reached his house first; then Golcho, Champ and finally Twab. Whether the others had a bath when they went in soaking wet we will never know, but Champ did. Jeannie was made to run the bath while his mum stripped him of his wet clothes in front of the fire and then threw a towel around him. It was only then that he realised that his two drawings had been ruined in the storm. To cheer him up his mum said he could always draw another picture.

While soaking in the lovely hot water, Champ relived the day's adventure. How many more places was he going to be taken to he wondered? That night in bed, while filling in his diary, he underlined his visit to Harry's Rock, Golcho's fear of the dark and how he himself had felt while in FitzHugh's wood. Life has so much to give he thought. He also underlined how grateful he was to his mum for allowing him to use his dad's fountain pen. Also underlined was the storm, the throwing of the spears, the swimming in Bersham, the waterfall and the crossing of the river with his shoes and socks on. He was still awake when his mum came up to bed. She popped in and said goodnight while tucking him in, and suggested he should go to sleep.

Part Four: Brymbo Pool, June, 1953

ALAN APPRECIATED HAVING EXTRA TUITION in his two favourite lessons, woodwork and sports, and decided he was going to concentrate on his other school lessons from now on. His mum was always telling him and Jeannie, 'Education is free and the future.'

Up till now Alan was still unbeaten on the school field and Mr Robinson, giving those who Alan was competing against a little head-start, made him dig down for that extra gear he was always talking about. Winning for Mr Robinson was important to Alan, so he listened to his every word and so wanted to impress him. Because school sports day was only four weeks away, Friday, 17th July, Alan, with his mother's permission, in order to keep up with his training, ran on the open roads after school for an hour, as suggested by Mr Robinson. And, because of this, he was unknowingly gaining a respectable reputation in the village. While running along certain roads around the area, those people who saw him would stop what they were doing and shout their encouragement as he went racing by. In school, both Mr Pritchard, and Mr Robinson were convinced that there would be trophies hanging on the school wall before the term was over, hence the extra tuition.

Mr Lloyd was impressed with Alan's woodwork and agreed that he could carry on making clothes maids for the time being. What the teacher did not know was, as much as they cost Alan 2s 6d, on getting them home his customers (his immediate neighbours) were paying five shillings for them, giving Alan 2s 6d profit. To complete his order book thus far another three were needed.

His mum's birthday had been two days ago, Thursday, 18 June, and had gone very well. It was so nice to see both sets of grandparents from Chester. What a surprise it had been when Alan and Jeannie had come home from school and to see them sitting there. Their mum had kept the visit a surprise. There was so much to talk about. It was hoped by

Doreen's parents that she, Alan and Jeannie would spend a weekend in Chester with them sometime. Whereas Doreen was all for it, Alan and Jeannie did not seem that enthusiastic. They both said later that they did not want to be away from their friends for a whole weekend.

But Alan was pleased to hear that the council had kept its promise and had demolished their old house along with the whole row. He was also told that the new road system and factory where Raleigh bikes were going to be made was well on the way and that he would not recognise the place. Even the old air-raid shelter had gone which Alan found hard to believe. He had often had a lot of fun in that, not that there was any comparison to Harry's Rock when it came to echo. The echo down Harry's Rock was really something.

Doreen's birthday party began with her being made to sit down, for once she was going to be waited on. Wearing the hats which Jeannie had made secretly, 'Happy Birthday' was sung not once, but twice. And as a treat, Granny Fletcher (more for the children than for her daughter) had made a birthday cake covered in thick chocolate. Everyone agreed it was delicious. When Jeannie asked why there were no candles on the cake, Doreen smiled and said she was no longer interested in candles. So when Jeannie politely asked how old her mum was, she was politely told to go away (she was never going to reveal that she was now thirty-four years old). But she was more than pleased with the birthday card which Alan and Jeannie had made for her. It depicted their back garden as it would be one day. Alan smiled when he saw their card in the centre of the other four which she had received, two from Chester, one from Aunty Mair next door (which had also been signed by Aunty Jinni across the road, Terry's mum) and one from someone called Sally who worked in the Co-op.

When Doreen opened her children's birthday card just after they had left for school she was amazed with Alan's poem. 'Roses are red, violets are blue, sugar is sweet and so are you.' It was the very poem his dad had always written on her birthday cards and she found that amazing. So, while she enjoyed her little cry and cup of tea, she re-read the poem and wondered if Alan had somehow inherited the verse or was it coincidence? She also liked his drawing of the house, washhouse and toilet, the path in front of the house, along with the piece of side garden which led up to the gate. Then there was the lawn with its three diamond-shaped flower beds, a path, a washing line (with washing on it) and finally a vegetable plot. This was one birthday card that was not going to be thrown out.

Tears also began to flow when she opened their present. Between them, Alan and Jeannie had saved up and bought her a woollen scarf from Gracie's shop in Coedpoeth. The lady behind the counter had told them that it was very attractive. It was Jeannie who had wrapped up the broach which Mr Lloyd had made out of the broken piece of green glass that Alan found in the Woods river. He had not only secured it onto a metal pin, but it now looked like a proper heart. Thinking it was lovely and something which she would not have minded having one herself, Jeannie had wrapped it up in a little box she had found amongst her doll's things. For his initiative, Alan had been given a pat on the back by Mr Lloyd who said he was glad he was able to help and that his mother was sure to like it. And she did very much.

Delighted with her presents, Doreen had to dry her eyes more than once before she could thank everyone properly for everything she had received. Her in-laws, the Fletchers, gave her a half-pound box of Black Magic, with a brand spanking new five pound note inside their card. From her parents she received a pair of shoes, two pairs of nylons, plus another five pound note – there was never enough money available for a struggling single mother.

The party went well and was enjoyed by one and all in the time that remained before the visitors from Chester had to leave. It was crucial that they caught the twenty past nine Maggie-Johnson's bus or they would miss their Chester connection, the last bus being ten-minutes to ten.

Escorting them to the bus stop and seeing them on to the bus and waving them off, Alan pointed out to his mum and sister that the road they could see this side of Llidiart Fanny Farm was the actual road that would take you to the wood. He also pointed out the green gates and the five-bar gate, with its companion oak tree which was a favourite of his. His mum did not let on that she knew of the woods road and the green gates.

But, because it was a pleasant evening, the Fletcher's took the long way home. As they strolled along Heol Offa, they came across four young girls playing hopscotch. Knowing them by name, Jeannie said

'Hello,' as they passed by. They then turned right into what was going to be Heol Glyndŵr. The houses were coming along nicely, as was the road and the two parapets. Families would soon be moving in.

Eighty yards on, they turned right into Heol Islwyn. While passing Twab's house, Alan wondered if he, Sparrow and Golcho were still out somewhere or whether they had gone in as it was after half-past nine and getting dark? There was no sign of Golcho either when they passed his house, which confirmed that the lads were out doing something, somewhere.

Alan mentioned in passing that their garden was going to look something like Golcho's garden when it was finished. He again hoped Golcho's dad did not mind him pinching his idea. While walking up Heol Wen, Doreen, with all the building that was going on, said the Adwy was going to be bigger than Coedpoeth one day. When they entered their house, Doreen locked the back door and put the kettle on and said she was going to make them all a nice bedtime drink of Oxo.

During July, August and September, Champ was taken to a host of places he had never seen before. Places like Pantwyll, a lovely gorge which you had to pass through to reach Minera Mountain, through which the river Clywedog ran. The only problem with visiting Pantwyll was the Coedpoeth lads, led by Barry Rowlands; Pantwyll was their territory. But for reasons unknown, the Saturday morning that Champ was taken there, there was no sign of the Coedpoeth lads, so they brazenly swam in their pool. How cheeky was that? Even so, a good half-hour was had in the pool which was in truth no better that their pool on Alum's side of the woods. It was a little deeper, but that was all. When they had splashed around enough, Golcho suggested they should go on to Minera Mountain where they spent the rest of that day, it being Champ's first visit. But sadly they missed the winberries which had either been picked by children and made into winberry pies or eaten by the hordes of sheep that roamed over the mountain. But a good game of Commandos was had. Champ was also shown several peat bogs, where a Coedpoeth lad, Robert (Bertie) Jones had fallen in and sunk up to his waist. That little incident had apparently taken place when several Coedpoeth lads had decided to play truant and, as they roamed over the mountain, Bertie had fallen into the peat bog that was being studied. The story was that it took his mates quite a while to get him out, and because he stank to high heaven, was made to walk behind them as they made their way home. He wondered what Bertie had told his parents? Children did not go to school and then come home covered in foul smelling mud.

Champ was also taken to Southsea Park, where a good time was had on the swings, slide and roundabout. While strolling down Southsea Hill (which was as steep and long as Fron Hill), he was amazed at the size of Southsea Bank, now that he was actually walking past it. It was gi-mungus. Sparrow explained that the bank was made up of the shale and slag that was dug up before the actual coal-seams were worked, adding that the pit was called Plas Power and apparently his dad had worked there as a miner for years.

Their route home that day was up Tan Lan, the little side road that Champ had been taken along when he went to Bersham, just before they stood on Offa's Dyke, where he had been given a lecture about King Offa, whom he had never heard of.

There was also a little exploring done in the old derelict house half way up Tan Lan, which no longer had a roof on it. There was ample evidence that it was being used by secret smokers and drinkers as there were cigarette stumps and empty beer bottles all over the floor of what had once been the living room.

Even Adwy woods had received a visit, another place that Champ quite liked, even though it was possible to hear the traffic go roaring past. It was not as quiet as their little woods, but before leaving that day, he asked and was shown the gooseberry bushes.

There was one place he was taken to which he immediately fell in love with, not that he did not fall in love with all the other places he was taken too. When he saw the little bridge and river down the Nant, where Twab had lived when he was younger, he went back that evening on his own and drew it. He studied the bridge for ages until he found the sketch he wanted. So, while sitting on a huge, flat stone listening to the river's gurgling sound as it made its way over and around the myriad of stones, a sound Champ was really in love with, he drew the bridge, the river and its two banks.

A black pipe about twelve inches in diameter, stretched across the river and was included in the drawing. He did not know what it was, only that it came out of one bank and disappeared into the opposite one. He wondered if Twab knew what it was? But he never got round to asking him and it remained a mystery.

Alan's drawing made the bridge appear to be in a better condition than the actual one, as there was no rust showing on it, nor any chunks of paint missing. Before going home he dared himself to walk across the black pipe. Sensing that he could do it, he climbed up on it from the road side, found his balance and, remembering how he had walked across the gate at Kynaston's farm a few months ago on the way to Bersham, he raised his arms to shoulder height and set off. He started off feeling quite safe, but had a change of mind when he was over the river. He could not afford to fall in the river or his mum would go berserk and his drawing would be ruined like the one he had made of the Woods bridge when they were caught out in that thunder storm. Despite stumbling a couple of times, he made it across but decided not to chance his luck again, ran up the field and crossed over the bridge and went home a different way. He had got to the Nant over Kynaston's fields, but went home via Rhos Berse Road, where he made a drawing of the turnstile they had pirouetted on when they went to Bersham.

Although it was the first week of October, the weather was holding up and Alan wondered what the rest of the month had in store for him and the lads. According to Gordon Morris (the boy who had put a dead rat in Cock Leg's waste-paper basket for giving him the cane and showing him up in class) his dad and all the other farmers in the area were praying for rain.

Alan had meticulously kept up with his diary, carefully recording everything in ink. One day he had seen Cock Leg filling her fountain pen from a jug of ink that was kept in her cupboard, so he took his dad's fountain pen to school and filled it up from different inkwells when she was not looking. His thinking being, 'If she can steal and get away with it, so can I.'

The long October evenings were warm and Alan, still on a 9.30 curfew (with Jeannie having to be in by nine) played out after tea once his homework and chores had been done. Jeannie, Wendy and Hazel were bosom pals now and, if they were not upstairs playing house or whatever, they were either on the field or in the road with the other village girls playing a host of games. Certain girls were allowed to play certain games with the boys – chase, stroke the bunny, tick (especially off-ground tick) – and Jeannie, Wendy and Hazel, along with the other village girls, very often joined in with the lads. Jeannie was told off one time while playing chase for only chasing Sparrow. She did not dare tell anyone, not even Wendy and Hazel, that she was still in love with him, not that Sparrow ever knew it. Apparently his wavy hair and blue eyes were lovelier than ever.

Alan was never in before 9.30, always staying out until the very last minute. If he was not playing around the village with the lads, he was drawing until it was either time to go in or there was not enough light. If the lads played with the other village kids, a variety of games were played, football, cricket, tennis, hide and seek, chase, to name but a few. But it was when running that Alan stood out above all the others.

Having done well in the school sports, he decided to try and make a little money on the side, accepting anyone's challenge of a race around the village if a little something was included to make it that much more interesting. The course was approximately two miles, starting from the lamp post at the bottom of Heol Wen from where they ran up to and along Lloft Wen Lane, then up the main road as far as the Bent's public house in Coedpoeth, then down Castle Road and Clay Hill, right along the Talwrn Road (as far as Llidiart Fanny Farm), right past the green gates, right into Heol Celyn and left into Heol Islwyn, with the finishing line being the lamp post from where the race had started. Alan won many a sixpence from his challengers and never went short of picture money while the racing lasted.

There was one game that united the sexes – chase. When there were at least ten people playing, there would be as many as three chasers who, armed with a big stick, would, after a count of ten, begin the hunt. The only rules were that you were not allowed to go beyond the village's known boundaries or go home without telling someone.

Champ and Co very often went home with stinging legs and backsides. When those being chased were surrounded by more than one chaser, drastic action had to be taken by running through someone's garden in the hope of getting away, or by climbing over the fence or privet hedge. But nine times out of ten that was where you were caught and whacked. But, at the end of the night, it was all deemed as good fun.

In Stroke the Bunny, the one who was on (the Bunny), with his or her eyes closed, had to guess who stroked his or her finger. Like chase, this game was best played with several people, the more the merrier. If the Bunny guessed wrong (which was often the case), he or she would be sent as far away as the green gates, a hundred yards away, and while there would have to count up to one hundred out loud to ensure that there was no cheating, and then, on returning, would have to begin the search again. Some hid in gateways, some in someone's garden, some behind parked cars (not that there were many cars in those days), while others ran as far as Heol Offa and made their way back through gardens that brought them out by the lamp post so that while the Bunny was out looking, you simply walked into base.

Last night's Bud Abbot and Lou Costello film, *Jack and the Beanstalk*, was very funny, especially when the little fat one first met the Giant. The cinema was in uproar for most of the film. Champ could not decide whether he liked them or Dean Martin and Jerry Lewis the best. He also began to like Errol Flynn just as much as Alan Ladd and wondered if they would ever make a film together. But there was no more time for thinking as it was time to get up. It was Saturday morning, the 3 October, and Champ was being taken to a place called Brymbo Pool.

The lads met up by the lamp post at the bottom of Heol Wen at the agreed time of ten o'clock. They were all armed with an empty Robertson's jam jar and a lengthy piece of string. They set off, but moments later, stopped dead in their tracks as Norman Williams, who lived three houses down from Sparrow, was demonstrating his latest four-wheeler truck to a potential buyer, Basil Davies, who was always on the lookout for a bargain. Standing close enough to hear what was being said, the lads heard Norman explaining the braking system. To stop, you simply scraped your feet along the ground until you stopped. Norman had not as yet come up with a better idea. Then, confidently, Norman set off down the pavement from outside his house to demonstrate just how good the truck was, with his potential buyer running alongside. Moments later both disappeared around the bend at the bottom of the road.

Turning to Champ, Sparrow explained that Norman was always banging away with his hammer and nails, making things and could turn his hand to anything. It was Norman who introduced the lads to 'bowlers' which were old bike wheels (with or without a tyre). Some of his customers preferred their bowler to have tyres on, as they ran silently. But others preferred the sound the bare wheel made while in contact with the road. Some preferred their bowler to have spokes in, while others did not care. The choice was theirs.

The lads strolled on down the pavement and, as they went around the corner, came across Norman who had crashed into Peter Evans's gateway and was, as the lads passed without saying a word, cursing like mad. The left, front wheel of his latest truck was badly buckled having hit the concrete gate post. There was no sign of Basil.

Racing past the green gates and up to and across the Talwrn Road, then turning left by Llidiart Fanny farm, the lads ran down the woods hill up to the bend where Twab pointed out several birds foraging in one of the many hazel bushes. Their excitement trebled when Champ spotted a much bigger bird which was black and white with a red patch on its head and rump, which appeared to be standing upright on the tree-trunk and pecking like mad. No one knew what it was other than it was most unusual. Champ was so smitten that he decided he was going to come here on his own sometime and hopefully draw that most fantastic bird.

The weather it seemed was again going to be kind to them. It was warm and sunny with not a cloud in the sky. While the others were frolicking about, Champ, now that the mysterious bird had flown away, was trying to take notice of the other birds. He still did not know what they all were, but he was watching chaffinches, green finches, gold finches, coal tits, great tits, blue tits, yellow hammers, gold crests, robins and blackbirds. Twab said they were woodland birds. Admiring them, Champ realised that each bird type had its own distinctive colour, plumage and shape. This he found very interesting and began to question why it was so? But before any answers came, Golcho suggested they have a quick swing on the Monster before going on to Brymbo Pool.

Approaching the dump with their jam jars tucked away in their jackets for safe keeping, and cursing the sulphurous emissions which were quite strong that morning, they each in turn slid down the wall of refuse on their heels and bums. Twab had the only problem when he hit a soft patch of refuse which caused a flurry of steam to belch out of the ground. At the bottom, he checked his jam jar. It was still whole. Happy, they raced on, but suddenly, voices were heard. Someone was using the swing.

To their horror, Terry, Frank, Ernie and Dave and a few other older lads from the village were in possession of the swing. Being told in no uncertain terms, well, very rude uncertain terms actually, that, no way would they be using the swing this morning, Twab and Co, not wishing to antagonise them, kept on going along the soggy path until they reached the hazel bushes that led down to the river. There they scrambled down the steep slope and reached the river, ever so thankful they had not been molested by you know who.

To make up for the disappointment of not being allowed on the swing, Twab cut down four lengths of hazel coppice from which he made spears. He quickly shaped and pointed them using his dad's jack-knife and they then set off along Alum's field throwing their spears at different targets. Suddenly, an awful lot of swearing filled the air and, judging by the amount of laughing and mickey taking that accompanied the bad language, it was obvious that someone had just fallen off the swing. Giggling, the lads all hoped it was Terry, Frank, Ernie or Dave that had just fallen off the swing. It did not matter who, as long as whoever it was, was badly scratched and bruised.

'I don't know about you lot,' said Twab laughing as loud as he dare, 'but all that swearing has just made my day.' Revenge was sometimes sweet, but rather than hang about they moved on.

Having thrown their spears at a cow pat some ten feet away, with the river on their right, it turned out that Sparrow had won the contest by several inches. Champ was second, Twab third and Golcho, who blamed a non-existant arm injury, was last.

While retrieving their spears, Sparrow caught sight of something that needed to be investigated. Safely crossing the river without getting his feet wet, he discovered just above the water line in the tufted grass what turned out to be an empty jenny wren's nest. Calling the others over to have a look, they all marvelled at the way the nest had been constructed. It was so expertly made and camouflaged and the young chicks, Champ mused, must have been very snug and warm when they were all together being fed and looked after by their parents. And the nest was so small. No wonder this bird is sometimes known as the two-fingered jenny wren.

Two minutes later, with the nest left intact, the lads raced up to the top of Alum's field, while keeping an eye out for the owner. Their aim was to see who could throw his spear down the field the furthest. They were all hoping that their spear would land somewhere over the river in the wood. Each gave it his best shot, and each spear landed in the wood. But, because there was no time to find out who the winner was (Brymbo Pool calling), the victor would have to wait until they next came this way when, if undisturbed, their spears, which were all marked differently, would remain where they were. But from looking down Alum's field, Twab was convinced that he was the winner, with Sparrow telling him he needed glasses if he thought so, as he had won by a mile. Champ and Golcho declined to argue as they both knew they had not won.

But getting to Brymbo Pool was going to be a problem. The problem was how were they going to reach the Woods wall without being seen by Terry, Frank, Ernie and Dave? They could either go the long way round, and most likely be chased by Alum, as they were more exposed on that route. Or they could try their luck and go back the way they had come in the hope that Terry and Co would ignore them.

In the end Twab decided they should go back the way they had come. If they used the gorse bushes which stretched almost up to the Woods wall, falling short by about twenty yards, where they would be exposed, they could be on their way again before you could say Jack Robinson. While Twab was explaining his plan, he thought he could smell smoke. Using the gorse bushes as cover, while Terry and Co mucked about, the lads sneaked their way closer to the wall. But suddenly there for anyone to see, was a plume of blue smoke spiralling up into the morning sky. Why had someone with Terry's knowledge of Alum made a fire? Twab and Co suddenly wanted to be away. Being on Alum's field with smoke rising was not a good idea. What to do? The Woods wall was less than twenty yards away, but how could they reach it without being seen?

Should they go up the field and possibly be seen and chased by Alum? No, that was out of the question. Twab decided he was going to take a chance and make a run for the Woods wall. On his countdown they broke cover and raced for the wall, hoping You-know-who did not spot them. But You-know-who did spot them. In fact You-know-who was swinging outwards and upwards on the Monster over the bushes and river when he spotted them and decided he was going to have some fun with them.

Seeing their jam jars glistening in the sun, and hoping to put the fear of God into them, he shouted, 'Oi, you lot, going to Brymbo pool then?' When he next appeared he added that they might just see them there. Encouraging his comrades they all shouted out a long, 'Yeaaaa, we just might.' Panicking because they'd been spotted, Twab gave the order, 'Every man for himself!' and there was a mad rush for the Woods wall.

When Terry next appeared over the river and bushes, he threatened them that, if they were not out of sight by the time he counted to ten, he was going to stake them to the ground and light a fire around them. He was only kidding of course, but the lads did not know that.

When Terry (who was hogging the swing) next appeared over the river, Twab yelled for Golcho to get a move on or they were going to leg it up the Fron Hill without him. Golcho was the last one up the wall simply because he had been pushed aside by the others in their bid to be up the wall first.

Urging his mates to join in with him, Terry began to shout that they were coming after them and 'God help anyone who is caught'!

When Golcho finally jumped off the wall onto the road, the lads legged it up the Fron Hill as fast as their legs could carry them. Half way up and panting for breath, but out of sight of Terry and his lot, the lads, hearing all the laughing coming from the woods, realised that Terry had been teasing them all along. But Twab was still puzzled as to why they had a fire on the go. The fire had actually been lit because there were several potatoes being cooked, along with three tins of Heinz Baked Beans. Terry and his lot were planning to spend the day in the wood, but as Twab knew, sending smoke into the air was not a good idea, especially if Alum was around.

Pleased that Terry was not after them, the lads sat on the grass verge to get their breath back. Having calmed down, Twab pointed out that Champ was about to venture into unknown territory, or virgin territory as Golcho put it. Which was true; Champ had never been this far up the Fron Hill in the three months he had lived in the Adwy, but he thought it was exciting.

Fully rested, the lads moved on. Twab suddenly remembered when he and Sparrow, as a joke, hid from Golcho, and told champ the story which had happened about a fortnight before Champ's arrival. The three of them had been playing on the Hafod side that day and when it began to get dark, decided to pack it in and go home. When they reached the road, Twab suggested they should each show how brave they were by going back into the wood as far as the little swing and while there shout 'Geronimo.'

Sick and tired of hearing the story, Golcho placed his hands over his ears, but because he could still hear what was being said, tried to put them off by screeching out Eddie Calvert's *Oh Mien Papa*. Knowing what he was doing, but determined the story was going to be told, Twab explained that because the idea was his, he would be the first to perform the brave deed, adding that it was one thing to be in the woods with your mates when it was getting dark, but another to be there on your own with only the trees for company.

Setting off, Twab strolled over to the swing some thirty yards into the wood and while swinging yelled out 'Geronimo,' loud enough to be heard. Satisfied with his performance he returned back to the road.

Sparrow went next. He walked down the first slope, then the second and third and because he was not afraid of the dark like someone he knew, meaning Golcho, and remembering their visit to Harry's Rock a few months previously, lit a fag, reached the swing, swung out and shouted 'Geronimo' and then made my way back to the road enjoying his smoke. On his way back, he even tried several times to blow one smoke ring through another but failed.

Because Sparrow teased Golcho about Harry's Rock when he got back, Golcho gave him the V sign. Sparrow said he could be as rude as he liked, but he was still unafraid of the dark, adding that it has never bothered him. Standing there, Twab pointed out that it was getting darker by the minute and that the sooner Golcho did the deed the sooner it would be over.

When Twab said he thought Golcho (who was still yelling out his *Oh Mien Papa*) began to wet himself, Golcho shouted back 'Oh no I never,' adding that he could hear every word that they were saying about him.

'Oh yes you were, Golch,' insisted Twab and Sparrow.

Refusing to be drawn in, Golcho kept his distance and remained silent. He did not really mind the story being told. In fact he was beginning to laugh himself as it unfolded. Going on, Sparrow said they both knew he was afraid, but Golcho, out of devilment shouted back, 'No I wasn't.' Whispering, Sparrow added, 'He was afraid we insisted he did it or we'd make him out a coward, and as Twab had already pointed out the longer he left it, the darker it was getting. So, making us promise not to run away, he finally set off.'

Both Twab and Sparrow began to belly laugh, knowing what was coming next. Sparrow said the moment Golcho was out of sight, he and Twab legged it up to the farm where they could hide in the bushes. Because Sparrow was laughing so much, he had to tell it in short bursts. 'What made it so funny …' is what he was trying to say, but both he and Twab were laughing their heads off, it being so funny at the time. But finally Sparrow managed to say, 'What made it so funny was, when Golcho shouted Ger….' He had to stop again. He was laughing so much; the story had to be put on hold again. The laughter became infectious and Champ joined in. It took several minutes for the laughing to peter out and when it did, Sparrow finally said, 'What made it so funny was, he must have shouted Geronimo as he was running down the first slope. Oh God it was funny.'

With that, Sparrow, Twab, and Champ burst out laughing again. The look on Golcho's face as he made his way down the first slope must have been one of sheer panic. But because the lads were laughing so much and feeling left out, Golcho caught up with them and joined in. For several minutes they all laughed their heads off. It was some time before Champ asked how it ended. Drying his eyes and throwing his arms around Golcho and squeezing him, Sparrow said, 'We teased him something rotten, didn't we my old mate?' Unable to deny it Golcho nodded. As they set off again up the Fron Hill, and after giving it some thought, Champ, who was feeling a little sorry for Golcho, said,

'Well, I know we've had a good laugh at Golcho's expense, but I'll tell you something, he's braver that me. I wouldn't have done something I was afraid of.'

Appreciating Champ's remark, Golcho turned to Twab and Sparrow and gave them his infamous top C from the *Student Prince* and, while hanging on to the note, gave them the V sign as well.

Fron Hill is approximately four hundred yards long from top to bottom, with three pathways leading off to various places. It is very steep with high hedges on both banks and oak trees that appear to be standing to attention like Roman centurions. It was a good sledge run in winter. Half way up, and having reached what you could call, I suppose, a crossroads, where two of the three paths led off, the lads, bar Champ, turned right. Seeing the view on the left and wanting to see more of it, he went and leaned against a five-bar gate and was amazed. The view was fantastic.

When the others came over and leaned on the gate with him they caught his mood and also stood there admiring the view of the entire Hafod side of the woods, along with most of Mr Williams's farm. The river could just be seen in places. The scene was so tranquil and, on the other side of the gate, the little path, which was a public right of way, not only split the field in two, but disappeared into a little tree lined gully. To their right was one half of the Fron Bank.

Moving on, the lads crossed over the road and hurried on past the entrance to Alum's farmyard. Several yards further along the public footpath, they again stopped to admire the view of the Dump side of their little wood, again seen in its entirety from the bridge all the way down to the old Plas Power colliery in Southsea.

Twab said the view will be ten times better in ten minutes time. Climbing over a makeshift stile (a wooden pallet standing on edge) the lads began to walk along a red shale path which had low cut hedges on either side. Again they came across a fantastic view of their little wood. The sun, having gone behind a small cloud, suddenly reappeared, not that they noticed. Nor did they see the flock of wild pigeons flying over their wood, because their attention was taken up with the enormity of the first of the two Fron Banks which, known as the red bank, was a mini mountain in Champ's eyes. It was the waste that had accumulated whilst digging out the coal. The Fron mine shaft was similar to, but much higher then Harry Rock's tunnel, most of them being high enough for both men and ponies to work in.

Champ was even more surprised when told there was an even bigger bank on the other side of this one, known as the Black Bank.

'Are you telling me,' Champ said pointing at the enormous mountain, 'that all that came out of the ground?'

'Yes,' said Sparrow, adding that it was just another closed down pit's slag heap. 'All this,' he said pointing at the red bank, 'came out of the ground.'

'The only difference,' said Golcho 'is that unlike Harry's Rock, all the shafts around here have been capped to prevent people from climbing down.'

'There's one such shaft at the end of this path,' said Twab pointing, 'Come on we'll show you.'

Running to the far end of the path which would take them into the village of Tan y Fron; the lads eventually came to a stop, with Golcho looking for a large enough stone. To their right, just inside Alum's field and circled off with fencing, was a disused, capped mine shaft.

'Come and see this, Champ,' said Golcho climbing over the fence. 'All these shafts that have been capped have this little hole for the gas to escape.'

Standing on the six-inches thick concrete cap and staring at a little hole in the centre, Champ watched as Golcho dropped his stone down the shaft. After what was an age, there was a loud crashing sound when it hit the bottom.

For Champ, the memory of Harry's Rock came flooding back, and he wondered why Harry's Rock had not been capped? Frightened of falling down the shaft (who was to say this cap would not suddenly break in two), Champ stepped off. 'Blimey,' he said, 'it must be twice as deep as Harry's Rock.'

'And the rest,' said Twab, adding that some shafts were miles deep.

'You want to hear the bang when a little Demon firework is dropped down one of these shafts,' said Sparrow. 'It's like a bomb going off.'

'And with a Jacky Jumper,' put in Golcho, 'you get several explosions going off one after the other. It's like being in that John Wayne film, *Sands of Iwo* ... something?'

'Is this cap safe?' Champ asked a little worried.

'Safe as houses,' said Golcho jumping up and down to prove it.

Again, because no one could say that it would not suddenly break in half and send them crashing down the shaft, Champ insisted they step off. He wanted them back on solid ground.

Pointing towards Southsea Bank, one of the last mines in the area to close down, Twab said this whole area was once a mining community. Curious, and looking at the enormous bank in front of them, Champ asked if they ever played on it.

'Not often,' said Twab scrunching up his face and shoulders. 'The reason is the Tan y Fron lads don't like it. If they see you, they chase you. If they catch you, they thump you.' With that he again scrunched up his face and shoulders.

'Oh, oh,' said Golcho pointing, 'look who's on the prowl.'

Seeing the plume of smoke from Terry's fire, Alum and an assistant were in hot pursuit. As the two men ran down the field in the hope of catching the perpetrators, Twab and the others wished there was some way of warning Terry that Alum was on his way.

'As much as I don't care for Terry and his lot,' said Twab, 'I wouldn't like to see them being caught.'

'Alum must be feeling brave today,' put in Sparrow, 'He normally only chases us little ones.' With his next breath he said, 'Look at what happened to little Barry Pritchard.'

'Why, what happened to little Barry Pritchard?' Champ asked curiously.

'He and his mates,' Sparrow explained, 'were swimming in the pool last year when Alum pounced on them. He caught little Barry and thrashed his legs with his stick.'

'Alum's very brave when it comes to seven-year-olds,' said Golcho adding, 'I bet when he sees how big Terry and his lot are he won't be so brave.'

Finishing off the story, Sparrow said Dave, who went around with Terry, Frank and Ernie, being Barry's older brother, went after Alum one day and found him ploughing the field by the Woods bridge and pelted him with stones.

There was no point in shouting to warn Terry as they were too far away; their fate was in the hands of the gods.

Not particularly bothered, Golcho said, 'Anyway, let's forget about them and see if there are any Tan y Fron lads around and climb the bank. But first let's show Champ the tree where that kid hanged himself all those years ago.'

'What?' said Champ as they raced back along the path.

Reaching the only tree on the path, a beautiful old oak, Champ was told that some poor soul, years ago, hanged himself on that very tree. No one knew why he did it, only that this was the actual tree. Keeping his thoughts to himself, Champ felt sorry for the tree. He could not understand why someone would want to hang himself on such a lovely tree. It was a magnificent specimen, one he would love to draw one day.

Moving on now that the tree had been explained, they scrambled through a gap in the hedge and came face to face with a wall of red shale. For a moment Champ thought he was standing at the bottom of a mountain. So, with their best foot forward, they began to climb up the steep slope. Their shoes were instantly filled with loose shale. Determined he was not going to fail, Champ grunted and groaned along with the others as they clawed their way up to the first ledge. There was a lot of slipping and sliding and it was a case of three steps forward and one back. But they eventually made it to the first level.

With so much height gained the view was fantastic. Not only could they see their woods, the village and Llidiart Fanny Farm, but they could also see smoke rising from several chimneys in the village, including Sparrow's and Golcho's. And they could see other villages as far away as Wrexham.

'Look,' said Champ pointing towards their woods. 'It's Terry and his lot scrambling up the Dump.'

Terry and his lot looked like ants from where they were, but the lads could just make out them scurrying up the dump having seen Alum and his assistant crossing the river. Suddenly they were seen running up the Woods hill and minutes later Alum and his assistant were seen walking back up the field. What the lads did not see was Alum dousing the fire and throwing the tins of beans and potatoes into the river.

'I'm glad they've got away,' said Twab, 'but we'll have to tease them about it in school on Monday.'

'Hey bugger,' Golcho piped up, 'what's this we. No way am I teasing them. I don't fancy another trip to the stink pipe thank you very much, because that's what will happen if we tease them.'

While they sat down to remove the shale from their shoes, Sparrow began to tell Champ about the fun that had been had on those two banks over the years. Interrupting, and wanting a little more of that fun, Golcho said, 'Well, there doesn't seem to be anyone around so let's go on a bit further.'

'Okay,' said Twab, adding for Champ's sake that they keep a sharp look out and be ready to run if they did come across any of the natives.

'Be ready to run where?' Champ asked.

'There,' said Golcho pointing towards their woods. 'Back down, onto the path and across Alum's field. He'll be too tired to chase us now.'

'Let's show Champ here how we jump off a cliff,' put in Sparrow.

So with that they began to climb the second of the three steep slopes. Again their shoes filled up with shale, and again there was a lot of slipping and sliding (and cursing, but not under their breath) as they struggled on, but they finally reached the second level. Roads had been constructed for the lorries that were taking the shale away for the construction of new roads and this red bank was slowly shrinking.

'I hope they're not taking the whole bank away,' said Golcho as he looked around, 'or we won't be able to play here any more.'

Reaching one of the man-made roads, they raced along while watching out for danger in the form of Tan y Fron lads. Suddenly they reached a massive pile of what Twab called clinkers. Climbing up and over them as a short-cut to reach the third level, just as steep as the previous two, Sparrow mentioned in passing that all the little caves in the clinkers would make good places to hide in.

After much giggling and mickey taking, due to the slipping and sliding back down the slope (it being just as steep as the other two), they reached the third level somewhat out of breath. Climbing up a loose shale bank was not easy. Looking back towards their village, Sparrow pointed out the view and several minutes were spent admiring it. Sparrow then pointed out how big their village was going to be when all the building was finished. From this vantage point the overall picture of how the Adwy was going to be developed could be seen. But it was sad to see all the fields they (apart from Champ) once played in slowly disappearing. The way things were going there were not going to be any fields left. In his, 'I told you so' voice, Twab for the umpteenth time reiterated that the village extension meant the loss of its fields. Could they not see why he did not want their village to expand, the losses being too great?

As much as Sparrow and Champ gave it some thought, it was too philosophical for Golcho. Bringing the mood back to more important things, he pointed out the thin strip of their little woods where so many hours had been spent in fun. Golcho was chuffed at being able to see their village, Southsea, Brynteg, Caego and New Broughton, as well as

Coedpoeth, the Smelt, and Minera. There were still plenty of fields left he insisted.

Still looking for a good place to jump off, the lads followed a well trodden path and shortly came across an area that had been made into a dirt track by the local lads. What fun they must have had, Champ thought, riding their bikes full pelt up and down the steep slopes and uneven ground. Sparrow reckoned they were dare devils. Alert and convinced there were no Tan y Fron lads around, the boys again began to look for a suitable place to jump off.

So again after much slipping, sliding and laughing, while making it as awkward as possible for the one next to you, by trying to push him down the last and final slope, they reached the summit, again out of breath. Several minutes of recuperating were again spent in looking at the magnificent view.

Appreciating the slight breeze, the lads had a 360° view and could see way beyond their own village. In fact they could see for what Twab said was hundreds of miles. Being on the summit of this fantastic red bank, Champ had his first view of the Black Bank. It was even higher than the one they were standing on, and it certainly was black.

It was sheer coincidence that both Twab and Champ had Edmund Hillary and Sherpa Tensing in mind, trying to imagine how they must have felt while standing on top of the world when they climbed Mount Everest about three months previously. It must have been a fantastic sight. When it was mentioned that two men had stood on top of the highest mountain in the world, Golcho said he would not have gone; it would have been too cold for him, plus he had read or heard somewhere that a creature that they were calling the Abominable Snowman lived there. He had no intention of ever meeting it, thank you very much. So instead, and eager to be doing the business, he said breaking Twab and Champ's reverie, 'Come on, 'let's find a good ledge to jump off.'

They soon found a slope that was to their liking, quite steep and undisturbed, ideal for jumping into.

As a budding artist, Champ was amazed at the different colours of shale there were. There were greys, blues and browns, as well as the overall reddish brown. He thought it was very picturesque. Twab, looking down the slope that had been chosen to jump into, which had at least a ten to twelve foot drop, said, 'Right lads, I don't have to tell you to keep your eyes peeled out for danger, but bags me jumping first.'

Stepping out of the way, Sparrow, Champ and Golcho watched as their leader walked several strides backwards, rubbing his hands. You could see in his face that he was eager to jump. He then scrunched up his face and ran towards the edge and leapt into the abyss. As he fell silently through the air towards the ground, having to suppress the urge to scream out, his stomach racing up into his throat, giving him the tummy-tickles, Twab thought it was every bit as good as being on the Monster. Suddenly he was sliding down the loose shale unhurt. He wished his time in the air could have been longer, it being more or less over the moment you jumped. Determined he was going to have another jump, he began what he knew was going to be the difficult task of climbing back up the slope, there being nothing to hang on to, or grab a hold of.

Seconds later, Sparrow jumped, and with the same emotions as Twab had just had, was soon sliding down the loose shale unhurt, determined that he too was going to have a second jump.

Golcho went next, but forgot all about the rule of being quiet. As he leapt into the abyss with eyes as big as saucers, his yahoo was as loud as his infamous top C and lasted for the full time he was in the air.

Twab (who was on his hands and knees struggling up the slope, the shale being so loose that he was sliding back down, with Sparrow on all fours just behind him and struggling to catch up) began to panic. Calling Golcho a 'Dozy so and so,' Sparrow accused him of trying to let the Tan y Fron lads know that they were on their bank. Giggling, Golcho told him to pipe down. All he could think of was climbing up this very awkward slope and having another jump.

When Twab finally reached the top and struggled over the edge on his belly (it being so awkward, there being nothing to hold on to) he told Golcho, who had caught up to Sparrow and was fighting it out with him to be the next one to climb over the edge, not to be so noisy.

Ready to jump, Champ, having chosen another slope that had not been disturbed, wanting to be the one who disturbed it, and thinking it was a shame that he was going to break up the pretty colours, but wanting to jump, ran towards the edge and leaped into the air and immediately began to feel his stomach racing up into his throat. It was a marvellous feeling. It reminded him of his one and only ride on the Big Wheel in Blackpool.

Like the others, he too wished his time in the air was longer, because no sooner did you leap than you were knee deep in shale and sliding down the slope. But for the next half hour the lads enjoyed repeatedly jumping off the cliff.

Slightly worried, Twab then decided that enough was enough. It was silly to over stay their welcome. Surely there were Tan y Fron lads around at this time of day? So, while making a game of it, the lads thoroughly enjoyed their running back down the slopes, slipping, sliding and laughing, and hoping not to fall. For reason's no one could make out, their jam-jars were not only still intact, but had also gathered a certain amount of red dust.

By taking a different route, they were soon back on the road with their shoes once again full of shale. They then sat on a grass verge at the top of the Fron Hill with their shoes and socks off, removing the last of the shale from in between their toes. While assessing the last three-quarters of an hour, it was agreed that it had been great fun and should be done again and quite soon.

But in fear of being seen by the Tan y Fron lads, Twab, now that they were shod once again, hurried his men along the Fron's only road. The Fron and Tan y Fron lads turned nasty with outsiders caught on their beloved banks.

A hundred yards on, with the Fron banks well behind them, and feeling much safer from attack, their urgent strides became a nice steady stroll. While walking along the road, with a hedge and ditch on their right, Champ asked if anyone knew what the lovely smell was that he was picking up. No one knew, but after a sniffing investigation of the flowers on route, trying to avoid the insects, especially the wasps, the scent they were trying to identify was that of a creamy white fluffy flower on long stalks which was very prominent; the flowers that had caught Champ's attention when they were being visited by all the insects you could think of – it was Meadow Sweet.

Now that the question had been solved, their next search as they walked along was to see what birds could be spotted other than the rooks, jackdaws and magpies that had already been identified.

Having travelled some eighty yards, and approaching an S-bend, a terrible stench suddenly knocked them for six. Tŷ Cerrig Farm was just up ahead. Coming out of the bend on this little winding back road, with Tŷ Cerrig Farm now in sight, the reason for the horrible smell was evident to everyone. The road, for about twenty yards on either side of the farm's main entrance, it being in a slight hollow, was flooded with what Twab called 'slurry.' The stench was horrendous, much worse than Mr Lloyd's glue in school. Everyone stopped at the edge of the green, slimy pool, and they all agreed that the farmer (Mr Tŷ Cerrig himself) should be shot for allowing this to happen. It was a public road for Pete's sake.

'So how do we cross?' Golcho asked.

No one answered for ages, but seeing a possible way across, Twab said they were going to have to find a way up to the fence, which was supporting the holly hedge that ran in front of the house, and hope that it would take their weight, adding there was no other way unless they walked through the smelly goo. He then asked, while scratching his head, if any of them had a better idea?

No one did. The green, gooey slime looked too deep to walk through without Wellingtons, and would be over their shoes.

Outraged with the mess and wishing to check the depth, Golcho tossed a stone into the goo. As predicted it was much too deep to walk through. Golcho said nothing, but was very angry. Sparrow then tossed several more stones into it, causing it to smell even more. 'It's well over our shoes,' he confirmed while shaking his head.

So it was decided that Twab's plan was the only way. They had to somehow reach the wire fence that supported the holly hedge. It looked like the prickly leaves were going to be a problem. So, in single file with Twab leading, with the green slime up to their laces, they each in turn trod very lightly and carefully up the slightly inclined bank until they reached the wire fence. The only thing in their favour was the fact that the ground they were now on was slightly higher than the road, which was something. Placing both feet on the bottom rung that held the fence together, which was quite sturdy, and while hoping to avoid the holly hedge's prickly leaves, Twab set off making sure that he knew where he was putting his feet. His time was slow, but when he jumped off at the half-way mark and tip-toed across the entrance (it being drier due to it being higher ground), he again stepped onto the wire fence and made his way very carefully across the last stretch of soggy ground. Having seen how it was done, Golcho went next, then Champ. Sparrow, as Tail-end Charlie, seeing the wire had buckled some, hoped it was going to last long enough for him to get across. He made it safely to the half-way stage and, like the others, tip-toed across the entrance, and like the others used the wire for the last stretch. When he stepped off the fence, Golcho had to be calmed down. He was so annoyed with the farmer that he wanted to throw stones at the farmhouse windows in protest for the mess on the road. It was Sparrow who finally consoled him when he said that he hoped someone would chop the farmer's balls off. Golcho laughed at the idea, but wished he could have thrown a couple of stones.

It was so nice being back on dry land. Reaching the T-junction some fifty yards further on, they all cleaned the goo off their shoes with clumps of grass. That done, they turned left up a fairly steep hill. Half way up, Golcho mentioned how nice it was to be away from that horrible smell and still wished he could have thrown stones at the house windows. One broken window would have sufficed he said.

The tall overgrown hedge on their left which was blocking their view suddenly petered out and became iron railings, revealing acres and acres of open fields, with grazing cattle in lovely countryside. Walking in silence, each was inwardly appreciating the splendour of his surroundings, while at the same time enjoying the lovely sunshine and the skylark that was singing its head off in the field on their side. They each tried to find it, but no one did. All they knew was that there was a skylark singing its head off somewhere above them.

Suddenly Sparrow announced that he could see it. Telling him to point it out and failing to see the blasted bird, Twab, followed the others and began to believe that Sparrow was telling porkies yet again.

'There it is,' said Sparrow pointing. 'Can't you see it; you must be blind.' He knew he was winding everyone up.

'I can hear it, but I can't see it,' is what everyone said.

Ending the prank, Sparrow suggested they move on or they would never get to Brymbo Pool at that rate. The weather was still being kind to them and the sun was beaming down from a cloudless sky. Even the breeze was gentle and warm.

Twab noticed some birds in the field opposite and pointed them out. There were several crows and magpies feeding in the distance. But on their side of the road, the blasted skylark that only Sparrow could see, was still twittering away. Suddenly they saw some blackbirds, thrushes and goldfinches all busy foraging for food and a robin was spotted perched on a post.

Thanks to the lads, Champ now knew the difference between a jackdaw, a rook and carrion crows. The jackdaw had a grey head and nape, and was the smallest of the three. The rook had a massive, grey beak, with fingers on the end of its wings. The carrion crow had a shiny, black beak and fluffy trousers.

Having reached the top of the hill they strolled along the flat and, on reaching a gateway, decided to have a rest. Twab pointed out a tractor in the distance. It was Mr Williams, raking one of his fields. In doing, so he was causing a huge cloud of dust to rise up into the air. As they watched, Twab casually mentioned that he would not have minded being a farmer when he grew up.

'Farming's not for me,' said Sparrow, kicking the bottom of the gate. Because the gate was rotten he was trying to see how much of it he could break off. 'I'm going down the pit.'

'Yea, me too,' said Golcho, 'I'm going down Bersham with my dad, and I want a snapping-tin just like his, the type you clip onto your belt.'

'What about you, Champ,' Sparrow asked. 'What are you going to do when you leave school?'

'I don't mind what I do at first,' said Champ enthusiastically, 'but when I'm eighteen and old enough I'm going in the army the way my dad did.'

'Oh, so is your dad's a soldier then?' Sparrow asked.

'He was. He was a sergeant major in the Royal Artillery.'

'So where is he now?' Twab asked, 'We've never seen him.'

'He was killed in the war.'

'Oh,' said everyone, wishing the question had not been asked. After several moments of feeling uncomfortable, Golcho suggested they get going or they would never get to Brymbo Pool. So, with their jam jars safely tucked in their jumpers, they set off.

Knowing Brymbo Pool was not that far away, and keeping well away from the barbed wire fence on their left, they again stopped to admire the view. When Champ asked if the village in the distance was their village he was told it was. There was a good view of Castle Road and the pond where Twab caught his tadpoles. Champ then asked why there was a cloud hovering over the village like the one Mr Williams was creating with his tractor?

'It's like what we told you when we took you down the woods the first time,' said Twab. 'Everyone in the village burns logs with their coal.' He then pointed out the Talwrn, the Smelt and Minera. They too had clouds hanging over them. Twab then went on to say that if and when his dad brought home a tree branch which he often did, it was him who had to saw it into logs.

'Yea, it's the same in our house,' said Sparrow and Golcho.

While Champ was pondering this, Sparrow noticed just how close to them a small herd of heifers had approached. They had stopped grazing and slowly made their way up to the fence. Those at the front leaned over the top barb and began to sniff the lads. All of them were snorting and blowing. Golcho waved his arms at them in order to frighten them, but all they did was move away. Regaining their courage, the animals they moved in again as if determined they were going to sniff the lads.

Golcho's second attempt at shooing them away also failed. All they did this time was jerk their heads back in a quick movement before moving in again.

'Bugger off,' Golcho told them from his side of the fence. 'Go on, bugger off'. He then noticed the strings of snot dribbling from their nostrils. 'Ugh,' he said cringing, 'look at the dirty buggers licking all that snot, ugh.'

For a dare, the lads grabbed Golcho's arms and frog marched him forward, saying they were going to rub his face in all that snot … and, believing they meant it, Golcho began to kick, swear and struggle. But the more he did, the more the lads held on to him. Belting out, and holding onto his infamous top C from the *Student Prince*, Golcho was not only released, but the heifers panicked and began to kick and thrash about. In the chaos that followed, and with his sense of humour kicking in, Golcho blasted out another piercing top C.

The lads then suddenly realised that things were not as they should be. The heifers were kicking their back legs into the air and were mooing ever so loudly. And things did not come right when they got Golcho to shut up. Because of the trouble he had caused by his stupid singing, Golcho was made to look at what he had done. His stupid top C had caused the animals to stampede. While half way through his, 'Oh bloody 'ell,' he ran off with the lads chasing after him. The only one who was still laughing was Sparrow who thought the situation was so funny. There they were, running as fast as they could on the road, with the heifers in the field running along with them.

After a while, Sparrow too began to see the danger they could be in and tried to run a little faster. Golcho felt he was running for his life. The heifers were not only running parallel to them on their side of the fence (kicking and thrashing about), but their mooing was causing other cows in other fields to join in. Suddenly it was like being in a Wild West film when the herd has stampeded.

Panicking, the lads ran on knowing that if they were caught by the farmer, it would mean a trip to the court house in Wrexham. It was as if all hell had broken loose – all because of Golcho's infamous top C.

'You've done it this time Golch,' Twab yelled out when he caught up to him, 'you and your stupid *Student Prince*.' Golcho was too frightened to answer back. He, along with the others just kept on running. Even Twab and Sparrow, who were still some way behind Champ, having overtaken Golcho, were panicking. They each made a left hand bend in the road and racing on listened to the thunder of hooves on their left and wished it was not happening. Their plan to take Champ to Brymbo Pool was simple enough. All they wanted was a little fishing, have a game or two and then get home in time for tea. Where was the harm in that? But between Terry and his lot, the mess by Tŷ Cerrig Farm and now this, their day was certainly far from being simple.

Twab and Sparrow watched as Champ raced away. He had obviously found that special gear he was always going on about and was nearing the only house on this stretch of road and the hill which they were all going to have to run up. Unbeknown to them, the occupants of the house, an old couple in their eighties, had a little Jack Russell called Monty which had witnessed the event which caused the heifers to stampede. Not having had the pleasure of killing a rat recently, Monty decided that he was going to jump over the gate and see if he could bite at least one of these four yobs that were running towards him.

Monty, who was getting on in years, regarded anything that ran as a yob and potential biting material.

Seeing the dog was trying to jump over the gate and believing it would bite him if it did, Champ said a little prayer, but it was not answered and the dog jumped the gate and began to bark its head off. For reasons known only to Monty himself, he let Champ pass before running into the middle of the road and barking the place down while waiting for the other three to approach him. Monty's tail went stiff. The situation for Twab, Sparrow and Golcho was: mad cows to the rear and coming up fast and a yapping dog, which was more than likely going to bite at least one of them, to their front. Unbeknown to them however, the heifers had stopped stampeding; having reached the electric fence and knowing it gave a nasty bite, they went back to doing what they did best, chewing grass.

Running nearer to the yapping dog, Twab gave the order that no one was to stop for anything. It was Rule No 3, every man for himself. They were to keep running no matter what. Ironically, as much as Monty was kicked at, shooed away and sworn at, and as much as he ran in and out of the lads' legs, he failed to nip anyone which for him was most annoying. One nip would have made his day. Hearing the chaos that Monty was causing, his owner, Mr Jones, came out and rescued the lads by ordering Monty to 'Get in this house.' But Monty went instead in search of a rat in the barn.

Grateful to the old gentleman (but still angry with the dog), the lads raced on up the hill puffing and panting. Champ, with his amazing speed, had already reached the crossroads and not knowing which way to go, was sitting on the grass verge. He watched as Twab and Sparrow (puffing and panting) raced up the hill and flopped down beside him. By the time Golcho came in, also puffing and panting, Champ, Sparrow and Twab were laughing their heads off. Their laugher was from the nervous tension they had built up. As funny as it would have seemed to a bystander, seeing them laughing for no apparent reason, all four were shaking inside, so much so that the laughter went on for several minutes. It was Champ who finally asked what the Dickens happened back there? Golcho told him while wiping the tears from his eyes. He put all the blame on Twab and Sparrow for trying to rub his face in all that snot. He actually called them 'Silly buggers.'

'Did you see all that snot,' said Sparrow, 'it was dribbling every-where?'

'And they were licking it up,' said Golcho, 'the dirty buggers.'

After several minutes of laughing, glad they were safe, Twab said, 'I tell you what, that is definitely the best chase we've ever had from cows. It's even better than the one we had while crossing Alum's field last year.' That incident had occurred about three weeks before Champ's arrival. The lads were crossing Alum's fields on their way to do some work on the dam, when suddenly and out of the blue, the cows, which had been grazing only moments ago, gave chase. What the boys did not know was that a third calf had just been born and cows do not like strangers around their little ones, so they gave chase.

'What would those heifers have done had they caught us?' Champ asked. No one knew exactly, but everyone was trying to imagine what might have happened. The mood was suddenly somber and boister-ous. Sombre because they each had visions of being in hospital with broken bones and then being taken to Wrexham police station. Who knows, they could have gone to gaol. Boisterous, because thank God none of that was going to happen. Their being safe and sound was why they laughing their heads off.

When the laughing eventually died out, Twab suggested that they moved on. Halfway along the road heading towards a farm, just a stone's throw away from Brymbo Pool, Golcho noticed that there were cows in the fields on both sides of the road. To keep an eye on them (one encounter with cows was enough for one day) he ran up the little embankment every now and then to check that they were behaving themselves. They were. They were mature cows, and grazing.

Champ in the meantime was being given some advice by Twab in the art of fishing with a jam jar (the secret being in the way you cast out) when Sparrow, who was lagging behind, shouted to say he had found an empty blackbird's nest. But no one was interested. Had it been found two weeks earlier when it was home to four chicks, that would have been interesting.

When Sparrow caught up with the others, Golcho was pointing out the mirage on the road just this side of the farm to Twab and Champ. Not that Champ could see it and it had to be explained to him that, on hot days, you could see little pools of water on the road which looked like pools of water, shimmering like they did in the films when the hero was lost and dying of thirst. When at last Champ could see it, which took ages, he became rather excited, never having seen a mirage before. And yes, it was shimmering. When he asked what caused it, Golcho said it was something to do with the day being hot.

For several minutes they all stared at the mirage. It really did look like a pool of water and, if you had never seen one before, you would be fooled into thinking that it was a pool of water. Sparrow pointed out that the closer you go to it, the quicker it disappeared. He did not know why that was, other than it did. When they reached it, it was gone.

Sparrow then asked if they wanted to know one of his secrets, passed onto him by his dad. When they all said they did, he told them to close their eyes tight so that no light could be seen. They were then told to apply a little pressure on their eyeballs with their thumb and forefinger and *voila*, they would see a lovely yellow colour that changed into different shapes. To everyone's surprise they did see what Sparrow predicted they would see.

They were then told that if they scrunched their eyes up and applied different pressures to their eyes, the yellow colour would change into other colours. And again they did. It was fantastic.

Telling them another secret, Sparrow said that if they stared really hard, without blinking, at a tree they were approaching, for at least a minute, and then closed their eyes, they would still see an image of the tree or whatever it was they had stared at. And again it worked. Everyone stared at a tree while Twab counted out a hundred and, when they closed their eyes, once again the tree appeared for several moments before it disappeared. It was amazing.

Having told enough secrets for one day, Sparrow suggested they should move on and, reaching the farm, they turned left and raced along a dirt path just wide enough for a tractor. A hundred yards on, taking a sharp right-hand bend they came face to face with Brymbo Pool.

This was not one pool but two, surrounded by the countryside that Champ knew he would be drawing one day. The only thing that separated the pools was the tractor path they were standing on. To their left, running the full length of the path, was a wire-netting fence behind which was the larger of the two pools, the one they had come to fish in.

Beyond the pool were fields that were covered in flowering gorse bushes. It was a lovely sight. On their right, and again running the full length of the path and beyond, was a prickly hedge that encircled the smaller pool which was affectionately known as the 'hot pool' on account of the steam that was always rising from it.

Apparently the small pool supplied the local steelworks with water which having been heated up, returned via pipes and ducts. The T-junction at the far end of the path would take them home if they turned left, or to the village of Brymbo and elsewhere if they turned right. Champ thought the view of the pool they had come to fish, whose water was rippling along its northern shore, was fantastic. Golcho who was willing to bet a shilling that there was more gorse here than in Alum's field.

To the left of where they were going to be fishing and surrounded by gorse bushes in flower, was an old broken-down band stand which in its heyday had been very popular. Between the bandstand and the shore line was the pump house which supplied the water to the local steelworks. On their left, well away from the pool, was a huge bottle-shaped structure, affectionately known as The Bottle. Champ was beginning to wish he had brought his sketchpad and coloured pencils. He would have been quite happy to have sketched while the lads fished.

The smaller pool that always gave off steam, was very polluted, not that the local lads who used it as a swimming pool cared. The main pool (the one with the fish in) was there to top up this hot pool if and when its level dropped. It was according to Twab, the property of the local steelworks.

'Cor-blimey,' is all Champ could say while trying to take it all in.

'Come on, let's get fishing,' said Golcho as he ran down the path. Going after him, they all ran to the far end of the pool and wriggled under the barbed-wire fence. They then approached the pool on their left. Champ thought it looked like a sheet of glass. There was hardly a ripple to be seen.

They each tied their string to their respective jam jars and, finding a vacant catch hole in the grass for any fish caught, after telling Champ the best way to do it, all very carefully cast out their jam jars. The technique entailed:

(1) Tying the string around the neck of the jar.

(2) Very carefully casting the jar out so that the thick bottom landed on the water.

(3) As it bobbed in the water, pulling on the string so that the water seeped in.

(4) As the jar sank, preying that lady luck was on your side, because if she was not and the jar hit a stone and smashed, you ended up being a nuisance to the others.

A silence came over the lads as they watched the little shoals of minnows swimming up and down the shore line. If and when a shoal of fish swam up to any one of the jars, the individual felt he was being teased, because they would swim up to their jar, but would not go in. When this occurred, the individual would lean forward, take up the slack string, ready to pull the jar out should any fish enter it. But today, the fish were cagey. To them this massive see-through object in front of them was a mystery. They had never seen a Robertson's jam jar before. They did not know that they would be thrown back at the end of the day because of the chemicals in tap water which would kill them and so there was no point in taking them home.

Suddenly, several fish were taking notice of Twab's jar.

'Could be in luck fellows,' he said as the fish swam up to his jar, wriggling their tails like mad as if wondering what on earth this massive see-through object could be? No one said anything as there were fish swimming around their jars as well. Suddenly three fish were at the entrance of Twab's jar. Willing them to go in, he tensed up and prepared to pull out. 'Go in, go on,' he whispered. To his delight one did enter, followed by another, then another, but as quick as a flash swam out again. Cursing, Twab ordered them to go back in. Not only did the same three fish go back in, but another two followed them. There were now five fish in his jar. With all the slack taken up, he yanked the jar out of the water and saw that only one fish had managed to escape. The other four were swimming in circles around the bottom of his jar.

'Yahoo,' he yelled, 'first catch to me.'

To prevent their strings from floating away, the lads weighted them with stones and then went over to have a look at Twab's catch. The four fish were still swimming around giving the impression that they were head butting the jar. Twab, with the others watching, placed them in his catch hole, making sure they had enough water, then cast out again and the atmosphere calmed down.

Moments later, Sparrow pulled one out, and after showing it to everyone placed it in his catch hole, again making sure the fish had enough water.

Securing their lines with stones, Twab and Sparrow went over to see how Champ and Golcho were doing. As they neared, a shoal of about twenty fish approached Champ's jar.

'Be ready to pull Champ,' said Sparrow feeling the expert fisherman.

'Take up all the slack and be ready to pull,' Twab advised.

Excited and nervous at the same time, Champ watched as two fish entered his jar then a third.

'Pull,' said Sparrow.

Champ yanked his jar out, but when they looked inside it was empty.

'You were too slow,' Twab told him. 'Never mind, better luck next time.'

'Got one – no, two,' yelled an excited Golcho.

'Make your mind up, Golch,' Sparrow teased, 'Is it one or two?'

Golcho never answered. He was much too busy pouring his single fish into his catch hole and making sure it had enough water. Glad he was not the last one to land a fish, he strolled over to Champ and, like the others, hoped it would not be too long before he caught a fish.

Minutes later, Golcho pulled another three out, and while placing them in his catch hole with his other one, shouted, 'Hey, my luck's in.' But Golcho's luck was not in, it was about to run out. Casting out, his jar hit the water alright, and sank alright, but fell on a stone and smashed. Cursing he reeled in his string, undid the knot and placed it in his pocket for use again. He then went over to Twab and complained that his jar had just smashed.

'I know,' said Twab who was just about to pull out, 'I heard you cursing. Now go and pester someone else.'

Given the cold shoulder by the others as well, Golcho strolled past the pump house and made for the old broken down bandstand. Climbing up the three steps, he began to toss over the top rusty rail which had somehow managed to hang on to some of its original blue paint. Spotting an old rusty Duraglit tin under a nearby gorse bush, Golcho fished it out and placed it on one of the few remaining steel knobs that encircled the bandstand and used it for target practice. Throwing stones at the tin, he remembered the time when, as a baby, he and his family had come here to listen to one of the many brass bands that played here on Sunday afternoons. Golcho smiled when he remembered the pram he was in at the time. Its two back wheels, slightly larger than the two front ones. As there were no more babies after him, it ended up as a truck several years later. But suddenly his reverie was broken. Sparrow was joining him as his jar had also smashed.

After some ten minutes of throwing stones at Golcho's rusty tin, Sparrow, with Golcho in tow, convinced the other two that fishing was boring and that they would have more fun playing in and around the old Bottle.

Agreeing, they all returned their fish to the pool. Twab won the competition, having caught eight. He beat Sparrow by two. Champ and Golcho had caught three each. Twab and Champ hid their jars under some gorse bushes for the next time then raced after Sparrow and Golcho who were already making their way over to the Bottle.

The Bottle was a huge, free-standing building, shaped like a funnel that was roughly forty-feet high with an inside base that was some thirty feet in diameter. There were two openings. One, a small doorway and the other a large, elongated window half-way up the west-facing wall. The top section tapered off to about ten feet in diameter and was open to the elements. Three quarters of the way up the inside wall was a ledge wide enough for a person to walk on. The Bottle was a favourite nesting place for several kinds of birds, including kestrels. Whereas the kestrels nested at the top, the smaller birds, the robins and dunnocks made their nests almost at ground level.

According to Twab, the Bottle was once a drying kiln for the now closed down Caello brickworks, but Sparrow did not think so. He seemed to think it was something to do with candles. Golcho thought it was something to do with the steelworks, it being so close to the two pools. The truth was nobody knew.

Approaching the Bottle which was slowly being hemmed in by all the encroaching vegetation, Champ was amazed at its size and all the gorse bushes in the area. The smell reminded him of something, but he just could not put a finger on it, but it was very pleasant. Reaching the Bottle, a quick look around confirmed there were no Brymbo lads hiding in the bushes. Then the lads then began to relax. Suddenly the smell that Champ was having trouble with came to him, 'Coconuts,' he yelled out.

'What's he on about?' asked Golcho.

'All these yellow flowers,' said Champ, 'smell of coconuts.'

When everyone agreed with him, the first game was decided upon. They were going to play tick, with Sparrow as the chaser.

Twab, Champ and Golcho ran into the Bottle and, choosing one of the four struts that braced the wall, began to climb up. Moments later they were standing on the ledge that ran all the way around the building. From there they could hear Sparrow coming to the end of his count of one hundred, letting them know he was coming whether they were ready or not. He ran into the building and saw them looking down at him from the ledge.

As usual, Golcho began to tease Sparrow by saying he was not going to catch them. Then Twab had an idea. He suddenly wanted Champ as the chaser to play a joke on him. It was suddenly imperative that Champ should be the chaser.

When Sparrow was half-way up his strut, Twab ordered everyone to climb down. Seeing this, Sparrow just watched while hanging on. It did not make sense. They were making it easy for him. So with everyone back on the ground, Sparrow scurried back down and ticked Twab. Carrying on with his plan, Twab then suggested that they played hide and seek instead, and that Champ should be the seeker because of his not knowing the area. Twab said it would make the game that much more interesting.

So, as Champ closed his eyes and began to count slowly up to a hundred, the others ran off with Twab explaining his plan to them. Inside the Bottle Champ counted and listened as they ran away. Suddenly he could not hear them anymore and he had only counted up to fifty-three. What he did not know was that his having to count up to a hundred, slowly, was giving the lads time to scramble under a clump of gorse bushes some distance away where there had once been a cellar.

In its then state of disrepair, this was an ideal hiding place. It was eight-feet long, three feet wide and three feet deep – perfect for hiding in. On reaching the gorse bushes they each in turn scrambled into the den and waited.

Having finished his count, Champ stepped out of the Bottle and began to search the area by walking around the outside of the building, but saw nothing. He then began to search the nearby bushes, unaware that he was being watched. Moving away from the Bottle, and in the wrong direction, Champ searched the bushes but could find no trace of them. He searched and searched, but it was as if they had gone home. Fed up and knowing shouting them would be a waste of time, he realised they had played a joke on him. Champ decided to turn it around and play one on them.

He knew there was no point in shouting for them to show themselves. That would only encourage them to keep their cover. So he casually walked away, under the pretence that he was still searching but in fact was going back to the pool to do a bit more fishing. Golcho, after what seemed like ages, said, 'Where the hell is he? He should have found us by now?'

Thinking he could hear a voice, Sparrow told Golcho to 'Shush,' or they would be found.

'I think he's stopped looking for us,' said Twab.

Thinking Twab was right, and as quietly as he could, Golcho climbed out of the den and began to search the area. There was no sign of Champ. One by one the other two left the den to search for the elusive 'Scarlet Pimpernel'. They searched everywhere and finally ended up back by the Bottle with no sign of Champ. Golcho began to shout. 'Champ, where are you?' But Champ, who was happily fishing declined to answer.

'Champ,' yelled Twab, 'wherever you are, answer me. That's an order.'

Having a hunch, Sparrow walked over to some high ground which gave an overall view of the area, and called the others to come and see. 'Look,' he said, 'he's only buggered off back to the pool and is fishing.'

'The crafty sod,' said Twab realising his joke had backfired.

'Let's thrown him in the pool head first,' suggested Golcho.

Champ was fishing alright, but not for fish. What was more

important than catching any fish was a good overall view of the pool. Seeing the lads approaching and trying to play it cool with one eye on the fishing, the other on the lads, he knew they would have some form of revenge in mind. Some thirty feet away and trying to be casual, Sparrow said, 'You crafty old bugger, you've had us looking everywhere for you and here you are, fishing.'

Champ said nothing. He was more interested in what they had in mind. He shifted his weight so as to have them in full view all the time.

'Yea, fair play,' said Golcho, 'you fooled us. There we were, thinking you were looking for us and all the time you were fishing.' He began to laugh.

It was Twab's silence that put Champ on red alert. He was convinced more than ever that they had something up their sleeves for him.

Pulling his jar out of the water, Champ placed it at the ready. It was to be his first line of defence. A chase was inevitable, but because of Champ's great speed, Twab had given instructions that no one was to charge until he gave the order and then they were to rush him and overpower him. Sod his judo.

As the gap between them closed, Champ began to get the jitters. He knew something was up in the way they were trying to be casual. They were acting as if nothing had happened and that was not like them. 'Why do I get the feeling you lot are miffed with me?' said Champ gripping his jam jar. Golcho, who could stand it no longer, shouted, 'Get the little sod.' Rushing forward the three of them were suddenly stopped dead in their tracks, more puzzled than surprised.

Activating his first line of defence, Champ had thrown the water from his jam jar, not so much as at them, as above them. The plan was to startle them just long enough for him to scramble up the embankment and make his getaway. As they all scurried about trying to avoid the dousing they were likely to get, Champ scarpered up the embankment and ran off in the direction of the Pump House.

'You sneaky sod,' Golcho yelled as they began to wipe themselves down.

'You'll pay for that,' shouted Sparrow, 'you see if you don't.'

Letting out a victory yahoo, Champ ran past the Pump House and headed for the bandstand, laughing at the look on their faces when they realised they were going to be a little wet. He knew for certain now that he would be in trouble if they were to catch him. But because the lads were hot on his tail, having run along the shoreline and then scrambled up the embankment, Champ ran to the right of the bandstand and found there was nowhere else to run. There were too many bushes and brambles blocking his way. He was trapped, or so the lads thought.

Twab ordered Golcho to stay with him. They would go to the right. Sending Sparrow to the left, the plan was to trap Champ and carry out Golcho's suggestion of throwing him into the pool head first.

Seeing their ploy, Champ encouraged them to come and get him by pulling faces at them. Like that first day in school, when Terry and his lot were coming for him, he had a plan. At the last moment (just as the lads thought they had him) he jumped up, and with one hand on the bottom rung of the bandstand, rolled under the lower rail. Springing to his feet he raced across the old clapped-out stage whose concrete base was crumbling, and leapt through the gap where the middle and top rail had once been. Landing in the crouch position to buffer the impact, he made his escape. He ran back past the Pump-House and, turning left, went along the grass verge parallel to the pool, heading for the barbed-wire fence. To tease his pursuers he slowed down and allowed them to come within striking distance of him then, when they thought they had him, sped away laughing which made them angrier by the minute.

'That bugger's making me angry,' said Twab who only swore when angry.

'Don't worry,' said Sparrow indicating the pool with his head, 'he's going in there when we catch him.'

'If we catch him,' put in Golcho.

Reaching the wire fence Champ fell to the ground in order to roll under the bottom rung, but as he did so his right-hand sleeve caught in a barb. Seeing this, the lads moved in for the kill. With Golcho's cry of 'We've got you now you little sod,' ringing in his ears, Champ untangled his sleeve, but caught his trousers on another barb. 'Oh, oh,' he murmured, realising they were too close for comfort. With three pairs of hands reaching down to grab him, he decided on some drastic action. Knowing there would be a telling off when he got home, Champ yanked himself free and thus created a three-inch tear.

His worrying about the telling off he was going to be having off his mum only stopped when Twab's hand grabbed his right arm. But when Twab felt the barb scratching his hand he quickly let go. Champ completed his roll to freedom.

He then raced along the red shale tractor path backwards while referring to them as slow coaches, meaning they would never catch him now.

'When we do catch you,' Golcho yelled, his head indicating at the pool, 'it's in there you're going, head bloody first.'

Watching the lads in turn rolling under the bottom barb, Champ shouted back that if they caught him they would not have to throw him in, he would jump in. When Sparrow rolled under the fence, he being the last, Twab called a meeting. 'Right lads,' he said angrily, 'we run him until we catch him, okay?' Both Sparrow and Golcho nodded and so set off at full pelt. Champ again allowed them to come within striking distance of him and then sped away laughing. On their second attempt at catching him, Champ again slowed down by pretending to fall this time, but just when they thought they had him, Champ again sped away knowing he was making them angry. Realising they were never going to catch him and carry out Golcho's wish of throwing him in the pool head first, Twab, puffing and panting, and with the agreement of the other two, called off the chase. During the arm shaking, the Roman Way, Golcho saw several lads at the top of the path just standing around. 'Oh, oh,' he said, 'could be trouble.'

Five Brymbo lads, whose ages ranged from thirteen to fifteen, possibly sixteen, were definitely blocking their way. It was always a dangerous time when two sets of lads from different villages met up. There was never any explanation given, but nine times out of ten a confrontation of some kind broke out which usually ended in violence.

'What we gonna do?' Golcho asked.

'I think we should make a run for it the other way' said Sparrow.

'I don't think so,' said Champ, 'look behind.'

Coming up from the rear were three more Brymbo lads.

With the pool on their right and a prickly hedge that was too high to climb over on their left, there was nowhere for them to run.

'We'll just have to hope they let us pass,' said Golcho with fingers crossed.

Twab agreed but felt they would not do so. 'Come on then,' he said, 'let's see what happens. Let's see if they will let us pass?'

Acting like they were not bothered, they set off talking amongst themselves. Twab pointed out how lovely the two swans on the far side of the pool were as they swam through the water. Hearing the sound of running feet behind them, Twab gave the order to see if they could get past the dodos up front. Setting off at a fast pace, Twab again gave the order that rule three was to be implemented if need be.

'What is rule three?' Champ asked, never having heard it before.

'It's every man for himself,' Twab replied, not believing for a minute that they would be allowed to pass. And he was right. The five Brymbo lads had no intentions of letting them pass. 'You lot aren't going anywhere,' one of them shouted and as Twab and Co tried to force their way past the Brymbo lads, they were overpowered and captured. Moments later the other three completed the trap.

When all the pushing and shoving and threatening ceased, one of the Brymbo lads said. 'So, what are you lot doing here?' Before any answer was given the same lad said, 'So where you from?' Again before an answer was given the same lad said, 'So who are you?'

With that, one of the lads at the back came forward. 'First things first lads,' he said with authority.

Twab thought he knew this lad from somewhere?

'Well kid,' Sparrow was asked 'Where you from?'

'The Adwy,' said Sparrow to prevent being hit.

'Is that so?' said the one who had obviously taken over. Turning to Golcho he asked if they were all from the Adwy.

'Yes, we are,' said Twab having decided he was going to show this Brymbo lad that he too was a leader of men.

'Speak when you're spoken to kid or you'll get a thick ear,' said the Brymbo lad looking at Twab. After a long stare he said, 'Do I know you?' Twab suddenly remembered who this Brymbo lad was and shook his head. But in truth he did know him. There was a big fight down by the school canteen between this lad and Terry some time last year with Terry being the outright winner when he landed a good right-cross, splitting his opponent's lip and causing him to bleed like a pig. Realising it would be foolish to mention the fight at this precise moment, Twab scrunched his face up at Sparrow and Golcho, hoping they would not mention the fight which they too had witnessed. Even Champ understood Twab's meaning.

The fight had occurred because Terry had caught this Brymbo lad bullying a first year who just happened to be an Adwy lad. Terry took it upon himself to show him that bullying an Adwy lad would not be tolerated. Suddenly Twab remembered his name, Tony something. He also remembered how bloody his face had been when Terry had finished with him and began to fear that Tony would want some sort of revenge if he realized he was present at the fight.

Sparrow telling him that they were from the Adwy had not been in their favour. Crossing his fingers Twab hoped for the best.

'So what we going to do with them?' someone asked.

'Well, for a start they can empty their pockets out,' said Tony.

'That's stealing,' said Champ.

'Shut you face kid,' said Tony, adding that he knew it was stealing.

'For that,' Tony said, 'we'll start with you. Empty your pockets out, kid.' But when Champ refused, Tony said he would not tell him again. Champ placed his hands in his pockets and just stood there. The fact that there was nothing of value in his pockets was not the point, there was a principle involved. Champ was adamant that he was not going to be bullied or robbed.

'C'mon kid,' yelled Tony, 'we haven't got all day.' While waiting for this stubborn Adwy kid to empty his pockets out, Tony ordered his other prisoners to empty their pockets out as well.

'I'm not emptying mine,' said a defiant Champ, 'you can all get lost and anyway there's only a dirty hanky in mine full of snot.'

'There's nothing in mine either,' said Golcho jumping on the bandwagon.

'Nor mine,' put in Sparrow.

Believing he had not been recognised and wanting to keep it that way, Twab, with fingers crossed, said nothing. Sparrow was then picked out and frisked. Tony went through his pockets and discovered a packet of eight Woodbines and a few matches. Turning to Champ he said angrily, 'So, there's nothing in your pockets, huh?' Sparrow was slapped across the head for telling lies. Tony said that everyone in the Adwy told lies. Nodding to his mates he yelled 'Search um.'

Having been searched, Sparrow was thrown to one side. Twab,

Champ and Golcho were slapped and punched rather viciously about the head and body and were then pushed to the ground.

'We can do this the hard way or the easy way,' said Tony looming over them 'Make's no difference to me.'

'Why don't you all get lost and leave us alone?' said an angry Champ. 'You think you're clever picking on ... ' But he never finished. Tony began to slap him about the head. 'I can see you want this done the hard way, kid,' said Tony. When he had finished slapping Champ he turned to his pals and told them not to just stand there, but was to go through their prisoners' pockets. While Twab and Golcho were being searched, Tony decided that he was personally going to search the mouthy one and began to take his coat off. Seeing his chance and remembering what his Uncle Dave had said one time, Champ waited until Tony's coat was half way down his arms then leapt into action? His uncle's teaching was about to be put to the test.

Champ turned side on to Tony and stamped on his left foot as hard as he could and, when the coat fell to the floor, grabbed his right wrist and, with his fingers pointing upwards, placed him in a wrist lock. He made sure that Tony's little finger was in the twelve o'clock position, thus locking the elbow and shoulder, thus preventing Tony from moving either to his left or to his right. Champ then applied pressure to his wrist by pushing his hand forward forcing him onto his right knee and held him there firmly. Seeing Tony's mates racing forward, Champ ordered them back or else. To prove he meant business, he applied more pressure to Tony's wrist by again pushing his hand forward. Tony yelped in pain as the pressure increased.

Now that he was in control of the situation, Champ ordered Twab, Sparrow and Golcho to make a run for it. When they refused, he ordered them, saying he would be alright. As they made a run for it, he kept the pressure on Tony's wrist by pushing the hand forward with his thumbs. Champ had the bully boy fully immobilised. The more Tony struggled, the more pain he found himself in. Bewildered, Tony found it painfully amazing that he was unable to move to his left or right, that his whole arm was locked solid.

Suddenly Tony's friends began to inch forward again. Seeing this, Champ applied a little 'on/off' pressure to Tony's wrist, telling him to tell his friends to back off, or else.

'Do as he says,' said Tony, who was clearly in pain.

Champ had a quick peep up the pathway while maintaining his hold on Tony. There was no sign of his friends. Pleased that they were out of danger, Champ noticed that Tony's mates were again inching forward.

'I won't tell you lot again to keep back,' said Champ applying more on/off pressure to Tony's wrist, making him squirm, then decided the message would be much better coming from Tony himself.

'Okay Tony, ready when you are,' said Champ realising his mates were only a couple of yards away,' Tell um to back off.'

'Do as he says,' Tony ordered, 'he's breaking my wrist.' He then let out a couple of squeals to let them know he was not joking.

'What you don't understand,' said Champ, 'is that I can make Tony do anything I want, can't I Tony.' To prove his point, Champ applied some on/off pressure.

'Yes, yes, yes.' Tony yelled out.

'Just to prove I'm not telling porkies,' said Champ wanting to humiliate him. 'Tony will now raise his left arm.'

Tony complied.

'Tony will now lower his left arm and place it on his head.' Tony complied.

'Now tell your friends why you're doing this,' demanded Champ.

'Because I'm in pain, that's why,' Tony yelled out.

'It's called judo fellows, and believe me I'm an expert, young as I am. Don't let my size or age fool you.'

'Being an expert isn't going to help you when we get our hands on you pal,' said one of the bullies.

'I hope you like hospital food, kid,' another one shouted.

'You're only making it worse for Tony,' said Champ applying a little more on/off pressure to Tony's wrist, causing him to yell out again.

'Back off fellows, I can't take much more of this. It's really hurting.'

The lads did as they were told and backed off several yards. With another look up the path to make doubly sure that there was no sign of Twab, Sparrow or Golcho, Champ, with a feeling they may have sneaked back said. 'Right, now listen to me, all of you. I'm only going to say this once. If you don't want Tony's wrist broken, which I will if I have to, you are to walk away to the end of the lane. Then one of you is to come back with a wet cloth to wrap around Tony's wrist. Is that clear? I'll be staying with him until I see just one of you returning. If I see more than one of you, well, it'll be a long time before Tony ever uses a pen again, now get going.'

Champ watched them walk away, then leaning over Tony said, 'In the meantime, I'll have my friend's fags and matches back.'

Tony very carefully reached into his left-hand jacket pocket on the floor and retrieved the said items which Champ took and said, 'Tony, I know you're mad at me, but I'm going to let you go in a minute, but before I do, please take this advice. When your friend has wrapped whatever he's going to use around your wrist, just go home and rest it. It's not broken. If you keep a wet cloth on it, you should be alright.'

Champ slowly eased the pressure off Tony's wrist, and allowed him to wriggle his fingers in order to get the circulation going. Champ then released him completely.

Tony instantly cradled his arm and wrist. Even though his right foot was still throbbing, his wrist was more painful. While clutching Sparrow's fags and matches in his hands and walking backwards ready to run, Champ said, 'See you.'

'Oh you'll see me, kid,' said Tony nursing his wrist. 'You'll see me alright when you're not expecting it. Then I'll show you what I can do.'

When Champ saw Tony's friends running up the path, he turned and raced after Twab, Sparrow and Golcho. With one last look over his shoulder, he saw Tony and his lot not coming after him, but walking away for which he was ever so grateful.

Feeling good Champ dug down deep for that special gear and raced after his three best friends catching up with them up near Ty Cerrig Farm as they were just about to again use the wire fence to cross over the pool of green slime. After greeting Champ, and while waiting for Sparrow who, as tail-end-Charlie, was the last to come across the wire, Golcho asked Twab for permission to throw a stone at the farmer's window, but was refused. They had been in enough trouble for one day.

That night in bed, Champ meticulously filled in the day's events in his diary. His encounter with Tony was underlined three times.

Part Five: The White Hand, October, 1953

ALAN COULD NOT UNDERSTAND WHY HE WAS AWAKE SO EARLY. He had no idea of the time other than it was still dark outside and it was Saturday morning once again. My goodness, the weeks were flying by. Lying there he suddenly remembered last Sunday's confrontation with those Brymbo lads and hoped Tony's wrist was okay. There was no reason why it should not be, but as he lay there in the dark all snuggled up under the warm bedclothes, he could not help but feel pleased with himself for saving the day with his judo. Reliving the event he remembered how it had begun, how the Brymbo lads had blocked their path and were going to rob them. Highway robbery was as alive and well in 1953 as it had been in Dick Turpin's day.

Alan smiled when he remembered the look on the faces of the Brymbo lads when he grabbed Tony's wrist and put him in a wrist lock. How he had squealed and his mates had backed off, and how the lads showed their appreciation when he caught up with them by the 'Smelly Farm' as Golcho was now calling it. Wow, they sure made a fuss of me, he mused. Smiling, Alan said a big thank you to his Uncle Dave in Chester for teaching him judo. It certainly worked.

He then began to think about the bird he had seen the previous Sunday morning while going down the Woods hill with the lads on their way to Brymbo Pool, before they had their confrontation with Terry and Co. He remembered that it had a red splodge on its head and rump. So strong was the memory, he decided he was going to do something about it right now. Normally he had to be dragged out of bed at the weekend but he jumped up and got dressed. With no idea of the time, other than that the sky was beginning to brighten, he tip-toed into Jeannie's little box room for her pencil case. But where was it being kept these days? Failing to find it, and knowing there would be a telling off, he put the light on and shook his sister, 'Jeannie,' he whispered. 'Wake up.' When there was no response he shook her again, this time

230

a little more aggressively. 'Jeannie, wake up,' he whispered.

Slowly, Jeannie's head appeared from under the bedclothes. With one eye open, and seeing who it was, and squinting because of the light, she, being rather annoyed, asked him rather what he wanted?

'Where's your pencil case?' he whispered.

After a long pause with still only the one eye open, Jeannie asked him why he wanted it. Then barked at him to go back to sleep. He shushed her and told her to keep her voice down or she was going to wake their mum up. 'I just want to borrow a pencil.'

'Why?'

'Because I'm going down the woods to draw a special bird.'

'Use your own pencils and draw one off the roof,' Jeannie croaked.

'Are you going to wake up or what?' he asked as he again shook her. Pleading he said. 'I want to borrow your pencils because they're better than mine. I want to draw a bird that only lives in the woods. It's a bird I've never seen before, so please wake up and show me where your pencils are.'

'They're in my satchel,' Jeannie scoffed.

'So where's your satchel?' he asked, slowly loosing his patience.

Jeannie, who was trying desperately to go back to sleep, knew she was not going to be allowed to do so until she gave him her pencil case. Huffing, she threw back the bed clothes and stomped out of bed. Still huffing to let him know she was angry with him, she walked over to her dresser, pulled open the top drawer and unfolded her satchel. Rummaging inside she found what she was looking for. 'Here,' she said handing him her pencil case, 'Now can I go back to sleep?'

'Oh thanks, Sis,' he said, smiling as he helped her back into bed. Tucking her in and kissing her cheek, he switched off the light and tip-toed down the stairs with the pencil case. Seeing the time was only five past five caused him to be a little excited. He had never been up this early before. This was a first and it was exciting; cold, but exciting. He put the pencil case into his jerkin pocket and then shoved his sketch book up his jumper for safe keeping. He had a quick drink of milk out of the bottle and shivered. My goodness it was cold. Then he put his shoes on and, as quietly as he could, unlocked the back door. All the previous times he had unlocked the back door it had never once squeaked, but it did now. Hoping it did not wake his mum, he stepped out and re-locked it, again hoping it did not disturb his mum.

Reaching the front door, he very gently pushed the letterbox lid in, and it also squeaked, but determined he was going down to the woods, he shoved the key through the gap knowing it would not made a noise on account of it falling onto the mat.

My, how different the garden appeared in the morning light. How different everything seemed in the morning light. With never having seen this time of day before, he was amazed that the ground was covered in what he suspected was dew, never having seen it before. Even the gate, which he opened and closed ever so quietly because of the click it made, was covered in dew. He very excitedly tip-toed down Heol Wen, then, when he reached the corner house's privet hedge, across the way from Golcho's house, he was spellbound. In the dawn light, and running the full length of the hedge, were hundreds of shimmering spider's webs. So mesmerising were they that he was immediately drawn to them. How simple and complex they were. How intricate and delicate they looked. Who taught the spiders to weave such finery? He remembered the spider's webs in the Bottle last Sunday, which he had thought nothing of, but these, covered in dew, were fantastically different. But for all their charm and appearance, he knew they were deadly traps designed to catch insects.

Knowing he was going to have to draw one, Alan took out his sketch pad and pencil case, and studying one of the webs close up, suddenly realised they were all the same size and design. He thought that was incredible.

Choosing one, he drew it slightly larger than life. When he was satisfied with it, he drew some hedge background. Pleased with his work, he moved on while tucking his sketch pad back up his jumper.

As he made his way down Heol Islwyn, with Sparrow's house on his left, he thought for one moment of knocking Sparrow up to see if he wanted to join him. But when he thought of the trouble it might cause, he changed his mind. He did not want anything to go wrong this morning.

When he approached the green gates, he crossed over the road and leaned on the five-bar gate by the oak tree which he had come to love. Peering over the top bar he was again stopped dead in his tracks. The fields, as far as the eye could see, including Llidiart Fanny Farm and the Fron Bank in the distance, sights he had seen hundreds of times before, all seemed different in this early morning light. Even the crows feeding in the middle of the field seemed different.

His arms were wet from leaning on the gate's top bar, it being covered in dew. He was drawn to the oak tree which he thought of as his and noticed for the first time how deeply furrowed its bark was. Some grooves were longer than others, while others were deeper. Suddenly a movement caught his eye. He was totally amazed as he watched little dewdrops crashing into one another causing a little rivulet to fill up a particular crevice in the bark. It was fantastic to watch. He then noticed that it was going on all over the trunk. It was so amazing to see nature in action. Even the grass just inside the field was amazing. Each and every blade was covered in dewdrops that looked like diamonds. Stewart Granger and Debra Kerr and a hoard of spear chanting natives in *King Solomon's Mines*, came to mind, and all those diamonds in that deep, dark cave in which they were trapped and where they were meant to die.

As with the spiders' webs, Alan knew he had to draw this scene. No way was he going to allow the moment to be lost. Out came the pencil case and sketchbook. With all these wonders here for the sketching, he knew he was going to be getting up early again. How different things look in the morning light.

Climbing over the gate, he crouched down and began to draw a single blade of grass covered in dew drops. Half way through the drawing he stopped and tried to count the dewdrops which really did look like diamonds clinging to the blade. He counted fifty, then went back to his drawing. Each blade was strewn with minute droplets of moisture and he shook his head in wonder. When he was satisfied with his drawing, he drew a patch of shimmering grass in what little light there was before climbing back over the gate and, on a clean page, trying to capture the dewdrops that were still running into one another on the tree trunk. It took a while to draw what he was after, but when it was finished he was rather pleased with the fact that he had managed to draw a single dew drop running into another one and then filling up a given crevice, then going on to fill up another one, and so on. It was amazing. With a sigh of satisfaction, he put his pencil case and sketchbook away, leaned on the gate again and thought how wonderful it was to be there.

He was not what you would call a slow walker, but that morning, with the dawn light slowly increasing, it took him all of ten minutes to reach Llidiart Fanny Farm which was no more than two hundred yards away.

The hedge, which ran up to the unique metal railings with its hooked-over top that belonged to Llidiart Fanny Farm, similar to the one by Golcho's house, was given an extra look, as it too had hundreds of spiders' webs covered in dew with some of the dewdrops sliding down the hedge and soaking the soil, albeit one drop at a time. Again, how wonderful was that?

When he reached the farm, even the shippon's windows, which had not been cleaned in years, looked different in the dawn light. The hundreds of webs that were clinging to the window frames stood out very prominently, shimmering in the morning light. A small black and white bird whose type Alan had yet to learn (it was a pied wagtail) was bobbing its long tail as it ran up and down the building's apex looking for something to eat.

When he entered the Woods road and looked over the hedge and fields, and then at Minera Mountain which was in silhouette, Alan saw a huge bank of cloud rising above it which had hints of gray, white and pink in it. From there he walked up to, and down the Woods hill, his mind full of wonderful thoughts. He smiled as he walked through the tunnel effect the trees made, which Golch was now calling Champ's tunnel. Moments later he was approaching the S-bend where, the previous weekend, he had seen the red bird he was hoping to draw that morning. He searched the trees and bushes for several minutes, but saw no trace of it or any other bird for that matter and wondered whether they were up at that time of day? But he had seen the little black and white bird on the farm's roof, and the crows in the field opposite the green gates, so they were up, but where was the red bird?

While pondering where they could be, he inspected Jeannie's pencil case. Inside were two black, leaded pencils with excellent points on them, an all important eraser and pencil sharpener, plus several coloured pencils, including two blues (one dark one light) two greens (one dark one light), a yellow, an orange and a brown; but the one that brought a smile to his face was the red one. That was the one (even though there would only be two splotches used – one on the bird's head and the other on its rump) that would make this getting up early worth while.

He suddenly shivered, but was determined the damp was not going to lower his spirits. He was convinced he would find the bird, and it would be the red pencil that brought it to life. So he again began to search the trees and bushes. As the light increased, so did the little chirps and tweets. The birds were suddenly everywhere. Seeing movement, Alan watched whatever it was hop and fly from branch to branch, from tree to tree. Suddenly, and without warning, a flock of rooks took to the air. It happened so quickly it made him jump. What was silence a moment ago was now pandemonium. The sky was full of squawking birds flying overhead in circles. At first it was exciting, but as it went on, it became a little annoying. They were not only disturbing him, but were, he imagined, disturbing everything else that was awake at that moment. He began to think it was all unnecessary and feared the noise would frighten every bird and creature away for miles.

For several moments he was of a mind to shout at them, to tell them to shut up and be quiet, then realised their squawking was not of his doing and it could only mean that they were doing what they always did in the morning.

He wondered whether they did that every morning, or was it just because he was there disturbing them? He watched them as they flew in circles over the canopy, landing on certain nests and then, for whatever reason, repeat the exercise. Then, as suddenly as it had started, it ended, except for the odd squawk here and there. The wood was once again more or less bathed in silence which was wonderful, until an unseen aeroplane shattered the silence again.

Going into the S-bend, the blue-tits, the great tits, the chaffinches and all the other small birds could now be seen and heard. Alan watched them as they all went about their business looking for food. How important food was to every living thing he thought to himself. Just then, a blue tit landed on a branch and began to search both sides of a leaf for insects. Alan held back a giggle when he saw another blue tit hanging upside down on a leaf, pecking away at something. Suddenly, a blackbird flew past him at what appeared to be a hundred miles an hour, just missing him and causing his eyes to enlarge as big as saucers. The bird was twittering like mad at something. Coming out of the S-bend, Alan saw a bird on the road just his side of the bridge, eating what he thought was gravel – some birds did eat gravel to aid their digestion. Then, not ten feet away, a robin perched on a branch and began to sing its lovely melodious song. Alan stood very still and listened. The robin's blending in with all the other birds songs was magical and he wondered if it would stay still long enough for him to draw it. As he reached for his pencil case it flew away.

Some thirty minutes later and having fallen in love with the dawn chorus (never having experienced it before) there was still no sign of the red bird. Alan then noticed that the wild flowers were all closed up, as if deciding whether or not to come out? But he knew they would show themselves as the day progressed, especially when the sun shone down on them. Then they would show off their wonderful colours and be visited by all the insects.

He had not yet told anyone in case he was laughed at, that the dandelion was becoming one of his favourite flowers. He decided he was going to save up and buy himself a magnifying glass so as to be able to see the parts of the flowers that could not be seen with the naked eye. He believed that would open up a completely different world for him. Back in Chester, especially in May when the dandelions were in profusion, he used to lob their heads off for fun. But not any more. For one thing, thanks to Twab's dad, he now knew that insects fed on them as well as all the other wild flowers, pollinating a lot of our food which was very important.

Stepping onto the Dump and looking at yesterday's refuse down in the hollow, bottles, tin-cans and cinders, Alan thought he could smell smoke above the toxic fumes that were seeping out of the ground. He stepped back onto the road and sniffed the air. It was definitely smoke that he could smell and it was coming from the Hafod side. Putting his sketch book and pencil case away, he decided to go and investigate.

Using the bank as cover he made his way to the Woods entrance and again sniffed the air. It was smoke alright, of that there was no doubt. But it was the fact that he could smell smoke at this time of the day that bothered him. What to do? Should he go back and raise the alarm and risk being told off if it turned out to be a false alarm? Or should he investigate alone? If it was a fire burning out of control, so much time would be lost in running home to raise the alarm. The fire could have burned down so much of the woods. With the thought of never being able to play there again, he decided he was going to tackle the blaze himself.

Slipping into the wood he made his way down the first two slopes and managed to scratch his leg on the holly bush that Golcho was still threatening to cut down. Ignoring the scratch he again sniffed the air; the smoke was stronger – meaning there was a fire. He had visions of trees burning away like mad and crashing down. It was up to him to save the day.

Silently, keeping to the path, he moved on. Ever since coming to live in the Adwy, which he thought was the most beautiful village in the world, he, thanks to the lads, had learned at least one thing – you always walk through a wood in silence.

Reaching where the path split into two with no sign of any fire, he thought he could hear some strange voices. Hiding behind a tree and believing the fire may have been deliberately started, he dashed forward and crouched behind a big holly bush. Suddenly, he could not believe his ears. Here, in his little wood with the time something like six o'clock in the morning, someone was being told that 'Cha' was ready.' Equally amazing was the reply. 'Oi'll be back in a jiffy so oi whill.'

Alan was flabbergasted, but schooled enough to know that was how the Irish spoke. But what were Irish people doing in his little wood?

'See that yew are, or it whill be cold so it whill,' said the voice that announced 'Cha was ready.'

'Whill yew stop your fussing,' said the second voice, 'haven't oi just said oi'll be back in a jiffy, so oi whill.'

Even though his heart was racing, Alan could not help chuckling at their accent. In his search for a better viewing position, he trod on a dead twig that snapped under his weight. He hit the deck, hoping the noise had not been heard, but it had. Alan began to panic. Someone was approaching.

'Be-jabers,' a voice said when it was almost on top of him. 'Yew'd better come out and show yourself so you'd better or oil shoot you with my little gun so oi whill.'

Frightened, Alan raised his hands in the air and gave himself up.

Seeing it was a boy, the man, who was heavily bearded and rather tall and stout, removed his thick woolly hat and while scratching his head, shouted back to his companion. 'Well, oil be, tis only a youngster so it is.'

When Alan reached the man, with his hands still up, he pleaded for his life. 'Please don't shoot me mister. I won't tell anyone I've seen you, honest.'

Realising Alan was frightened, the bearded man motioned for him to lower his hands then said, 'Now don't yew go a tinking that oi've got a gun cause I haven't, so oi haven't.' laughing, he shouted, 'Michael O'Flynn, will yew come and see what oi've found?'

Turning back to the boy the bearded man said, 'And what would your name be oi'm a tinking?'

'Alan,' Alan answered, 'Alan Fletcher. I'm twelve years old and I live in the village just behind us.'

'Ah, twill be the one we passed tru only last noight so it whill, so it whill.'

Showing Alan the piece of wood he thought was a gun, the man with the beard said, 'There's no reason why yew should be afraid, so there isn't. This little piece of wood here doesn't shoot bullets so it doesn't.' With that he gave out a little chuckle. But being serious again and towering over Alan with his hands resting on his knees, he said, 'Would yew be brave enough oi'm a tinking, to step into our little camp and share some tea with us?'

Alan felt it would be safer if he did.

When they entered the camp, Alan, with the big man's hand on his shoulder acknowledged the other man who was kneeling down seeing to their breakfast with a nod of his head. He was then invited to sit on an old rotting tree trunk by the fire, the one he had sat on many times while in the woods with the lads. It was only a stone's throw away from were Golcho's Christmas trees were growing. The smell of bacon was so delicious it was making Alan feel hungry.

After nodding a second time to the man who was seeing to breakfast, Alan found his courage and said, 'Excuse me, but are you tramps?'

'Would it frighten yew if we was?' asked the bearded man still standing.

'I don't think so,' said Alan looking up at him and then across at the other man who was pouring out two cups of funny-smelling tea.

'I knew a tramp when I lived in Chester. He was a nice man who used to come around on his bike and for sixpence would sharpen knives, scissors and axes for you on a sharpening stone.'

The man who was kneeling offered Alan, who was staring at him, a drink from his cup. Alan took a few sips and thanked the man, even though it tasted awful. Alan thought it tasted of nettles. He handed it back.

Smiling the man said, 'Moi name is Michael O'Flynn, and this big giant of a man who found you is my good friend Patrick O'Donagan. We're from the Emerald Isle across the water.'

'Michael O'Flynn,' said Patrick O'Donagan, who was leaning over so as to be at Alan's level, 'say hello to master Alan Fletcher from the village just behoind us; the one we passed tru only loist noight.' With that he stood upright. Michael O'Flynn leaned away from the fire and shook hands with Alan. Alan then shook hands with Patrick O'Donagan. 'I'm very pleased to meet you,' he said, noticing that both men had huge hands.

Nodding and acknowledging Alan's remark, Patrick O'Donagan said 'And why would a twelve-year-old boy be out of his bed so early in the morning oi'm a tinking?'

Warming his hands on the fire and rubbing them and enjoying the smell of the bacon sizzling on the open fire Alan said, 'I've come to draw a special bird. One I'd never seen till last Sunday. I don't know what it's called, but it's about the same size as a magpie without a tail. I was being taken to Brymbo Pool when we spotted it.' Using his hands to measure the bird Alan said, 'It's mostly black and white, but I like it because it's got a red blob on its head and underneath.'

Taking a drink of tea then handing it over to Alan, Patrick O'Donagan said, 'Oi'm a tinking it whill be the greater spotted wood-pecker that you'll be after.' Looking across at Michael O'Flynn he said, 'Now didn't we see the very bird only loist noight?'

'That we did Patrick O'Donagan,' said Michael O'Flynn, 'That we did.' Handing the tea back, Alan reached for his sketch book and showed the two men his morning's work; the spider's web, the shimmering grass and the colliding dew drops on the oak tree. 'I drew these on my way here this morning.'

'Ah, tis a wonderful gift he has, is that not so Patrick O'Donagan,' said Michael O'Flynn looking at the drawings. Turning to Alan he said, 'Yew must use this gift the good Lord has given yew wisely. Yew must draw all His little creatures and trees and mountains and rivers and anything yew see as beautiful, so yew must.'

Alan nodded his agreement, but the smell of their thick bacon butties which were just about to be eaten, was so powerful that they were making him feel hungrier still, to the point where he was becoming a little fidgety. Actually his tummy was rumbling. Sensing his hunger, each man broke off a corner of his sandwich and offered it to their guest of honour. Feeling he was robbing them of their breakfast, Alan tried to refuse their offer, but having his hair ruffled, was told to take them and enjoy them. Alan tucked in.

'Yew eat up this good food my little leprechaun,' said Patrick O'Donagan grinning, 'or oil shoot yew with my little gun so I whill.'

When Alan began to chew the delicious food, he found he could not stop giggling. Both he and his empty stomach were so grateful.

When the meal was over, both men lit their pipes, and whilst enjoying their smoke and with the fire made up, they listened to Alan's story of how he and his three best pals climbed down Harry's Rock a few months ago and then swam in Bersham waterfall in the afternoon and how it was all written down in his diary. When the two men emptied their pipes and put them away, they invited Alan to see if they could find the greater spotted woodpecker.

When a chaffinch was spotted and sketched, the two men marveled at the speed and accuracy of Alan's drawing, as they were again when a robin and a blackbird were sketched. Explaining how the background would be filled in later, Alan was again told he had been given a wonderful gift by God.

Realizing the greater spotted woodpecker was not in the area, they returned to camp. When Michael O'Flynn poured out their nettle tea and saw to the fire, Alan asked for their attention. Because they had been so kind to him, he wondered if they would mind him drawing them sitting by their fire as a thank you.

'Well oil be,' said a smiling Patrick O'Donagan. He removed his thick woolly hat, and after combing his hair with his fingers, he dampened down his thick, bushy eyebrows with a little spittle and straightened his beard. When he was ready he said. 'Yes, oi would surly loike to be drawn sitting by moi fire, so oi whould.'

'So too whould oi,' said Michael O'Flynn as he too groomed himself.

Some twenty minutes later, Alan showed them his drawing. It showed the two men sitting side on to a blazing fire, watching over four rashers of bacon sizzling away on their home-made spit, with a billy can of steaming tea.

Feeling all emotional and having to wipe his eyes Patrick O'Donagan said, 'Oi've never known such a wonderful gift before, so oi haven't. Here Michael O'Flynn,' he said handing the drawing over, 'Whill yew take a look at yourself and myself sitting boi this fire.'

Michael O'Flynn was also taken aback with their young guest's accuracy with a pencil. The moment had well and truly been captured, as had the background, including a couple of oak trees thrown in for good measure. The picture, after being looked at for several minutes was then put away in Patrick O'Donagan's wallet for safe keeping. Alan was then given some twenty minutes of funny stories relating to their travels and way of life.

Answering Alan's original question, 'Are you tramps?' both men said they were and had been living the life ever since the war ended eight years before. With God's sky as their roof and his countryside as their larder, they bothered no one. They simply went about their business as happy as a pair of larks.

Alan felt it was time to go home. He hoped his mother would not be too worried about finding the back door key in the hall and him not in bed. The two men escorted him to the road, and as one shook his hand and the other ruffled his hair, he was again told that he was to capture everything dear to him on paper. The two men watched as he ran up the Woods hill.

'Alan Fletcher, don't you ever go out of this house again without letting me know where it is you're going. Is that understood?' said a very relieved Mrs Fletcher whose eyes were welling up.

With his head bowed, Alan did not know why his mum was so angry until she explained how worried she had been when she saw the back door key on the hall floor. She was furious with him, but held her anger back. Seeing the error of not having left a note, Alan apologised and said he was very sorry for worrying her, adding that it would never happen again. Pulling him and Jeannie (who also felt a little guilty for lending him her pencils) to her and hugging them, Doreen said, 'What if those two men had not been friendly?'

Making full eye contact with her children, she explained that there were people out there who took young children away and … . But she could not bring herself to say anymore. 'You two are so precious to me. You're all I've got.'

With one arm around each of them and hugging them again, and in a somewhat calmer frame of mind, she said, 'Now that I've had my say, and to avoid this happening again, you must promise to tell me where it is you are going, every time, is that understood?' Both nodded and said they would always tell her where they were going from now on.

Pulling away from his mum, and seeing the concern on her face and trying to make light of it, Alan said, 'There was no need to worry Mum; my running would have gotten me out of trouble.' But when she saw the state of his shoes and socks, which were soaking wet, Doreen's smile vanished. 'Well Alan,' she bellowed, 'your feet are soaking wet. How on earth am I going to get your shoes ready for school tomorrow?'

'Oh Mum,' Alan murmured under his breath, 'they're only wet, it isn't as if they're going to fall apart.'

Turning to Jeannie, not exactly shouting, Doreen said. 'Jeannie, get your brother a pair of dry stockings from the dresser, and you my lad,' she said pointing to his shoes and socks, 'get them off, now.'

Because he was not taking them off fast enough, Doreen sat him down on a chair and rather abruptly pulled them off for him, and in a slightly more raised voice (actually she was shouting at him now) said, 'I can see you going down with pneumonia my lad, you see if you don't.'

Appreciating the dry socks and shoes, his Sunday best, Alan sat by the fire trying to remember the last time he had seen his mum so angry. But having already eaten, he somehow was not relishing his runny egg and toasted soldiers that morning.

Later, with Twab, Sparrow and Golcho in the washhouse with him, with his stomach bulging from having eaten his breakfast, and having told his story, Champ said, 'I'm not telling porkies, everything I've said is true, honest, cross my heart and hope to die.'

Opening the washhouse door to make sure there was no one

listening (especially his mum) Champ closed the door and retold his story about Patrick O'Donagan and Michael O'Flynn. Seeing they were still unconvinced, he said, 'Well, there's only one thing for it. You'll have to come down the woods with me and I'll introduce you to them.'

'Okay,' said Twab checking on the others, 'let's go.'

Alan explained to his mum (who was washing his dirty socks in the sink) that he and the lads were just going for a walk now that the sun had finally come out. No way was he telling her that he was going back down the woods. As a last thought he decided to take his sketch pad and Jeannie's pencil case, just in case.

'Don't be late for dinner. We're having beef today,' she said with a smile. Alan stretched up and kissed her cheek. 'Thanks Mum, can't wait, see you later.'

'Bye, Mrs F,' shouted the lads in turn. Because of Twab, both Sparrow and Golcho were now referring to Champ's mum as Mrs F.

Closing the gate, the lads ran down Heol Wen, turned left by Golcho's house into Heol Islwyn and then right by Norman Williams's place into Heol Celyn and then left again at the T-junction with Heol Offa. From there they walked on past the green gates and up to the Talwrn road. Crossing over and turning left at the farm they raced on as far as the Woods hill. While walking down the hill, Champ began to describe the size and shape of Patrick O'Donagan with his thick bushy beard and woolly hat. Reaching the S-bend, Champ said, 'This is where I began to smell the smoke from their fire.'

'Well there's no smoke now,' said Sparrow sniffing the air.

'He's right,' said Golcho, with Twab agreeing.

'You just come with me,' said Champ confidently. 'I'll show you.'

Thirty yards in the wood, retracing his steps of earlier that morning, Champ began to feel that something was wrong. There was no hint of the two men or a fire. 'This is where I first heard their voices,' said Champ scratching his head, puzzled. 'See, there's the holly bush I hid behind, and there's the twig I trod on.'

So where was Patrick O'Donagan and Michael O'Flynn?

Reaching the now abandoned camp, Champ pointed to the log he had sat on only a few hours before, the one he had sat on dozen's of times, but there was no trace of the fire, the fire that had boiled their nettle tea and grilled their bacon. Nor was there any sign of the stones that had encircled the fire.

'I think you've been dreaming,' said Twab grinning.

Champ was speechless. He then realised that the two men had moved on and left the place as they had found it. What was it they said about God's countryside being their back-yard and garden? Smiling to himself he wished them good luck and hoped their God was with them. He was very impressed with them for respecting the land the way they did. He has learned that lessen back in June when he was first taken down the woods.

'Hey gang,' said Sparrow breaking the silence. 'Look what I've found?'

Crouching, Sparrow (the ever-ready detective) had found evidence of a fire. The ground where the fire had been was still warm, 'Looks like Champ was telling the truth after all.'

'There you are,' said Champ all smiles. 'See, I wasn't telling porkies.'

Lighting two halves of a Turf cigarette (the shop having run out of Woodbines) and preferring Turf as apposed to Robin, Compass, Park Drive or even Player's Weights, Sparrow handed Golcho his half (he could not tell the difference between the brands). Sparrow then asked Champ to tell them the story again.

Sitting cross legged, Indian style, with Sparrow and Golcho blowing their smoke at the flies to keep them at bay, Champ obliged them very enthusiastically and retold his story and ended with, 'And thanks to my two very good Irish friends, I now know that bird we saw last weekend on our way to Brymbo Pool was the greater spotted woodpecker.'

At that very moment, in a tree not fifty feet away, the unmistakable drumming sound of the greater spotted woodpecker was heard by one and all. When they located it, Champ asked the lads to be very still while he, if it was at all possible, crept up on the bird. Reaching what was considered a safe enough distance, and for once, with a marvelous view, there being no branch or leaf in the way, Champ put the bird's image down on his sketch pad. While he was filling in the background the bird flew to another tree and was lost to sight. But Champ was pleased with what he had caught of the bird.

Returning back to his mates and showing them his drawing, Champ proceeded to colour it in, while listening to some adventure which involved Sparrow nicking three swedes from Alum's field one dark night so as to make Halloween masks. It was Golcho who remarked how life-like the drawing was.

Meeting up after dinner, it was decided that a quiet day was going to be had down the woods, staying close to home. If the truth be known, the previous Sunday's clash with the Brymbo lads was still fresh in everyone's mind. Even though Champ had got the better of Tony with his judo, neither he or the lads fancied the idea of ever meeting up with him again. So, with no plans as such, the lads casually made their way down to their little woods.

At the green gates, Golcho, (after having a peep through the little spy hole that Champ discovered a couple of weeks earlier when they were messing about at being Frankenstein monsters) asked Champ what that lovely smell was when they called for him.

'That was me mum's cooking,' said Champ. 'We had beef today with potatos, carrots and gravy and peas out of a tin. I love those peas out of a tin as much as Twab here loves his ponchmipe.'

'And that's exactly what we had,' said Twab grinning like a Cheshire cat, 'lovely ponchmipe and plenty of it.'

'Did you have sausage with it?' Champ asked.

'No, rabbit,' said Twab licking his lips.

'So what did you have, Sparrow?' Champ asked.

'Meat pie with all the trimmings and soaked in gravy.'

'What about you Golch, what did you have?' Twab asked.

Looking gloomy, Golcho said they could not afford meat now that his dad was off work having hurt his back.

'So what did you have?' Sparrow asked a little impatiently.

'Butty jam.'

When Golcho tried to apologise for not having a proper Sunday dinner, Sparrow, smiling, said he loved butty jam. And before anyone could say another word on the subject, both Twab and Champ also said that they loved butty jams and would have swapped dinners with Golcho anytime.

Everyone agreed that Golcho's was the better dinner. Champ could even remember the time when Billy Watts from Chester (the same Billy Watts that climbed up onto the removal vans bumper to see inside the cab the day they came to live in the Adwy) would go to school with just a butty sugar.

When they reached the Talwrn road, Twab suggested that they have a change of scenery and go to the woods via Southsea Bank as he wanted to see how the hazel nuts were coming on. Golcho thought it was a good idea, remembering Twab's promise to Champ's mum of giving her a bag of hazel nuts and chestnuts when they were ready. So they ambled on past the farm and up to the top of Southsea Hill, about five hundred yards away. There was no racing today on account of Champ's stomach being too full – with two breakfasts and a dinner. But there on their far left for all to see in all its splendour was Tan y Fron bank, showing off its best side and a small section of the village itself. But facing them was the slightly bigger Southsea Bank, also showing a small section of Southsea and the nearby village of Brynteg. Champ was told as they began to stroll down Southsea Hill that the ice-cream man that usually came on a Sunday, whose ice-cream was for nicer than Lewis's ice cream, came from Brynteg and that his name was Mr Richards, who also had a milk bar in the village, although they did not go there. When Champ asked why, he was told that they stayed away on account of the Brynteg lads who, like the Tan y Fron lads and the Brymbo lads, chased away anyone who ventured into their village. That was the way it was everywhere.

Southsea Hill, Champ noted was very much like the Fron Hill, long, slightly curved and steep with low cut hedges. During their discussion while walking everyone agreed that it was not fair on the nesting birds the way the farmers were cutting their hedgerows low. Blackbirds, thrushes and robins, to name only three, prefered high, wild-looking hedges, but the trend was for low-cut hedgerows. Twab had heard in school that Britain was beginning to follow European farming practices and wished to stay as we were with high hedges and smaller fields; Europe had low hedges and enormous fields. Some of their fields were six times the size of British fields said Twab, adding that he could see us having trouble with Europe in the future.

Sparrow likened the trend to the new hair style that was in fashion at the moment, the crew-cut. He said he did not care if Mr Pritchard was telling everyone that the crew cut was the healthiest of the hair styles. No way was he cutting off his wavy-hair. He did not want to look like the GIs he saw in the war films or people who are in gaol. Champ wondered what Jeannie's response would be if Sparrow suddenly turned up with a crew cut. Would he still be the love of her life?

Thirty yards down Southsea Hill they came to a man-made gap in the hedge and scrambled through into what was once Plas Power Colliery, but now known as Southsea Bank. Like the Fron Bank, this was a mini mountain of shale, dug up and dumped before the pit went into coal production. Waiting for Sparrow to emerge, his jacket having caught on a branch, Golcho and Twab between them pointed out all the hazel nuts to Champ.

The hedge on their left belonging to Llidiart Fanny Farm and ran as far as the eye could see, never failing to produce a good crop of nuts, Champ was told there were always plenty to be had, even after the squirrels and jays had taken their share.

Champ was told that in its day, Plas Power Colliery had produced more coal than any of the others mines in the area that had closed down.

Twab climbed onto Golcho's back and reached up for a branch that was loaded with nuts and pulled off a cluster of three. Champ watched as he cracked one open with his teeth and was then given the still growing nut to taste.

'Mmm, it's lovely and sweet,' said Champ chewing it with his front teeth. Asking when they would be ready to harvest, he was told November.

'We all collect them and store them in brown paper bags for Christmas,' said Golcho, adding that he always has his after his Christmas dinner.

Moving on they made their way along a make-shift, uneven road where they eventually reached the now derelict pit head.

'Not that long ago,' said Golcho, 'this place was alive with men, on the surface and below ground, but now, as you can see,' he said pointing at the dereliction, 'It's empty.'

There was no evidence as to where the two shafts had been, but there were several empty buildings whose windows had been smashed. And there were bits of rusty machinery and wagons strewn about the place.

At the far end of what was once a busy and well kept yard, a man and boy were digging up coal. And when it was seen what they were digging up, Twab thought he too was going to be having some of this free bounty. He already knew where there was an old pram that would do very nicely for carting the coal.

Golcho then began to throw stones at an old doorway which ended up as a game. Each one of them in turn had to try and knock out a small piece of glass in the top right-hand corner of the door. But after several throws, the game was abandoned on account of the target being too small.

Moving on they scrambled over several shale banks and came across more abandoned machinery, but their aim now was the river which Golcho was the only one who managed to cross without getting his feet wet. Sparrow slipped on a mossy stone, Twab sank several inches in a mud hole, and Champ completely misjudged his jump and plunged in the water with both feet.

Now that they were in Alum's bottom field, one they had not previously been in that year, they began to rub their hands when they saw the quantity of nuts growing on the hazel bushes. Like the ones by the road these too were showing promise. That year's crop was going to be a bumper one. That being so, Golcho suggested they should check on the chestnuts down Nant Mill as soon as possible, which was agreed.

Champ could see why this area was no good for playing in. It was much too boggy. In places there were pools of what looked like rusty water mixed in with the mud. The evidence that Alum's cows were trashing the place was everywhere. You had to be careful where you trod. One false move and you would sink into the mud well over your shoes. As Sparrow said, the place was best left to the cows and birds and whatever else lived there.

Because his feet were already wet, Sparrow walked through the river to fetch what looked like a seven-foot long pole. A young fir tree that had been stripped of its branches was just lying there. Picking it up, he wondered how on earth a fir tree got there in the first place. There were no fir trees around. But he quickly found a use for it. Without saying a word to anyone, he pole vaulted over the river. The moment he was in the air, the lads, seeing the potential began to yahoo. Sparrow then ran at the river and, jabbing the pole in at about the half-way mark, sailed through the air and landed safely back in the field, having allowed for the fact that the bank was a little higher than the river. Had he not judged it right and collided with the bank, he would have ended up in water that would have been up to his knees.

Showing off, Sparrow then vaulted back over the river, knowing very well that he was going to have to share his find. No way would he be allowed to have it all too himself. The others would definitely want to have a go. When he began to vault over this and that on the other side of the river, Twab, with hands on hips to show he meant business, ordered him to vault back so that they could have a go. Sparrow grudgingly complied.

Twab took the pole off him and walked back several yards. Raising the front end, he ran up to the edge of the field and stabbed the pole into the middle of the river and sailed over the water. He thought it was fantastic. His return vault was also successful. Next to go was Golcho. His there and back flight was also successful, as was Champ's when his turn came.

They then made their way up river, vaulting over this and that, nettle beds, small bushes, strands of briar, but mostly across the river, with not too many mishaps under their belts. Golcho began to feel a little uneasy though when Sparrow suggested that they should try and vault across the swimming pool. He thought it was much too wide.

Reaching the pool and deciding that vaulting across the shallow end was going to be easy-peasy, well fairly easy-peasy, Sparrow announced that he was going to be the first one who attempted such a brave deed. It was his pole and idea after all.

So, with the adrenalin pumping and looking ever so serious, Sparrow said, 'Well gang, if I fall in and drown, tell me mam and dad how it was, that I died bravely.' As an afterthought he said, 'Oh, and tell them to put plenty of blue bells on my grave when they come out in the spring.'

'Get on with it, Joe Soap,' said Golcho who was still not happy with this crazy idea, 'let's all see you make a fool of yourself.'

Sparrow, with pole in hand and ready to go, shook Twab's hand, then Champ's, then Golcho's. With one last afterthought he said. 'I'm also doing this brave deed in honour of our little gang, the Shanghai Bombers.'

Being all official and feeling he ought to say something, and with

Champ looking on, Twab said. 'You are a brave man, my man, and should you drown in your attempt at vaulting this great river,' he pointed at the pool, 'you will be honoured by us, and yea, we will tell your mam and dad about the blue bells.' Twab had to suppress a giggle. He suddenly remembered Golcho's joke about Robin Hood and the Sheriff. He had a vision of Sparrow thrashing about in the water and then being buried in the roof next to Robin Hood.

'Get on with it,' said a despondent Golcho, still unhappy with the idea.

Sparrow took several strides up the field, turned and, facing the river, psyched himself up by hyperventilating.

'Hang on Sparrow,' yelled Golcho urgently; 'before you drown yourself, hand over your fags and matches as they're hard to light when wet!'

Sparrow thought for a moment, then handed them over. But while staring at the pool again, all psyched up and telling himself he could do this, his concentration broke. Running his left hand up and down the pole, psyching himself up, he splintered his thumb. 'Ouch,' he cried as he pulled the sliver of wood out with his teeth. Seeing it was bleeding he licked up a blob of blood.

Eager to see his friend make a fool of himself, not minding if he did drown, Golcho, trying to ridicule Sparrow said, 'C'mon you dozy so and so, we're all waiting to see you fall in.'

Determined to prove Golcho wrong, Sparrow, with the end of the pole raised, ran full pelt at the river while at the same time lowering the tip. This is it, he thought. Victory would be handshakes and congratulations, whereas failure would be being laughed at. He ran at the pool, aimed the pole as far as he could across the water and rammed it in. He felt his whole body rise up into air as he sailed across the six or so feet of water. It was so exhilarating. He compared it to swinging on the Monster, but his landing was about a foot short. Golcho burst out laughing.

Yes, he was wet from the knees down, and yes he was laughed at, but when he explained that he had not actually fallen, his failed attempt was suddenly seen as a success. All the laughing and teasing petered out and was suddenly turned into congratulations. Golcho cursed under his breath, knowing he would be expected to try.

Sparrow threw the pole onto the bank and climbed out of the water all fired up. Facing his comrades he said, 'Well, who's next?'

'I am,' said Twab.

'You needn't think I'm doing it,' said Golcho making his feelings known, 'because I'm not.' Because all the attention was on Twab, Golcho was ignored.

With pole in hand, Twab walked up to the starting point, turned, and like Sparrow, psyched himself up. When he was ready he let out a yahoo, raised the tip of the pole in the air and raced towards the water. Running the short distance, and like Sparrow, he too aimed the pole as far as he could across the river, and like Sparrow, he too sailed over the expanse of water, landing more or less where Sparrow had landed, about a foot away from the bank.

Wet from the knees down but pleased, Twab also saw his attempt as a success. Climbing up the embankment, helped and congratulated by Sparrow, Twab shook his soaking wet feet and shouted across, 'Whose next?'

'I am,' said Champ. In the time it took Twab to throw the pole across, Champ had a vision of having to stand in front of his mum to explain why his shoes and socks were wet again. 'I've got to make it across,' he told himself as he walked up to the starting point. The pole was not that heavy, and it would be really something if he did make it across. He had to or his mum would kill him.

Knowing he was next, Golcho was frantic. Not only did he not want to do it, but he did not have the confidence. But there were Twab and Sparrow telling him that he could do it, whereas Golcho knew he could not, wishing he was somewhere else.

With the thought of his mum yelling at him again for being wet through, Champ raced towards the pool. There was not enough time to finish the first line of the 23rd Psalm (The Lord is my shepherd, I shall not want) and he ran on with Sparrow and Twab's encouragement ringing in his ears. Suddenly it was time to do something. The pole was rammed in and he leapt into the air. He too found it exhilarating, and he too failed to get across, landing more or less in the same spot as Sparrow and Twab. Cursing under his breath, (he could see mum's angry face yelling at him), he nevertheless congratulated himself for not falling in completely. Passing one end of the pole to Twab, he was yanked out of the water and, looking at the state of his shoes and socks, let out his victory cry.

Looking across the pool at Golcho while Twab was throwing the pole across for him, Champ said, 'You can do it Golch. You can.' Trying to encourage him, Champ suggested he think of it as those nettles back there. The ones he jumped over with ease. Golcho had been against this stupid idea from the moment Sparrow suggested it. Yes, he was taller than them by several inches, which was ideal for scrumping apples or reaching up for something, but what good was the extra height now? He also knew he would not be allowed to back out, so, with that in mind, he picked up the pole and strolled up to the starting point.

Realising he was stalling Twab called, 'C'mon Golch, you can do it.'

'I'm coming,' Golcho yelled back over his shoulder.

'Well get a move on,' said Sparrow trying to rile him.

Reaching the starting point and turning, Golcho let out a very weak 'Geronimo' and began to run. The lads began to shout and egg him on as he raced towards the water. But, when it was time to jump, he rammed in the pole – and froze. After a few moments of silence Sparrow said, 'What was all that about, Golch?' then burst out laughing. Thinking it might not be so bad, looking across at his mates and feeling a little more confident, Golcho said, 'Okay fellow's that was just a trial run. Now I'll do it.' All fired up and bursting with confidence he ran back up to the starting point.

'This could be it,' said Twab as he and the others watched Golcho psyching himself up the way Sparrow had by hyperventilating.

'C'mon gang,' said Twab, 'let's give the lad some encouragement.'

While chanting, 'Come on Golch, come on Golch,' they began to clap their hands as well when they saw their friend getting himself ready. But his second attempt ended up exactly like his first. He ran at the water, rammed in the pole and again froze – as he did with his third and fourth attempts. He simply was not happy doing this.

Fed up and slightly angry, Twab ordered Golcho to jump or they would throw him in head first, the way he had wanted to throw Champ in Brymbo Pool only a few weeks ago. Sparrow said he was going if he was not going to jump.

'Hang-on fellows,' Golcho pleaded, 'This time.' All fired up again, he ran up to and beyond the starting point.

'Where's he going now?' Sparrow asked shaking his head.

Laughing, Twab said, 'Leave him be, let's see what he does.'

'C'mon Golch,' shouted Champ, 'you can do it. I know you can, and we are waiting to go. So show these two how it should be done.'

Having run way beyond the original starting point, Golcho turned, and having a good old swear in place of 'Geronimo' to boost his ego, he ran at the pool. As he ran, with the end of the pole in the air as the others had done, the lads cheered him on, but noticed he was running at an angle. He was running, not for the shallow end as they had, but towards the dam. What was he playing at? But before he could be warned, he rammed in the pole and leapt. Sadly, he did not put enough effort into the jump. For what seemed like ages, he clung to the pole for all his worth, feeling as if the world had stopped or was about to. Knowing the worst was about to happen, he began to say a prayer as he begun to fall to his left, and the dam, the deepest part of the pool. Laughter and cheering was the last thing he heard as he went under.

Standing up and coughing from swallowing some water, and very angry, Golcho blanked out all the laugher and teasing and threw the pole over the dam as far as he could. Refusing any help from anyone he scrambled up the bank and yelled, 'Well I hope you're all satisfied now that I'm soaked to the skin. That's been the plan all along, hasn't it – you and this bloody stupid vaulting.' He took his coat off and began to wring it out, 'You're always making me do things I don't want to. Look at me; I'm in a right bloody mess. I can't go home like this, me mam will kill me with me dad on the sick.'

Feeling guiltier than the others, Sparrow told him not to worry as they would get a fire going to dry him out.

'What good's a bloody fire?' Golcho yelled.

In trying to console him as he stood there dripping wet and soaked to the skin, Twab said, 'We're all wet as well.'

'Yea but only from the bloody knees down,' screamed Golcho. 'I'm soaked to the bloody skin.'

'C'mon everyone,' said Champ, 'All this talking is not going to get a fire going. Golcho's right, he is soaked to the skin.' With that, Twab led them into the wood where they soon found a suitable place to make a fire. While Golcho stripped off, the others gathered firewood.

'Oh no,' said Sparrow. 'We can't make a fire. Guess who's got the fags and matches?' Sparrow pointed at Golcho, squatting there, shivering.

'Oh no,' said Twab.

With Sparrow and Champ looking on, Twab approached Golcho and said, 'Golch, where's the matches.'

'Ohhh, that's all I bloody need,' said Golcho as he produced a soggy packet of Turf and a box of matches from his pocket. 'That's all I bloody need.'

'Give um to me,' said Champ. Opening the soggy fag packet he saw all but one half of the cigarettes had spoiled. The matches had also had a good soaking.

Choosing one he said, 'Carry on with the fire lads we may be in luck.' He then began to rub the match head very gently in the soft hair on the back of his head, hoping this would dry out the wet phosphorus. Champ said he had seen one of his old mates in Chester doing this. With his fingers crossed he said, 'Let's hope it works.'

When a good mound of sticks had been built up, Golcho was on his haunches with Champ and Sparrow's coats wrapped around him. Having rubbed the match head for ages it was time to see if it would strike, the moment of truth. Also on their haunches around the pile of sticks, Twab and Sparrow watched as Champ very gently scrapped the match head along the surface of a very dry stone. It made a scratching sound but was it dry enough? With all the fluff from their pockets squeezed into a little loose bundle and in a convenient spot amongst the sticks, Champ struck the match. It lit, but the phosphorus head split into two halves. One half fizzled out while the other dropped out of sight. Believing it to be out, the lads gave up and fell back on their haunches. They all cursed under their breath, except Golcho who swore out loud, very loud. As already mentioned, he used swear words more so than the others, and he certainly used them that day while reiterating that his mum was going to kill him when he got home and saw the state he was in. All because Sparrow wanted to vault over the bloody river.

Twab was just about to say 'Sorry' when a thin veil of blue smoke appeared. With everyone wanting to take charge, Champ yelled for everyone to leave well alone. 'Let it find its own way for a moment or two,' he insisted. 'If we mess with it, it'll go out.' To everyone's delight the smoke suddenly thickened. Cheers rang out when a tiny flame appeared and, feeding the flame with stalks of dry grass, Champ ordered the lads, bar Golcho, to move back so as to give him room in which to manoeuvrer. In less than a minute the fire was showing promise.

Sending Twab and Sparrow out for more dry sticks and seeing Golcho smiling, Champ said, 'Don't worry, we'll soon have you dry my old mate.' Ten minutes on the fire was blazing and Golcho watched as Twab and Sparrow between them rung out his clothes and passed them to Champ who placed them very carefully around the fire to dry. The inside of Golcho's coat was held up to the flames and it was not long before it began to steam then it began to dry.

Golcho was given the very important job of drying out the ciggies. Some twenty minutes on, with his vest and shirt as good as dried, Golcho put them back on, but his trousers, jacket and socks still needed more drying time. Feeling chuffed at the way things were going, Golcho announced that the ciggies were now okay and that he was going to have one to settle his nerves. Choosing the one that had not been completely soiled, he broke it in half, lit the two ends with a twig from the fire and then passed the half that had been soiled over to Sparrow.

As they sat around the fire drying their own shoes and socks, Sparrow's attempt at emulating Terry became the entertainment. All three watched as he tried to complete the task. Champ thought at one stage that he was going to do it, actually blow one smoke ring through another. He was just about to congratulate him, but realised more practice was needed. The only distraction to Sparrow's deed was when someone checked on their clothes as everyone was willing him to succeed.

Thirty minutes on and deciding that his pants and jacket were now dry enough, Golcho dressed in front of what was now a good roaring fire. But even so, he knew he would be in trouble when he went home. His mum would know he had fallen in the water on account of his jacket and trousers being all wrinkled.

As they sat around the fire and talked about what they were going to be doing tonight, Twab reached for a stick and with his dad's jack-knife began to whittle. As he did so, Sparrow asked him to show Champ how they hid things.

'How you what?' said Champ puzzled.

'How we hide things,' said Sparrow, insisting Twab show him.

Twab put his stick down and looked for a piece of suitable ground. Choosing a grassy area, and on his knees, he began to show Champ what they do when they had something to hide. He pushed the blade into the soft earth up to the hilt and cut out a small circle of about six inches in diameter. Using the blade he loosened the earth by going round and round until the clump was loose enough to be lifted out. He then cut off the clump of grass and very carefully placed it on the ground as it would be needed later. He then cleaned out the hole and lined it with leaves. A stone was placed inside, the grass top was replaced and ruffled to make it look undisturbed and then he said, '*Viola*, the safest place in the world.'

Champ removed the grass top and inspected it. 'Why, it's brilliant,' he said as he replaced the top and ruffled the grass, making it invisible again.

'It's very important that you remember where you've dug it,' said Sparrow. 'I buried some money once and I still haven't found it. There's a two bob piece safely hidden in the field the top side of Arthur Tattoo's house.'

Deciding it was time to go, the fire was doused by everyone weeing on it and the ashes scattered, their policy being to always leave the place as they found it. When Champ asked where this policy came from, no one could remember the film they had seen it in, other than it starred Cornel Wild as a trapper. Champ liked the idea.

While they were weeing on the fire, Twab was again laughed at because of the way he was still covering his thing. As much as Twab thought it was the thing to do, Golcho thought it was hilarious. The way he laughed, you would not have thought he had fallen in the water.

Not wanting to go home just yet, the lads spent what was left of the afternoon down the woods. But Golcho again burst out laughing when Twab suggested they strip off and have a good old water fight, arguing that the weather was nice and when again would they have the pool to themselves.

'Well you lot can have a swim,' said Golcho cadging a ciggy off Sparrow. 'I'm going for a swing. I've had enough water for one day, thank you very much.' Golcho never seemed to have any cigarettes and only smoked when Sparrow supplied him with one.

Deciding Golcho had a point, that enough water had been had for one day, the lads had a tremendous amount of fun on the Monster. It started off civil enough, each one swinging out individually, but as always, the antics crept in. Twab tried to hog the swing, Sparrow did some showing off, Golcho still refused to swing outwards and upwards and Champ had a go at being Tony Curtis when he had completed a triple somersault in the film *Trapeze*. About an hour later they decided it was time for home. Their bellies were telling them that it was time for tea.

When they met up after tea, Twab announced that he could not go far as he had to run an errand for his mum at 7.30 sharp. To pass the time he and Golcho joined in a game of marbles with some village lads just outside his house.

Sparrow and Champ played off the ground tick for a while before swarming up the lamppost and swinging from the two cross bars to see who could hang on the longest. Sparrow, while hanging there dangling his feet, announced that he was just popping home to check on his last year's conkers and invited Champ to go along with him.

When they reached Sparrow's house, Champ was told to wait at the bottom of the garden while Sparrow disappeared into the house. Moments later he emerged with an old biscuit tin. Crouching he removed the lid. To Champ's horror it was full of cow muck. When Champ realized what Sparrow was about to do, he scrunched up his face in amazement. He thought Sparrow was loosing his marbles when he began to rummage in the tin with a stick looking for last year's conkers. Finding one, and taking hold of it, he cleaned it up with a clump of grass and gave it the thumb test to check its hardness. He smiled when he realised that it was as hard as it could be, 'Good,' he said smiling like a Cheshire cat. 'They're hard enough.'

Searching for another one, then another, and giving them the thumb test, he found that all were in good condition and as hard as rocks. He handed one to Champ, who on smelling it asked why conkers were put in cow muck?

'It makes um go hard,' said Sparrow pushing them back in the dung.

'So how does cow muck make conkers go hard?' Champ asked, puzzled.

'Don't know, just does,' said Sparrow replacing the lid.

Satisfied with what nature was doing for him, he put the tin back in its hiding place at the back of the broom closet, next to the pantry. He and Champ then met up with Twab and Golcho who were still playing marbles. When Champ asked if his mum minded him keeping conkers in cow muck the house, Sparrow said she did not know about it. But she did. The only reason they were still there was that there was no smell; otherwise they would certainly have been slung out.

The lads then decided on a walk around the village. As they set off for the green gates, Champ, who still could not get his head around the fact that conkers were put in cow muck said, 'Do any of you know why conkers are put in cow-muck?'

'I've already told him,' said Sparrow, vexed for not being believed.

'Conkers placed in cow muck are mysteriously hardened,' said Golcho. 'No one knows why, but they just do.' Had Mrs Price, Golcho's next-door neighbour and a somewhat nosy parker, not been standing in her gateway when the lads passed by, Golcho would have said 'cow shit' instead of 'cow muck.' Swearing down the woods, or while going over the fields, was one thing, but swearing with the chance of being heard by such a nosy parker as Mrs Price was something else entirely. Had he said the 'S' word, the news of it would have reached his mum's ears well before it was time to go in, and he would have been kept in for the rest of the night.

Anyway, to finish off the story as to why conkers went hard in cow muck, Golcho said that everyone did it, so that when it was time for conkers again, out they came, and the secret was, to only take on those who only had this year's conkers. That way, your conker could become a champion conker. Twab here, last year, had a 26er before it was smashed.

'Is that right?' Champ asked.

'Yea,' said Twab puckering his lips the way he did when he was chuffed.

'Well, you've told me some weird things in your time,' said Champ, 'but putting conkers in cow muck takes the biscuit.'

'Takes the what?' said Twab with a straight face.

'Takes the biscuit,' reiterated Champ. It was only when the others burst out laughing and began to shove and push him from one to the other did Champ realise that he was being teased.

Guessing it was time to go on his mum's errand, Twab said he would see them in the morning. When Champ asked why their motto, 'All for one and one for all' was not being implemented, it was Sparrow who explained that when Twab goes on such an errand for his mum, he goes alone.

Twab had told the lads ages before Champ's arrival that some things are meant to be private, including the type of errand he was about to run.

'Right then,' said Golcho as they watched Twab running away, 'Shall we go to my house and play with my train set?'

'Ooh, yea,' said Sparrow remembering the last time. 'Let's see if I can't crash it again,' he said teasing.

'I'm going home fellows if you don't mind,' said Champ. 'I want to do some work on some wild flowers I'm drawing?'

Reaching Golcho's gate, Mr Jones, Golcho's dad, on account of his bad back, was sitting in a chair by the front door enjoying a smoke, while watching the world go by. Mr Jones was usually a very pleasant man and had once repaired a sledge for Twab which was in need of a couple of nails in one of the runners. So Golcho's dad was alright as far as Twab was concerned.

Returning Mr Jones's wave and admiring his front garden, especially the flowers he had put in the big diamond shape in the lawn, Champ said his goodnight and made his way up Heol Wen and home.

He still intended to have three small diamond shapes in his back garden with flowers in and had already started to dig the front garden, but it was hard going. Being new houses meant that a lot of rubble had been buried and he was already digging up all sorts of things, bricks, slates, breeze blocks, bits of wood, which were made into sticks for the fire. He even dug up a trowel that one of the brickies had obviously lost.

At twenty past nine exactly, Twab's special knock was heard on Champ's back door. Mrs Fletcher almost jumped out of her skin. Knowing who it was, she wondered what on earth Malcolm could want at this time of night.

'I'll go,' said Alan putting his green coloured pencil down. But his mum's stern look told him to stay where he was. Looking across at her brother, Jeannie, also putting her pencil down, whispered; 'I wonder what he wants at this time of night?'

Alan scrunched his face up to mean he did not know.

'Hello, who is it?' said Mrs Fletcher being cautious?

'It's me and the lads Mrs F,' said Twab, 'can we have a quick word with Champ please, It's very important?'

Unlocking the door, Mrs Fletcher invited the lads in. Jumping up from his chair by the fire, Champ went into the back kitchen to meet them. 'What's up?' he asked while looking at his mum. Knowing she unhappy about this late call, he asked them if they knew what the time was? Seeing they wanted privacy, Mrs Fletcher left them to it. Twab asked if they could talk in the washhouse.

'No you can't,' shouted Mrs Fletcher from the living room. 'It's too late for that, close the door if you want privacy.'

'So what's up?' Alan asked while closing the door.

'I can't tell you here. It's too incredible. You won't believe it,' said Twab.

'If it's that important,' said Mrs Fletcher opening the door, 'then go upstairs to Alan's room and no jumping on the bed like last time or I'll skin you all alive. Is that understood?'

As they filed into the living room, Twab nodded his appreciation and thanked Mrs F, saying it was much appreciated.

Still hopelessly in love with Sparrow and his lovely wavy hair, Jeannie smiled at him while she and her mum escorted them to the bottom of the stairs and watched as they raced up like a herd of elephants. Mrs Fletcher, worried about her lino, knew it would not last long with that kind of treatment.

'I wonder what it's all about,' Jeannie finally said. When she heard her brother's bedroom door being closed, she suggested she go up and listen.

Also wondering what it was about, Mrs Fletcher told Jeannie not to be so horrid, adding that people did not listen at doors anymore. But as they made their way back to the fire she would have given anything to be a fly on her son's bedroom wall.

The lads all flopped down on Champ's bed. Twab sat up straight and looked a bit peaky (so Alan thought) 'Well, what's going on?' he asked.

'Do you believe in ghosts?' Sparrow asked.

'No! You know I don't, why?'

'Well,' said Golcho with a straight face, 'Twab here has just seen one on his way home from the errand he's had to run.'

Turning to Twab who was biting his lower lip, Champ said, 'Is this true?'

Twab nodded then gave a seedy sounding, 'Yea.'

Shoving Sparrow to one side so as to be able to sit next to Twab, Champ put an arm around his leader and explained that ghosts were not real.

'Well this one is,' insisted Golcho. 'Our Twab here saw one while sneaking through Bryn Celyn Farm.'

'Twab,' said Champ, but before he could speak, Twab responded, 'It's true. I have seen a ghost. As you know, I had to run an errand for me mam earlier. Well, on the way back I took a short cut through Bryn Celyn Farm. As I tip-toed past the last building, the wind got up and I saw a white hand waving at me.' After a long silence he said, 'I think it wanted to kill me.'

'So what did you do?' Champ asked who did not believe in ghosts.

'He bloody well legged it is what he did,' said Golcho laughing then apologised for swearing.

'After calling in to see me mum about the errand,' said Twab, 'I called for these two and then we came here.'

Sitting up Sparrow said. 'Twab only wants us to go back with him to see it for ourselves.'

Scratching his head, Champ had a quick peep through the curtains. He said he did not think he would be allowed out as it was already going dark.

'Well at least go and ask your mum,' said Twab. 'It's only half past nine. This is something I think we should investigate.'

Mrs Fletcher and Jeannie could not help hearing the lads stomping down the stairs. Again she thought they sounded like a herd of elephants.

While the goodnights were being said, Mrs Fletcher overheard Sparrow whispering to Alan that they would wait for him by the gate.

Closing the door and locking it Doreen said, 'Alan, what's all this about waiting for you by the gate?'

Nervously Alan asked his mum to sit down. 'Mum,' he began, 'we have a rule where if something important crops up, we all have to go, and something really important has cropped up. I can't tell you what it is. If I do I'll be thrown out of the gang, but Twab says its men's work and is very important.'

With eyes closed, fingers crossed and his face all screwed up and swallowing hard, Alan said, 'Mum I have to go out for at least half an hour.'

Mrs. Fletcher's first instinct was to say 'No,' adding that it would be pitch black in half an hour. But pulling Alan to her she said, 'As long as you're telling me the truth and not some made up nonsense then you can go.' Kissing Alan with trembling lips she said. 'Your dad will never die while you draw breath.'

Not knowing what she meant by that he gave her a big hug. Knowing she would not be able to speak without crying, she returned her son's hug, dried her eyes and told him to be careful. Thanking her, Alan put on his shoes and jacket and was gone.

Having witnessed the scene, and not fully understanding, Jeannie kissed her mum and allowed her to cry on her shoulder. It was just like being grown up.

Outside, the lads ran down Heol Wen, turned right by Golcho's house into Heol Islwyn, on past Twab's house and the lamp post, then the end house where Richard the lad who worked for Oswald lived. But there they slowed down and quietly made their way up to the T junction.

As they approached the only house in this new batch of houses that was occupied at that moment, they passed very quietly as they did not want to disturb the occupant who was none other than Griff, Mr Griffiths, the new village Bobby who had recently arrived and was settling in. Tip-toeing across the road that was going to be named Heol Glyndŵr in a few month's time, the lads ran down a dirt path that linked up with one of the lower fields belonging to the Bryn Celyn Farm. Using the hedge as cover, Twab instructed everyone to be very wary as they were now on dangerous ground.

'Right lads,' he whispered, 'stay close to me and keep your eyes peeled for anything unusual.'

'Like what?' Golcho asked making sure he was somewhere in the middle.

No one answered, but in single file and in the dark, they made their way up the field towards the farm's out buildings. Suddenly, and to everyone's delight, the moon came out from behind a thick bank of cloud. Taking advantage of the extra light and still using the hedge as cover, the lads ran the rest of the way up the field.

With their target in sight, Twab ordered everyone to crouch down. They could just make out what were once cowsheds. Twab pointed out that the ghost, or White Hand, was in the end building. All eyes strained, all ears pricked up to see if any clues could be picked up, but none were.

'We need to be a little closer,' whispered Champ.

'I think we're close enough,' whispered Golcho gripping Sparrow's arm.

'Okay,' whispered Twab, 'let's crawl as far as that old, broken-down tin sheeting. That should be close enough to give us good cover.'

As their leader Twab crawled away with Champ close behind him and Golcho behind him, with Sparrow as Tail-end Charlie behind him. Several yards further on, Twab stopped and told the others to gather round.

'You see that doorway?' he whispered, pointing towards the end building, 'Well, that's where the ghost is. That's where its white hand beckoned me over to kill me.'

'How do you know it wanted to kill you?' asked Golcho.

'Why else would a ghost call you over?' said Twab, shaking his head at such a dumb question. It was time Golcho grew up. He was only six months away from being a teenager. In fact they were all only six months away from becoming teenagers when he thought about it.

'We'll have a better view when we reach the tin sheeting,' whispered Sparrow who was a little fed up with Golcho gripping his arm so tight.

Wishing he was somewhere else Golcho said nothing.

'Okay, let's go,' whispered Twab.

Still crouching as they made their way over to the tin sheeting, and with only a few feet to go, the lads suddenly panicked and froze to the ground. A voice and the slamming of a door were heard. After some thought, while putting his men at ease, Twab whispered that it was probably the old man going for a pint.

'He'll be as drunk as a skunk when he gets back,' giggled Sparrow, knocking Golcho's arm away. Because of nerves, the giggling went on and was soon out of control. Fearing they would be discovered, Twab sternly reminded everyone of why they were there. 'C'mon fellows,' he whispered, 'stop this nonsense, it's not funny. Pull yourselves together, that's an order.'

So with order reestablished, the lads waited a few moments then, with the moon coming out from behind a bank of cloud, they moved on. Moments later, having had several nettle stings, they reached the tin sheeting.

Twab re-told his story of how earlier he had seen a white hand waving at him as he sneaked past the last building, convinced it wanted to kill him. 'I'm sure it wanted to kill me,' he insisted.

'Oh, these bloody nettles,' Golcho sighed. 'Pass me a dock leaf someone'

'Stop moaning Golcho,' whispered Twab as loud as he dared. 'We've all been stung and there's only you complaining. As a Shanghai Bomber you're supposed to be tough.' Shifting his weight he asked if anyone had any ideas.

Wanting to get back at Twab, Golcho mentioned, that perhaps the ghost was there to stop the likes of him from sneaking through somewhere he should not have been sneaking through, adding that he was trespassing.

'Yea, just like we're trespassing now,' Sparrow pointed out.

'Forget the trespassing,' whispered Twab somewhat irritated. 'This is serious work we're here to do.'

Peering over the tin sheeting which was leaning slightly to one side as if it was about to fall down, the lads concentrated on the last building. Gripping Golcho's arm, Twab, rather excited said, 'Look, over there, there it is!'

All eyes were glued on the doorway of the last building.

'I can't see it,' whispered Sparrow, again complaining the way Golcho was gripping his arm. Twab was pleased that Golcho was gripping Sparrow's arm. Now he knew what he had gone through when they were down Harry's Rock the other month. Golcho had a grip of steel when nervous.

'I can't see it either,' whispered Champ.

Golcho did not even look.

Twab told them to look at the door and window of the end building for a white hand waving up and down. Suddenly the moon went behind a bank of cloud and plunged them into total darkness. Golcho again remembered that Bud Abbot and Lou Costello film where they met the Mummy, which did not help.

Twab suggested they take advantage of the darkness and move up to an old building that seemed to be on its last lags about twenty feet away. They each in turn wriggled along the ground with Twab leading. 'That's better,' he whispered when they all came in. 'So what are we gonna do?'

'Get out of here if we had any sense,' whispered Golcho gripping Sparrow's arm for the umpteenth time.

The moon suddenly emerged from behind the bank of cloud and flooded the area with its eerie, ghostly light. The said door and window, where according to Twab the ghosts white hand would appear, was clearly visible. Suddenly the wind got up. 'There it is,' whispered Twab as loud as he dared. Pointing at the apparition, he said it was in the window to the right of the door and then asked if they could see it? Everyone saw it, causing all their pulses to race, with Golcho's racing the fastest. But as quickly as it appeared, it disappeared. Everyone watched in anticipation. Finally, Twab, who was beginning to think that the lads were beginning to think he had been telling pork pies said, 'Well, did you see it?'

Everyone said yes.

'So there really is a ghost and not just some figment of my imagination?' Twab said in his, 'I told you so' voice. Again everyone said yes. Running back down to the tin-sheeting and crouching behind it, and after a second and third sighting of the white hand, they tried to decide what to do. Golcho's suggested they should ignore it and go home. But how was this creature from the underworld going to be dealt with if they did that? No, that was out.

After several minutes, with no one putting any suggestion forward, Champ, thinking his time was up, said, 'Listen fellows, I promised my mum I'd only be half an hour. I'm going to have to go or I'll be in trouble.'

'Yea, me to,' said Golcho feeling he could have hugged Champ.

'I tell you what then,' said Sparrow, 'Let's go home, have a good think as to what to do, and meet up tomorrow morning by Twab's gate.'

Everyone nodded. With one last look at the building and with no white hand in sight whatsoever, they headed for home. Sparrow added as they walked back down the field that he had a feeling that it would still be there tomorrow.

Sunday morning at ten o'clock precisely the lads met up by Twab's gate. A quick hello was given to some younger children who just happened to be passing and then the subject of last night cropped up.

'Well, anyone got any ideas?' Sparrow asked.

Twab gave everyone time to say something, but when no one did, he said, 'I suggest we go there now and see what we can see.'

'We can't do that,' said Golcho, 'Its day-time, we'll be chased away.'

'Only if we're seen,' said Twab trying to rouse them, adding that they were the fearless Shanghai Bombers, ready for battle at any time. It was the 'being ready for battle at any time' that roused them. Reaching Heol Glyndŵr and Griff's house, and making sure he was not around, they crossed over the road and raced along the path. In the field, and again using the hedge as cover, they raced up the field as far as the tin sheeting that they had used the previous evening. Seeing no one, they raced up to the broken down, south facing wall, which in its day had been an outside lavatory. From there they stared at the next to last building. There was no sign of any ghost or white hand.

As little as six months before, cows had been housed and milked in the two buildings the lads were gazing at. Chickens, ducks and pigs roamed all over the cobbled yard that separated the lads from where the ghost had first been seen, but with the Council passing plans to expand the village, Bryn Celyn Farm, along with other little farms in the area, had given up some of its land in the name of progress. After several moments of staring at the two end buildings Champ said, 'I somehow don't think we're going to see anything. What do you think?'

'Yea, you could be right Champ,' said Twab, 'but we had to be sure.'

With one last look to see if there was any sign of any ghost, Twab said, 'Well, there's only one thing for it, we'll have to come back tonight and see if it shows up again, and if it does we'll pelt it with stones.'

Nodding, everyone agreed. Sneaking back down the field with one last look at the buildings, Twab said, 'Until tonight then.'

With their Sunday dinners over, the lads met up by the lamp post at the bottom of Heol Wen. After some idle chit-chat, they made their way down to the woods which they entered on the Hafod side, and made for the river. They were going to bomb some German warships, but the idea fizzled out. No one was interested.

They crossed over the river and sat on the edge of Mr Williams's field. No one spoke. There was nothing to say. Suddenly, to cheer himself up, Champ began to flick stones at Sparrow's feet. Seeing how much it was annoying him, Twab and Golcho joined in. Sparrow chose to ignore it until he was hit on the ankle. 'Ouch,' he cried, accusing Golcho of being the culprit. Sparrow threatened everyone to pack it in or he would start throwing bigger stones at them.

Flopping onto his back with his hands behind his head, wanting to get something off his chest, Champ said, 'Listen, I know what we saw last night was a little scary, but I don't think it is a ghost.'

No one spoke for some time until Twab said, 'Well, it wasn't Father Christmas.'

'You don't believe in Father Christmas,' said Golcho. But with his next breath he said he wished it was, adding that it would make going back tonight a lot happier. Giggling he said, 'I could have given him my Christmas list.'

'So what do you think it is then Champ?' Sparrow asked.

'I don't know, but like I said last night, I don't believe in ghosts and things that go wandering about in the night. I think that, when you die, you go in the ground and stay there. How can you get up and go wandering about?'

'Just because you don't believe in ghosts, Champ,' said Twab, 'doesn't mean there aren't any.'

'They've been seen by hundreds of people.' said Sparrow.

'My Aunty Betty,' said Golcho, 'used to work where there was one and had to give the job up because the house was haunted. She said this woman would appear at the top of the stairs dressed in old fashioned clothes and would then walk through the wall, so there.'

Remembering the story, Sparrow said, 'Yea, I remember Golcho telling us about it at the time. And it was in the *News of the World*.' Sparrow then asked Twab if he still remembered it? Twab could even tell them where they were when Golcho told them the story. It was by the green gates one dark night. He also remembered how fast they had all run to the nearest lamp post after the story had been told. 'So you see Champ,' said Twab a little cocky, 'there are such things as ghosts.'

Realising there was no point in arguing, Champ said nothing, but in the silence that followed their minds could think of nothing but the supernatural.

In fact, they thought of nothing but the supernatural for the rest of the day until it was 9 o'clock and time to go again. Standing by the lamppost by Twab's gate in the wonderful yellow light that was so comforting, the lads reiterated their plan of pelting the ghost should it appear with stones then run like hell.

Shaking arms (the Roman way) and with the Musketeers oath of 'All for one and one for all' thrown in for good measure they set off.

Stepping out of the street light which was so comforting they plodded on nervously, especially Golcho. Tip-toeing past Griff's house they crossed over the road and raced along the path and entered the Bryn Celyn field.

Everyone was pleased to see the full moon. At least they would have some light to see where they were going. 'Looks like we'll have the moon for some time,' said Golcho as he positioned himself in the middle, 'there's not many clouds about so we should be okay.'

Using the hedge as cover the way any good Roman soldier or any one of the Musketeers would have, they made their way up the field. But suddenly they were plunged into total darkness. A cloud, from nowhere covered the moon. Minutes later the moon re-appeared. 'Quick lads,' said Twab, 'if we get a move on we can be at the top of the field before that next lot of cloud comes in.'

As quietly as circumstances would allow, they raced up the field. Running through a section of tall grass which bordered the field, they fell to the ground. With one eye on the building, Twab ordered every-one to look for stones.

'How do we find stones in the dark,' moaned Golcho whose heart wasn't in this operation. He began to wonder why he'd bothered to come along. In fact he wished he was back by Twab's gate being bathed in that lovely yellow light.

Ignoring him, Twab went one way, while Champ went another. Golcho accompanied Sparrow so as to protect him, or so he said.

Knowing it was a porky; Sparrow allowed his friend to tag along and for once didn't try to wind him up.

After groping in the dark for several minutes they met up again. The nine stones collected were shared out equally, two each, with Twab keeping the odd one for luck. He then gave the order to follow him as quietly as they could.

Reaching the tin sheeting, then the broken down south facing wall, Twab said, 'Right lads, this is it, you all know what to do. Golch, you throw first.'

'Sod off,' whispered Golcho, 'you throw first, it's your ghost.'

Twab saw red and decided he was going to show Golcho up for the cowardly coward he is. He'd refused to obey a direct order. How dare he, that was court-martial offence, so he said as loudly as he dared, 'Okay Golch, to show you how brave he is, Sparrow will throw first.'

'Sparrow will not throw first,' whispered Sparrow, 'it's like Golcho said; it's your ghost, so you throw first.'

Getting angrier by the minute Twab said, 'Champ, show this lot how brave you are and throw first.'

'Mmm,' whispered Champ. 'The lads do have a point here Twab. It is your ghost and we all think you should have the pleasure of throwing first.'

'Here, here,' whispered Golcho who thought that was telling him.

'You bunch of cowards,' said Twab, again whispering as loud as he dare. 'I'll show you why I'm the leader of this gang. All of you; watch and learn. You lot think it's easy being a leader, well let me tell you ...'

'Get on with it,' said Golcho sniggering. He was beginning to enjoy the fact that Twab was loosing his bottle.

Deciding he was going to reprimand Golcho for being insubordinate as well as being a coward when all this was over Twab stepped out from behind the south facing wall and prepared to throw.

'Can you see it,' asked Sparrow, feeling somewhat safe behind the wall.

'No,' said Twab staring into the darkness about to cast the first stone.

'Hang on,' said Champ, 'the moon's about to show itself' Moments later the area was lit up with eerie moonlight as if someone had switched a light on.

'Can you see it now?' Golcho asked innocently. But Twab, who was going to reprimand him for, for, for something which he'd forgotten at the moment but knew he was going to be told off said, 'Get your backside over here and see for yourself, Golcho.' Knowing that Twab rarely swore or lost his rag, Golcho stepped out and joined his leader on the firing line, then put it to him that, 'Shouldn't the other two should be on the firing line with us as well?' Whatever happened to 'All for one and all that?'

'You're right Golch,' said Twab. 'You two,' he ordered, 'get yourselves out here at the double.' Moments later four pairs of eyes were staring into the eerie night to see if they could see an eerie ghost.

'Perhaps it's gone back to hell,' whispered Golcho who was getting more frightened by the minute. They were after all dealing with the unknown.

After several minutes and whispering Sparrow said, 'Golcho could be right you know. We've been here for ages now and it hasn't shown up.'

'I hope it doesn't,' whispered Golcho.

Champ was just about to remind everyone that ghosts don't exist when the wind suddenly got up.

'Look,' said Twab realizing he'd shouted too loud, 'there it is.'

Everyone saw it and everyone including Champ ran back and hid behind the south facing wall. Golcho wanted to run as far as the tin sheeting but Twab stopped him and reminded him that he is a Shanghai Bomber for Pete's sake.

Sneaking back to the firing line and nervously gripping his stone, Twab said it was time to do battle with this thing from hell. So taking a deep breath he said, 'The moment I throw, you lot throw as well, is that clear?' In his trying to ridicule Champ, Twab said, 'So, they don't exist, huh. Then what's that thing over there, clever-clogs?'

Champ ignored him. It wasn't worth arguing about. Stepping out and lining up for battle with the moon again coming out from behind a bank of cloud, Champ, Sparrow and Golcho stood alongside their leader, all for one and one for all as it were. But just as Twab was about to throw, Golcho asked what he thought was a simple question, 'What do we do if it's got magic powers?'

That stopped everyone in their tracks. 'What do you mean what do we do if it's got magic powers?' said Twab lowering his arm.

'What do we do if it's got magic powers and does things to people who throw stones at it,' said Golcho, tutting Twab for not understanding English.

Frustrated and wanting to get on with it, Twab whispered rather loudly, 'Will someone please tell me what he's talking about.'

'Take no notice of him,' whispered Sparrow, 'throw your stone and have done with it.' But having given the question some thought Twab said, 'Hang on Sparrow, don't get your knickers in a twist let's hear him out.'

'I think what Golcho means,' said Champ, 'is what happens if we throw our stones at it and it comes after us and does things to us?'

'Yea, that's what I mean,' said Golcho rather loudly.

No one spoke but everyone followed Twab back to the south facing wall so as to have a little think about it. Everyone waited for someone to say something, but when no one said anything Twab said, 'Someone, say something.'

'Like what,' said Champ wondering what the time was? Any later than nine-thirty and he'd be in a spot of bother with his mum.

'I don't know,' said Twab who was both angry and frustrated. He felt the situation was getting out of hand. They'd come here to do battle with a creature from hell, not to bicker about whether it's got magic powers or not.

'One of you, take a look to see if it's still there,' said Twab.

'There's no sign of it,' said Golcho rather pleased with himself for volunteering. Moments later everyone agreed there was no sign of it, but, as they all stared at the end building a gust of wind blew across their faces. 'Oh bloody 'ell,' said Golcho again rather loudly, 'it's there now.'

All four watched as this thing from hell waved its white hand at them as if beckoning them to go over and be killed. And the more the wind blew the more Golcho panicked. Suddenly with his nerves stretched as far as he was going to allow them to be stretched he yelled, 'Argh!!! It's coming after us, I'm off.'

Golcho, with the others hard on his heels raced on down the field keeping close to the hedge, not that cover or being a shanghai Bomber mattered any more. No one was interested in cover now. At the bottom of the field they all ran along the path, past Griff's house and didn't stop until they reached Twab's gate and the wonderful yellow glow of the streetlight, that wonderful and glorious street light.

When everyone had calmed down, it was agreed that plans would have to be made in school tomorrow as it was time to go in now.

For the full duration of the three play-time periods in school the next day, nothing but battle tactics where discussed. Sitting in the hollow down by the canteen out of sight of everyone, (well almost everyone) the lads racked their brains for a solution to their problem. But as hard as they tried, they could not agree on anyone solution in dealing with this thing from hell.

Golcho suggested they tell Griff the policeman and have done with it. Sparrow on the other hand suggested that they bring Terry, Frank, Ernie and Dave in, arguing that there's safety in numbers.

Champ who thought that things that go bump in the night was nonsense, said very little on the subject, so, on the way home from school, having spent all day on the problem, with Jeannie and her two friends, Hazel and Wendy in tow some way behind, it was decided that they would use Twab's original plan of pelting it with stones and send it back to hell where it came from.

When Twab opened his gate and was greeted by Queenie who was always waiting for him at this time of day, he ordered that they all meet up after tea at 6.30 to gather stones for later on.

Waiting for any battle to begin is nerve racking, and this one, this one with this creature from hell was no exception. Twab, would you believe had to go and call for the lads at 6.30 as no one had turned up.

And he was ashamed with their excuses.

Golcho thought he had a cold coming on and thought he ought to be in bed.

Even Sparrow who usually followed Twab's orders without question challenged his leader on this one; throwing stones at something as formidable as a ghost. What was he thinking of?

And then there was, 'I don't believe in ghosts' Champ, who thought the whole thing was silly. But Twab, with his quality of leadership rallied his men with the promise of their names and pictures being in all the papers, especially the one that everyone reads, the News of the World.

Asking them to picture the scene, Twab bamboozled them with

fanciful headline as, 'Four brave Adwy youths save world from Hell
Demon - four brave youths to meet Mr Churchill - four brave youths to
have tea with the New Queen. And it worked with Sparrow and
Golcho, but Champ, who didn't believe in ghosts and things just went
along with it as any good soldier would.

Suddenly it was 8-30 and time to go. With their pockets filled with
stones, it was time to show this creature from hell that four Shanghai
Bombers from the Adwy, in Coedpoeth, in North Wales were prepared
to do battle with it.

So engrossed in their mission were they that no one saw Griff the
policeman standing in his gateway. 'Good evening lads,' he said
startling them, 'and where would you four be off to on a night like
this?'

Stunned and somewhat speechless, the lads finally pushed Sparrow
to the front with Twab insisting he tell the good policeman where they
were going.

'Oh, hello Mr Griffiths,' said Sparrow fumbling his words. 'It's a
lovely night isn't it?'

'It is,' said Griff straightening, 'but you still haven't told me where
it is you're going.'

Searching for an answer but failing to find one, Sparrow decided to
tell the biggest lie he could think of and hoped to get away with it. 'We
were on the point of going home, Mr Griffiths,' he began, but moving
in the way you do when telling someone a secret he said, 'but first, we
have to make sure that the village is safe.' Looking up and down the
street he whispered, 'From Martians, like the ones in my Dan Dare
comic.'

Joining in with Sparrow's most fantastic lie, and to a policeman,
Golcho added, 'They're easily recognized, Mr Griffiths because they
have these massive green heads and big bulging eyes.'

'Well,' said Griff going along with it. It was harmless enough plus
the fact that he too red Dan Dare comics as a youngster. 'Should you
come across them,' he said looking up and down the street, 'you come
and let me know immediately.'

Griff stubbed out his cigarette; said goodnight to the lads and went
indoors not realizing that their pockets were bulging with stones.

Not believing they had managed to get away with it, Twab

complemented both Sparrow and Golcho. 'That was good work, you two, but phew, it was close.'

'That's the best lie I've ever heard,' said Champ, 'and to a Bobby.'

Feeling chuffed with himself, Sparrow scrunched his face up the way Twab will pucker his lips when he's said something worth saying.

They raced along the path and entered the Bryn Celyn field. And like last night they used the hedge as cover. When they reached the tin-sheeting they prepared for battle. Each member of the gang had a stone in each hand ready to throw. 'Right lads, we all know what to do, so let's get on with it,' said Twab.

With no sign of any clouds and with a full moon they tip-toed up to the old tumbled down South facing wall. In the eerie moonlight and ready to do battle, the lads listened as Twab counted down. On 3, everyone tensed. On 2, everyone gripped his stone, and on 1, they all stepped out from behind the wall and taking aim prepared to fire, but there was no sign of the ghost.

It was Golcho who asked rather nervously, 'Where is it?'

'Don't worry Golch,' whispered Twab, 'it'll show when it's ready.'

'Well I wish it would hurry up,' said Sparrow who was fed up with all this now, and was cold, and was beginning to think that Champ could be right in not believing in ghosts and things.

Twab was just about to reprimand Sparrow for moaning, when the wind got up. 'There it is, lads,' he said, 'just like I predicted.' The white hand from hell was waving at them as if daring them to throw their stones. Taking several deep breaths, Twab whispered, 'Right lads, all for one and one for all?'

All agreed except Golcho.

All fired up and ready to face the enemy Twab said, 'On my count lads, one, two,' but before three was reached, Golcho again pointed out that they still didn't know whether this ghost from hell had any magic powers or not.

Everyone lowered their arms and ran back to the safety of the broken down south facing wall.

'Listen you lot,' scowled an angry Twab, but before he could begin what was going to be a telling off, Sparrow said, 'Don't you go shouting at us, it's Golcho who's causing all the trouble, so shout at him.'

'Look here Golcho' said Twab, inches from his face, 'we're here to get rid of a monster from hell, not to be frightened out of our pants, so pull yourself together man and let's get on with it.' That's told him, Twab thought.

Twab stepped out from behind the south facing wall and cast the first stone. Moments later the sound of a stone rolling down some tin sheeting was heard.

Laughing his head off, Golcho said he'd missed by a mile. Sparrow and Champ suppressed their giggles; Twab was naggy enough as it was. But he had missed by a mile.

In trying to save face, Twab said he threw that stone to see if there would be a response, adding that he'd missed by a mile deliberately.

'Bollocks,' said Golcho laughing out. 'You're just as frightened as I am.'

Golcho's use of the B word always made Sparrow laugh (not that he didn't use it himself from time to time) but knowing now was not the best time to laugh; and he was dying to so he stepped out from behind the wall and cast his stone. It hit some door, but like Twab's stone there was no response.

Encouraged by this, the others joined in and pelted the monster from hell with their stones even though they couldn't see what it was they were aiming at. The monster from hell had disappeared. But suddenly a window smashed.

Panicking, the lads ran back to the safety of the tin sheeting. 'Who the bloody hell was that,' asked Golcho leaning against the wall. No one answered; everyone, including Champ was too busy feeling fidgety and nervously laughing.

'Well,' said Twab at last, 'we've found out one thing.'

'What's that?' Champ asked.

'That it doesn't have any magic powers. Nothing's happened. We're not in hell or anything. So let's go back and blast it to kingdom come.'

With a second volley of stones thrown, and another broken window, and once again behind the safety of the tin sheeting, the lads assessed the situation. It was concluded by all, except Golcho, that the ghost did not have any magic powers to speak of, other than it could show itself and then disappear.

Creeping back up to the south facing wall with stones in hand, the wind suddenly began to gust. The lads watched as the white hand waved at them as if saying, 'come on, if you think you're brave'. But after several minutes of serious staring at this creature from hell, the wind dropped, causing the white hand to disappear. Moments later the wind got up again, causing the white hand to resume its waving. 'That's odd,' said Sparrow, 'why is it the ghost only appears when the wind gets up?'

Scratching their heads at the mystery, they watched the white hand wave in the wind then disappear when the wind dropped.

Was it somehow connected with the wind? 'One of us is going to have to go across there and take a look,' said Twab.

'Well don't look at me,' said Golcho emphatically.

'We'll do this fair and square,' said Twab. 'Shortest straw goes.'

'Oh no you don't,' said Golcho even more determined. 'I'm not falling for that one again. I wouldn't trust you lot as far as I could throw you.'

'Okay,' said Twab turning to Sparrow and Champ. 'It'll have to be one of us then seeing as Golcho is a cowardly coward.'

'Why don't we all go, including Golcho?' said Champ.

'Good thinking Champ,' said Twab, 'Yes, we'll all go. I was wondering when one of you lot would think of that. I have to think of everything.'

'I'm not going,' Golcho insisted. 'Sod you; you can shove all that nonsense of 'all for one and one for all' where the monkey shoves his nuts. Do you realize what we're dealing with here for Pete's sake?'

'Okay then,' said Twab, 'point taken. You stay here on your own and keep nicks for any other ghosts that may be in the area.'

'There aren't any other ghosts in the area,' said Golcho, 'you're just saying that to frighten me. I know you lot.'

'We don't know that for sure do we,' said Twab in retaliation, adding, that was why they had to go over to find out.

Suddenly realizing he could end up being on his own, and in the dark, and with the possibility of other ghosts being around; Golcho had a sudden change of mind. 'Yea, I suppose you're right Twab. We should stick together you know, all for one and all that.'

'Right then,' said Twab, 'now that's been settled who's going to lead?'

'You are,' said Sparrow, 'you're the leader; you always lead.'

'Yea, well it's about time one of you lot led for a change.' said Twab.

'You're just as scared as I am,' Golcho reiterated.

'No I'm not,' insisted Twab. 'It's just that I'd like one of you to lead for a change, that's all.'

'Oh yes you are,' insisted Golcho.

'No I'm not,' said Twab raising his voice.

'Stop bickering,' said Champ, 'I'll lead.'

So with that Champ, Twab, Golcho, and Sparrow as tail end Charley, ventured across the remaining twenty feet of open yard. Half way across with the white hand waving at them like mad, Champ, for devilment said if the ghost was going to make a move, now would be the best time.

'Pack it in Champ,' whispered Golcho, 'I'm pissing me pants as it is.'

With that Sparrow began to giggle which caused Golcho to giggle. Then, as panic set in, they all ran back to the safety of the old broken down south facing wall. When the giggling stopped, Sparrow said he was sorry for giggling, but could see Golcho pissing his pants.

Admitting that he wasn't that far off from messing his pants, Golcho said that if they didn't get a move on he would have to go home to use the lavvy.

Allowing for the laughter to peter out, to get it out of the system as it were, Twab restored order. 'Right lads,' he said, 'same line up as before only this time we do the business, okay.'

'I knew you were going to say that,' said Sparrow not relishing being tail end Charley tonight.

'Stop griping, Sparrow,' said Twab. 'You're always tale end charley. Right lads, let's do it.'

As they stepped out from behind the south facing wall, the wind began to howl again. Golcho, in the middle, turned to Sparrow on the end and rubbing it in said he was glad he wasn't tale end Charlie.

Two strides on, he again turned to Sparrow and said, again winding him up, 'It'll be either you or Champ who gets picked off first.'

'Shut up Golch,' said Sparrow showing signs of nervousness.

Giggling, with Harry's Rock in mind, Golcho said, 'I wonder what these White Hand things do to you when they've get you in hell.'

'I won't tell you again Golch,' said Sparrow nervously.

Knowing Sparrow's nerves were playing up, Golcho, beginning to enjoy himself said, 'I wonder when it is they throw you in the fire.'

Sensing Sparrow's twitchiness, Golcho had to suppress a giggle. He knew Sparrow was biting.

'Twab,' whispered Sparrow from the back, 'tell Golcho to shut up.'

'Golcho, shut up,' whispered Twab staring ahead. 'That's an order.'

'All of you shut up,' whispered Champ. 'Come on, we're almost there.'

Turning to Sparrow, Golcho said, 'Get ready to be picked off.'

Thumping Golcho in the back causing him to laugh out Sparrow said, 'Pack it in, Golcho, I mean it.'

'Satan's got little ugly things that gouge your eyes out before they throw you in the fire,' said Golcho trying to imagine the fear in Sparrow's eyes.

'That's it,' said Sparrow, 'I'm off.'

Laughing out, Golcho, more than pleased that he'd got his own back on Sparrow for when they were down Harry's Rock that time, shrieked out his infamous top C. from the Student Prince and held on to the note for several moments, that is until everyone began to run.

A moment later he too was racing after them laughing his head off.

Racing down to the bottom of the field with Griff's house in view at the end of the path, (they could at least call on him) Golcho was given a right telling off, but he was enjoying himself too much to worry about it. He'd gotten his own back on them for when they were down Harry's Rock. Revenge is sweet Golcho told him-self over and over. It's just a question of biding your time.

So when they finished scragging Golcho, Twab said that this problem was going to be sorted out tonight one way or the other.

No one knew for sure what that meant, but with Golcho's promise to behave and do his duty the way any good Shanghai Bomber should, they made their way back up the field.

Stepping out from behind the south facing wall with the wind still howling, and with their stones at the ready just in case, they carefully approached the White Hand, this creature from hell who'd come to Earth to torment them.

But when they saw what they saw, Champ (as leader) with Twab behind him, with Golcho behind him, and with Sparrow as tail end Charley, they all burst out laughing. They couldn't believe what they were looking at.

This ghost, or white hand; this creature from hell, sent here to destroy the Earth was nothing more than a piece of chicken-wire which had come loose. Stuck to it was a piece of white cardboard which flapped when the wind caught it.

As much as they all felt a little silly, no one admitted it. What was that saying about dignity at all times. There was nothing to do now but to go home.

So they emptied their pockets of stones and did just that. When Alan went in, he was given a slight telling off for being ten minutes late. Jeannie had to be in on time and Alan was told that he too had to be in on time in future.

When he told his mum that the crisis was over, she smiled and told him to drink his nightly cup of Oxo and then get himself to bed.

In bed Alan reached for his diary and completed the episode which had kept him and the lads on their toes for a couple of nights. But how ironic it was that the Ghost from hell was nothing more than a piece of cardboard stuck to a piece of chicken wire?

If and when that episode was ever mentioned, and it was mentioned quite often as they went through life, that little episode where they thought they were fighting a creature from hell was always referred to as, 'The White Hand.'

Part Six: Winter, December, 1953

WHILE WAITING FOR THE LADS TO CALL, as another carol-singing session was on the cards, Alan, slumped in his chair by the fire reached for his diary. Seeing the time was seven o'clock, there being a few more minutes before Twab would come knocking on the back door, he began to read July's entries. How much warmer it was then.

He smiled as he relived the school's sports day on the 17th, which took place on the Pentwyn fields just below the junior school. And the day went well. Thanks to Alan, Dek Dooley and John Hughes (the same John Hughes who gave Twab and Sparrow their nicknames) there were three trophies hanging on the school wall with everyone saying there would have been a fourth had Ada Goodwin not sprained her ankle just prior to the long-jump finals. Everyone said Ada would have won hands down. She was most upset with her injury.

Alan had been over the moon winning his two races, the 200 and 400 yards, but sadly the relay team, where he was the anchor man, was disqualified. Penygelli' first runner, a third year, slipped and fell on the first bend, but like Mr Robinson said, 'Don't worry team there's always next year.'

Dek Dooley from Tan y Fron had won the high jump, clearing 3 feet 3 inches, with John Hughes, a fifth year, the best javelin thrower on the day. John had won by seven inches. At the end of the day, Penygelli boasted three firsts, three seconds and one third with the remaining three contestants coming nowhere. But again like Mr Robinson said, 'Don't worry team, there's always next year.'

What a nice man Mr Robinson was turning out to be. Champ liked him as much as he did Mr Pritchard. Mr Lloyd too was a different teacher now that Alan had taken an interest in his passion, astronomy. At the end of a woodwork lesson he would hand Alan a sheet of paper on which a winter constellation had been drawn with the names of the alpha stars printed ever so neatly above the main stars. It was so easy to follow. Then with a brief explanation given and understood, and being told to wrap up well and enjoy himself, Alan would then be sent on to his next lesson on the understanding that he reported back as soon as the said stars had been located, when a discussion of a few minutes would be entered into. Alan could now find Ursa Major (the Plough) and Cassiopeia (a constellation so easy to find on account of it resembling a giant W in the winter and an M in the summer). Both constellations are overhead all year round and are easy to find. Orion, Gemini, Taurus and the Pleiades, three gem constellations of the winter sky, had also been pointed out to Alan via the slips of paper. One day, Mr Lloyd had surprised him with a book entitled *Planets and Constellations* and suggested that he join the library in Coedpoeth for free access to a host of other astronomical books.

According to Mr Lloyd, the best time for astronomy was the winter months. Alan was told that, if he wrapped himself up on a moonless night when there were not too many clouds about, the sky would be ablaze with shimmering points of light. If he looked carefully he would see that the stars were not all white. Some were red, some were blue while others were yellow or orange. Alan was flabbergasted when Mr Lloyd said that the star's colour represented its age. If it was red, he was to think of it as an old-age pensioner having burned off all its hydrogen gas. But if the star was blue, he was to think of it as a youngster. Yellow or orange stars are about halfway through their life with millions of years of hydrogen gas still left to burn. Mr Lloyd also pointed out that our sun would carry on burning for another five billion years before it exploded.

It took Alan ages to convince the lads that he was not fraternising with the enemy. Mr Lloyd, he said, was giving him knowledge that he wanted, but could still be an awful man when he chose to be.

While reading through July's entries, he remembered all the fun he and the lads had while bringing in the hay with Mr Williams. For an old man, Mr Williams had lots of energy and was always playing a joke on someone. His favourite was to catch someone off guard and soak him with milk straight from the cow he just happened to be milking by hand at the time. Like Twab, Sparrow and Golcho, he was now very fond of Mr Williams and his two dogs, Meg and Bess. He made a fuss of them if and when they were down the Hafod and was spotted by them. He also enjoyed pay day for helping to bring in the hay. His pockets and jumper were filled with sweet tasting apples and pears, when they were ripe.

The Saturday afternoon they were chased all the way to Southsea by Alum, with Champ in tow, made for good reading and would not be forgotten in a hurry. It was almost a repeat of the time Alum had chased the lads through Southsea before Champ had come on the scene. While they were splashing about in their swimming pool, as naked as the day they were born, Alum had sneaked up on them and was again accused of being born out of wedlock, and again it was Golcho who had the blame. He apparently yelled it out at the top of his voice and the man was so enraged that he gave chase. It is not easy trying to dress and run while at the same time being chased by an irate farmer!

Champ was ever so grateful to the lads for pointing out certain wild foods that were often eaten when out and about. There were dandelion leaves and flowers, sorrel leaves, burdock leaves, hawthorn leaves, elderberry leaves to name five, but when it came to the berries, wild strawberry, hawthorn, raspberry, gooseberry, elderberry, and winberries, it was fantastic. But it was the blackberries in the autumn that Champ craved. Many times while out with the lads and seeing a briar bush full of the succulent berries, they went home with stained fingers. Alan was amazed that his fingers were not stained black as one would have thought, but were if fact stained a light purple. Several times he had taken Jeannie out with him to feast on the succulent berries as she also loved them. The only pies that were ever made with blackberries were those made when Mrs Fletcher went out and picked the blackberries herself. Alan and Jeannie ate them raw, first blowing on them to remove any little grub that just happened to be feeding on them.

He turned back a few pages and read his entry for 7th April, where he asked Mr Lloyd if he could somehow stick the heart-shaped piece of glass he had found in their little river on his first ever visit to their little woods onto something so as to make it into a broach for his mum's birthday. Mr Lloyd very kindly obliged him while form 2X was having a woodwork lesson. But there was no mention in the diary that Jeannie had wanted a similar broach, and that it was high time he got off his backside and fulfilled his promise or her coloured pencils were suddenly going to be unavailable to him.

Then there was the Saturday morning when he and lads barged into Gracie's shop in Coedpoeth and asked to see the snake belts. And his luck was in. Alan was able to buy one exactly the same as the lads for two shillings.

He then read the entry for 8th June, when Richard Trematick and Basil Davies, wanting a closer look at the latest acquisition to the music room, a violin, broke into the classroom while everyone was having dinner in the canteen, and between them broke a string. Miss Griffiths had gone wild when she found out who the culprits were and wanted them expelled.

Then there was the telling off he received for tearing his trousers when he and the lads had visited Brymbo Pool. That was the day they met up with the Brymbo lads who were going to rob them; when Champ saved the day with his judo. And the way his mum went on when she saw the tear! She was so angry, Alan though he was going to be expelled from the home.

Then there was all the coal he and Twab had picked from Southsea Bank. Between them they half filled their coal houses. But it was hard work getting the coal home as it was mostly up hill. It was only when the pram broke that the coal picking stopped, but what fun was had on their way to Southsea Bank. With Twab in the pram, Champ would push him as fast as he could along the pavement, just missing lamp posts and gateways that were open. Champ loved the look of panic on Twab's face when he would let go of the handle and begin to walk, but would then run like the devil and catch him just as he was about to crash into something. Then there was the bouncing off the parapet and steering so wildly that the pram sometimes ended up on two wheels. Of course, when it was Champ's turn in the pram, Twab would do the same only worse. Sparrow and Golcho were not interested in the coal picking. Their dads being miners meant they had more coal than they knew what to do with.

Then there was the time when Sparrow was offered a packet of ten Woodbine by John Hughes if he would deliver a letter to someone in Tan y Fron. It was only when Sparrow quoted the Musketeers motto of, 'All for all and one for all,' that the others decided to go with him. How they managed to deliver the letter, unseen by the Tan y Fron lads was a mystery. When Golcho suggested they play on the Black Bank for half an hour he was regarded an idiot.

He was reminded of a Wednesday morning in assembly when Mr Samuels, in his cap and gown, called out certain names and caned them in front of the whole school for having played truant the previous day. How they were found out was unbelievable. Mr Lloyd, testing his latest home-made telescope on Minera Mountain spotted one, then another, then another until he saw eight pupils from Penygelli who should have been in school. All of them were given six of the best.

Golcho's Taid, who apparently understood the weather more than most, knew when there was going to be a storm. Alan could not remember what brought on the conversation, but it ended with Golcho insisting that his Taid was always asked if there was going to be rain, wind or snow.

Alan read his underlined entry for the 12th October, the thunderstorm to beat all thunderstorms, which took place in the early hours and went on for ages. The rain had carried on lashing his bedroom window well after the thunder and lightening had ceased. And the lightening lit up his bedroom, even though the curtains were drawn, and the thunder, if it did not clap, sounded like cannon fire. And how one clap just went on and on, and Jeannie rushed into his room and jumped into bed with him and shoved her head under the bedclothes. Their mum went downstairs and turned the mirror over the fireplace to face the wall, as apparently did everyone else in the village. And that reminded him of the two houses that went on fire in Heol y Gelli on the last day of October. What a night that was; the whole sky had lit up with the blaze. Alan, Jeannie and their mum had watched it from her bedroom. Some of the houses in Heol Wen, including theirs, were bombarded with bits of breeze block flying off the burning houses. It took three fire engines to put the fire out, but long before their arrived, the people of the Adwy had rallied round and did what they could for the house that was burning the least. It was said that people had run into the house, grabbed whatever they could and, having carried the said item to the bottom of the garden, ran back into the house for something else. A fair amount of furniture and other things were saved. But when the fire brigade turned up, the chief fireman had ordered everyone to leave the scene as it was now their responsibility.

Next morning, while on their way to school, Alan and Jeannie, having met up with Twab, Sparrow, Golcho and most of the other village children, walked past the ruined buildings as slowly as they could. The occupier of the house that was the least burned was heard asking a fireman if he or any of his colleagues had found a banana-shaped mouth organ. Later that day, parcels of clothing were gathered for the two unfortunate families who were re-housed a few miles away in a village called Gwersyllt while the council rebuilt their houses.

On a lighter note, Alan read his entry for 5th November and how it literally went off with a bang. The lads, along with the other village children, had joined forces with the bigger lads, led by Terry and Co, to build what some said was the biggest bonfire to date. The building of it had begun on the first weekend of October. Champ had enjoyed going down to the woods with the bigger lads on the weekends and dragging branches that had been cut down to the designated area which, to his delight, was just inside the field the top side of his house. As the 5th drew nearer, most of the children, including the lads, went around the village with old worn out corn-meal sacks given them by Oswald, whose shop was in between Lloft Wen Lane and Rhos Berse Road and gathered up all the dead leaves that littered the streets, and especially the Woods floor where there was an endless supply. These leaves were kept in the gatherers' washhouses in order to keep them dry, as were all the old newspapers and the like. In the week leading up to bonfire night, everyone went around knocking on doors to ask if there was any old rubbish that could be used for the bonfire – old doors, furniture, tyres, lino; anything that would burn was accepted and taken away. He enjoyed guarding the ever-growing bonfire. After school, once his chores were done, he and the lads, along with the other village children, including certain girls, took turns to guard the bonfire from the kids from neighbouring villages as, according to Twab, they would come along and set the bonfire alight and then run away having done the evil deed. In retaliation, it was the responsibility of every kid in the Adwy, including certain girls, to see to it that the bonfires belonging to the evil doers were also burned down before bonfire night. All this was done in the name of tradition.

Twab had suggested that a den be made in the bonfire for those who were on guard duty. Not only did it give cover and shelter, and a certain amount of comfort when on guard duty, but it also frightened the life out of any would-be arsonist. The arsonists, who usually came in pairs, would approach the bonfire with dirty deeds in mind and, when they were close enough, would be yelled and screamed at, and threatened by the guards. It was funny to hear them yelling out their obscenities while running away as if the devil himself was after them.

On the 5th, all the sacks of newspapers, leaves, lino, and cardboard, as well as some car tyres were shoved into the den and with a gallon of dirty engine oil that had been donated, the fire was lit. For once it did not rain. The cheers went up as the flames took hold, and when the crowd was big enough the fun and games began. The night started off with what fireworks there were being let off, some sensibly, with others like Little Demons, Cannons and Jacky-jumpers, not so sensibly. A Jacky Jumper thrown into a crowd made people scatter. For about half an hour, those around the bonfire enjoyed the fireworks being let off and there was smoke everywhere. As the night wore on, a few grown ups with small children came along. Any fireworks they brought were then appreciated by everyone. Jeannie, having arranged to meet up with Wendy and Hazel, ran over to meet them and their parents when she saw them approaching. The games that were played were: chase, tick, stroke the bunny and, for those a little more daring, there was catch a girl, kiss a girl.

When the fire began to settle down, the grown ups began to sing songs not heard since the war. Songs such as, *Well Meet Again. Keep the Home Fires Burning* and *Run Rabbit Run*, filled the air. And there was also a great deal of laughter. Mrs Fletcher, like most of the adults, brought a few potatos that were cooked in the fire and then dished out when they were ready. Everyone seemed to enjoy blowing on a potato that was burnt to a cinder on one side and almost raw on the other.

Champ had enjoyed himself very much. Seeing the sparks rising up from the fire when a stick was thrown in had fascinated him. The bigger the stick, the more sparks which would float along before fizzling out. Twab had suggested they move into the shadows and watch for any rockets being let off from other bonfires in the area. Several trails were seen lighting up the night sky and numerous bangs were heard. The artist in Champ was amazed when he saw the many patches of orange from the other bonfires in the area lighting up the sky. Black and orange was a lovely colour combination, he decided. But what really impressed him was what Sparrow pointed out, how a banger that was some way off, flashed and then banged, depending on how far away it is. Mr Ellis, the maths teacher (who also taught science) was only talking about that phenomenon the previous week, but how different it was to talk about it in the classroom and to actually witness it.

Around 9.30, with the fire a shrunken mass of embers giving off a dull reddish glow, some of the grown ups said their goodnights and left. Jeannie said goodnight to her friends when their parents decided to leave. It seems that Wendy's dad wanted the last hour in the pub. When Jeannie asked her mum if she could stay out a little longer with Alan and the lads, she was allowed an extra half hour. Sitting around the fire enjoying what heat there was, Champ, like the others had stinging eyes and smelled of smoke, was asked what his thoughts were. The only word he could think of was, 'Wow.'

Terry and Co, who lit the fire were not too much of a nuisance. Someone heard them say that they were going to make a nuisance of themselves around someone else's bonfire and so off they went.

A couple of nights later, poor old Golcho had gone down with the flu and was bed ridden for a few days. As he improved, Champ and Co paid him several visits in the evenings. During one such visit, judging from the laughing that was coming from his bedroom, his mum knew that he was on the mend and oh my, how the smile on his face disappeared when he was told, 'Its school for you on Monday morning, my lad.' But it was nice having him back on his feet. The lads all agreed that the three nights he was bed ridden had not been the same without him. Twab compared it to having a piece of jig-saw missing, the picture was being complete. Golcho was so pleased when it was explained to him that he was a vital part of their little gang.

Now that the warm weather had been replaced with freezing winds, the lads only stayed out for an hour or so in the evenings. Alan, in the company of his mother and sister, with a rip roaring fire on the go, continued with his studies. Now that he was a member of Coedpoeth library, he discovered that Mr Hughes, the librarian, was only the father of Mr Ken Hughes, the metalwork teacher. But, as much as the lads befriended Mr Hughes senior, he would not allow them to go upstairs to play snooker. The ruling was that you had to be fourteen to play the game. They all said they would be back in two years time. 'You do that,' said Mr Hughes, 'you'll be made most welcome.'

Meanwhile, Alan's studies, thanks to the library, included woodland birds, wild flowers of Great Britain and astronomy. On clear nights, with Mr Lloyd's slips of paper having ceased, and having studied his library book on astronomy after tea, he would wrap up warm and spend some time outdoors looking for a particular star or constellation and, when he found it, would rush indoors excitedly and try and persuade his mum and Jeannie to come and have a look. More often than not, Jeannie, because of the cold weather, would refuse to budge from the fire. His mum however would brave the cold for a few moments and then return to the fire.

From studying the wild flower book, he had a better understanding of why the leaves changed colour and fell in the autumn, and why certain plants went to sleep in the winter, as well as a few other things he wished he had not learned. He felt that all this discovering was taking some of the magic out of what nature had to offer. But how wise his mother was when she said, 'The truth once learned must be accepted.' Twab's prediction that their little wood would be spectacular in the autumn when the leaves changed colour, was absolutely correct. As promised their little wood was transformed from something that was already special to something that was really special. The colours were – Wow! As twelve year olds, the lads did not know how to describe the phenomenon other than 'Wow.' How the trees managed to produce so many leaves in the first place was something of a mystery to them, especially to Alan who was amazed at the many different shapes of leaves, and the special way they had of falling to the ground when discarded by the tree. Some floated down, while others swirled, swooped or span. But however they fell, it was fascinating to watch.

Alan went back to 15th October and re-read the day he explained to the lads that he wanted some time on his own down the woods. When they asked why, he said he wanted to make some drawings of the leaves changing colour before it ended. His request was granted. While on the Hafod side of the wood, he drew certain trees and bushes. Then he drew their leaves, sometimes while they were on the tree, sometimes while falling, and sometimes while on the ground. The floor of the wood, now that most of the trees were bare, looked like a multi-coloured carpet, in places a foot deep. He particularly enjoyed drawing the holly leaf with its very intricate collection of prickles, but not having the right shade of green to do it justice, it remained as a pencil drawing.

Of all the sketches he drew, the one that took his mum's fancy the most was the one of a blackberry being nibbled at by a little field mouse. Mrs Fletcher insisted it was hers and in fact she had it framed. Alan had said that he felt so privileged to be able to draw the little creature that was not ten feet away. Its coat was so shiny he told his mum and Jeannie.

As much as his sister always moaned about him using her pencils, she was always the first one to congratulate him and it was she who suggested that they make their mum a special calendar for Christmas. Alan agreed to draw twelve coloured pictures depicting the twelve months which Jeannie would make into a calendar.

Alan then read the entry for 15th December when, according to the lads, it was time to go carol singing. Anytime before then would only end up with you being told to 'Go away, it's too early.'

It was also on the 15th, just before tea, that Alan and Jeannie went out and chopped down a lovely holly Christmas tree. He had spotted one a few weeks earlier in the field at the top side of their house. Not only was it a lovely shape and covered with berries, but it was several inches taller than the two of them. It was kept in the washhouse until the 19th, the last school day of 1953. Coming home on that day, he and Jeannie were thrilled to see their house so transformed. The tree, which had been placed in a bucket that had been wrapped in Christmas paper, stood in the corner to the left of the front window and looked wonderful. It was decorated with tinsel, cotton wool and bits of decoration that Doreen had bought when Dave her husband was still alive, and Christmassy things that Jeannie had made over the years. Also dangling from the branches were three bars of chocolate, three apples and oranges, a few sherbet lollipops, sticks of licorice, chocolate coins, Spanish-wood and three small presents. Not only were the trimmings up, but balloons were dangling from the ceiling on lengths of string. Sprigs of holly decorated every picture frame making the room look so Christmassy. To top it all off there was a lovely smell coming from the cooker – their mum had made them their favourite lobscouse pie for tea. Christmas was only six days away.

That last day in school had been a little weird. Miss Williams had wished everyone a happy Christmas and, when the bell finally rang, everyone cheered and got away with it. All the discipline which Miss Williams always demanded somehow went out the window with everyone yelling and shouting as they raced, not walked, out of the classroom for the last time. There would be no more school for two whole weeks, which was fantastic.

Alan then read the entry for 22nd December, what a day that had been. It had rained all day and kept everyone in. When the rain finally stopped, around teatime, the weather turned very cold and mum had said the country was in the grip of winter.

Alan's only regret in all this was, had they moved from Chester a week earlier, on 1st June, he would have had a wonderful time with the lads on Coronation day when the street parties had been fantastic. The fun and games on that day were great, and the quantity of cakes, buns and pop that was had was also fantastic. Golcho said that he had never seen so many ice buns and bragged that he had eaten most of them. When given one he would ask for another, saying it was for his sister who was too ill to be out, and it worked. Champ said he would have loved to have seen certain people under the wing of a certain Mr Lewis (who was nicknamed Gwilym Spongecake) who, with a few others all dressed up in animal costumes made by Mrs Lewis, had apparently waltzed about amongst the crowd with buckets asking for donations for needy children while the different carnival bands marched in procession. There was something like eight floats with eight carnival queens all hoping to win.

There had also been a piece of glass that mystified everyone. If you held it a certain way you would see all the colours of the rainbow and all who saw them were told that the glass was magic. Alan closed his diary and, while trying to work out how a piece of glass could give off the colours of the rainbow, Twab's unmistakable knock could be heard at his back door. It was 7.30 and they were venturing out again on another Christmas carol session.

Letting the lads in, Mrs Fletcher invited them over to the fire. All three hugged the heat having said 'Hello' to Jeannie who was dressing up one of her dolls. They then began to secretly compare Champ's trimmings to their own, deciding theirs were better as two of Champ's balloons were already going down. While comparing the tree to theirs, again thinking their own was better, they heard Mrs F trying to persuade Alan to stay in.

'It's freezing out there,' she remarked, with Champ saying he would be alright. Actually, he complained that she was making him feel like a wally in front of the lads. Realising she was not going to get him to stay in, but determined she was going to have some say in the matter she said. 'Well at least put this scarf on; see, the lads are well covered up.'

'You're right there Mrs F,' said Twab, 'its brass monkey weather out there tonight. Don't know what I'd do without me balaclava.'

Sparrow also had on his balaclava. Instead of a balaclava, Golcho had one of his dad's old flat caps on, with his mum's scarf wrapped around it. He did not care how funny he looked, and yes, Sparrow had laughed at him. The main thing was, his ears were covered up and that was all that mattered. He also had his socks pulled up as far as they would go. But, being in short trousers, their knees were exposed and frozen.

Twab took the scarf off Mrs F and wrapped it around Champ's neck. When Champ tucked it inside his jumper, Twab told him to think of all the lovely dosh they would be making and asked him what he was going to spend his money on? Alan was so excited, he did not know.

Seeing they were ready for off, his mum told everyone to behave themselves and have a nice time. As she and Jeannie escorted them to the door, she placed her hands on Alan's shoulders, pulled him to her and whispered that he was to come home if the cold was too much. She saw them through the back door, quickly locked it and took her place back by the fire with her library book. Both she and Jeannie had been encouraged by Alan to join the library, but as yet, Jeannie was not interested in books. Who would look after her dolls and things if she was stuck in some book? Doreen was reading *A Tale of Two Cities* by Charles Dickens.

Closing the gate, the lads walked down Heol Wen as fast as they could so as to keep warm. The weather was freezing that night. They raced on and reached their first customer, a privately owned house on New Road. Champ had already been told that private houses were the better payers. They crept down the yard so as not to disturb the dog, a little Jack Russell, and stopped by the big front door where they began their programme with *Once in Royal David's City*, which caused the dog to start barking. But they all smiled when they heard the dog being told to be quiet, and again when they heard the little girl telling her mummy that they had carol singers and, not being told to go away, they knew their luck was in.

Giving the thumbs up Twab said, 'Looks like we're in fellows, keep it up.'

With the rest of their program completed (*Away in a Manger, O Come All Ye Faithful* and *We Wish You a Merry Christmas*), the door was knocked. When it opened, Sparrow was given a silver sixpence. This was truly a good start to the night. The lady of the house was thanked very much and wished a happy Christmas. 'Thank you boys,' she said, 'that was very nice. You will close the gate, won't you? Thank you and good night.'

Closing the gate and with sixpence in the kitty, the cold suddenly was not that cold. Crossing the road another favourite house was chosen where each was given tuppence for the same programme. Old Mr and Mrs Jones in the end house, both in their 80s, give them an apple each, plus a three-penny bit in money. Completing the block of houses, eight in all, their earnings jumped up to 3s 8d and they moved up New Road and sang for several more houses while making their way up to the old Co-op, opposite Lloft Wen Lane. Of the seven houses that were on the shale path that took them to Harry's Rock, only five paid out. But three houses on the main road gave generously. So too did Mrs Glasspool, whose orchard the lads had scrumped not three months before.

Their next customer, Roberts the chippy did not open the door to them, even though the light was on. They must have been out, because they were always paid well when singing carols there. According to Griff the policeman people were leaving the light on while out as it supposedly deterred burglars.

Crossing over the road, the lads were going to try their luck with the Three Mile Inn public house. No sooner had they began their first carol than the pub door opened and the landlady, Mrs Doris Evans, invited them in. Once inside, the lads waited while Mrs Evans ordered everyone to be quiet. Then with all eyes on them, they started to sing their programme. When they saw the collection jar, a pint glass, being passed around, they sang their hearts out. With the last line of *We Wish You a Merry Christmas* the audience, having sung along with them, gave them a tumultuous round of applause, plus a pint glass almost full to the top with money. Stuffing the coins into their pockets, the boys could see the collection included silver tanners as well as a couple of shillings and three-penny bits. Oh, this was indeed a good night. While the lads were thanking their audience and wishing everyone a final happy Christmas, and being teased by neighbours they knew, and taking a quick sip of beer that was offered, they at last stepped out into the freezing cold with the intention of singing for the Grosvernor Arms, fifty yards up the road.

But, as they ran the short distance with their pockets jangling with money, they found their luck had run out. Someone (actually, Billy Deakin) was giving his audience a terrible rendition of *Oh Come All Ye Faithful*. So, eager to earn some more money, they moved on towards Coedpoeth, but had a poor response as they were unknowingly singing for houses that had already been visited by Billy and others.

Rubbing his freezing hands, Twab put it to the vote to see if they wanted to carry on singing or go back to his lovely warm house and share out the money. Everyone agreed it was cold and that sharing out the money was a better idea. Each felt he had made a small fortune.

As they passed the Adwy chapel's cemetery, rustling the money in their pockets with big grins on their faces, they suddenly felt something on their faces which felt like rain.

'Well I'll go to the foot of our stairs,' said Golcho, 'you're not going to believe this but it's raining.' But a moment later their faces were beaming when they realised it wasn't raining, it was snowing. Yahooing and dancing about as the flakes kissed their faces, and glad to see the white stuff again, the lads raced up to the street light and watched the tiny flakes glistening as they fell. Minutes later, bigger and better flakes were falling with the promise of sticking. All fired up they raced on to Twab's house. As they ran along Lloft Wen Lane Champ was told some of the fun they would have in a day or two, sledging, sliding, snowballing and so on, when hopefully a foot of snow had fallen.

Bursting in through the back door, Twab invited the lads in and informed his family that it was snowing outside. Mrs Smith looked through the window and moaned. She was not too good on her feet in the snow, and Twab's three sisters, Brenda, Hillary and Pamela, in their rush to see the snow, were shouted at by their mum for not closing the door and all the heat was escaping. Queenie stood up, yawned once, completed three circles as dogs do from time to time, then lay down again. Mr Smith was in the pub on the Talwrn road.

Pushing the table cloth up, the lads, with Brenda, Hillary and Pamela looking on, emptied their pockets out and began to separate and stack the different coins. There were pennies, halfpennies, three-penny bits, silver tanners, and two, (which no one could believe) shillings, which caused a lot of excitement. After several counts, it was decided that the total was £1 4s 0^1/2d, giving the lads six shillings each. After tossing up for the odd half-penny, Golcho's face lit up when it was handed to him.

With their six shillings safely tucked away in their pockets, Sparrow, Golcho and Champ, escorted to the gate by Twab and Queenie, went home. It was still snowing. While seeing them, Twab scraped the ground in the hope of making a snowball to throw at his mates, but they were out of reach by the time he had made one, so he threw it at Queenie who enjoyed the excitement.

Reaching Heol Wen, the lads said their goodnights and Sparrow ran on eager to count his money again. Golcho ran up his yard to do the same.

Reaching his back door and beginning to look like a snowman, Champ began to sing, *We Wish You a Merry Christmas*, but before the first line was finished, the door opened. 'Oh my goodness,' said his mum startled. 'Jeannie,' she cried, 'come and see the snow?'

Jeannie's face lit up when she saw the light covering of snow. Eager to feel the flakes on her skin, she kicked off her right slipper and raised her dress. She watched with delight as the snow flakes ran down her leg and melted while tickling her.

Feeling the cold, Mrs Fletcher told them to come in and close the door, adding that the snow would still be there in the morning. Making a snowball, Alan handed it to Jeannie and then made one for himself. Daring Jeannie to step out, they threw their snowballs at the garden fence. Both missed, but it was such a joy to know that it was snowing as they remembered the fun they could have when there was a blanket of snow on the ground.

Removing his wet clothes, Alan took his place by the fire, and while warming his backside told his mum and sister how the night had progressed. He began by telling them just how good the lads singing voices were and that it was Golcho's harmonies that highlighted their performance.

Deciding that three cups of Oxo would go down a treat, Mrs Fletcher asked Alan to put the story on hold while she brewed up. While Doreen put the kettle on, Jeannie reached in the pantry for three cups. Sipping their lovely, hot drink while hugging the fire (it being too late to put another shovel of coal on, it being too near bedtime) Alan told the rest of his story. How they had to sing their carols inside the smoky Three Mile Inn, and how the pub was packed, and how the money was collected in a pint glass, and how some houses had paid more than others and how one old couple had given them an apple each as well as thruppence. He convinced his mum and sister that a good time had been had and added that the cold was soon forgotten when the money started to roll in.

Now that everyone was nice and warm, thanks to the Oxo, and with the story told, Alan asked his mum to stand up. Telling her to open both hands, he dug deep into his pocket and placed all his carol singing money into her palms.

'Mum,' he said smiling, 'this is what we've each earned tonight. There's a fortune to be had out there. You were lucky if you made sixpence in Chester.'

Placing the money on the table, Doreen asked Jeannie to help count it.

'How much is there?' Jeannie asked looking at the pile of coins.

'Count it and see,' said Alan.

After two counts and looking at her mother, Jeannie said, 'Goodness me, there's six shillings in all.'

Instructing Jeannie to pick up all she could, with Alan picking up the rest and telling his mum to hold out both hands, Alan said, 'Mum, I'd like you to have this to buy a bottle of that sherry stuff you like.' When Doreen tried to refuse, Alan ordered her to take it. She deserved it.

To the delight of every child in the village Sunday morning saw a good covering of snow. How different the village and surrounding countryside looked. Everywhere looked like a Christmas card. Alan and Jeannie were already wrapped up warm and making a snowman when Twab and Golcho called.

'We're going down the woods when we pick Sparrow up,' said Twab as he and Golcho, also wrapped up, joined in the making of the snowman. 'Are you coming with us Champ?' Jeannie was rather hoping her brother was going to spend the morning with her, but when their eyes met, she said while hiding her disappointment. 'No, I don't mind, you go, I'm getting cold anyway.' While he went in the house to tell his mum where they were going, Twab and Golcho began to snowball Jeannie who gave as good as she got. The snowman, because of its size (a good two feet at the base, and standing some four-feet tall) had more or less emptied the garden of snow.

There was a slightly smaller snowman in Aunty Mair's garden, but there was no sign of Bryn or his two sisters. Meanwhile, Sparrow, anticipating the lads calling for him, was waiting for them on the corner of Heol Celyn.

Sledge marks were already evident by Norman Williams's gateway leading down the hill. Reaching the green gates while sliding as best they could and frolicking about in Norman's sledge tracks, (Norman was no doubt heading for Fron Hill) the lads looked out across the fields to admire the view and saw the farmer from Llidiart Fanny Farm delivering food to his cows in his tractor and trailer. The cows were running alongside the trailer, mooing rather loudly, impatient to be at the food. Grinning, Twab asked Golcho if that was how it was in his house when his mum called dinner. Calling Twab a cheeky sod, and picking up a handful of snow, Golcho splashed it in his face, with Sparrow and Champ joining in. Suddenly it was a free for all snowball fight with snow finding its way down their necks. Their antics and frolicking about went on all the way up to Llidiart Fanny and only stopped at the top of the Woods hill when Champ spotted an ideal first picture for his mother's calendar. He had seen the scene hundreds of times before, but somehow the snow made it much more magical. A stout oak tree, surrounded by hazel and holy bushes, all covered in snow stood out. The hazel's lower branches were almost touching the ground with the amount of snow they had to bear. He knew that the hazel and holly were going to be in the first of three winter scenes in his mum's calendar. Wanting to be alone for a few minutes so as to capture the scene, he made the excuse that he wanted a wee and said he would catch them up.

Watching his pals running down the Woods hill teasing each other, Champ focused on the scene before him. Slowly and carefully he memorised the image. The picture was breathtaking by itself, but was strengthened with all the bird sounds he could hear. For several minutes he concentrated on the view until the picture was locked in his mind's eye. Aesthetically satisfied, he chased after his friends running along side Norman Williams' sledge tracks.

Knowing the three sets of jumbled up footprints were those of his three best friends, Champ was suddenly aware that they were nowhere to be seen. What were they up to? Arming himself with two snowballs and on red alert, he wondered where the attack was going to come from.

Approaching the S-bend, with no indication that the lads had scrambled up the bank, he supposed the attack could come from the Dump side, but again there were no footprints to suggest this. Norman's tracks and their jumbled up footprints continued into the S-bend. Wondering where they could be, he twice thought the attack was on, but it was only dollops of snow falling from the trees somewhere to his right. The thuds that were being made startled him and he began to giggle, having a vision of several pairs of arms and legs flopping about in a huge pile of snow.

Going into the S-bend Champ saw in the corner of his eye a white object hurtling down on him, then a second and a third. The aerial attack had begun. In a matter of moments (long before any decision could be made) he was being pelted with snowballs. They were hitting him in the chest, shoulders, on the legs, arms and head.

To protect himself he fell to the ground and rolled up into a tight ball like a hedgehog. For a while he began to think there was a small army attacking him, even his shout of surrender did not stop the barrage; it just went on and on until they finally ran out of snowballs. Yahooing the lads showed themselves.

To Champs amazement they had entered the woods and somehow managed to scramble up the sloping bank into Mr Moss's field which over looked the road. Seeing Champ just standing there staring at something, they had made their snowballs and waited patiently for their victim to arrive.

Looking up at them while brushing all the snow off, Champ, who a moment ago resembled a snowman, asked whether they had anything else up their sleeves? Twab, who was a little unsteady on his feet, said the attack was over, adding 'It had been a good attack, hadn't it?' Seeing Twab was a little unsteady on his feet and knowing he was going to fall, Golcho gave him a friendly nudge to help him on his way. Twab yelled out as he rolled down the bank and everyone laughed as he gathered speed while at the same time clearing the snow away. He only stopped when he slid off the bank and hit the road. Picking himself up and while brushing the snow off, he threatened Golcho with what he was going to do to him when he caught him. Twab then watched as Golcho, thanks to a friendly nudge form Sparrow, began to slide down the bank on his heels and bum. He too thudded to a stop when he slid off the bank and onto the road.

Not giving the lads time to pelt him with snowballs, Sparrow slid down the bank that had been cleared of snow and, seeing the wide path that had been made, suggested they hire themselves out as snow ploughs. But it took a free-for-all snowball fight before peace was established.

Coming out of the S-bend and seeing the crenulated bridge with its two walls leading up Fron Hill, Fron Banks and the surrounding fields and hedgerows, which belonged to Alum and old Mr Williams, covered in a blanket of snow, they all decided it a fantastic sight that would never be forgotten. A moment later, they all trampled their way down to the bridge where they each cleared a patch of snow for themselves to lean on by flaking it off with their bare hands. The snow cascaded down onto the snow that was already covering most of the frozen river. They stared at what little of the river that could be seen under the sheet of ice. When Golcho commented that the running water looked like bubbles as it trickled along, everyone agreed, but they all knew it too would soon be frozen solid.

Then, with Sparrow going first, they each carefully slid down the concrete strut on the left hand side of the bridge. While waiting for the others to follow, Sparrow tested the ice and declared it was not safe to stand on. It not only creaked under his weight, but cracked. One by one the others joined him and were all in awe of the view. What a difference a covering of snow made to things that they saw all the time. The lads had seen this particular view hundreds of times, but how different it all looked now that snow had fallen. Everyone agreed that a tree looked nice in the spring, summer and autumn, but winter snow seemed to give it that something special that made you look at it differently. Champ especially liked how a covering of snow seems to make everywhere quiet.

The lads suddenly turned their attention to the little stretch of free-running water under the bridge. There was no sign of it freezing and for about ten feet, unhampered by snow or ice, the water ran free and gurgled as it always did. Golcho scooped up a large handful of snow and hurled it at the water where it splashed and became trapped when it reached the wall of snow on the other side.

While Champ and Twab weed on the ice to see if it would melt, Sparrow and Golcho scrambled back up the concrete strut to the road. Looking over the bridge wall, and seeing the other two still watching the river, they decided to have a private snowball fight. Twab and Champ in the meantime, seeing how prominent their breath was, were having a competition to see who could make the best breath rings. Each tried to blow one breath ring through another, but failed miserably. They then realised that Sparrow had set himself a hard task in trying to emulate Terry with the cigarette-smoke rings. It was only when Sparrow and Golcho began to drop handfuls of snow on them from the bridge that they scrambled back up the strut, which was not easy now that the layer of snow had been disturbed.

Back on the road, they made for the Woods entrance on their right in virgin snow. They each liked the crunching sound of the snow when it was walked on. It was an unique sound. They then compared the different patterns that their Wellingtons were making, and the size of their feet. It turned out that Twab had the biggest feet.

Entering the Hafod side, they each in turn used Twab's footprints to walk in for the full length of the first slope. The snow was up to the tops of their Wellingtons and when they reached the holy bush that part blocked the path on the second slope, the one that Golcho had still not cut down, Twab knocked all the snow off it, as he did not want snow falling on him. They then made their way down the rest of the second and third slopes by making their own tracks.

Whoever it was that mentioned how peaceful it was mistaken. A blackbird flew past, tutting like mad. A sparrow tried to mimic it, his tut, tut, tutting was actually very good.

All agreed that it was both exciting and a little eerie to be in the wood with all the snow on the ground. It also gave them a sense of adventure, knowing their footprints were the only ones around.

It was Golcho who mentioned that there was no sign of Norman Williams who they had thought would be sledging down Fron Hill. For a moment they wondered where on earth he could be, but only for a moment. Before you could say Jack Robinson, they were plodding deeper into the wood with Norman completely forgotten.

Had they ventured onto the Dump side of the wood, they would have seen Norman who was there simply minding his own business, sitting on his sledge, contemplating. He too was in awe of the scene he was looking at. Not even the lads frolicking about less than thirty feet away bothered him in the least.

Reaching the little swing (that swung them across the river) and because of the snow drifting over their Wellies, Golcho suggested they should go back to the road and make their way up Fron Hill, and climb over the little wall into Mr Williams's field where they could roll snowballs down the steep slope.

It took a good half hour to reach the top of Mr Williams's field, but when they did, Twab and Golcho, took on Sparrow and Champ to see who could make the biggest snowball to be rolled down the rather steep slope.

They frantically began to roll their little snowballs around the field making them bigger and bigger. When they could roll them no more, they pushed them to the starting point and, on Twab's command, rolled them over the crimp and cheered as they gathered momentum and grew larger and larger before finally crashing into the river and breaking up. It was so much fun it was done all over again. They cheered and argued that their snowball was going the fastest, as a second set of them went rolling down the field and crashed into the river, followed by another two and then another two.

Suddenly, the game came to an end as there was no more snow in the immediate area. But when they saw the intertwining tracks they had made all agreed a good time had been had. In later years, Champ felt certain that the design of the famous Spaghetti Junction road interchange was based on the tracks they made in the snow that day.

Because of all the activity, no one noticed the weather until Sparrow threw a snowball at Twab hitting him in the chest. It was starting to snow. Shaking his head at Sparrow which said, 'I wouldn't do that again unless you want a thump', Twab, rubbing his hands to keep them warm, said he was ready for home as he thought the weather was going to get worse. Plus he was hungry.

'Yea, I'm ready for my dinner as well,' said Golcho.

They ran back to the little wall and climbed over. Back on the road, with one last look at the design they had made on the field, they crunched their way down to the bridge where they had a long look at their snowballs all splattered out across the river. With no more to do, they set off up the Woods hill for home.

As the snow was undisturbed, apart from the tracks that they had made, walking up the hill was easy. Champ began to knock the snow off the bushes he came across by gently kicking them at their base. Seeing the fun he was having the others joined in. The game was, you had to kick the bush as low down as you could and then get your foot away before the snow fell on it. The fascination for Champ, and then the others, was seeing the snow crack before it fell away and by the time the had reached the top of the hill, all the bushes on both sides of the road had been freed from their snowy prisons.

It was only when Twab announced that he was getting even hungrier that two things were noticed – they were all covered in snow as it was snowing rather heavily and all the tracks they had made when they came that way were gone, buried by the fresh snow. Laughing and looking at his mates, Golcho likened them to the Abominable Snowman and began to prance about with everyone laughing. More laughter erupted when, in a free for all, everyone tried to shove snow down each others neck. But, after several minutes of fooling around and realizing they were getting whiter and whiter, it was deemed that they should get a move on and get home.

When Alan reached home, instead of going in, he stood in the garden for ages trying to work out why all this snow was suddenly affecting him. He thought long and hard about it as the snow began to cover him. There was no more playing out that day; it was five o'clock and dark when it finally stopped snowing, not that it ever really got dark when there was snow on the ground. On this occasion there was at least a six-inch covering and no tracks or footprints could be seen anywhere. Everywhere was white, giving off a radiance and calmness that only a heavy fall of snow can give. All sounds were muted, which Alan thought was marvelous.

Worried that Jeannie was still in Wendy's house three doors up from the Grosvernor Arms, Doreen asked Alan if he would accompany her to bring her home. His offer of going himself for her was rejected. 'We'll both go,' his mum said.

Wendy's house, less than half-a-mile away, seemed much further that day due to the snowy conditions but Alan enjoyed walking through the new snow along the path leading to Lloft Wen Lane. It was fun and he was an explorer in the Antarctic. But that could not be said for his mum who was worried that it might start snowing again. He thought there was an awfully strange atmosphere as there was no traffic on the main road which was covered in a blanket of snow. Usually cars and lorries would be shooting past, but not today, not in this weather. The road was completely empty. In fact, he and his mum were the only people out.

Reaching Wendy's house, and having to shove the gate open even though the little path up to the front door had been cleared, he knocked the snow off the brass knocker and ran-tanned the door to be sure of being heard. Hoping it was someone to collect Jeannie, Mrs Pritchard opened the door and invited them in. She said Wendy's dad was just about to take Jeannie home, having just this minute returned from taking Hazel home. Then she went on about how bad the weather was before walking through the narrow hallway and informing Jeannie that her mum and brother were there to take her home. Jeannie greeted them and then excitedly asked how deep the snow was?

'Its deep enough,' her mum told her.

With the offer of a cup of tea refused, in case it began to snow again, Jeannie and Wendy said farewell to each other with Jeannie dying to get outside. Back on the road and realising that the street lighting, which was on, was not needed due to the covering of snow, Mrs Fletcher and her family set off for home. After a few yards, Alan pointed out to Jeannie that their foot prints were the only ones to be seen. They plodded on past the Grosvernor Arms, the Adwy Chapel and cemetery, the Three Mile Inn, Roberts's chippie and Glyn's shop, but as they approached Lloft Wen Lane, he pointed out how lovely the wall was having lost its crenellated look due to the snow. Mrs Fletcher then pointed out the house of her friend, Sally, on the other side of the road. 'Oh,' said Alan, who then informed her that Sally was one of those who had paid sixpence when they sang the carols.

Turning left into Lloft Wen Lane and having to face the drifting snow again, Alan suggested they should walk in their previously-made footsteps, with Jeannie walking in his, but it did not make walking any easier. Trampling along, he pointed out how much brighter it was on account of the snow, even though it was going dark, but Jeannie shrugged and said she was not bothered as she had now had enough of the snow and just wanted to get home. The excitement of it had worn off.

Suddenly Alan stopped. Something had caught his eye. He ignored it at first, but then was suddenly curious. 'Hang on,' he said, 'I'm sure I saw something back there in the snow.' Walking back, he began to sift through the snow with the tips of his Wellingtons.

'What did you see?' Jeannie asked while snuggled behind her mum so as to avoid the chill wind. She was freezing.

'Whatever it was,' said Alan pushing the snow with his foot, 'It's gone now.' Just then he saw something sparkling. He picked it up and shook off the snow that was clinging to it. Holding it up for all to see he said, 'Well, well, well, I've found a watch.'

Asking to see it, Mrs Fletcher held it up to her ear. 'It's a ladies watch, and it's ticking.' Looking up and down the lane she said, 'It's only just been lost, I'd say. It must belong to the person who made these prints.' She pointed to a set of prints. 'Someone's going to be awfully disappointed when they realise they've lost their watch.'

'Not to worry Mum,' said Alan, 'you have it as a Christmas prezzy.'

'No,' said Mrs Fletcher, 'That's not right.' Looking at the watch again, she said, 'We'll call in at Mr Griffith's house and hand it over. Being a policeman he'll know what to do with it.'

'Why?' asked Alan. 'I found it.'

'Yes, I know you did, but it doesn't belong to you. It most probably belongs to this person.' Mrs Fletcher again pointed at the new set of prints.

While climbing over the stile which was covered in snow, Mrs Fletcher explained that if it was not claimed in three months then it would become his property, but not before.

Griff, the policeman thanked them for their honesty and said he would personally deliver it if it was not claimed in the next three months.

Reaching home, Alan made the fire up with a shovel full of coal and a good sized log. While their tea was being made, egg and chips with bread and butter, Jeannie set the table while Alan again cleared the yard of snow. After tea, when the pots had been washed and put away, Doreen read a little more of *A Tale of Two Cities*, while Jeannie played with her dolls. Alan was waiting for seven o'clock.

At seven o'clock, he said he was going to meet the lads as there was another carol singing session on the cards. While waiting for Sparrow on the corner of Heol Wen the lads made a slide, there being an ideal dip in the road for that purpose, and it was up and running in no time due to the icy conditions. Knowing there was a slide on the go by the amount of yahooing he could hear, and finishing off a thick butty jam, Sparrow licked his sticky fingers clean and raced up to the lads. There he waited his turn to run at the slide and join in the fun. On completing his run, he ran to the back of the queue for a second go.

Champ could not understand why he always ended up going backwards about halfway along the slide. Starting off was okay, then, at about the half way mark, he would begin to turn to his left, loose his balance and fall. It was Sparrow who pointed out his error. His feet were in the wrong position. Instead of having his feet more or less in the direction he was going, they were at too much of an angle which was causing him loose his balance. With the fault corrected, he then completed the full length of the slide on his next run. And what a difference not falling over made but, as Twab said, Christmas Eve was only two nights away and they were not there to enjoy themselves, they were there to earn money. Telling them to go on and saying he would catch them up, Champ, now that he knew how to slide without falling over, wanted a few more rides. After being told not to be too long, he ran at the slide and rode down the icy path several times. Pleased that he could now slide properly, he had one last run before running after the lads who he caught up with by Griff's house on Heol Glyndŵr.

Golcho's request that they sing carols for Griff was turned down. He did not know of anyone who had sung carols for a policeman before and thought they would be the talk of the town if they did. But his request was still turned down. While Golcho argued that they would have been able to boast about singing carols for a Bobby when school started up again in the new year, Twab wanted nothing to do with it again turned down the request, adding that he did not want to hear another word about it. Neither did Sparrow or Champ. Singing carols for a copper, what next?

Champ then remembered the night when they were doing battle with the White Hand and Sparrow and Golcho had told Griff the best lie he had ever heard, that they were checking to see if there were any Martians about. That entry like, so many others in his diary, had been duly underlined.

Deciding to stay local, the lads sang their carols for the twelve houses that made up Heol Offa. As five of the twelve houses refused to give anything, saying they had already given once that evening, and the other seven hardly gave anything at all, and the night was bitterly cold they decided there was no point in staying out any longer for such low wages. Back they went to Twab's house with the night's takings of two shillings and eight pence, which gave them eight pence each. Golcho said it was better than nothing. They could at least go to the pictures and have an ice-cream.

With their goodnights said to Twab's mum and sisters, and while Golcho began to walk up Twab's yard, both Champ and Sparrow pelted him with bits of ice, the snow being too frozen now to make a proper snowball. When they reached Heol Wen, Champ and Golcho began to throw bits of ice at Sparrow who had said goodnight. Sparrow then legged it down the road. Knowing he would have ice thrown at him, Golcho ran up his yard and was indoors before it could happen.

When Alan walked into his house, having had several more goes on the slide to finish the night off, Jeannie was already in bed. Sitting next to his mum, enjoying his bedtime drink of Oxo, he tried to find a way of asking for a favour as he wanted to go down the woods early, and he wanted to be there alone. He wanted to see if being there on his own would solve the riddle of why the snow was having such an effect on him? Swallowing the last of his Oxo and knowing what he was about to say was not exactly true, there being a little porky involved, he said, 'Mum, would you be angry if I got up early in the morning and went down the woods on my own?' There, he had said it.

'Why on earth would you want to do that?' his mum asked puzzled.

'Well, since we've been in the Adwy, I've changed,' he said (which was true). 'I love nature so much now. I want to learn everything there is to learn about it. For instance, I would love to see the woods early in the morning before anyone else has been there and filled the place up with their tracks. I imagine it would be very beautiful and peaceful. And I'd have a better chance of seeing any animals or birds if there were any. When I got up early that time and sneaked out, it made you angry and you worried, but, oh Mum, something's happening to me and I don't know what.'

Thinking he had said enough, he decided he was not going to mention how the snow was affecting him, the main reason for wanting to be down the woods. There was a lot of working out to be done before mentioning the snow.

Hugging him and realising he was growing up, Doreen said, 'Well thank you for asking.' Hugging him again she said, 'I promised your dad a long time ago that I would never stand in your way in such matters. Your dad knew these times would come. He was a very special man and I loved him dearly.'

She hugged him again and then holding him at arm's length said, 'Now I don't have to tell you to be careful, do I?'

'Noooo,' he replied. Hugging his mum, he said he would be very careful.

'Right then,' she said, smiling, 'just come home when you're ready.'

Next morning he was nudged three times before he opened his eyes. 'Are you still going down the woods?' his mum asked.

Nodding and yawning, he asked what the time was.

'It's just coming up to six o' clock and it's freezing out there.' Leaning over the bed and seeing he was falling back to sleep, his mum said in a low voice, 'Are you going or shall I leave you to go back to sleep?'

'I'm going,' Alan chirped up as he went into another long, noisy yawn.

'Don't be so noisy or you'll wake our Jeannie up,' whispered his mum. Prodding him, she said quietly, 'Come on now, let's have you up.'

Alan jumped out of bed, dressed and crept downstairs thinking his mum had gone back to bed, but was pleasantly surprised when he saw the light on and heard sounds coming from the back kitchen. Closing the hall door as quietly as he could as it still creaked a little after all this time, he said, 'I didn't mean for you to be up as well Mum.'

'Knowing you my lad,' said Doreen from the back kitchen, 'you would have gone out without anything warm inside you. Wrap that blanket around you and then sit yourself down. I'll have a nice warm drink for you in a minute.'

Although Alan was fully dressed, he was still cold even with the blanket wrapped around him. Wanting to check on the weather he pulled the curtains apart and noticed all the window panes were covered in Jack Frost patterns. They were so intricate and he marveled at them.

'Here you are,' said his mum handing him a glass of warm milk. Sitting down she told him to drink it as it would warm him up.

She watched as he devoured the warm drink. She was so proud of him. Also wrapped in a blanket and hugging a freshly-filled hot water bottle, his mother was going back to bed until Jeannie woke up. Ruffling his hair she said, 'You should be alright. It hasn't snowed any more during the night and your Wellingtons and extra socks are by the back door.'

When Alan finished his drink and began to lick the inside of his glass, his mum, wondering where on earth he had learned that, took it off him and placed it on the table. Going into the back kitchen with him she helped him on with his extra socks and Wellingtons and said, 'Now don't get too cold, but I hope you enjoy yourself.'

All ready to go, he stepped into the freezing cold Christmas Eve morning. With the spare key in the outside lavvy in case he came home before anyone was up, and knowing his mum was freezing, he was amazed to see so many icicles hanging from the washhouse guttering. He had never noticed them before. He told his mum to go in as he would be alright and it was too cold to be standing in the doorway. As quietly as he could, he crunched his way up the path and through the gate. In the stillness he heard his mum tapping her bedroom window. Waving back, he pretended it was not that cold – but it was.

It had not snowed during the night, but what snow there was, was very compacted and crunchy, and it was freezing cold. Because of the time of day, the noise of his crunching feet was carrying and sounded like there was an invisible man walking along side of him.

On the corner of Heol Wen he saw that last night's slide was still intact and, now able to slide without falling over, ran at it and enjoyed the ride. Moving down Heol Islwyn he began to pound his rapidly cooling feet in the hope of keeping them warm.

Alan turned right into Heol Celyn, and then left into Heol Offa. He then passed the green gates and crossed over the Talwrn road. Turning left by Llidiart Fanny, he was, moments later, where he wanted to be, at the top of the Woods hill.

Stopping to admire the scenery, his attention was drawn to the first winter scene of his mother's calendar, an oak tree with its companion bushes. Because he'd rushed here, his breath was quite prominent and while he stood in the early morning silence, puffing slightly, he tried to emulate Sparrow, who was, as you know trying to emulate Terry.

Champ tried to blow a breath ring through another but failed. He then began to see and feel the reason for his being here at this unearthly hour. The visual was easy enough to explain, it was beautiful, and he was now interested in nature, which he put down to his growing up. But why was he again feeling the way he felt in his garden yesterday – that was the mystery? Why was all this snow affecting him? It had never bothered him in Chester. He pondered the problem for several minutes trying to work it out, but its meaning was still lost to him no matter how hard he tried to resolve it.

Because it was too cold to just stand there, he gave up and instead began to admire the scene he had drawn for his mum's calendar. It was breathtaking even now. While staring at what was January's picture, that strange feeling which he could not explain was again upon him. Why? Was it because he was living in the Adwy? Was it because he was growing up? Was it because he had never seen snow on this scale before? Yes, there was snow in Chester but it never seemed to last long, plus the snow ploughs were always on the go. He somehow did not think the answer was going to come on this visit. January's drawing was simple enough. All it was was an oak tree and some bushes covered in snow. But why was it more than eye catching. If only the answer would come.

While taking in the moment, his eyes were everywhere, on the snow-laden trees, on the bushes, on the bank, on the frozen hedgerow that stood over and somehow protected the little woods road.

He suddenly heard a sound, so faint it sounded like someone was sprinkling salt on a lettuce leaf. He quickly located the source and watched in amazement as the very fine particles of snow began to bathe the bushes with such finesse. What a delicate sound it was. He then noticed little animal tracks running alongside and up the bank. They appeared to be running in all directions. Alan wondered what could have made them? He decided there were three sets of little feet all jumbled up, crisscrossing one another. How many more were hidden in the bushes he wondered and how clearly they were imprinted in the frozen snow? They looked like fossils, but unlike fossils, he knew these prints would soon be gone.

The tiny tracks were so perfect he knew he would never forget them. He then spotted some bird tracks. Crouching down to have a closer look, and after comparing them to the animal tracks, Alan noticed that some of the birds' tracks were bigger than others. But whatever their size they all had one thing in common; a back claw. Alan suddenly realized its significance; it aided the bird when perching. It was for all the world like a thumb for gripping. Alan was so chuffed for having worked that out for himself.

Suddenly remembering the greater spotted woodpecker, he wondered if its tracks were amongst those on display and decided they were. He then wondered when he was going to have his next sighting of what was becoming his favourite bird; not that he did not like the buzzards and jays and all the other birds. He decided he liked them all.

Suddenly the sound of his breathing began to fascinate him. He stood there in the morning silence, listening to his breath being sucked into his lungs via his nostrils and then released back into the atmosphere. But the mystery was where did the spent breath (the carbon dioxide) go? One moment it was so prominent and visible, almost as thick as cigarette smoke, then it was gone, but gone where? Alan wondered if any of the lads would know the answer to the mystery.

But the other sound he was hearing from time to time was no mystery. It was his feet crunching the snow when he moved or shifted position. But it was still a puzzle as to why the snow was making him feel the way he was feeling. What was churning up this strange feeling that he had never had before yesterday? And just as important, why was it being churned up? All this because he had stood in his back garden pleased with the depth of snow. It was crazy.

Then he remembered that day in FitzHugh's wood, when he was taken to Bersham waterfall. The feeling he had then, was very similar to the one he had now. Was it because he was in a more densely-populated wood?

It was the same with the river. Was it because the river was so much wider and stronger than their little woods river? That, and now this, he felt were somehow connected. It had to be, but why? But the answer would not come.

With Twab's teaching imprinted on his mind (never be noisy when in the woods) his feet nevertheless crunched their way down the Woods hill. Reaching the S-bend he stopped at the spot where less than twenty-four hours before Twab, Golcho and Sparrow had pelted him with snowballs. He smiled when he remembered how Twab, and then Golcho, having been given friendly nudges rolly-pollied down the bank. The evidence of their rolly-pollying was gone, but not the memories which, like so many others, would stay with him for the rest of his life.

He entered the Hafod side of the Wood by the only entrance he had used ever since coming to live in the Adwy. He also remembered his first ever visit to this fantastic place. It was 13th June, 1953, a Saturday morning, not six months ago. Wow, was it nearly six months ago. Gosh, how time was flying by.

The feeling of being completely surrounded by trees and bushes for the first time in his life was simply out of this world.

He made his way down the first slope through the deep snow, then the second, with its holly bush that usually scratched your leg, the one that Golcho was still threatening to chop down, then the third one and was suddenly in the first of the clearings where the trees thinned out a little. How much longer it had taken him to travel the short distance on account of the snow. Normally it would have taken seconds to reach this first of several clearings. The snow, where not frozen was almost to the tops of his Wellingtons.

How different the trees were now that they were naked. But knowing their leaves would be growing back in the spring; Alan trudged on to where the path split into two lesser ones and again enjoyed the scene and serenity.

It was so wonderful being tuned into nature's frequency, listening to sounds that most people did not take any notice of.

Alan decided he liked the sound of snow breaking away from a given branch and then crashing into a bush, thus freeing it from its snowy covering. But that was nothing to the rumble it made when sliding off a roof and crashing into the garden with a deep thud, which Alan thought was an avalanche when he first saw it happen, like the other day when he saw it tumbling off Aunty Jinni's house. It was all over in seconds, but the rumble it made was incredible.

He could just make out little audible tweets and whits of birds as they scuttled around in the deep, hard-packed snow for something to eat. As much as he could not see them he knew they would be watching him, but they had nothing to fear, he would not harm them for the world.

The solitude was so enjoyable. As he looked around his little wood, he remembered times here with his three best friends, Twab as leader, Sparrow who was forever winding Golcho up, and Golcho who was always retaliating. He marveled at the fun and games they had been had in this little wood, knowing they would be played out again. Alan suddenly remembered his first day in school when he swore his allegiance to the Shanghai Bombers and decided that he was going to give that same allegiance to nature from now on.

Closing his eyes and with his arms splayed out above his head, he vowed that from this moment on he would protect the animals to the best of his ability. When he lowered his arms he felt ten feet tall.

Moving on in order to keep warm, he trudged his way over to where he had met his two Irish friends, Patrick O'Donagan and Michael O'Flynn. Wondering where they could be on such a morning, Alan wished them a happy Christmas. Trudging through the deep snow (it was everywhere up to the tops of his Wellingtons) he made his way down to the river. As he prepared to leap across the unseen river, a loud thud startled him. He knew what it was, a clump of snow falling from a tree. Alan crossed over the frozen river, knocked all the snow off the branches he had to pass under and then wriggled through the middle strand of the barbed-wire fence and stepped into Mr Williams's field. He trudged along what he thought was the edge of the river, but several times misjudged his step and fell thigh deep into a drift. Unperturbed, he began to make his way over to the Hafod Bridge which was a hard slog. One minute the snow was hard enough to support his weight, the next it was not, which slowed him down. But as he struggled on it began to snow.

He stopped and looked upwards, closing his eyes and smiling as the flakes kissed and tickled his face. How gentle they were. Minutes later, it began to snow more heavily and, not only was he becoming a snowman, but he was also being enveloped in a mist that suddenly appeared from nowhere. He thought the moment was truly magnificent. Not only was he in a silence that he had never known before, but he was also being snowed upon, and was disappearing into a mist that was closing in around him.

As the landscape began to disappear, and being just a teeny-weenie bit mystified, he decided it was a privilege being there at that moment. There was no point in trying to make any sense of it. It was too beautiful a moment to even try. He was simply going to accept and enjoy it. It was clearly a one-off event which brought him no nearer to solving the problem of why the snow was affecting him. While being snowed upon and slowly disappearing in this magical mist, he decided he was not going to worry about it again. But he did hope that perhaps one day the answer to this and a hundred other unanswered questions would come.

While standing there in Mr Williams's field, mesmerised, Alan claimed the moment and shortly afterwards set off for home. It was only when he reached the top of the Woods hill, after some twenty minutes of hard slog, that another miracle happen. He could not believe it but he walked out of the mist into beautiful sunshine. Had he been standing on top of Fron Bank, he would have seen that the whole of his little Woods was shrouded in mist with only the tallest trees showing through. The vision he created in his mind's eye was magical.

The moment he reached home he reached for his diary and wrote down the morning's adventure while it was still fresh in his mind. He still could not get over the fact that he had walked out of the mist into brilliant sunshine. He did not think he would ever forget that.

While enjoying his dinner and the fire, he told his mum and Jeannie all about his morning's adventure. Jeannie said she would have gone with him had she known, but when she asked if he was afraid when the mist came down, he replied, 'No,' adding that it was so magical, it felt as if a door had opened. When Jeannie asked what he meant, Alan said he did not know, but that was how it felt. He did not know it then but his life was altered forever. Like the mist and sunshine at the top of the Woods hill, it was an experience he would never forgot. He tried many a winter-time to re-open that door, but it never did, it was a one off.

After dinner, Jeannie asked to see Alan upstairs, where, in her bedroom, she showed him their finished calendar. He praised her for putting it together; there was a picture for each of the twelve months. Now that he had seen it, it was going to be wrapped up in an old copy of the *News of the World*.

'Alan,' his mum called from the bottom of the stairs, startling them both, 'the lads are here.'

Twab gave Jeannie a quick 'hello' when they came downstairs, but told Champ to get his coat on, as according to Sparrow there was sledging going on down Fron Hill. Champ scrunched his face up. He was in an awkward situation. With his mum in the back kitchen he whispered that he had promised to spend some time with Jeannie this afternoon as they had a few prezzies to wrap up.

'Oh, you can do that tonight,' Twab whispered back. 'Anyway, who said anything about leaving Jeannie behind? She can come with us if she wants to.'

'Ooh, yes please,' said Jeannie excitedly. 'I'd love to.'

'Right then, that's settled,' said Twab, 'Get your coats on.'

While the lads were warming their backsides by the fire, Twab, having said hello to Mrs F, who was very busy in the back kitchen, listened as Golcho asked her if she would like to come along and do some sledging. When Sparrow saw the look on Mrs F's face, he said nothing. He could see how busy she was preparing for Christmas and was surprised that Golcho was not told off for being presumptuous.

Helping Jeannie on with her coat, and in response to Golcho's invitation, Mrs F asked him, 'Who do you think will do all the Christmas preparations for me while I go sledging down Fron Hill?'

As much as it sounded like a telling off, it was not. She was just stating a fact.

Wishing he had not asked the question, Golcho moved away from the fire as his legs were burning and everyone was ready for off.

'See you Mrs F,' the lads all shouted as they scrambled through the door, pushing Jeannie out first, but not before she also shouted, 'See you Mrs F.'

Telling Alan to keep an eye on his sister and closing the door, Doreen went over to the front window and watched as Twab led his little gang of five through the gate and down the road. By the time they had reached the top of the Woods hill, everyone, including Jeannie, had been snowballed. 'Look Jeannie,' said Alan pointing to some trees, 'do you recognise them?'

'Ooh yes,' she answered. 'It's January in our mum's calendar.' She thought his drawing was very good.

Coming out of the S-bend, they were surprised to see several children from the village, as well as children from the Talwrn, all sledging down Mr Williams's field and not down Fron Hill as Sparrow had said. They part slid, part walked and part ran down to the bridge and then raced up Fron Hill as far as the little wall, which was devoid of snow because of all the people that had climbed over it. They each in turn climbed over into the field. Alan and Jeannie, never having seen anything quite like this before, were amazed at all the fun that was being had by everyone. There were screams and yahoos of joy everywhere. Some sledges were already speeding down the field, with their excited passengers hanging on for dear life, while others, having completed their ride, were being pulled back up the field in haste for yet another run. But which ever way the sledges were travelling, a lot of fun was being had.

'It looks like it's a free for all,' said Golcho.

'What does that mean?' asked Champ.

'It means you help someone to pull their sledge back up the field,' said Sparrow, 'that way you get a free ride. Watch, I'll show you.' Trudging down the field to one of the village lads who was struggling with his sledge and, with a simple nod of heads to mean the deal was on, he grabbed hold of the rope and helped Neville and Glyn Williams to pull their sledge back up to the top of the field. When it was turned around, Neville jumped on, followed by Glyn and Sparrow then pushed them and the sledge over the crimp. When enough speed was had, he jumped on. As they raced on down the field, his yahoo, along with that of Neville and Glyn, was heard above all the others.

'That's how it's done,' said Twab as he raced over to help Arthur Davies.

Golcho chose Selwyn Pugh and John Hughes.

Telling Jeannie to stay put, Champ chose a new lad to the village, Alun Roberts, or Ali Cabbage as he was known, who lived in the corner house that Champ had been shown around the day he was taken to Harry's Rock, which meant he lived across the way from Griff the policeman.

What bad luck having to live so close to a policeman Champ thought, as they hauled the sledge back up the field. But while it was being turned around ready for the next run, Jeannie was called over and told to sit at the back of Ali Cabbage and hold on for dear life. Pushing like mad, Champ pushed them over the crimp and, as they started down the slope, with Jeannie's heart racing, he jumped on. 'Hang on Jeannie,' he yelled as they went speeding down the field, stopping just feet away from the river. Not that they would have fallen in as the river was frozen. But moments later, Golcho and his partners, Selwyn Pugh and John Hughes, came crashing in.

The fun and games were played out in brilliant sunshine until it began to cloud over some two hours later by which time the temperature had also plummeted. Because of the cold and wet from plunging into the snow from time to time, the lads, and especially Jeannie, were ready for home.

They trudged back through the Hafod and, never having seen the place before, Jeannie said how lovely the area was, adding that she would be coming here with her friends in the spring when all the snow was gone. She particularly liked the Hafod bridge and the area that was becoming a picnic area. She could see herself and her friends, along with other children, playing happily in the warm, summer sunshine. Her mind was made up even more when she was told how lovely it was in the spring with all the daffodils and primroses.

They made their way up the path to Mr Williams's farm in single file. Jeannie walked next to Sparrow and they each in turn scrambled over the stile which had a good six-inch covering of snow. There was no sign of Mr Williams, or the two dogs, but they quickly realised that they were faced with a snow drift that appeared to go on and on, all the way along the farm's outer buildings, including the hay loft where the lads had so much fun only a few months ago. Sparrow bet the drift went as far as the Talwrn road.

Seeing the worried look on Jeannie's face prompted Champ to ask Sparrow if he would link hands with him so as to carry her through the drift. But Sparrow being Sparrow caused Jeannie's heart to flutter when he asked her if she wanted a piggy-back. Eagerly, with the help of Twab and Golcho, Jeannie jumped onto Sparrow's back and, after much wriggling about to make herself more comfortable they set off. They cautiously approached and stepped into the drift which was very deep and, as they plodded on, Twab began to wonder how deep it was going to be.

'We'll find out when Sparrow and Jeannie disappear!' said Golcho grinning while trying to shove snow down Sparrow's neck.

'Pack it in Golch,' said Sparrow as he felt the cold snow on his skin. 'You're going to make me …' But it was too late, he did not have time to finish the sentence as he slipped and fell, throwing Jeannie into a dollop of lose snow. Picking himself up, and with revenge in mind, he gave chase.

'Wait for me,' yelled Jeannie, as Golcho tried to make his escape. 'I want to be the one who puts the snow down his neck.'

Realising he was running the wrong way (he was heading into the drift), Golcho asked for mercy and gave himself up. But knowing there was not going to be any mercy he dropped to his knees, rolled up into a ball and waited for whatever punishment was doled out. Laughing and with clumps of snow in hand, Sparrow and Jeannie struggled into the drift after him. Feeling like a condemned man and seeing the situation as being unfair, Golcho stood up, grabbed Jeannie, pushed her into the drift and made a run for it.

Not wanting to miss out in the fun, Twab and Champ joined in the chase and Golcho was soon captured. The snow being so deep there was nowhere for him to run and, not only was he pelted with snowballs, but Jeannie suggested that he should lean over and carry her on his back donkey style. With Twab and Sparrow seeing to that she did not fall off, she was carried with Champ leading the procession the way they did in Egypt.

'Listen everyone,' she said, 'we're in a snowy desert and I am your very beautiful Queen and you have to obey me or you'll be thrown you to the lions.'

With Queen Jeannie on his back, with her legs dangling on either side of him, and with Champ leading and shouting 'Mush,' they set off across this Welsh-Egyptian desert which was very cold and wet, not hot and sunny. They had not gone five yards when Queen Jeannie felt she had been insulted and she punished Golcho for his remark by smacking his backside as hard as she could with her gloved hand. She also informed him that he was going to be thrown to the lions.

'Ouch,' Golcho cried out half laughing, 'tell her to stop it. I was only joking when I said she weighs a ton.'

As he trudged through the 'desert' as ordered by Queen Jeannie, Golcho, for devilment, threw her into the snow, not once, but twice, but got away with it saying , 'I'm sorry your majesty, I slipped.'

With order restored and about twenty minutes of hard slog behind them, they stepped out of the drift. Had Sparrow insisted on betting, he would have lost as the drift petered out well before they reached the Talwrn road. Once on the road and having dismounted from Golcho's back, Jeannie joined in with the antics of sliding and snowballing each other.

When they reached Sparrow's house, he said his goodbyes adding that he would see them after tea. Golcho did likewise when they reached Heol Wen. But Twab set off for home, his walk suddenly became a run as the first of several snowballs went whizzing past his ears. When he was out of range he made a single snowball and just threw it. He never thought for a moment it would hit anyone, but it did. It struck Champ on the head. Twab laughed and ran off when he saw Champ making a snowball to throw back. Champ threw his snowball, but Twab was way out of range. Turning to Jeannie he said, 'Come on Sis, let's go home.'

'Oh, Mum,' said Jeannie when she and Alan began to remove their wet clothes, 'I wish I was a boy. They have much more fun than us girls.' Jeannie chatted all through their meal, telling her mum everything that had happened. How Golcho was made to carry her on his back, how she had sat on a sledge and raced down the field, how Mr Williams had let them play in the hay loft and how they had filled up their pockets with fruit when it was ripe. 'He doesn't mind you being on his land. Oh, why couldn't I have been a boy.' It took ages for her to calm down.

Whereas Jeannie stayed in after tea as she knew Wendy and Hazel were calling, Alan met up with the lads by Twab's house and helped to make a slide on the corner of Heol y Gelli. Like Heol Wen, the sun hardly ever shone on the street across the way from Twab's house. After some twenty minutes of sliding down the road in every position possible, Ali Cabbage (the lad Champ had teamed up with that afternoon while sledging down Mr Williams's field) let it be known there was some good sledging to be had on Heol Glyndŵr shortly, and that they were all welcome to go along. As a thank you, Ali Cabbage was told to sit on his sledge while they gave him a free ride as far as Heol Glyndŵr. It worked out that Golcho also ended up on the sledge, while Twab and Sparrow pulled from the front and Champ pushed from behind, using Golcho's shoulders to push against.

Having made their way up Heol y Gelli, they turned left into what was going to be Heol Cadfan. When they reached the T-junction with Heol Glyndŵr, they met four lads with sledges who said they had come to have a good time.

The evening's fun began with the sledge owners sledging down the steep hill on their own but, after a couple of runs, Ali Cabbage offered Golcho the chance to ride with him, which meant that Golcho had to lie on top of him which he did. When they returned to the starting point, Ali Cabbage suggested to the other sledge owners that they should also carry a passenger as it was much more fun.

Twab, Sparrow, and Champ pushed their chosen sledge (with its owner safely aboard) and guided it down Heol Glyndŵr as fast as they could. When enough speed had been reached, they jumped onto the owner's back and enjoyed the ride down Heol Glyndŵr. Golcho stayed with Ali Cabbage.

It was great speeding down the hill with occupied houses on both sides of the street. It was also great hearing the crunching sound that the sledges made as they sped along the hard, packed snow. As the evening wore on, two of the sledge owners who were feeling the cold went home, leaving just two sledges and six people. Someone suggested the two sledges should be tied together, but no one knew how to do it. As Ali Cabbage, Golcho, and Jimmy (the owner of the second sledge) set off down the hill, Twab, Sparrow and Champ raced after them with one idea in mind – to jump on Jimmy's back. As Twab made his move, Sparrow read his mind and pushed him to one side. When Sparrow then attempted to jump on Jimmy's back, Champ sent him flying into a pile of hard snow that lined the side of the street. The snow plough had been around that afternoon which meant that all the streets in the village were edged with piles of hard, dirty snow. Because of all the pushing and shoving, no one got to jump on Jimmy's back and on reaching the bottom at a fair speed, Jimmy, Golcho, and Ali Cabbage ended up crashing into the embankment of Ty'n y Coed Farm and thought it great fun.

Everyone helped in some way, getting the two sledges back up to the top of Heol Glyndŵr for a second run. It was then suggested that it be turned into a game. The sledge owners agreed. The sledge owners, safely on and ready to go, were pushed as far as Lloft Wen Lane then, as their speed increased, Twab, Sparrow and Golcho began to fight for a place. Trying to jump on, Sparrow pushed Twab flying, causing him to stumble. But Twab then pushed Sparrow so hard that he sent him sprawling into the pile of snow at the edge of the road. Getting up and giving chase, Sparrow plunged head first onto Jimmy's speeding sledge, knocking Champ clean off. But long before Sparrow had finished his yahooing, he was thrown off again and landed in a pile of snow. What fun Christmas Eve was turning out to be.

Trying jump on, both Champ and Twab began scrapping with Sparrow, who was trying to prevent them from doing so. Suddenly the sledges came to an abrupt stop as they slammed into the embankment of Ty'n y Coed Farm, again throwing the occupants into the snow. With everyone agreeing that having to fight for a place was great fun, the sledges were eagerly hauled back up the hill.

For their third run with everyone fired up, it was decided that the sledge owners should now also have to fight for a place. So, as the two empty sledges began to gather speed, everyone made a mad dash to jump on. There was so much shoving, pushing and tripping going on that the still empty sledges ran into the snow pile at the side of the road. When they were straightened up, Golcho, and Jimmy quickly jumped on and the others chased after them. They were halfway down Heol Glyndŵr before anyone else managed to jump on. Twab jumped on Jimmy's back, with Sparrow on Golcho's. Moments later they again crashed into Ty'n y Coed's embankment.

There was so much laughing going on the lads were drawing attention to themselves. People on their way to the pub, seeing the fun they were having, stopped to watch. Two recently married men wanted to join in the fun, but were stopped by their wives. When the sledges slammed into a pile of snow outside Griff's house, the lads, as well as the spectators, laughed so much that Griff himself came out to see what the commotion was. But when he saw how much fun was being had, he actually commented to a group of spectators that he wished he was their age again. As the evening wore on, the cold finally got to the lads and with one last run, the party broke up.

Everyone said their goodnights, and after wishing everyone a Merry Christmas, Champ and Co ended up by Twab's gate. His invitation to spend some time in his house was turned down. They all said they were too cold and wet. Shaking arms, the Roman way, they all wished each other a Merry Christmas and went home having had so much fun.

'Well Alan,' said his mum when he walked in, 'you're soaked through.' Helping him to remove his wet clothes, she shouted up to Jeannie who was in the bath, not to empty the water away as her brother was going to need it. Stoking up the fire, she sat Alan down as near to the flames as she dared and removed his shoes and socks for him while he took off his jumper and shirt. He left his vest on, as the fire was not exactly throwing out a lot of heat.

'I can see you in bed over Christmas with pneumonia my lad,' said his mum, 'You're cold as well as wet.'

'Oh Mum, you wouldn't believe the fun we've had tonight sledging down Heol Glyndŵr. Even Griff wished he was our age again when he saw the fun we were having.'

While he was telling his mum about the antics that were used in trying to jump on the sledges, Jeannie was heard coming down stairs. Moments later, she too was standing by the fire in her nightgown and slippers, with a towel wrapped around her head, listening to her brother's stories.

Prodding Alan on the shoulder, his mum said, 'You my lad, bath.

Now. And don't take all the hot water, I want a bath later.'

Looking forward to his bath, Alan raced upstairs. In the bathroom he threw off his pants and vest, and stepped into the lovely hot water. Sitting in the bath he splashed the water all over himself. He topped it up a little with some hot water then, stretching out, sang what words he knew of his favourite song, Frankie Laine's *Cool Water*. Half way through the song he stopped singing and began to think about his trip down to the woods that morning. There was nothing nicer than wallowing in the bath and thinking. Now that he was lovely and warm, he began to think about all the animal and bird tracks he had seen at the top of the Woods hill and wondered if it was Christmas for them as well.

Then he remembered being in Mr Williams's field with the snow well over his Wellingtons, and how he stood there, in the falling snow as the mist closed in on him. The fact that he had fallen into several drifts up to his thighs did not once seem dangerous to him. He actually enjoyed it. He imagined that it was like that for anyone going to the North Pole.

When he again attempted trying to solve his problem as to why the snow was affecting him, he gave up. It was too much for him and he began to wonder why his attitude to the animals was so different to that of the lads. It was obvious that Sparrow did not feel the way he did. Sparrow was for ever shooting at them with his catapult. Twab went rabbiting with his dad and would eat them. Golcho was always throwing sticks and stones at any animal he came across. So why did they not feel the way he did?

His reverie was suddenly broken. His mum was knocking on the bathroom door. 'Come-on love,' she said, 'Don't be too long, our Jeannie's falling asleep and I want a bath.'

Ten minutes later, Doreen was enjoying her bath and Alan was downstairs trying to make the occasion as exciting as he could for Jeannie. 'Remember,' he said 'once you're in bed, you have to go to sleep as quickly as you can. And whatever you do, don't wake up while he's in the room or you'll end up with nothing.'

'Ooh,' said Jeannie snuggling up to her brother. 'Isn't it exciting?' With so many nice thoughts in her head, she said she was going upstairs as she could not keep her eyes open. 'See you in the morning when *He's* been.'

When Jeannie reached the top of the stairs, the bathroom door opened.

'Are you off to bed love?'

'Yes, Mum, I'm falling asleep.'

'Just give me a minute. I'll come and tuck you in.'

Doreen shouted down to ask Alan to remove Jeannie's brick from the oven, wrap it in the brown paper on the chair and bring it up. Then he was to make her a cup of tea. Doreen dressed and, with a towel around her head, tucked Jeannie in. She was asleep within minutes. Twenty minutes later, with his hot brick warming his feet, Alan was also tucked in. As he said his goodnight, his mum switched off the light and closed his door.

He lay there thinking about this and that. With heavy eye-lids, he turned over to go to sleep, but after some time, he turned onto his other side. After several minutes he realised that he was not comfortable and turned over again. He could not settle, but knew it was not the occasion that was keeping him awake, and for a few minutes he began to envy Jeannie who was fast asleep.

He suddenly realised what the problem was that was keeping him awake, and knew it was not going to go away. He lay there with his feet on the brick, not knowing why his feelings were different to the lads when it came to the animals. Nor did he know why he was going down the woods on his own at such a ridiculous hour? And why were the flowers and trees suddenly so important to him? They never used to be. In Chester he had completely ignored them. Failing to come up with an answer, and knowing his mum was still downstairs, he got up.

Knowing it was Alan who was coming down stairs, Doreen, when he popped his head around the door said, 'Shouldn't you be asleep?'

'Am I in trouble?' he asked.

'Of course not, silly,' said Doreen beckoning him over? 'It's not like you to be awake so late.' When no answer came, she asked what was wrong.

He pulled up a chair and sat next to his mum. After a while he said, 'I seem to be all mixed up Mum.'

'Do you want to talk about it?'

Finally, finding a starting point, he said he had never cared about the animals and things when they lived in Chester, so why was it different living in the Adwy?

'It's not a question of where you live,' said Doreen stroking his hair. Wrapping her coat around him she said, 'You've simply reached another stage in your life. You're growing up, that's all. Perhaps living here has helped in some way, but you are on a wonderful journey that everyone has to take. First you are born, then you begin to grow, and while you are growing you pass through different stages until you reach maturity.' Pulling him to her, she added that he was growing up into a fine young man. He would be thirteen and a teenager the following year and he already had some lovely traits. It was not something to worry about. It was, in fact, a journey to be enjoyed.

He thanked his mum for the information. Everything suddenly made sense. He then asked her to talk about his dad.

'Oh, and what would you like to hear?'

'Anything.'

Pouring a small sherry and cuddling him, Doreen began to tell him how she first met her husband at the local dance hall in Chester a long time ago. She was asked to dance and found dancing with his dad to be very good. On their second date they learned each others names. They had lovely times and he wanted to be a soldier.

With his head now on his mum's lap and trying to stay awake, Alan enjoyed everything he was being told, but twenty minutes later he was back in bed and fast asleep. Popping downstairs for a moment, Doreen left a glass of sherry and a mince pie for 'You know who'.

'He's been. He's been,' Jeannie announced to the Fletcher household. Thinking this might be Jeannie's last year of believing in Father Christmas, Doreen, who had been awake for ages listening for any noise from her room, was determined she was not going to miss it. She was going to make the most of it.

Jeannie ran into her mum's bedroom with her presents and jumped under the bedclothes. Excited she said, 'Oh, I wonder what he's given me?' While she was ripping the Christmas paper off the first of her presents, Alan, walked in with his presents and also jumped under the bedclothes.

'Oh, look, look what he's brought me,' said Jeannie holding up the present for all to see. 'How did Father Christmas know I needed a new satchel?'

'Father Christmas knows everything,' said Alan, half watching his sister examining the satchel while ripping the paper off the first of his presents.

'Oh, thank you Father Christmas,' said Jeannie as she tore the paper off another present.

'There you are our Jeannie,' said her mum, 'He even knew you were in need of a new pair of slippers and bed socks.'

'Oh, isn't Father Christmas wonderful?' said Doreen, as Jeannie struggled to put on her bed socks. She would have put her slippers on as well had her mum let her. Jeannie's next present was her favourite comic annual, *Bunty*. She had also been given a small box of Black Magic chocolates, a set of coloured pencils and two drawing and colouring-in books. Her Christmas stocking contained an apple, an orange, and some hazel nuts. But her final present was really appreciated. Because she was always cold in bed, winter or summer, she had always wanted her very own rubber hot-water bottle. Father Christmas had left her very own red, rubber hot-water bottle. Holding it up for all to see she said she could not wait for tonight to try it out.

'C'mon our Alan,' Jeannie said excitedly clutching her hot water bottle. 'Let's see what he's left you?'

Ripping the rest of the paper off his half-opened present, Alan found had been given a box of coloured pencils and a good quality sketch book.

'Good old Father Christmas,' said Jeannie, her eyes all scrunched up. Teasing, she said perhaps she could have her pencils to herself now? Alan pulled his tongue at her and screwed up his face. He then smiled and said his thank you to Father Christmas. While opening a second present, he could not guess what it could be. The only clues were, it was small and pliable. He was therefore was gob-smacked when he saw what he had been given. Father Christmas had given him an 8 x 30 monocular, complete with carrying case. Sitting there with his mouth open, he could not think of anything to say.

Seeing the pleasure on her son's face and squeezing his hand, Doreen said, 'Well I declare, Father Christmas even knows our Alan has taken up bird watching and star gazing.'

Alan leaned across the bed and, pushing Jeannie out of the way, kissed his mum. So too did Jeannie. While thanking Father Christmas again, Alan whispered to his mum that it must have cost a fortune. But hearing his every word, Jeannie told him not to be so silly. Father Christmas made everything himself and gave them away. You did not have to pay for them. Only shopkeepers make you pay for things.

With that settled, and guessing what his third present was from its shape, Alan opened it and showed Jeannie that he too had been given a red, hot-water bottle. To make sure they did not get them mixed up, Jeannie said she was going to tie a piece of ribbon on hers.

Alan slipped out of the bed for his mum's present which was in the airing cupboard at the top of the stairs (not that Doreen had not spotted it). Moments later, and back under the bed clothes, he handed it over.

Jumping out of bed, Jeannie ordered her mum not to open Alan's present until she had retrieved her present from her built-in wardrobe (again it had been found, but ignored by her mum). Both presents were wrapped up very neatly in the previous Sunday's *News of the World*. Both of the children watched as their mum tore the paper off Jeannie's present. 'Why thank you both,' she said, knowing they had bought this present between them. 'Thank you very much,' she said thoroughly examining the slippers. 'They're lovely.'

'We're glad you like them,' said Jeannie, 'your old ones had holes in them and so we thought it wasn't fair that Father Christmas only gave presents to children, so we bought you these slippers from Gracie's shop in Coedpoeth. They only cost … '

'That'll do Jeannie,' said Alan, grinning. 'I'm sure Mum doesn't want to know all the details.'

Kissing Jeannie, Doreen thanked her very much for choosing the style and colour. Doreen was then ordered to open her second present, which she thought was a book. But when the paper was tore off and the twelve pictures seriously looked at and appreciated, Doreen said it was a lovely present, adding that this was one calendar that was not going to be thrown away at the end of the year. She said she was going to keep it for ever.

> January's picture was a tree and bushes the top of the Woods hill.
> February was the S-bend.
> March (the last of the snowy scenes) was the Woods bridge and Fron Hill.

April was the Woods on the Hafod side, as seen from the top of Mr Williams's field, with a stretch of the river where the piece of glass was found that was made into a broach for his mum.

May was the Hafod bridge, depicting all the spring flowers.

June was Mr Williams's farm.

July was Brymbo pool.

August was the Fron banks.

September was their swimming pool on the Dump side of the woods.

October was the Monster swing.

November was their back garden, when completed.

December was their mum sitting in their back garden in a deckchair surrounded by flowers.

Leaning over and hugging them both, Doreen thanked them very much.

'I tell you what,' said Alan, 'you stay here while I go and get a fire going.'

'A cup of tea for me and Mum would be nice,' Jeannie hinted.

Downstairs, with his jerkin on over his pyjama-top, it being so cold, Alan set to work. The cinders were put to one side while the ash went into the bucket. The ash was going on the yard between the back door, the coal-house, and the outside lavatory, as there was an icy patch there where someone could fall on. With the coal-bucket and sticks at the ready, he put a layer of newspaper in the bottom of the grate, then placed a good handful of sticks on the paper and then topped it off with a shovel full of coal. Then with a single match he lit both the fire and the gas ring.

While waiting for the kettle to boil, having empted the tea pot and milked and sugared the cups, he put his Wellingtons on and stepped outside into the freezing cold and tried out his 8 x 30 monocular. It was amazing. Everything was so much closer. He did not know where to look first and finally settled on some chimney pots on Sparrow's street. He noticed that one of the pots was cracked which could not be seen with the naked eye. He thought that was phenomenal.

He then checked all the other chimney pots on Sparrow's street. They all appeared to be alright. He then focused on the tree at the bottom of next door's garden. How different it looked when compared to the summer when it was in leaf. Suddenly, something caught his eye. A robin flew out of the tree and landed on one of the posts at the bottom of the garden. Alan adjusted the focus and stared at the bird which suddenly dropped to the ground, pecked at something and then returned to the post.

He stared at the little bird and felt he could reach out and touch it. Never in his life had he seen a bird this close up. There was so much detail. He marveled at the birds little stabbing beak and decided he would not like to be a worm. Then he focused on the bird's famous red breast, which was, he thought, more of a rusty colour than red. The bird's brown speckled flight feathers were so lovely to look at. When he looked at the bird's eyes, he thought they were cold and lifeless, not how you would think of a robin, really. He remembered seeing a coloured photograph of a great white shark once and its eyes were just like those of the robin, cold and lifeless.

Suddenly he heard the kettle boiling its head off. A pot of tea was made and, with a few biscuits each, breakfast was had in bed.

Now that all the excitement of unwrapping Christmas presents was over and knowing the fire would be blazing away downstairs, the Fletchers got up and dressed. With her new slippers on, Doreen, after a second cup of tea and a warm by the fire with a cardigan on (it was freezing in the back kitchen), began to prepare their Christmas dinner by peeling the potatoes in warm water.

Sitting at the table, Jeannie began to colour in one of her colouring-in books. All wrapped up and trying to ignore the cold, Alan was in the field above their house with his monocular looking at everything. It was a lovely sunny morning, but the sun was too low down to give off any heat. The fact that there were no clouds in the sky only added to the cold. Icicles were still clinging hard and fast to the gutters of certain houses.

Alan was watching a blackbird feeding on some holly berries when Jeannie informed him that their dinner was ready. Was it one o'clock already? Kicking off his Wellingtons by the back door and appreciating the warmth coming from the living room, he stepped in and sniffed the aroma of the food. When he saw the table, the Christmas dinner looked so inviting. His mum had placed before them a feast fit for a king. To keep the living room warm, Alan banked up the fire with a shovelful of coal and a log and then washed his hands.

Sitting at the table, he smiled at the meal that was set out before them. Both his and Jeannie's mouths began to water when their mum began to carve the bird. With their plates piled up with chicken, potatoes (roasted and boiled) carrots, sprouts and Alan's favourite, peas out of a tin, and with a traditional Christmas pudding to follow, they pulled their crackers, put on the brightly-coloured paper hats and tucked in. But not before Alan and Jeannie thanked their mum for all the hard work she had put in, making the meal.

At about five past two, the lads came calling. All were carrying air rifles. Stepping in and wishing everyone a Happy Christmas and noticing a balloon had gone down completely, Twab proudly showed Champ his brand new Diana air rifle. Sparrow and Golcho's were last year's presents. Leaning the guns against the wall the way they had seen it done in some western, the lads entered the living room and said hello to Jeannie and her mum, whereupon they were each given a mince pie. While munching away they began to look at Jeannie's presents. Sparrow, still the love of her life accepted a coffee-flavoured Black Magic chocolate from Jeannie. Twab hinted for, and was given, another mince pie. Golcho, having hugged the fire, sat down and began to colour in the picture that Jeannie had made a start on. She was just about to tell him off, but hesitated, it was Christmas after all. Peace on earth and goodwill to all men.

It was only when they stepped into the garden that they appreciated Champ's main present. After they had all had a look through the glass, Twab announced that they were going down the woods. Champ explained to his mum that they were off now, and that he would be back well before it went dark. He was looking forward to the chicken leg and sandwiches he knew he would be having for tea.

It was not until they reached the green gates that the lads began to fire their rifles. They had each been warned by their parents not to shoot them while walking through the village. Not that they dared with Griff on the prowl. While they shot at simple targets (tree branches and a huge stone that jutted out from the hedge) Champ scanned the field for birds with his 8 x 30. He was watched a flock of rooks pecking at the frozen ground with their massive beaks, but their plumage was something else. It looked blue, not black.

When he refused a couple of pot shots, they moved on. At the top of the Woods hill, Sparrow stopped and took aim at something. Curious, Champ looked to see what his target was. Several jackdaws were hoping about in the branches just above their heads.

Sparrow fired, but his pellet hit the branch just below the birds and they flew away. He cursed for missing, quickly broke the barrel, inserted another lead pellet and snapped it shut looking around for another target.

'Hey, bugger,' said Golcho, angrily. 'Why didn't you say you had some live targets? We could have all had a pot shot at them.'

'Keep your hair on Golch,' Sparrow told him, while looking to see if there were any more birds around. 'There'll be plenty more when we reach the woods.'

Noticing Champ was quiet, Twab asked if anything was wrong?

'I hope you're not going to be shooting the birds just for the fun of it?'

'Of course we are,' said Sparrow, 'what's the problem?'

'Me liking them,' said Champ. 'I vowed yesterday morning that I was going to protect the birds and things to the best of my ability from now on.'

'Ignore him,' said Sparrow.

Agreeing with Sparrow, Golcho said they always shot birds when they were out with their rifles, adding, what were rifles for if not for shooting birds?

'I hope you're not going to try and stop us,' said Sparrow.

Reaching the woods and making their way down the first slope, crunching the hard-packed snow, Champ, saw something that could be shot. 'Hey fellows,' he said, 'there's some good targets for you to shoot at.' Champ pointed at the icicles that were clinging to the arch of the bridge.

'Good spotting, Champ,' said Twab.

'You go and shoot them while I go and see if I can find the greater spotted woodpecker. We'll meet up later by the little swing.'

With that, Twab, Sparrow and Golcho raced on towards the river to see who would be the first to have a pot-shot at the biggest icicle. With several stops, looking at this and that, Champ finally reached the little swing and began to search the trees and bushes for any signs of life. One minute he was looking at a chaffinch, then a greenfinch, then a blue tit. On the ground he spotted a wren and a robin. But there was neither sight nor sound of the greater spotted woodpecker, but his fingers were crossed. Then he heard the lads by the bridge, yelling out when a target was hit. He also heard the pings and zips that the pellets made when the rifles were fired. It was a mystery why the sound carried the way it did in this environment.

Some thirty minutes later, having destroyed all the icicles, Twab, Sparrow and Golcho met up with Champ by the little swing.

Champ asked how they'd got on.

'We sure as hell shot them icicles to pieces, partner,' said Golcho in a most terrible John Wayne accent. With that, Twab and Sparrow began to shoot at a near by tree just to hear the sound of their pellets hitting it. They, as did Golcho, loved the sound their pellets made when they smacked into a tree.

'Here, Champ,' said Golcho offering him his rifle. 'Let's see how good you are with an airgun.'

Taking the rifle, Champ joined in with Twab and Sparrow. The target was a bough on the big oak that housed the little swing.

Twab felt good when his pellet made a ping sound and hit the target.

Sparrow's pellet also made a ping sound and hit the target.

Champ's pellet, also made a ping sound and hit the target.

The start of an icicle hanging from a branch of another tree was chosen as the next target, with Sparrow being the only one who failed to chip a piece off it with his first shot. But he got it with a second shot, only to be teased by Twab.

Suddenly, Sparrow saw a little blue tit perched in a holy bush some thirty feet away. Without a word to anyone, he took aim and fired. His pellet pinged away and hit the target. The little blue tit was dead before it hit the ground.

Yelling his excitement, Sparrow rushed over to claim his prize. Trudging through the crunchy deep snow, he began to search the area. His cry of, 'I've found it,' shattered the silence. Smiling with delight he brought the dead bird back for everyone to see.

Twab was the first one to hold it. He then gave it to Golcho who also had a good look at it. But while all the congratulations were being given, Champ, who was seething, aimed an angry stare at Sparrow.

'Pretty little thing isn't it,' said Golcho as he handed it back to Sparrow, who then wiped some blood off his gloved hand. Sparrow held the bird out for Champ, 'Here,' he said, 'take it, it won't bite you, it's still warm.'

Champ cupped the bird in his hands and admired it. He loved its blue head, yellow breast, and its little beak. Its eyes were closed and as Sparrow had said, it was still warm. When he looked, there was blood on his gloved hand. With no more to do, he trampled through the crunchy snow to where the bird had been shot. There, he dug a little grave in the ice with his right hand. He then wrapped the bird up in his handkerchief and buried it, marking the grave with a stick.

Angry, Champ went over to Sparrow and, grabbing his right hand, forced him to his knees in a painful wrist lock. Sparrow fell to his knees still clutching his rifle. Champ disarmed him and threw his rifle away. Sparrow was then placed in a strangle hold from behind where he began to choke and gasp for breath. Seeing how serious this was, Twab, with Golcho's backing said, 'Leave him be Champ. He's only done what Golcho or I would have done.'

But before Twab could say another word, Champ told him and Golcho to back off, as this was between him and Sparrow. Champ applied a little more pressure to Sparrow's neck, cutting off his air supply even more. He wanted him to feel really uncomfortable.

'I want him to know that he's done wrong killing that bird,' said Champ. The more Sparrow struggled, the more Champ held onto him. When Sparrow began to choke, Champ eased off and allowed him to get up. But, not finished with him, he made a fist and with his middle knuckle protruding, knowing it hurts, and punched his friend in the solar-plexus. Crying out in pain, Sparrow fell to the ground holding his stomach. 'Hey you, you sod,' he screamed, 'that hurt.'

Ready to hit him again Champ said, 'I'm glad it did. I also imagine that's what the bird said just before it died.'

'That wasn't fair Champ,' said Golcho, 'using that judo thing on him.'

'Neither was it fair for the bird, Golch,' said Champ. 'What chance has a bird got against a rifle? Go on, tell me that.'

'No one hits a friend,' said Twab.

'Oh yes they do,' Champ insisted, 'When they kill birds for pleasure.'

When no one said anything, Champ began to walk away.

'Where are you going?' Twab asked.

Champ never answered.

Reaching home and with his 8 x 30 monocular, he spent the rest of Christmas Day searching the hedgerows in the fields above Heol Wen. The death of that little blue tit was still heavy on his mind.

At 7.15, his mum, who was looking forward to going out for the evening, said, 'Well how do I look?'

'You look lovely,' replied Alan and Jeannie.

'Are you two going to be alright?'

'Yes Mum,' insisted Alan, 'you just go and enjoy yourself.'

'I'm only next door if you want me.'

'Jeannie,' said Alan grinning, 'help me push our mum out.'

Alan and Jeannie had agreed to look after Bryn and his two sisters from next door for the night while their mum, along with several other grown-ups whooped it up 'party style' in Aunty Mair's house. There were to be no children. Alan smiled at the thought of his mum being a little tipsy.

As the night wore on and with all the singing and laughing that was heard coming from next door, Alan knew his mum was having a lovely time.

Boxing Day saw Alan and Jeannie in the field's above the house. He was not only showing her the different bird tracks in the snow, but also wanted her to look at the birds through his monocular to see how different they looked. Jeannie was amazed at how much detail was revealed from looking through the glass and stayed with her brother until she could stand the cold no longer. Because of the cold she asked if she could go home as she was expecting Wendy and Hazel anytime now. Alan, however, decided to spend the day bird watching and hopefully, sketching them. He drew a robin, a chaffinch and a wren.

Whereas the first two were easy to draw (they being more in the open), the little wren was much more difficult and would only show itself for a moment or two before darting back into the hedge where it never stopped moving. But its image was captured. Alan decided that he loved all birds, they being so different in colour, shape and size.

It was coming up to five o'clock and getting dark when Alan heard someone approaching. He knew who it was.

'Your mum told us you where you were,' said Twab. 'She also told us to tell you that your tea is ready,' he added.

When asked how he was and what had he been doing, Champ explained that he had been bird watching for most of the day and then showed the lads the drawings he had made. While admitting that they were good, Twab said they had come to see him about the birds and Sparrow had something he wanted to say.

Walking up to Champ, Sparrow said he was very sorry about yesterday, adding that it will never happen again. Champ looked Sparrow squarely in the eyes and said, 'Honest, you mean it, no more shooting birds?'

'Honest, no more shooting birds.'

While shaking arms with Sparrow, the Roman way, Champ turned to Twab and Golcho and said, 'And what about you two?'

Both promised that there would be no more shooting birds from now on. There was so much arm shaking, the Roman way, that it took Sparrow ages to tell them that he heard there was more sledging down Heol Glyndŵr going on tonight, and why did they not just go along and see what happened. The air filled up with, 'All for one, and one for all.'

Epilogue

The lads were to remain friends for the rest of their lives. They did go to play snooker when they were fourteen and they each found a job when they left school and for a time put their wage packets on the table and each received ten shillings a week pocket money. But when they were eighteen and more grown up, their lives changed. They were introduced to many things which had previously been denied to them. With an extra seven shillings and six pence pocket money, they then had the pleasure of going to the pictures in Wrexham on the bus. They were also able to go in a pub of their choice for a pint of beer, which they did. They could even afford to go out with girls on their extra pocket money allowance, which they also did. They all took their responsibilities very seriously; they saved their money and worked hard at their jobs.

Twab did become a farmer for a while, but found he could make more money as a labourer in the building trade. Sparrow and Golcho eventually did go down the pit and became miners Champ went into the Army and, like his dad, became an NCO. In 1978, aged 27, he left the army and went to work for the RSPB.

One by one they fell in love, married and began families of their own. They became responsible citizens of the Adwy. They even reached old age still as friends. And 'All for one and one for all,' was how it remained for the four lads who were once known as Champ and Co.

In her seventies, and suffering with arthritis, Doreen Fletcher moved away from Heol Wen, the house having three bedrooms was too much for her, especially the stairs. She was given a pensioner's bungalow, built on the very field where Champ and Co, as twelve year olds, did battle with what they called the White Hand or the Ghost from hell. Bryn Celyn Farm where the incident occurred is now a privately house, with the outbuildings used as council garages.

As for Jeannie, she too fell in love, married a man named Smith (who was no relation to Twab) and became a mum. Like Alan, she still lives in the village, and they both keep an eye on her mum with several visits a week. When Jeannie went back to work, she trained as a teacher, and for a while taught in the junior school.

The Top School which Jeannie and Alan attended was burned down by an arsonist in 1973 and is today a sports complex. Sparrow insists he knew who the culprit was, but vowed never to tell.

The two classrooms where Miss Williams and Mr Robinson taught are still standing. So too is Mr Lloyd's woodwork shop and Mr Ken Hughes' metalwork shop although the main building has long gone. Tennis courts are now located where Mr Samuels and his staff once ruled with an iron rod.

The very thing that Twab as a twelve-year-old did not want to happen, happened. The Adwy did merge with Coedpoeth, the Talwrn and the Smelt and the four individual villages are now gone forever. So much building went on, and is still going on today, that what were once small villages surrounded by fields and hedgerows.

When Twab was asked recently how he felt about his village being so large, he replied that it was almost as big as Wrexham now. What he did not say was that all the fields that he, Sparrow and Golcho used to roam over and play in as ten-year-olds, two years before Champ arrived on the scene, are all gone, every single one of them. He could remember fields and hedgerows in Heol Wen where Champ and Golcho once lived and he used to think of the Adwy as an island, surrounded by a sea of green.

When he thought about it, Twab realised so many other things had also gone, like Southsea Bank, where a colliery once thrived. All the shale that was Southsea Bank and most of the Tan y Fron Banks went into the making of motorways. Ty'n y Coed Farm for a while was a thriving garden centre. The green gates are no longer there; where they once stood with barbed-wire running along the top of them, is now a small, privately owned housing estate. The five-bar gate across the way is still there, but not the original one. Even the oak tree that Champ thought of as his has long gone.

Alum's farm on Fron Hill has been altered so much that it's nothing like it was when Champ and Co were youngsters. Alum, of course has gone, but at least they have not started to build on what were once his fields – yet.

The Three Mile Inn, where Twab and the lads sang carol's back in 1953, is today a house. Also gone is the Adwy Chapel. Roberts the builder bought it and knocked it down, apparently wanting the stone to build a house for himself and his family. The grave-yard belonging to the chapel that Mrs Fletcher thought was a disgrace is still a disgrace. It has never been tidied up.

The Grosvernor Arms, where Champ and Co did most of their early drinking as young men is now closed and boarded up and is now a private house.

All the shops the lads thought were important are gone, barring Lingard's. Back in 1953 there was Oswald's, the Co-op, Glyn's, Roberts (with its chippy), Fords, Lingard's and Gracie's, plus other shops in Coedpoeth.

Old Mr Williams's farm is now where horses are bred and stabled. The well, which the lads deemed secret has gone, filled in. Actually, because of all the vegetation there is no evidence today that there ever was a well there.

The Woods river, where so many Adwy children swam and had the time of their lives is nothing more than a trickle these days; its only visitors today are cows. Most of the river edges are so overgrown that the river itself is hardly seen.

Worst of all, the little wood where so much fun was had by the lads, where so much time was spent, especially in the school holidays, has also gone. One day in 1955, the lads tried to enter the Woods, but men with big saws and axes told them that all the trees were coming down and that they and everyone else was now barred from entering. Champ and Co went home that day devastated. They did not believe it until they went to see for themselves when the men had gone home for the day. The first trees to come down had red Xs painted on them. The next day, and on a daily basis, the trees, were cut down one by one and taken away on lorries. In just three weeks the Woods was gone forever. Today the area is so different. Even the lie of the land is different. Holly, hazel and blackthorn now stand where once deciduous trees dominated. The carpets of wood anemone, blue bells, snow drops, primroses, lesser celandine, common spotted orchids, ragged robin, buttercups, daisies, butterbur, coltsfoot and a host of other wild flowers, have been taken over by briar, nettle and scrub. Cattle have devastated the area. Today when it rains, it resembles a bog more than a wood.

Champ, or Taid as he is referred to these days, pondered while having his tea the other day whether he should put it down on paper for those who would like to know how it once was. When he conferred with Cynthia, his wife, she thought it was a good idea. He spent the rest of the day reading his diaries from the 1950s and came up with a brilliant idea – which he called 'Champ & Co'.